I DID A BAD THING

LOUISE JENSEN

ONE PLACE. MANY STORIES

HQ
An imprint of HarperCollins*Publishers* Ltd
1 London Bridge Street
London SE1 9GF

www.harpercollins.co.uk

HarperCollins*Publishers*
Macken House, 39/40 Mayor Street Upper
Dublin 1, D01 C9W8, Ireland

This edition 2026

26 27 28 29 30 LBC 7 6 5 4 3
First published in Great Britain by HQ,
an imprint of HarperCollins*Publishers* Ltd 2026

ISBN: 978-0-00-873230-1

Typeset in Sabon LT Pro by HarperCollins*Publishers* India

This novel is entirely a work of fiction. The names, characters and incidents portrayed in it are the work of the author's imagination. Any resemblance to actual persons, living or dead, events or localities is entirely coincidental.

Printed and Bound in the United States

Praise for Louise Jensen

'Wow, I hardly stopped to take a breath . . . Intricate plotting, incredible pace, and a wonderful weaving of past and present'
Andrea Mara

'So good, raced through it in a day! Creepy and compelling, another great impossible-to-put-down thriller from the fabulous Louise Jensen'
B A Paris

'Louise Jensen is the master of suspense . . . Taut, atmospheric and utterly compulsive'
Kia Abdullah

'A twisty tale of family complexities and high-risk secrets from an author who rarely disappoints'
Daily Mail, Ones to Watch

'Thrilling'
Crime Monthly

'This is a nicely put together thriller shot through with panache'
The Observer

'Twisting, turning, breathless ride to the end'
Woman & Home

'Edge-of-the-seat propulsive psychological thriller'
The Courier

'Red herrings will boggle the mind and you'll be left open-mouthed by the turn of events'
Woman's Weekly

'A compelling page-turner'
Bella

Louise Jensen has sold approaching two million copies of her International Number One psychological thrillers. Her novels have also been translated into twenty-five languages and are for sale in over thirty territories. Louise's books have been featured on the *USA Today* and *Wall Street Journal* Bestseller's List and have been optioned for TV and film. Louise's books have been nominated for various awards including, the Goodreads Debut Award, *The Guardian's* 'Not the Booker' prize, best Polish thriller of 2018. She has also been listed for two CWA (Crime Writing Association) Dagger Awards. When Louise isn't writing thrillers, she turns her hand to penning love stories under the name Amelia Henley, along with writing short stories for magazines.

Follow Louise on Instagram @fabricating_fiction and Facebook @fabricatingfiction

Also by Louise Jensen

The Woman Next Door
The Liar
The Intruders
The Fall
All For You
The Stolen Sisters
The Family
The Gift
The Sister
The Surrogate
The Date

Writing as Amelia Henley

From Now On
The Art of Loving You
The Life We Almost Had

*For my dear friends Clare and Cheryl,
I'm glad none of our childhood escapades
could be posted online . . .*

Author's Note

Although not the central focus of the story, this novel touches on themes of suicide and grief as part of a wider narrative. While the act itself is not depicted, the emotional effects are explored. If you find this subject difficult, please do read with care.

Louise x

Prologue

Blood has a taste.

A smell.

It catches at the back of my throat. I'm in the bath on my hands and knees, retching again. Crimson-tinged water helter-skelters down the plug hole. Despite the steam rising, I'm shivering.

Oh, God.

There's so much blood. I think that after this, whenever I close my eyes, I'll see it.

I can't breathe.

The acrylic is slippery as I rock back and forth. Whimpering.

What have I done?

Panic skitters around every cell in my body. I'm hot and cold.

I can't breathe.

Shaking, shaking. I don't know what to do but I need to do something to hide the evidence from the children.

From everyone.

Thoughts of the kids bring another tidal wave of panic.

What have I done?

I try to calm myself. Remind myself that everything I do – everything I've done – is for them. To keep them safe.

Focus.

It takes a gargantuan effort to push myself back onto my heels. From the soap dish, I grab the brush I usually use to get the mud from my nails when I've been gardening. I scrub and scrub. Registering on some level that it hurts but welcoming the pain, feeling as though I deserve it.

Eventually, I raise my hands and examine the palms for blood, turn them over and check my nails.

Clean now.

But I don't think I'll ever really feel clean again.

A noise?

My stomach lurches. Has someone come home? I can't let anyone see me like this.

Especially not the kids.

It's this fierce maternal instinct that drives me to my feet. My legs feel too weak to support me and it takes a moment before I can step out of the bath, one hand against the tiles, steadying myself. Almost crumbling as I catch sight of the droplets of water left behind, pink now instead of red. Again, my mouth floods with bile.

Swallowing hard, I wrap a towel around myself, creep over to the door on tiptoes. Crack it open.

I'm motionless.

Listening.

But all I can hear is my own frantic heartbeat. My pulse whooshing in my ears.

'Hello?' I call out. 'Lottie? Chris?'

Thick silence wraps itself around me. Suffocating.

I can't breathe.

My heart thud-thud-thuds.

I hear something.

Behind me.

I start, spinning around. But it's just the last of the blood-tinged water being sucked down the plug hole.

I turn away from it. Turn away from my guilt.

I need a plan.

Focus.

Where is my mobile?

I hurry out of the bathroom. A knot of anxiety tightening in my stomach. I hadn't had anywhere else to go at the time I had moved into this modern glass house, and I'd thought how lucky I was. The patchwork of countryside surrounding it is stunning. But now I see it for what it is.

Too isolated.

Too conspicuous.

Because here's the thing. The transparent walls might allow me an unobstructed view of the outside, but it also allows unseen eyes to peer in. Frightened, my gaze is drawn to the darkness as I hurry towards my bedroom, but with the lights illuminating the landing, all I can see is my own pale face staring back at me.

My guilty face.

All at once I feel such a sharp pang of longing for the life I had before I accidentally became a viral sensation, when I was unknown, invisible – but you can't change the past, can you? No matter how desperately you want to.

Can't rewind a month, a year, two years.

Not even just two hours. If I could, then I wouldn't have . . .

Focus.

I drag my attention away from the windows because, even if there is someone lurking out there in the shadows, someone who has seen the terrible thing I've done, I can't do anything about that now.

But there *are* things I can do.

Have to do.

My mobile is on my pillow. My hand trembles as I pick it up. I haven't changed my screensaver in ages. In the photo,

Sean has his arm slung around my shoulders, the kids crowded either side of us. It was taken years ago.

Before . . . everything.

We had laden our wicker basket with food and set off to a pick-your-own-sunflowers field. The air had been fragrant: sweet and spicy, a warm breeze kissing my bare arms. Despite slathering myself with sun cream, the scorching August sunshine had drawn freckles on my skin.

Charlotte had turned cartwheels amongst the bright-yellow flowers until Chris had slapped her on the shoulder. 'Tag. You're it.' She'd raced after Sean, hands outstretched, trying to catch him. I'd filmed them, their feet pounding against the dry earth, dust clouds trailing in their wake. Even then, I was obsessed with filming everything. Sudden loss had left me with a fierce desire to try and hold on to each perfect moment.

Later, we had sprawled over a red tartan blanket and feasted on plump, juicy strawberries, and a Victoria sponge I'd made, spread thickly with pale buttercream and sprinkled with pastel hundreds and thousands because, well, just because the kids liked them.

I had angled my phone to take a picture so that we were all gazing upwards, chins tilted towards the clear blue sky.

We look so happy. How had we gone from that to . . . to . . .

I taste the blood as I drag in air.

I message the kids: **Sorry I'm going to be a little late. I'm not feeling well.**

That much, at least, is the truth.

I dress hurriedly. Black jeans. Black long-sleeved t-shirt. Hair tucked under my baseball cap.

Outside, the air is biting. My breath clouds in front of me. Despite the temperature, it's a clear evening. There's a velvety blanket stretched above, popping with stars. Before

I climb into my car, I take a moment to look up, overcome, because it's one of those things you take for granted, isn't it? The sky. The moon. That, whatever happens to us, the world will keep spinning, even though mine has again been thrust violently off its axis.

The car park is deserted when I slowly pull into it, turning off my headlights. There's the smell of hot oil and onions in the air from the burger place at the bottom of the road. A dull thud-thud-thud of bass coming from a club.

A crash.

My heart leaps into my mouth. In the distance, a cat darts out from behind the skip. Hurrying, I clench my car keys in my fist, ready to defend myself, wondering if I'll always feel this sense of being on high alert. Pre-empting danger around every corner.

When I reach the skip, I take a furtive look over my shoulder before tossing the bin bag amongst the other rubbish. Alongside the dress I had been wearing are our stripy beach towels and the Little Mermaid bathmat all splattered with blood. Charlotte had grown out of Disney years before but somehow the mat had stayed. Perhaps I have been clinging on to the last trace of her childhood before it fades away altogether. Perhaps we both have been because when Chris teases her about it and I offer to throw it away she won't let me.

And then I get back in my car, planning to head home and apply make-up with a shaking hand before joining my family and pretending to be normal.

Pretending is something I'm good at.

I've been doing it for years.

If I'd been paying attention, I might have noticed the glow of blue lights as I approached our house.

As it is, I am so distracted, on autopilot really, when I spot two police cars. There's a policeman leaning against the bonnet of one, talking into a radio.

Our eyes meet and my mouth instantly dries.

There's the click of my door opening.

My numb fingers fumbling for the catch on my seat belt.

And the words.

Oh god, those words.

'Mia Finch, I'm arresting you on suspicion of murder.'

Dark spots flicker in front of my eyes. Vision tunnelling. Sounds muffled.

Words running into each other except the one that's all-consuming.

Murder.

I can't make sense of it. I can't make sense of anything.

How did I get here?

But I know how I got here.

I know how my story began.

Once upon a time, I had fallen in love.

But as I'm led into the police car, a hand covering the top of my head as I duck inside, I don't know how my story will end.

PART ONE

Chapter 1

***Who's Watching You* Documentary**

Jake Lawler (host): Welcome to *Who's Watching You* – the most factual true crime series on TV. Today we're looking at a case I'm sure you're all aware of. There's a lot to unpack with the Finch family tragedy. (pauses for effect) A *lot*. The nation has been gripped by the rise, and subsequent fall, of the social media stars who seemed to have it all. (gestures to a photo of the family on the screen behind him)

The Finch family YouTube channel had over a hundred thousand subscribers at the height of their posts. This figure has risen dramatically after these past few weeks, although it's not as though they can post new content anymore, is it?

On average, their most recent videos have six-figure views. But not everybody watching was doing so because they rooted for the family after everything they'd been through. (walks to camera)

It's like this. Even if you have a small, private Facebook account and believe your posts can only be viewed by family and friends . . . can you be sure? (small, sad shake of head)

Even if you're certain your privacy settings are watertight, how can you trust there aren't lurkers? Shadows hidden amongst the brightness of your grid. (pauses)

Do you use social media? Do *you* really know who's behind the likes and the comments on your page? Do *you* really know who's watching you?(holds solemn expression)

Because you can bet your life, *somebody* probably is. And something as innocuous as Mia's desire to share part of herself with the public, however good her intentions to help other people were, has led to a twisted tale of tragedy and betrayal. We have stalking, blackmail, three deaths, multiple arrests and murder. And don't forget *that* shocking confession. Join in the conversation with #WWY. (hashtag flashes up on screen)

We'll be interviewing those connected with the case, but first, even though it's sad looking at this footage, knowing that not every member of the Finch family is alive today, (hand covers heart) we need to go back ten years and find out where it all began.

(cut to a shaky home video of Sean, Mia, Mia's mum Beverley, along with Sean's sister Esther. In front of them, fidgeting with excitement, Esther's kids Daisy and

Felix, and a much younger Chris and Lottie Finch, stand in front of a modest house, waving.)

'Hello, we're the Finch family. Welcome to our home.'

The siblings nudge each other, laughing.

'Go on,' whispers Mia, smiling.

(fade into another image, a different house; blue and white police tape flapping in the breeze; zoom in on a blood stain)

(voiceover from the children from original video: 'If you love what you see, don't forget to like and subscribe')

@Avocadomonkey Oh, they look so normal there. It's really sad seeing them like that #WWY

@Lamadrama23 Finally! This is going to be SO good!!!

@Blackcat1970 I don't agree with using tragedy for entertainment

@Jamie2983 And yet here you are

Chapter 2

Mia

Nine months before the documentary airs

Once I watched a video on YouTube of a female elephant fighting off a crocodile that was trying to attack her calf. As the calf screamed in terror, his mum had stomped and bellowed, driving the crocodile back, her distress palpable until her child was out of danger. Then she gently wrapped her trunk around her baby and pulled him close to her, keeping him safe.

If I could pull Lottie to me and keep her safe, I would.

I would fight crocodiles and lions with my bare hands for my daughter.

As it is, though, I'm fighting with my GP because I know something is seriously wrong with her.

I know.

This is not an innocuous childhood bug, the spring virus that is going around, or her having eaten too many Easter eggs, or any of the other things he's suggesting to me. Yes, he's right that Lottie is fifteen and teenagers can be lazy, but this lethargy isn't the usual weekend *mum-I-want-to lie-in-bed-till-midday* kind. This is several weeks of . . . something.

'Her gums bled when she brushed her teeth this morning and she has so many bruises.' I point out the ones on her legs to the doctor while Lottie sits, listless and pale, the sleeves of her black hoodie tugged down over her hands. Her nails are short, bitten, purple varnish chipped.

'So how do you feel, Charlotte?' Dr Corcoran asks.

'Dunno.' She shrugs. 'Knackered.'

'Are you one of these vegans?'

'Nah.'

'And have your periods been heavier than normal?'

Lottie shakes her head.

'We eat plenty of iron-rich foods.' I'm defensive.

'I wasn't suggesting you don't, Mrs Finch.' He focuses on Lottie again. 'Any weight gain? Hair loss?'

'Nah.'

'If anything, she's lost weight,' I chip in. 'Her appetite has been non-existent.'

He gently feels the glands in Lottie's throat.

'Everything feels fine. You don't have any other symptoms of hypothyroidism. Are you sleeping okay?'

'Yeah.'

'Under any stress? How's school?'

'Fine.'

'And you're . . . What? Year ten? First year of GCSEs?'

'Yeah. We picked our options last year.'

'All that studying must be tiring. I don't think it's anything to be alarmed about.' He leans back in his chair and smiles. 'You might be a little low on iron so make sure you eat plenty of leafy green veg, and if you don't feel better in a—'

'No.' I shake my head. 'Her brother, Chris, is in the first

year of A levels and he's . . . he's . . . ' I swallow down the emotions that are rising. 'Can you do some bloods at least?'

He might know medicine, but I know my child, and I have a dark, swirling mass deep down in my gut. A maternal instinct I just can't ignore.

Without replying, he turns back to his keyboard and tap-tap-taps. I'm not sure if he's writing up our appointment notes or putting into place the next step.

I draw in a deep breath. The air heavy with bleach and antiseptic. It's been unseasonably warm for April and, in denim shorts, my bare legs are sticking to the hard plastic chair.

I shift uncomfortably. I've a strong urge to remove the spider plant from the windowsill with its browning unruly leaves, heft open the small sash and stick my head out, just to give myself a moment.

Just so I can breathe. Block out the incessant ringing of the phone from the reception area outside this door. My head is throbbing.

I'm frustrated and sad and frightened and horribly close to tears. I don't feel heard. He isn't *listening* to me. Ridiculously, for the second time this morning, I wish there is an adult who can take charge, but even though I don't always feel like it, at forty-four, I *am* the adult. Sometimes I wonder when I'll actually feel calm and capable. I always thought, growing up, that once you reached eighteen you'd have all the answers. I'm not sure I even know all the questions, but what I *do* know is that I won't be fobbed off as an over-anxious mother although that's how I feel.

'Dr Corcoran.' I straighten my spine. I will not leave this drab magnolia room with its harsh electric lights and grey wipeable chairs until I get a concrete plan of action. I think he realises I'm not going anywhere because, after pushing his keyboard away and taking a pointed glance at his watch, he sighs and says he'll find out the availability for blood tests.

My fingers cross automatically as he picks up his phone and speaks in a low voice to reception. I'm painfully aware that if I wanted blood tests I'd be told to ring at 8 a.m. the next morning, then the next, then the next. Appointments are as rare as my teenagers bringing their empty glasses out of their bedrooms and stacking them in the dishwasher. The system must work differently for a child, though, because he asks us to return to the waiting room until the nurse calls us.

'Everything okay, Mum?' Chris asks, still on the seat where we'd left him. At seventeen, his voice is so deep now it's sometimes a shock to hear it coming out of his mouth. In my mind, he's often the little boy who refused to take off the Batman cape. 'My little superhero', I used to call him, and this is true today. He should be at school, but he was worried about Lottie; there's only nineteen months between them and they've always been close in spite of being polar opposites. Whereas Lottie is colour and noise and mischief, he is a quiet black and white. He gazes up at me, serious, his long legs stretched out in front of him, crossed at the ankle. When he stands, he's taller than I am now. Almost taller than Sean, too.

'They're going to do a blood test to be certain, but Dr Corcoran doesn't think there's anything to worry about.' I lift my mouth into a smile. Lottie may be the one who wants to be an actor but I'm good at pretending. I think as a mum, you have to be, don't you?

Lottie slumps on one of the chairs, head resting against the wall, and one glance at the lack of colour in her cheeks spikes terror in my heart again. She's always been my get-up-and-go ray of sunshine. Ever since she could walk and talk I've been begging her to slow down, to quieten down. Now that she has, I can't bear it.

'You get off to school.' I force myself to smile brightly again at Chris. It's an important year for him. His mock A levels are coming up in a few weeks. He's been talking about being a vet and I was so proud when he said that. He's nurturing and it feels like a good career for him, but right now I don't care what my children will be when they're adults as long as they are happy.

Healthy.

'So, they took some blood.' I tilt my head to the side, cradling the phone between my cheek and my shoulder while I spoon Nescafé into a mug.

'What are they testing for?' I hear the concern in Esther's voice. She isn't solely my best friend; she's also my sister-in-law. We've been friends since we met at uni, but it wasn't until several years later, at her wedding, that I met her brother, Sean. They're incredibly close but in a different way to Esther and me.

'Oh, I'm not sure.' I'd been so intent on pushing for some sort of tests I didn't think to clarify what they were. 'Dr Corcoran mentioned Lottie's thyroid, and anaemia. I'm not sure what else.'

'I'm sure it's nothing to worry about. The kids are all under a lot of pressure.'

Esther's children, Felix and Daisy, are the same age as Lottie and Chris. Often they study together.

'You sound like Dr Corcoran.'

'Sorry, Mia. I didn't mean you aren't right to worry. I just didn't want you to, well, worry, you know?'

'I know. You're an idiot but I love you.'

'You're an idiot but I love you too.'

It's what we've always said to each other, ever since we

met as freshers, sharing a flat. We were getting ready for a night out, wrapped in tiny once-white towels while we did our make-up, when there was the blare of sirens outside. We couldn't see what was going on from our window, so Esther went rushing out to the corridor in search of the drama. When she didn't return, I followed her out onto the landing. The door slammed behind us, and we looked at each other in horror.

'Please tell me you put the door on the latch?' she asked.

'No. Do you have a key?'

'Where would I put a key?' She glanced down at her towel.

Our eyes met again, and I knew this would be a definitive moment. We'd only known each other a month and, although we'd really clicked, would our friendship endure walking through campus to student services, practically naked?

'You're an idiot,' she said before she started to laugh. 'But I love you.'

That's when I knew we'd always be friends.

Even though we see each other all the time, there's always something to talk about.

It's unfamiliar and unsettling that there's nothing else to say right now.

I'm in the kitchen, preparing a dinner that I hope Lottie can eat at least a little of. She's stretched across the sofa, streaming Bruce Springsteen through the Bluetooth speaker. She gets her taste in music from Sean. 'Born in the USA' blasts out too loud and usually I'd ask her to put her AirPods in, but I'm just thankful she's showing an interest in something. Our tabby cat stares out of the window, ears twitching. He's grown up with the kids. Chris had chosen him from a kitten and Lottie had named him Michael Finnegan because she used to love the rhyme so much. He's barely left the house since Lottie got sick, as though he senses something is wrong with her.

Chris is sprawled on his stomach, on the floor, textbooks spread out before him. I don't know how he can possibly focus. He's munched his way through an entire punnet of grapes. That boy is permanently hungry.

I don't hear the front door open and close, but Sean's voice drifts through before he appears beside me, kissing the back of my neck and plucking a piece of red pepper from the chopping board.

'How long did the doctor say the results will take?'

I had texted him straight after Lottie's appointment to let him know she'd had some tests.

'About five working days but it could be more or less.'

'Not too long then,' he says but it seems an age to me.

'Sean, I'm really worried about her.'

'I am too, but let's put things in perspective.'

'I'm not catastrophising. This isn't anything to do with my dad. *Look* at her.'

'I know. Sorry.' He gives my shoulders a squeeze.

I lost my father when I was young. He was seemingly strong and healthy, although that day he had complained of a headache. Mum gave him a glass of water and some paracetamol and took me swimming to give him some peace. When we came home he was still in his chair, but he'd slipped away. Just . . . gone. I'd shaken him, trying to wake him up. Even now I find it hard to process.

I glance over my shoulder before furtively grating aubergine and courgette – vegetables the children claim to hate – so I can sneak them into a Bolognese sauce. Although they're long past the toddler stage, my parenting technique can still consist of distraction, bribery and sleight of hand. Not like some of the channels I watch on YouTube of parents who are seemingly, effortlessly, doing it all.

It's my guilty pleasure. All of us mums perhaps have one once the kids are in bed. Wine o'clock, a soap opera, endless hours frittered away on Candy Crush.

Social media is mine. Sean tends to go to bed early; he's often up before the sun has properly brushed away the violet streaks of dawn. Sean is a health and safety executive, with his own business, but it means he has to travel.

Later that night, as I scroll, I sip Pinot, orange table lamp glowing, iPad balanced on my lap. A vanilla-scented candle flickering on the hearth. I hover over one of my favourites: 'Hi, I'm Harlow.' She's one of the biggest parenting channels with a high six-figure following and is quite the local celebrity. Her son, Marco, is the same age as Chris, although they have absolutely nothing in common. Marco goes to a private school. Harlow's husband, Javier, is a property developer. Their house is gorgeous. There's always a huge vase of fresh lilies on their marble worktop; she says Javier has them delivered to her every Friday.

Esther laughed at me when I told her how perfect Harlow's home is. 'Don't be so gullible. Appearances can be deceptive.' And I know that – god, I *know* that – but I'm both envious and entertained by the sparkle in everyone else's life while mine is . . . not dull exactly. Just ordinary.

I'd once tried to start my own YouTube channel on a whim. It was stupid. I had filmed the whole family outside our three-bedroomed terrace, waving at the camera. 'Hello, we're the Finch family. Welcome to our home. If you love what you see, don't forget to like and subscribe.'

I'd hesitated before posting it because . . . well, I didn't want to draw attention to myself, but then I thought *stop being silly*. Everyone has a skeleton in their closet, don't they, and they don't stop living their life because of it. Anyway, the kids had egged me on and, if I'm honest, I'd loved the rush of adrenaline I'd felt when I'd clicked to make the post public.

In the morning, I'd felt quite anxious and had reached for my phone before I'd even properly opened my eyes.

Zero views.

I'd put up another couple of videos after that, but I didn't really have anything to say.

I never bothered deleting the channel; it's still there. On a whim, I check it now. There are a grand total of about twelve views, and in truth, eleven of them were probably me.

I should get rid of my profile; I'm not using it.

But, really, if I leave it up, what harm can it do? It's lovely looking back at Lottie and Chris, Daisy and Felix before they grew so tall.

No. It shouldn't be there, just in case . . .

I jab at menu options on the screen, but it isn't obvious how to deactivate it and I'm not sure which email I used to set it up, or what my password might be.

Yawning, I add it to the 'To Do' list on my phone that never seems to shrink, but I never get around to deleting the video because, before I can, before I can tick anything else off my list, the bottom falls out of my world.

Chapter 3

Mia

I'm gripping Sean's hand so tightly it must hurt, but thankfully he doesn't once ask me to loosen my grip. It feels as though the world has let go of me and he's the only one keeping me from floating away.

'Aplastic anaemia,' I repeat for the third time, somehow hoping that if I voice the words aloud they will lose their power but, of course they don't, because I don't understand what they mean. Sometimes there's nothing as terrifying as the unknown, is there? A tremor of fear spreads through me, starting at my toes, feet moving of their own accord. Knees jiggling up and down. Fingers twitching until I'm shaking so hard my teeth are rattling together.

'It's a relief it isn't cancer or . . . ' Sean trails off as he sees the expression on Dr Chadha's face. Her mouth, bare of lipstick, in a thin, straight line. She looks too young to be a paediatric haematologist, and I have to stop myself demanding to see her qualifications. She has to be wrong, doesn't she?

'Is it serious?' I don't know why I'm asking, because of

course it is. We'd been called to the hospital once the results of Lottie's blood tests came through, so it can't be nothing, can it? But still, even as I sit here trembling, tears stinging behind my eyes, I hope.

'I wanted to see you both without Lottie because we can't be one hundred per cent certain until we've taken a biopsy, but the bloods, Lottie's bruises, fatigue, bleeding gums . . . Experience tells me that it's probable. More than probable.'

'But what is it?'

'It's a blood condition. The bone marrow and stem cells are no longer able to produce enough blood cells for the body to work normally.'

'Why?' Sean sounds so bewildered, so out of his depth. We both are. A tea trolley clatters past the door. Nurses chatter. Sharp angry blasts of a car horn sound outside the window, another bun fight in the car park, no doubt. Life is, somehow, going on, but I feel as though we're stuck in this moment, and my heart is racing, desperate to escape it.

When Lottie was a toddler she'd cover her eyes with her small hands – *if you can't see me, I'm not here*. I'm fighting the childish urge to cover my ears – *if I can't hear you, it can't be true.*

'It's impossible to pinpoint the exact cause. It can be inherited.'

'Inherited?' My mind travels to another place, another time. 'My dad died of a brain aneurysm, very suddenly. He was here and then he was gone.' I still recall exactly how I felt that day because fear is the one emotion that can return with a memory and have an overwhelming sense of realism. I feel that same fear again now.

'I'm sorry you lost your father, but there won't be a connection there. Sometimes AA can occur after a virus, sometimes it's linked to toxins, and often there's no obvious reason.'

'Toxins?' A flash of shame rockets through me. 'Is it something I've fed Lottie? What about pesticides? Or the cleaning products I use?'

'Mrs Finch.'

'Call me Mia, please.' Because if she calls me by my first name it will seem more like we're friends. Like we're in this together. It's such early days but I already know I need a strong team – Lottie needs a strong team – to fight this. Whatever *this* turns out to be.

'Mia. It won't be anything you've done. This isn't your fault.'

'But,' I flounder, looking around, needing something, someone to blame, because I can't help feeling that this is some sort of divine retribution. A punishment for the terrible thing I once did.

Dr Chadha's voice pulls me back to now. 'It's generally idiopathic.'

'Idiopathic?' I repeat.

'There's no known cause.'

'But it's not . . . I mean is it . . . ' I gaze at the doctor imploringly.

'Every case is individual, but it can be very serious.'

'But it's never—' there's a hard weight in my chest, making it hard for me to whisper '—fatal?'

Dr Chadha links her fingers together, resting them on the desk in front of us. 'On occasions, unfortunately, it can be, but we're a long way from that and we have lots of options.'

'You have medicine?' Sean asks and we exchange a look. Both of us knowing that the sticky pink Calpol Lottie still prefers over swallowing a paracetamol tablet for temperatures and sore throats won't be enough, but hoping that there's something similar out there that will cure it.

'There are various treatments but, look, let's not get

ahead of ourselves. I wanted you to be clear what it is I think we're dealing with. We'll carry out a biopsy—'

'You can't cut Lottie open.' The thought of it obliterates my senses and for a moment I don't know where I am or who I am, but I can feel myself swaying in my seat. I'm slipping under until I feel Sean's hand squeezing mine again. Shakily I lean forward for my glass of water.

'Are you okay, Mia?' Dr Chadha asks. I nod and she says, 'A biopsy isn't as terrifying as it sounds. We'll use an anaesthetic, so Lottie won't feel anything, and then insert a small needle into the bone. The lab will process the results quite quickly.'

The results, when they come, are exactly what Dr Chadha had pre-empted.

Aplastic anaemia.

'So, the bone marrow—' Sean's in fix-it mode. I can see it from the set of his jaw. Forever the practical one, tell him a problem and he finds a solution, always. 'Sorry, I don't think I'm sure what bone marrow actually is?'

Dr Chadha picks up a pen and draws on a piece of paper as she explains. Blood cells, platelets.

When she looks up to make sure we understand, she slides a box of tissues towards me. I hadn't even registered that I am crying. I think of Lottie alone in the waiting room, waiting to be called in and given this news, and I cry even harder.

I rocket from never having heard of aplastic anaemia to becoming an expert in a matter of days. Googling, always googling. Typing out lists of questions, which I now read from my phone.

I've read up on blood transfusions and immune suppressive therapy through AGT and ciclosporin, but neither of these is the route Dr Chadha wants to take.

'That's the route we might have once taken with children,' she explains. 'But they're very different to adults and do respond better to stronger treatment options.'

'A bone marrow transplant.' I've been half expecting it, but the word transplant almost gets stuck in my throat; it's scary, isn't it?

'It's the most likely treatment to lead to a normal blood count, without too many side effects, and it will eradicate the need for long-term medication.' She pauses. Holds me with her eyes. 'Often a sibling is the best match.'

The feelings that tear through me are indescribable and that's what I feel my emotions are doing, tearing me into pieces. Dr Chadha is holding out a possible solution, but I want to knock it out of her hands and stamp all over it. I can't put Chris through any unnecessary emotional distress or physical discomfort. I can't.

But then, fighting against this instinct is the desire to snatch the solution from Dr Chadha and slot it into place. Chris donates, Lottie recovers, and we all live happily ever after, don't we?

One look at Sean's anguished face and I know that he's battling against the same tidal wave of worry that I am.

I hunch over, elbows on my knees, feeling I might actually throw up.

Feeling I have no choice but to agree.

Lottie, though, once she's in the room, objects. 'No. I don't want Chris to miss any school. It's an important year.'

'I think it has to be his decision, Lotts. You'd do it for him,' Sean says.

'Will it hurt Chris?'

I wince as Lottie asks this, as though I am already feeling his pain.

'The first step to testing is to take some DNA and then if he's a basic match we'll take some blood.'

'But—'

'Lottie.' She turns her head towards me. Her ponytail is becoming loose, and I remember when I used to be the one to brush her hair every morning before school.

I can't decide if I want a plait or a bun today, Mummy.

It seemed like such a huge decision at the time. I wish it was all she had to worry about right now.

'It'll be up to Chris,' I reiterate, 'but we don't even know if your brother is a match yet.' I address the doctor. 'Can you test me at the same time?' I'm adamant we go through this together, as a family.

'And me.' Sean is firm.

'We will, but siblings are far more likely to be a match than a parent.'

'Thank you.' I'm grateful.

Perhaps Sean and I being tested is standard procedure and it shouldn't feel like a victory because, ultimately, we are all on the same side, we all want the same thing, and yet somehow it does. I allow myself a moment to feel that warm flush of triumph because I'm so scared I'll never feel it again.

Lottie's life – our lives – are going to change unimaginably. I'm learning that there are so many things I'll have to deal with. We'll likely need to isolate as Lottie's immune system will be compromised. I might not be able to visit Mum, which will be confusing for her. She's not long been living in the care home and, on the days she remembers who I am, I don't want her to think I've forgotten her. There's my job. I write content for an online magazine and my firm has already made so many redundancies thanks to AI. Still, I can figure everything out once Lottie is well again because I have to believe that Lottie *will* get better.

She will.

Won't she?

*　*　*

In our living room, Sean is explaining the potential transplant to Chris and Esther while Lottie scrolls through her mobile. She's obsessed with Instagram. Will she be allowed her phone in hospital? Will the signal interfere with the equipment? The handset be an infection risk? There is so much I still don't know. Although I've been known to nag her about her screen time, I don't want it to be another thing she loses.

As Sean talks, my eyes are drawn to our wedding photo. We're beaming at each other, the future full of possibilities. Chris is on my hip. His legs not quite hiding my pregnant belly. It wasn't until I was expecting Lottie I felt I needed the security, the stability of marriage. It seemed right somehow to cement our family of four together.

We were so happy, and we'd taken it for granted. Looking back, it perhaps became too fairytale perfect after the hard time we had been through. Those stories I used to tell Lottie, spinning straw into gold. But now everything is returning to straw. Decomposing.

I have to stay positive.

I wrench my gaze away from it but instead land on the picture taken earlier this year. We had been to the fair with Esther, Felix and Daisy. The cousins are hurtling down a giant inflatable slide, side by side, joy radiating from them. Even though it's slightly out of focus, I had framed it because now they're teenagers they are outgrowing things at an alarming rate and who knows if they'll ever whizz down a slide again. You often don't know when it's the last time for anything, do you? The last time they'll cuddle their teddy bear at night, the last time they'll want to be pushed on a swing. I've tried to treasure every moment, but—

Silence.

Sean has finished explaining about the potential transplant to Chris and Esther.

Then, Chris's indignant voice.

'Are you mental? Of course I'm going to be fucking tested.' He rarely swears, not in front of Sean and me anyway; his eyes are blazing. 'I can't believe you think I shouldn't be.'

'Yeah, well, basically, I just don't want you to fall behind at school,' Lottie says.

'Yeah, well, basically, I just don't want *you* to . . . to . . . .' He stops his sentence there, but we're all thinking it.

She might die.

'I'll be tested too,' Esther says.

'Are you sure?' The pinch of pressure in my forehead relaxes a little.

She puts her hands on her hips the way Chris had and says, with attitude, 'Are you mental? Of course I'm going to be fucking tested.'

Nothing should be funny right now but still we laugh.

'You're an idiot but I love you.' I hug her, hug everyone. Hope lifting my spirits.

A couple of days later, we return to the hospital.

I'm rummaging in my bag for a tissue when footsteps approach.

'Hello, Charlotte, I'm Alma Rutherford. I'm going to be your nurse today and, moving forward, I'll be your point of contact if you have any concerns or questions and Dr Chadha isn't available.'

I look up, my eyes lock with hers. An expression I can't read flickers across her face.

Alma?

Alma Rutherford?

Alma isn't a common name. Her surname is different though, her hair colour and style too. She's larger. Wears glasses. I'm not convinced it is her and she hasn't said she recognises me.

I study her as she scribbles things on a clipboard. Perhaps I'm mistaken; it probably isn't her. I haven't seen her for nearly sixteen years. Not since that night. It wasn't as if I knew her well.

I'm reading too much into a name because I've convinced myself, and I know it's irrational, that Lottie is being punished by some higher force as some kind of divine retribution because I didn't tell the truth to the police at that time.

Alma begins to run through what will happen this morning and I focus on what she's telling me, keeping my fingers crossed as she swabs my cheek for DNA.

And then we wait.

But still I wonder if it *is* the same Alma, my heart racing as I'm reminded of that night.

The police.

The lies.

Chapter 4

Who's Watching You Documentary

Jake Lawler (host): Our first guest is Alma Rutherford. Alma was Charlotte's assigned nurse and can give us a rare insight into the Finch family during the time of Lottie's illness, which, of course, I think it's fair to say, was the catalyst for everything that followed. Thanks for coming, Alma.

Alma Rutherford (nurse): (whispers) Thanks for, (clears throat) thanks for inviting me. (speaks louder) It's great to have the opportunity to raise awareness of bone marrow transplants. Not nearly enough people donate. I think it isn't because they don't care but because they're not really aware of how simple the process is. The lives it can potentially save. Now, with everything with the Finch family . . .

Lawler: Yes, let's talk about the Finches.

Rutherford: But I just wanted to say about the bone marrow register—

Lawler: We'll be sharing links to info about how people can donate. (smiles at the camera)

Rutherford: If I can just ex—

Lawler: (hand covers heart) Having a sick child is every parent's worst nightmare, isn't it? Is there any such thing as a typical reaction? Was the Finches' reaction typical?

Rutherford: (hesitation) Lottie was phenomenal. She had chemo to prepare her for the transplant. She lost her hair, but I never once saw her cry.

Lawler: And what about Mia and Sean during this time?

Rutherford: (shifts uncomfortably in seat) Everyone is different. I've pretty much seen it all. Couples who pull together, couples who can't take the strain and separate, families who blame each other. I've witnessed both mums and dads turn to drink, to religion, but there are also those who take it in their stride.

Lawler: And was there any indication when you met Mia, Sean and Chris as to what sort of family they'd be?

Rutherford: They seemed very committed to each other. Sean seemed like a good man despite what people online have said about him.

Lawler: And Mia? What were your first impressions of Mia?

Rutherford: (lowers gaze, pulls at a thread hanging from the end of her sleeve; the camera pans as her thumb and index finger nervously twist it around the little finger of her opposite hand) I thought I was here to explain aplastic anaemia to the viewers? To raise awareness of the importance of donating bone marrow?

Lawler: You are absolutely raising awareness but, of course, everyone is interested in your opinion of Mia and Sean. You had access to this family when they were under extraordinary pressure.

Rutherford: Yes. (close-up of her face as she frowns and crosses her arms)

Lawler: (smiles, leans forward) You must have amazing insight and empathy, being a nurse. Can I just say how much I (makes a sweeping gesture with his hand towards the crew) *we all* admire you, and how grateful we are to you and our wonderful NHS. I really value your opinion. What did you think when the news first broke?

Rutherford: (blushing; uncrosses arms and rests hands in lap) Let's just say it didn't surprise me, what happened.

Lawler: Really? (edges forward on his seat) Why?

Rutherford: I mean, when you know a member of the family has had an association with criminals in the past, you become . . . well, I didn't let it affect my care of Lottie.

Lawler: How did you know about that association?

Rutherford: (flustered; picks up the glass of water from the table, camera zooms in to see her hands tremble, water spilling) Everyone knows. It's been all over the papers.

Lawler: But you said knowing didn't affect your care of Lottie? Your care of Lottie was way before any of this came to light.

Rutherford: I just . . . (panicked glance at the camera) I just meant that I had a feeling something wasn't right with the Finches and then when it all came out in the papers it made sense.

(pause)

Lawler: Right. So you first met the Finches when Charlotte was admitted to the ward you worked on?

Rutherford: (hesitation. Eyes flicker around the studio) Umm. Yes.

Lawler: And Mia and Sean were married.

Rutherford: Yes.

Lawler: Have you ever been married, Alma?

Rutherford: No.

Lawler: Have you ever changed your surname, or has it always been Rutherford?

Rutherford: What? I . . . I don't see what—

Lawler: Our expert researchers have uncovered—

Rutherford: Stop. (colour drains from Rutherford's face) I thought I was here to talk about Lottie? To help other kids by getting the viewers to donate. I said I didn't want to talk about anything *but* her illness. *I told you*. (stalks off the stage, pulling microphone from t-shirt)

Lawler: (raises eyebrows) We'll see if we can persuade Alma to come back out later. For now, we'll go to a break.

@**Lamadrama23** That nurse is hiding something!!!

@**Blackcat1970** You're such a drama queen. I never judge anyone

@**Avocadomonkey** #WWY will reveal the facts. It always does. This series is EPIC

@**Jamie2983** Shame it's hosted by such a twat

Chapter 5

Mia

Alma's voice on the other end of the phone is both unexpected and unsettling.

'Hi, Mia. It wouldn't normally be me who rings but I got your number from the file because I wanted to call you myself.' She pauses.

It's her.

It is her.

She wants to talk about that night.

'Good news! You're a match.'

'Me?' I'm momentarily thrown. After everything we'd been told, I'd expected it to be Chris. We'd *all* expected it to be Chris. Despite this, Sean, Esther and I had been tested. Lewis, Esther's husband, had brought her to her appointment, but he'd chosen not to be tested himself.

'I don't like needles,' he had said. 'If I am a match and had to inject myself every day to prepare for the procedure I just couldn't cope.'

Esther had looked embarrassed, Sean had been furious, but I wasn't surprised.

I know what Lewis is.

Who he is.

But I can never tell.

'Yes,' Alma says again, 'you're a match, Mia.'

She gives me a moment to let it sink in.

I'm a match! Lottie is going to be fine.

My hopes soar, untethered, as high as the balloons that Mum and I had released when I was a child. Messages scrawled in my uneven handwriting and stuffed inside them. Before the days we knew how bad balloons were for the environment, of course. Even now I can recall excitement twisting inside me as I watched the red, green and yellow balloons become small dots swallowed by the sky, while I anticipated letters arriving for me from around the world. I had been so lonely since my dad had passed. But then came the stomach-dropping disappointment after days and weeks went by, and the rattle of the letterbox was never for me. The comfort of my mother's hand around mine as she reassured me there was still time for someone to write to me, '*Believing in something is the beginning of everything and, if it doesn't work, don't lose faith, my love. We can always try again.*'

'Alma, is this . . . is this a one-shot thing?' Doubts are already setting in. 'If it doesn't work then . . .'

'We'd like you all to come in tomorrow at two and we'll go through everything, but no –' her voice softens – 'there are options if this isn't successful. Try not to think about everything that can go wrong. Focus on all the things that can go right.'

After the call has ended I put my phone back down on the table but, strangely, my hand doesn't feel empty. If I close my eyes, I can still feel my mother's palm against mine, her fingers squeezing me gently.

'*Don't lose faith, my love. We can always try again.*'

* * *

36

Lottie is curled on the sofa, watching *500 Days of Summer*, her comfort movie, Michael Finnegan snoozing in the crook of her knees. Her blonde hair is tangled, damp from the shower that's exhausted her.

I pause the film, crouching down in front of her before she can protest. Our eyes meet, her blue ones the same shade as mine, holding a weariness that no fifteen-year-old should be familiar with. Gently, I brush her fringe away from her face. 'The hospital just rang.'

'Why?' She scrambles to sitting position, Michael Finnegan mewling loudly as he's disturbed.

'Lottie,' I begin, then stop, not quite sure how to frame it. I don't want to get her hopes up too much but, really, there's only one thing I can say. 'I'm a match.' I hold that information out to her like it's a precious gift.

Her whole face changes, lifts. 'I knew you would be.'

She flings her arms around my neck and squeezes me tightly. Her hair smells of rosemary shampoo.

'I knew you'd save me,' she says into my neck and, even as I tell her gently that we must take things one stage at a time, the heat of her optimism spreads through me like a sunrise, bright and warm.

'I can't wait to tell Daisy when she gets home from school.'

'If you're up to it, we can ask Esther and the kids over for a takeaway later?'

'Yeah, that'd be cool.'

I don't want to call it a last goodbye, but Lottie could be in hospital for a long time, and she won't be allowed many, if any, visitors until her immune system can cope with it.

No, not a goodbye; a 'see you later', that's all.

I text Esther to see if they can come.

* * *

While Lottie sleeps, I take the chance to visit my mum in Poppyfields, the care home we had carefully chosen for her. In the month she's been here she's barely left the room, but when I check and find it empty, her bathroom too, I fear the worst.

'Beverley is in the garden,' Sierra tells me as I rush out into the hallway. Most of the carers are lovely, but she isn't one of my favourites. She always seems too worried about her acrylic nails to help when the residents ask for it. Whenever I need to ask her something about Mum, she is usually watching something on her phone, twisting her long hair around her finger, all platinum beach waves and pink tips.

I find Mum wrapped in a cardigan, on a wrought-iron bench, watching the bees hovering around the lavender. It seems this is a day for new beginnings.

'Hello,' I say cautiously as I sit down next to her. I don't want to startle her by calling her Mum because sometimes when I say that she looks at me with such fear because she either doesn't remember she has a daughter or because I remain a child within her muddled mind. The worst thing, though, is when she asks where my dad is and I'm reminded how suddenly I lost him and that I'm losing her now too. For the longest time after he died, I was scared to let her out of my sight, scared that she'd be taken too. That fear of loss has never really left me. Although I was young, I blamed myself. Had I made too much noise and given him a headache? Not understanding what an aneurysm was. Mum blamed herself too, that if she hadn't left him then he'd still be here. She could have called an ambulance; he would have been saved. We'll never know if this is true, but that's the thing about irrational thoughts, isn't it? They shout louder than the ones that make sense.

We both look up at the sound of a plane. Shield our eyes as we watch it streak a frothy trail across the cornflower sky.

'I wonder where it's going?' Mum says. 'Imagine all those people going to a foreign county. Learning about another culture.'

'Today I was remembering that I once wanted a pen pal so I could write to someone far away and learn about their lives. I wrote notes and put them inside balloons and then released them, hoping they'd travel for miles.'

She turns to me and the recognition in her eyes makes my heart lift.

'Nobody wrote back for a long time,' she says. 'Six months, wasn't it?'

'Almost a year, and then, when I'd given up hope, I got a letter from Jon, and rather than living somewhere exotic, he lived ten miles away.'

'You should never give up hope,' Mum says, and it is such a fight to swallow down the lump in my throat. Knowing that she – we – are sharing the same memory but knowing that it will slip away again soon is heart-breaking as much as it is heart-making.

'How are Chris and Lottie?' she asks, and for a moment I cannot speak because I want to throw myself into my mother's arms and let all the emotion I bottle up at home come pouring out. I want to feel like a child again, pass the responsibility to an adult, if only for a short while.

'Chris and Lottie are both great,' I say, because what's the point of distressing her with the truth when she won't be able to hold on to it anyway? I chat about the kids, the exams they are studying for, silly quarrels they've had that I think will make her laugh, and they do.

'So, how old are your children?' she asks, and I tell her.

'Perhaps they'd like to put messages into balloons and release them into the sky. I did that once with my daughter, you know.'

And she is lost to me once more, but we have made a

new memory together today. One that I will treasure and maybe, just maybe, we'll be able to make some more.

As I walk back to my car, the words my mum had once said to me echo through time: '*Don't lose faith, my love.*'

A text. Esther.

We'll all be there later! Even Lewis!

It'd be great to see you all, I lie.

It's never great to see Lewis.

It's a constant reminder.

I did a bad thing.

Chapter 6

Mia

'Congratulations, donor!' Esther bustles into the kitchen and begins to unwrap the fish and chip supper she's brought with her. Lewis doesn't say hello; instead he positions himself in the corner, typing something into his phone. It drives Esther crazy that he's always working. Daisy and Felix take plates from the cupboard, clatter cutlery from the drawer.

'We're trying not to make too big a deal of it,' I say, although I cannot stop grinning. 'There's a long road ahead of us.'

'Hey, sis.' Sean squeezes into the kitchen and kisses Esther on the cheek. They hug tightly. They've always been protective of each other.

'Lewis.' Sean hesitates before approaching him and shaking his hand as though this is a formal meeting, and they haven't been related for over twenty years.

'Sorry you weren't a match,' Lewis says.

Sean's face clouds over.

'It's great that Mia is,' Esther says.

'I was speaking to Alma,' Lewis says.

'Alma?' My mouth dries. I swallow hard.

Don't mention that night.

Don't mention that night.

Don't mention that night.

'You know, Lottie's nurse?' Lewis looks amused as he raises his eyebrows.

'I wasn't aware you knew her?'

'I met her when I took Esther to be tested,' he says.

I'm desperate to ask him if that's the first time he's met her. If he thinks it is the same Alma, but, of course, I don't.

I can't.

'She was explaining the probabilities of finding a match. I was feeling bad I didn't get tested but she said it's far less likely that a non-blood relation would be a match.'

'Well, I am,' I say, 'so it doesn't matter that you didn't want to try. It's turned out all right in the end.' I fetch the vinegar from the cupboard.

'Anyway, I have to go,' Lewis announces.

'Go?' Esther looks dismayed. 'We barely see you anymore.'

Lewis waves his mobile. 'Work calls, I'm afraid. Sean, are you still wanting that meeting tomorrow?'

'Please,' Sean says. I see the pink rise on his neck. He hates the thought of asking Lewis for favours, but it was Esther's idea. She hadn't been snooping but she'd come across one of our bank statements when she was looking for a pen in the pile of papers I keep on the worktop.

'Are you guys okay?' she had asked.

Sean and I hadn't replied because the truth of it is we weren't okay at all. Sean's health and safety business has been struggling to find its feet again ever since Covid. It isn't that all the companies had shut down but so many people work from home now and his services aren't in demand the way he'd like them to be. We'd remortgaged because he'd wanted to keep paying Aleksander's wages as he'd employed him for so long. He thought the business would pick up again but, despite investing into new equipment to compete with a larger firm that began monopolising the contracts, the profits are eaten up by our debt repayments.

Esther's worried eyes had flickered between us when we hadn't answered. 'You must stop paying rent to me.'

'No.' Sean was proud.

'You took care of me when Dad died, Sean, and again when we lost Mum.'

'Because you're my sister and I love you.'

'Well, you're my brother and I love you so—'

'We're fine.' Sean had been adamant.

She'd chewed her lip. She knew what he was like. Feelings held close to his chest like a winning hand during a game of poker.

'Why don't I ask Lewis if he can recommend you for health and safety contacts?' she suggested. Lewis invested in businesses and some of them might need Sean's services.

'I don't need my little sister going cap in hand for me,' Sean had said but then he'd glanced at a photo of the kids on the fridge. 'But I'll set up a meeting and ask him.'

'Half past twelve?' Lewis says now.

Sean looks at me.

I nod. 'We can meet at the hospital; I'll bring Chris and Lottie.'

'Half past twelve is great, thanks.' Sean shakes his hand again.

'See you tomorrow then. I'll wish Lottie luck on my way out. See you later, kids.'

He doesn't kiss Esther goodbye as he hurries out of the kitchen.

Her face drops and for a moment the mood is low, but then Sean says, 'I'll have his fish then,' and grins, and I relax. This night is for Lottie, and I don't want anything, or anyone, to spoil it.

'You can't just hog his fish –' Esther picks herself up – 'don't be shellfish.'

'You calling me shellfish?' Sean makes pincers with his hands. 'Don't get crabby. Does salmon else want it?'

'You two are, like, totally the opposite of funny.' Felix shakes his head as he douses his food in vinegar.

'Then you're not herring what I'm herring,' Sean says. 'I'm hilarious.'

'Cod almighty.' Esther grabs a knife and fork.

The atmosphere is light as we all crowd into the living room. Seven of us fill the space. This is the house that Sean and Esther were brought up in. When their parents passed, they left it to both Sean and Esther, but as Esther already had a home with Lewis, Sean and I moved in with the kids. We pay Esther rent, though, for her share, even though she says we don't have to. She was so supportive when Sean wanted to remortgage after his business took such a hit during Covid.

'I can look after my big brother, for a change,' she had said. 'You've done enough for me over the years, Sean.'

We probably pay more in combined mortgage and rent than we would do if we lived somewhere else that was purely ours but it's home and we're very happy here.

I watch Lottie as she cracks the golden batter around her cod. She's as white as the fish inside. I hope this isn't too much for her.

As though she can read my thoughts, she says, 'I'm glad you're all here. I might not see you for weeks now, months.'

'I'll miss you, but we can FaceTime,' Daisy says.

'You'll be all right hanging out with Erika,' Lottie says

sadly. I know she likes Daisy's new friend Erika too. Lottie isn't in Erika and Daisy's class, but she had been upset when she found out Erika had lost her sister – *I can't imagine ever losing Chris* – but it's clear she's already feeling left out, so I'm pleased when Daisy says, 'I love Erika, but she isn't you. How long are you gonna have to isolate for?'

'I dunno exactly.' Lottie shrugs.

'We've an appointment tomorrow afternoon where they'll run through everything properly,' I say. 'Hopefully they'll start me on the drug to stimulate my extra cells, and we can get some sort of timeline for the donation and transplant.'

'It's so cool that you're literally, like, going to save Lottie's life, Aunt Mia,' Daisy says.

'Yeah. Some cultures would say you'll be indebted to your mum forever now, Lotts,' Felix says.

'No.' Chris points his fork at Felix. 'I think it's the person who saves someone's life is responsible for that life forever.'

'I think as a mum, we're responsible anyway,' Esther says.

'Yeah, but Aunt Mia doesn't have to donate just cos she's related to Lottie. It's cool.'

'My wife is remarkable.' Sean holds up his can of Diet Coke in a toast.

Everyone gazes at me as though I am the sun, the moon, the stars.

They don't know there are other shades to me that no one in this room has seen.

They see the wife. The mum.

They don't know about that night. They don't see the liar.

Chris is the first to finish eating. He wipes the grease from his mouth with the back of his hands and fiddles with his phone until the Bluetooth speaker streams Raye.

It's as though we have momentarily paused the nightmarish situation we are in; the house is full of chatter and laughter.

Possibility.

And love.

So much love.

Later, in bed, I say, 'I think everything is going to be okay.'

Sean strokes my hair, my head on his chest, and I'm lulled by the rise and fall of his rib cage. Creamy moonlight filters in through the crack in the curtains. 'Do you think?' There's a tremor in his voice and I reach up to his face; his cheeks are wet with tears. 'I don't know why I'm crying. It's such a relief you're a match and we can move forward, but I wish I could donate instead of you. I wish Lottie didn't have to go through this full stop. I wish—'

'Shh. Let's just have this moment. This hope. Tonight. We need this.'

I climb on top of him and kiss his tears away. Take his hands and place them on my breasts, my own hands travelling over his body, lower, lower. Partly hating myself for wanting this, wanting him, when Lottie is still sick, when nothing really has changed. But when everything around us has been falling apart and that one phone call from Alma has given us a chance to believe we can put it back together, I just want, however fleetingly, to feel normal again.

Then Sean is inside of me, and I want to weep. It feels like the first and the last time. I'm not sure if Lottie and I will have to isolate away from him. If the drugs I'll need to take will have side effects. I'm not certain of anything except, 'I love you.' My lips brush against his.

'I love you too. Always. Whatever—'

I silence him with another kiss.

'Everything *is* going to be okay,' I whisper. Needing, even if it's just for tonight, to believe that.

I was still scared of losing Lottie, of course, not realising then that I could – I would – lose everything.

Was that evening the last time we were happy as a family? One of the last few hours that Sean and I were happy as a couple? Looking back, I think it probably was.

Chapter 7

Mia

Although Chris, Lottie and I get to the hospital fifteen minutes before our appointment, Sean is already in the waiting room when we arrive. I see him before he sees us. He's slumped forward, elbows on his knees, head in his hands. It looks as though he has the whole weight of the world on his hunched shoulders. I hurry to reach him before the kids do. He won't be expecting us yet and I don't want Lottie to see just how worried he is. My own anxieties are tucked neatly away. Outwardly, we have to be as positive as we can for her. 'Sean?' I startle him as I touch his shoulder.

'You're early.' He quickly wipes his cheeks. Last night we'd all joked around as we ate fish and chips because we'd so desperately wanted things to be normal, if only for a couple of hours. Now, here with the harsh lights, the smell of disinfectant, the constant noise, is a stark reminder that things are anything but.

'Dad?' The uncertainty in Chris's voice pushes Lottie into my side, her fingers finding mine.

'I'm okay.' Sean smiles at both children in turn but

he doesn't look at me again. I can tell he's trying to hold himself together. Once we have all the information about the transplant process, and we know exactly what's going to happen, we'll feel better. Knowledge is power.

'I'm scared too,' Lottie says as she sits on his lap for the first time in years.

He wraps his arms around her. 'Don't be scared, Lotts. You're in the best possible place.'

'I don't want to be here at all.'

I notice the pallor of her skin. The rapid rise and fall of her chest. I crouch down in front of her and take her hands in mine. 'It'll be okay, Lottie. Breathe with me, slowly now. One. Two. Three. One. Two. Three.' We repeat this until her body has remembered the most fundamental of skills.

Then it's my breathing that quickens as Dr Chadha is calling us into her consulting room.

There has been so much information to take in, my head is still spinning when I'm home. I'm trying to keep a conversation going while we eat, but no one is in the mood for small talk. We pick at our Shepherds Pie.

'I'm going to bed.' Lottie presses her palms against the table as she stands. She sways. Today has drained the last of her energy.

'I'll come up with you.' I follow her up the stairs, arms spread, ready to catch her if she falls backwards, the way I used to when she was a toddler.

Back in the kitchen, Chris is loading the last of the plates into the dishwasher, while Sean sits, staring into space.

'Thanks, Chris.'

He yawns. ''S all right. I'm turning in now.'

'Okay.' I know turning in means he'll spend the next few hours sprawled across his mattress, scrolling through his phone. 'Night, night. Don't let the bedbugs bite.' Our eyes meet because we both know there are worse things than bedbugs coming for our family.

When he's left the room, I am alone with my husband, who is staring at nothing.

'Coffee?' I flip on the kettle.

'No.' Sean's voice is flat. 'I'm going to go to bed too.'

'Sean.' I sit opposite him and reach across the table for his hands. Instead of holding mine, he picks up his mobile and stands. 'Wait, I haven't even heard how your meeting with Lewis went. How did it go?'

For a minute I don't think he is going to answer but then he says, voice tight, 'He said no.'

'What? Why?' I'm stunned. It never crossed my mind he'd actually say no.

'Among other things, he said mixing business with family is a mistake. He doesn't think I can compete with that other firm in terms of service and pricing.'

Disappointment swirls in my gut but it's quickly replaced by anger. Lewis gave me a speech once about the importance of family and, although I know at the time he was all about saving his own skin, I've done what he wants for the past sixteen years. Isn't it time he helped me? Us?

I realise Sean is waiting for me to say something. I can't tell him what I'm really thinking, so instead I ask, 'Are you okay?'

He shrugs but to my relief he does sit back down. 'It's too much. All of it. Not just Lewis. I've learned things today that . . .' He can't look at me. He's trying so hard not to cry. All that 'men must be men and stiff upper lip' that his father lived by might have been the norm in the 1960s but it's not okay. Lewis slips back to the hidden place in the corner of my mind. He isn't the most important issue right now.

'I know hearing the intricate details of what Lottie has to go through was harrowing. You can cry if you want to.

I know it sounds horrendous. Everything that's coming up but—'

'I wish it could be me going through it instead of Lottie,' he says fiercely, thumping his chest with his fist. 'Me donating instead of you, but it can't be, can it?'

Sean glares at me as though it is somehow my fault.

'That shouldn't make you feel inadequate.'

'Who says that's how I feel?'

'I don't know how you feel. Tell me.'

He shakes his head. His lips clamped together either to keep his words or his tears inside. Perhaps both.

I've only seen him this way once before and that was when his mum died and he'd tried to keep all of his grief inside, supporting Esther while she fell apart, shutting me out in the process. He'd barely talked to me for months, but I loved him, understood him; we'd got through that, and we'll get through this. Esther had said that he'd been exactly the same when their father died when they were both teenagers. Sean doesn't often open up about his early years, but I've learned much about his childhood through Esther. Sometimes it's a bonus being married to my best friend's brother. I get an insight into him that I wouldn't otherwise have. Sometimes, though, during the tough times – because all relationships have tough times, don't they – I can feel quite lonely as I can't share everything with her and expect her to automatically take my side because, as close as Esther and I are, she's equally close to Sean. Probably more so, if I'm honest. Blood ties count for a lot, don't they?

'It doesn't matter which of us is donating. We're her parents and we both love her equally and will be there for her every step of the way. It's important that we're strong for her.'

I take his hand and this time he doesn't pull away. His

eyes are tired, his face drawn and I don't think I've ever loved him more than I do right now.

I'm hoping we can talk some more but then he tells me he's going to bed, and he trudges out of the kitchen, leaves me sitting alone, a cold space on my cheek where the warmth of his goodnight kiss should be.

There's the creak of our bedroom floorboards above me. Sean is so close, but he feels so far away.

He's coped well so far with the diagnosis, but everyone has a breaking point, don't they? Hearing what his little girl has to go through these next few months could well be his. I can be strong enough for us all.

I can.

I can't fix Lottie – I have to trust the doctors can – but is there something I can do to help Sean? I'm tempted to call Lewis, ask why he won't help Sean.

But I can't make Lewis invest in my husband, even though I know his deepest darkest secrets. Because, although I can't be certain, from the way he looks at me sometimes, I think he knows mine too.

Chapter 8

Mia

I pour out wine while I pour out my problems to Esther down the phone, choosing my words carefully, not wanting to come across as critical of her brother or her husband.

'Sean seemed so defeated earlier,' I tell her. 'I don't think because of Lewis, although that hasn't helped, of course. We've been given a detailed treatment plan for Lottie, and it sounds terrifying.' The hope that the treatment will work dangles in front of us – a carrot on a stick. We have to be the trudging donkey, however exhausted we become, never losing sight of it, never giving up.

'When my brother is scared he's going to lose something, he can deal with the practical issues but can't process the emotional fallout. Today, well, I guess it's made it even more real, hasn't it?'

'Yes, and I feel . . . ' I'm trying put into words the crushing pressure I feel because it's my bone marrow they're using. That even though Dr Chadha explained to me that there are other options if this isn't successful, I feel I'm ultimately responsible for saving my daughter. That when I think that I might let her down, let the whole family down, there's such a physical pain in my chest I'm scared I'm going to have a heart attack. That, each time I think that, it makes the pain worse because if I wasn't around then I wouldn't be able to donate, would I? That I *have* to stay healthy for Lottie. For us all. It's all on me. Everything. The stabbing pain comes again, and I inhale sharply and place my palm against my chest.

Esther is already talking about Sean again and I want to interrupt her because – just for five minutes, two minutes, one – I want it to be about me, but as a mum I'm used to coming bottom of the list of priorities, so I stay quiet, press my hand against the pain, and listen.

'When Dad was alive,' Esther says, 'he was very much the protector, and I think Sean feels he has to be the same. He probably feels guilty that Lottie is sick. It'll be okay. You're a strong unit. You know this will pass. Look after him, Mia, won't you?'

'Of course,' I tell her, when what I really want to say is who is going to look after me because I'm terrified I have no control over any of it.

'I've got to go and spend some time with the kids. Daisy and Felix are, well, it's hard to tell with Felix. I know he's worried about Lottie, but he isn't saying a lot. Daisy, though, is struggling. We're all struggling this end.'

And then she's gone and it's wrong to feel hurt that her concerns about her brother, her children, have come before me, her best friend, because I hadn't shared what I'm really feeling, but I suddenly feel so alone.

I draw my knees up to my chest and run a light finger down my shin bone, trying to picture the bone marrow inside. Is it good enough?

Am I good enough?

*   *   *

I turn on the TV. I'm obsessed with *Grand Designs* – imagine building your own house from the ground up – but turn it off when I can't focus on the episode.

I gulp down more Chardonnay. It's a cheap one from the corner shop and, rather than tasting of tropical fruits like the one I prefer from Tesco, there's a bitterness about it. Or perhaps it's my own bitterness I taste. The 'it's not fair' that constantly sits on my tongue.

The wine is cold but still the heat from the alcohol blooms through me, but it won't matter how many glasses I knock back, it'll never be enough to thaw the chilling panic inside me. We've only just started this journey and everyone in the family is in a separate room. I remind myself that it's usual for Chris and Lottie to spend evenings in their bedrooms, and that Sean always goes to bed earlier than me, but still, I am so lonely right now.

I reach for my phone and open up my YouTube app. My favourite parenting channel, 'Hi, I'm Harlow', is streaming. Harlow has over 2 million subscribers – I find it hard to imagine that many people.

'I'm live. Ask me anything,' she beams at the camera, and in that moment I wish I was her, with her glossy ponytail and her glossy life. As always, a huge vase of lilies on the marble worktop behind her.

The alcohol burns its way down my throat. I listen as she answers the questions in the comments.

When will my baby sleep through the night?

What if my child doesn't make friends at school?

Is it too soon to explain the facts of life to a ten-year-old?

All of the questions are . . . I don't want to say insignificant, because that seems cruel and every parent's concerns are valid and important, but what wouldn't I give to be worried about something else, anything else, rather than the fact that Lottie faces a long and rough road ahead of her. That she might not, potentially, survive the journey.

A sob escapes me.

I'm watching exactly the same video, sharing an identical experience with thousands of other viewers, but I feel so separate.

I want to feel connected. I type in the comments box.

My daughter has been diagnosed with aplastic anaemia, and I'm so scared she might die.

I'm utterly despairing, craving reassurance, kindness. For someone, even if it is a stranger, even if they aren't medically trained, to tell me that it's going to be okay.

Harlow reads out my comment, 'Yes, your daughter is absolutely going to die.' She grins, red lips revealing perfect white teeth. 'Not really. Goodness, overreacting much? Now calm down, because all of us mums have worries and it's silly to be scared. We are all in this together. We're all here for each other. I can promise you that your daughter will be absolutely fine. Anaemia is nothing. You can't die from it and sorry if that seemed like a cruel joke, it wasn't meant to be, but honestly, it's no big deal. Look at what you're feeding her, though. Popeye had the right idea with spinach. It's full of iron.' She raises her arm in a bicep curl, displaying her Pilates perfect muscles and then laughs.

She laughs.

My daughter might die, and she laughs.

I feel a slam to my guts, a punch of raw emotion.

The rational part of me knows that, if you're not aware of the disease, it can sound innocuous. Even though anaemia can be more far serious than some people think.

The rage inside me builds as I drain the last of the wine.

Fuck her.

Fuck her.

It's as though all the anger I feel about Lottie, my disappointment in Sean, unfurls inside me and transfers to Harlow.

I grab my phone. Open up my camera app. I know my hand is shaking, my voice. I'm a blubbering mess. There's probably snot coming out of my nose, but I don't care. All I care about is the flippant way Harlow has dismissed me. I've had too much to drink. I really should calm down, but I can't. I begin to film.

'My name is Mia. I'm mum to Charlotte – we all call her Lottie and she's . . . she's . . . There's this disease. You probably won't have heard about it. If I mention it you might even make a joke, laugh about it like Harlow did, but it *isn't* a joke. My daughter might di— she might di—' I can't say it.

I wipe my cheeks with the sleeve of my jumper and take some steadying breaths before I grab the nearest photo of Lottie and hold it up to the camera. 'This is my baby, she's just fifteen.'

I begin to explain what aplastic anaemia is. Lottie's symptoms. How I knew she was ill and how dismissive the GP was. Then I explain about the bone marrow transplant, what's to come.

'Lottie needs two weeks of conditioning treatment. That sounds harmless, right? It's actually going to be a high dose of chemotherapy. She's likely to feel sick – be sick – she might lose her hair. She'll be even more exhausted than she is already. I'm going to be experiencing lots of side effects too while I inject myself with the drugs to stimulate my cells so I can donate, but I've got to be by her side regardless. She'll have to stay in hospital, for weeks actually, maybe months after the transplant. Her immune system won't be working so she won't be allowed many visitors, and Harlow, Harlow said it's silly to be scared but . . .'

Everything torrents out of me and when I'm finished I upload the video to the channel I set up years ago but never really used. Then I drop a link to it in the comments on Harlow's livestream.

When I wake up, my mouth is dry, the lingering taste of alcohol sour upon my tongue. I groan as I reach for my phone, remembering my video. My cheeks heat with embarrassment as I fumble to open up the app. I'm going to delete it.

My head is muzzy, and I can't make sense of what I'm seeing as I stare at the figures on my channel. Overnight, my subscribers have leaped from one to 450.

There are so many comments on my video.

My stomach flips with nerves. I'm expecting them all to be fans of Harlow berating me but, to my surprise, the first comment is from @CharliesAngels. We love you, Finch family! We're here for you. #TeamLottie

I don't know who Charlie's Angels are, but I'm reminded of that old TV show where a group of three inspirational women, overseen by Charlie, fought crime. I used to watch it with my mum as a child and found it so empowering. I draw strength now from whoever this @CharliesAngels are as I scan through the rest of the comments.

So sorry your baby is sick. As a mum myself I can't imagine.

We're rooting for you.

Do keep us up to date with Lottie's progress.

My child is in hospital too. It can get lonely. Good luck.

I am comforted by the support.

Not by the hate, though. There are a few comments defending Harlow. I switch to her channel. The comments on her last video are mixed. Mostly complimentary until I'd posted the link to my video and then the criticism starts.

While I'm on her channel, another video loads.

'Guys.' She's pale. At first glance it looks like she isn't wearing any make-up, but I can see the carefully blended contour of her cheeks, the pale-pink lipstick, coats of mascara. 'I'm the first to hold my hands up when I've made a mistake. Last night, I made a joke when a mum—' momentarily she covers her face with her hands, ashamed '—one of us, told me her daughter was suffering with a disease I've never heard of. I want to learn. To do better. I'm inviting you, Mia, to come and chat to me.'

I feel a pang of sympathy for her.

'Mum?' Chris calls up the stairs. 'Are you coming down for breakfast?'

I shut off the video. Pull my dressing gown around me and trudge downstairs.

Sean is standing at the stove, scrambling eggs, his back to me, shoulders stiff. Lottie is picking nail varnish off her nails. The atmosphere is sombre. We're all aware that this is the last time we'll all eat together around the table for weeks or even months.

'So,' I'm dreading this, but I have to tell them in case they find out online, 'last night I posted a video about Lottie—'

'What?' she says.

'Well, about AA. So many people haven't heard of it.' The thought occurs to me, coming out of my mouth before it's fully formed. 'Actually, how would everyone feel, especially you, Lottie, if I documented your treatment on my channel?'

'What channel?' Chris frowns.

'YouTube.'

'You don't want to get involved in social media, Mum. It can be brutal.'

'But it might help other parents, other kids, going through something similar.' I'm thinking of the comments. 'I mean if just one person watching signs up to the bone marrow register.' As I'm voicing this I find myself feeling a flicker of hope. The sense that, instead of sitting around the hospital, waiting, endlessly waiting, worrying, I might have a purpose. I might be able to help others.

'No,' Sean says. 'It's private. I don't want Lottie—'

'Are you ashamed of me, Dad?' Lottie asks in a small voice.

'God, no. Of course not. But it's going to be tough enough for us all without making it even harder.'

'I agree with Dad,' Chris says. 'You need a thick skin for social media, Mum.'

'No one is going to say anything negative about a sick child.'

'You never know who's watching you,' Chris says.

'Lottie?' I say gently. 'This is all about you. It's completely understandable if you don't want to do it.'

'But you want to, Mum?' she asks. 'Do you really think we can help other people?'

'I think so,' I say. 'But you're more important than everyone else. Look, you don't have to decide right now. We can start anytime. Stop anytime.'

I guess, looking back, that's where it all started.

Chapter 9

Who's Watching You Documentary

Jake Lawler (host): Our next guest is Sharon Ackley, who got to know the Finch family through the hospital. Welcome, Sharon.

Sharon Ackley (parent): I'm so excited to be here. (sweeps long blonde hair over her shoulders)
   Can't believe I'm on telly. Hi kids (grins and blows a kiss to camera)

Lawler: Now, you met Mia during a very difficult time, didn't you?

Ackley: (frowns) The worst time, Jake. Can I call you Jake? (giggles, touches his knee)

Lawler: You can call me anytime (winks, touches his ear as though someone has spoken into it)
   I mean you can call me Jake, of course. Can you tell us a little of the circumstances around your meeting?

Ackley: Yes. My son, Beckham, this is him. (pulls at her t-shirt to show the face of a teenager with a GoFundMe link and QR code) He was in hospital too. I can't tell you, Jake . . . (shakes head) The worst experience ever. The worst. (sniffs)

Lawler: (passes her a tissue) Take your time.

Ackley: (dabs her eyes) I was in the canteen, and I saw Mia sat in the corner. I knew straight away she had a child in there too. It's a look, you know? That haunted, hollow look. I saw it in my own face when I looked in the mirror, so I recognised it in her. She was picking at a sandwich. Your appetite goes when you're under stress. She was barely eating it.

Lawler: What happened?

Ackley: Well, I was queuing up for my sausage, beans and chips. I stood next to that nurse, the one you had on earlier.

Lawler: Alma Rutherford?

Ackley: Yeah. I'd been waiting, literally, forever. I blame the government.

Lawler: You blame the government for the queue?

Ackley: Yeah. I may be pretty, but I can be political too. (pouts) Not enough funding for the NHS, see. Anyway, I stood there, all jostled by other people, everyone miserable as sin. Waiting with my grey plastic tray, for overcooked, overpriced grub to be slopped on me plate. I nudged her with me elbow, said, 'It's like a prison here, ain't it?' (sits back in seat dramatically, crosses arms)

Lawler: (frowns) Then what?

Ackley: Alma said, 'I can promise you this is *nothing* like prison.' I said, 'Oh, you been inside, have you?' I was only joking but . . . well, she didn't say nothing, but her face said *everything*. I nudged her again, 'Oh you have, haven't you?' She muttered, 'Mind your own business' and then put her tray down and left. Didn't even get her lunch.

Lawler: I don't see—

Ackley: I heard her interview with you from backstage. Talking about criminals. Knowing stuff about the Finch family before it were in the papers. She's a dark horse, that one. You want to be looking into her a bit more. Mark my words.

Lawler: Our brilliant researchers don't leave any stone uncovered. I believe you got to know Mia quite well?

Ackley: Yeah, I went and sat with her because there weren't any free tables.

I blame the government. I asked if she
wanted a chip to cheer her up. 'Want to
get off your phone,' I told her. 'All doom
and gloom. It's hard enough when you've
got a kiddie in here.'

Lawler: How did she respond?

Ackley: She didn't want a chip. She asked
if I watched her channel. I didn't know
what she meant but she said she thought
I might know that she had a child in hospital because of her YouTube. I told her
it were because my son were in too and I
recognised it in her. Mother to mother.

Lawler: Did you share experiences?

Ackley: I asked her to tell me about her
channel. She said she'd started it as a way
to raise awareness of this blood disorder
her daughter had. Couldn't believe that a
few weeks before she said she didn't have
any followers and now she was up to nearly
2k. She was documenting what life was like
in hospital, not just for people with the
same disease. I said I would love to have
found her channel before my Beckham ended
up here. I said her family must be really
proud of her. She went a bit quiet then.

Lawler: Did she respond to that at all?

Ackley: Yeah. Her eyes got all misty as
she said that she didn't think her husband were keen on her doing it but with-

out it she'd drive herself crazy, sitting around, waiting for tests and results, fearing the worst. She said her daughter slept a lot and it gave her something to focus on. I said, 'Don't worry, love, it's understandable you feel lonely.' I know what it's like being separated from your family. My fella weren't there either. She said that she felt really distant from everyone. She'd only just been allowed to the canteen. Couldn't go out this bubble thing her daughter was in cos of germs. It was obvious she was struggling. It looked like an effort for her to pick up her tray when she was leaving.

Lawler: So your first meeting—

Ackley: Only meeting.

Lawler: Sorry, (looks confused) I was under the impression that your child was on the same ward? That you'd met the whole family?

Ackley: Beckham weren't on no ward. He were just having his leg set after he broke it falling out of a tree. Silly sod. (covers mouth) Can I say sod? There's no free speech anymore, is there? I blame the government.

Lawler: So you never spoke to Mia again?

Ackley: Oh no, I reached out to her online. I wanted her to share my GoFundMe. I want to take Beckham to Disney in Florida. He went through so much. Thought she could relate, mums of kids in hospital.

Lawler: And how long was Beckham in hospital for?

Ackley: About nine hours, but it isn't the *length* of time, it's the *trauma*. Anyway, she never got back to me, but I had decided I didn't want to be friends with her anyway. That family were trouble. It weren't long after our meeting that the arrest happened. The *first* arrest. (screws up face) I don't associate with criminals. Half of them walk around amongst us, you know, cos there ain't enough room in the prisons. I blame the government. (points to t-shirt) Anyway, check out my GoFundMe—

Lawler: It's time for a break.

@Lamadrama23 Alma's reaction when Sharon mentioned prison!!!

@Blackcat1970 Shocking but we shouldn't jump to conclusions

@Jamie2983 Yeah, but not as shocking as naming your child Beckham. No wonder kids today are all in therapy. I blame the parents

@Avocadomonkey I blame the government #WWY

Chapter 10

Mia

Over three months.

It's been over three months since Lottie was admitted to hospital. I've been by her side as she lay listless and disinterested in the world around her. As she's been overwhelmed, unable to catch her breath. I take her hands, and we count our breathing together.

One.

Two.

Three.

Over three months that I have largely been separated from my family. And again, Sean is filling me in on things at home that normally I'd have dealt with.

'Where are you? You sound really faint?' I ask him.

'I'm driving,' he says. 'Hands free,' he adds quickly, knowing that, always a worrier, since Lottie fell sick I worry a million times more about everything, everyone. The world – my world – now full of hazards, dangers, that weren't there before.

'So, how did Chris get on at the dentist?' I ask him in

a low voice, aware that I'm in a hospital, not wanting to disturb anyone. I'm walking back from the canteen. Still hungry because I hadn't finished my sandwich. I had got chatting to a woman who shared my table. She tried to tell me that she knew exactly how I felt because her son had broken his leg. I wanted to weep. The worst thing of all is that I think she believed it. That we were the same.

I don't feel the same as anyone anymore. The trauma of this has become embedded in my blood, my skin, my bones, in the place where contentment used to sit. I'll always carry a low-level fear that everything I love could be snatched away at any moment.

Like my father was.

Like Lottie could have been.

'Chris didn't need any fillings,' Sean says. 'It was odd, though.'

'Odd how?'

'The receptionist knew who we were. She follows your channel.'

'I got another seven hundred subscribers after the last video.'

'She knew almost as much about Lottie's health as I do. She said she started following you after watching Harlow's video apologising to you. Her mum has actually looked into donating because of it.'

'That's amazing.'

Seeing how invested people have become in our family makes me feel as though I'm making a difference at a time I had felt so helpless, so hopeless. Every day I read my comments, and they fill me with a sense of purpose.

My son is sick, not with AA, but sharing your journey I don't feel so alone.

I'm going to donate bone marrow.

I don't want to donate bone marrow, but I went to blood donors for the first time because of Lottie. Paying it forward.

'It's great that someone who hadn't thought of registering before now has, but . . .'

I wait for Sean to finish his sentence. He doesn't.

'You don't like me oversharing.' It's a conversation we have over and over.

'No, but look, if Lottie remains okay with you doing it it's fine with me. I know it helps you. We cope in different ways, don't we?'

Sean's way of coping is to only want to talk about the practical. I can't remember the last time we talked about our emotions. Our relationship – never really a priority because the kids always have been – feels not irreparably broken but there are cracks that weren't there before. It isn't surprising with the distance between us, the pressure we're under. We'll get back to us eventually. Laugh, eventually.

It worries me that we don't feel as close as we did before, and there's a definite before and after to our lives, but I just know – hope – that once Lottie is home and we're all sleeping under the same roof, Sean and I in the same bed, things will go back to the way they were.

'Look, Mia, I've got to go. I'm pitching for a new contract.'

'Good luck.'

He's under so much strain. I need to generate an income. The online magazine I write for are holding my position open for me, but at the moment I'm unpaid. Once Lottie is home and I can focus, I'll start writing again; it isn't as though I need to go into an office. The lifestyle features I used to write all seem so trivial, though. Perhaps I could write something meatier. Something about us.

'Thanks. Speak later.'

'Okay. Love you.'

He doesn't say it back. I can't remember the last time he said it at all, but I don't dwell on it. I can't say definitively that Sean's behaviour is out of the ordinary, because there is nothing usual about this nightmare situation we have found ourselves in.

I switch my phone to camera mode. I'm going to record another video.

'We were so scared Lottie was going to die,' I say into the screen, which shakes with every step I take.

I keep my mobile close to my face, so I don't show any of the other children on the ward. There's a real mix of ages. I've seen many kids admitted since Lottie has been here. Sometimes they don't stay for long; I like to think those ones have been discharged, have recovered. The alternative is too horrible to think about. Anything that draws attention to mortality, Lottie's mortality, is something I try to avoid. That said, I've become close with some of the other mums. There's a camaraderie. We've all been thrust into a club that nobody wants to be a part of. I've seen it all. Parents crying silently into tissues, hunched over the basins in the toilets, trying to compose themselves, sometimes sobbing in front of their child because they just can't hold their emotions in. It isn't all moping around, though. There's laughter too. And love. So much love the air is thick with it. I've been privileged to witness parents arriving with beaming smiles, trailing helium balloons, come to usher their child home. The nurses clapping when they leave. It must be impossible for them to not get attached to the kids. Alma spends so much time with Lottie. More so than with other kids, I think.

Once I heard her tell Lottie, 'Once I thought I'd have a daughter just like you,' and I thought it was sweet.

'But –' I smile into the camera as I walk past the cartoon mural – 'look at Lottie now.' I've already peeked through the window and seen the other three beds aren't occupied right now. I'd never feature anyone on my channel without both the child and the parents' consent.

Lottie is no longer in isolation and is sitting in the chair next to her bed, engrossed in a Colleen Hoover novel. It's from the pile of books that Daisy's friend, Erika, kindly sent for her. 'Mum!' She jumps when she sees me, grabs the baseball cap on her lap and shoves it onto her head.

'Sorry.' I stop filming and perch on the bed. 'You don't need to be embarrassed, though. Your hair is growing back and, even if it wasn't, you're so beautiful, Lottie.'

'It's just . . . weird.'

'Me filming, or your hair?'

'Both.' She fiddles with her book, turning over the corner of the page she was reading.

'You know, we're helping an awful lot of people.'

'Yeah, I know.'

'Dad just said that when he took Chris to the dentist, the receptionist said her mum was looking into donating bone marrow. Because of you.'

'That's cool.' She hesitates. 'The channel means a lot to you, Mum, doesn't it?'

'It doesn't mean as much to me as you.' I put down my phone and feel a twist of guilt. 'I meant it when I said we can stop any time you're uncomfortable. We have raised awareness of AA, even if it's in a small way.'

I've been documenting everything we've been through, from us isolating for two weeks before the transplant, me injecting myself daily so I could donate, the transplant itself, Lottie's recovery so far.

Although Sean isn't keen on me sharing our family, Esther has been my biggest supporter, sharing links on all of her socials #proudaunt. She says it's really helped her understand what we're all going through.

'It isn't just about AA though, is it? That woman has commented again, the one whose son is sick but with a different illness.'

'Yes, I saw that.'

'She says it's comforting to know she's not alone.'

I choose my words carefully because I never want Lottie to feel that anything is her fault. 'When you were diagnosed I felt confused and frightened and horribly alone. Yes, I know I have your dad, and Esther, and Chris, and I think we probably all felt the same. It was as though, all of a sudden, everyone had a healthy child but me and . . . ' It's hard to know how to phrase it. 'It wasn't that I'd wish an illness on anyone, adult or child, but . . . it felt quite isolating. And then here—' I gesture around the ward '—we've seen that this is normal for a lot of parents, this is their life, their challenge. It's a whole new world that we weren't really aware of.'

'Or didn't want to think about.'

'Yes, that's true. We all know hospitals exist but until what's between their four walls directly affects us, it isn't perhaps something we dwell on. We take so much for granted. I didn't know who to turn to, who to talk to.'

'And it made you feel better? Talking?'

'It did. It still does.' Suddenly I'm choked up. 'I don't feel that perhaps I've made any sort of difference in life so far. You and Chris are my greatest achievements and I'm so proud of you both but outside of being a mum . . . ' I swallow, feeling the swell of my throat. 'I feel I'm making a difference, Lotts. However small. Those with AA or those who know someone with an illness, it's an odd thing to say, but we all feel like a family somehow.'

'Not just those with an illness.' She grins.

'Charlie's Angels?'

'Charlie's Angels.'

I don't know if it really is a group of people or just one, but they've been a regular viewer since the start, and as theirs was the first comment I ever read, I have a soft spot for them too. I almost feel as though I know them, but of course I don't.

'I don't know why most of the people watch.'

'Because you're authentic. Honest. That's basically why people like watching you.'

Honest.

Oh, if my darling girl ever found out I'd looked directly at that police officer and lied.

'Okay,' she says.

'Okay what?'

She slides the baseball cap off her head.

'Are you sure?'

'Yeah, because there are other kids that might need chemo.'

I begin to record.

'So today, Lottie is bravely showing us her head.'

'Mum! It's hardly brave.'

'I think it is.'

'You think everything I do is amazing.'

'It is.'

'You're such a loser.' She grins. 'Anyways –' she tilts her head forward and runs her hand over her scalp – 'you can see that it's been . . . three and a half months?'

'Fourteen weeks and four days.'

'Whatever. And my hair is like, well, it's this weird colour coming through. Dunno if it will stay this way. Hey, Alma?' Lottie calls across the room where Alma is fetching a blood pressure monitor. I lower the camera as she comes over. She's made it clear she doesn't want to be featured online.

'You said my hair might be different?'

'It could change texture. You never know, you might have curls.'

'That might be cool. I'd look completely different. I'd go back to school and my mates won't know me.'

'It'd be like wearing a disguise,' Alma says, turning so she looks directly at me. 'Not everyone wants to be recognised, do they?'

A shiver shimmies down my spine. Alma and I have never acknowledged we recognise each other. I'm still not entirely convinced it is her. There have been times when Lottie has talked about her Uncle Lewis and I've watched her face for some kind of reaction, but there hasn't been anything.

I tell myself over and over that it cannot be her, but the way she's looking at me catapults me back to that night.

The flashing lights of the police car.

The metal click of the handcuffs.

Chapter 11

Mia

Sleeping in my own bed is something I used to take for granted. I had been Goldilocks fussy with my pillows – not too hard, not too soft. Always using Comfort fabric softener on my white sheets because my mum had.

Now, though, it's a novelty to wake up with Sean. Lottie is due to be discharged soon and, although the worst is over, I still feel that drumbeat of guilt for sleeping at home rather than at the hospital.

I prop myself up on my elbow and study my husband. His face holds faint lines that weren't there before. The hair at his temples brushed with grey. Even though he's asleep, there are dark bags under his eyes. I touch his chest lightly. He stirs, automatically reaching for his phone. We never used to have phones in the bedroom. Now they're always with us, never on silent. He scrolls through something I cannot see because he has angled the screen away from me.

'Morning,' I say softly.

'Morning.' He doesn't glance at me as he shifts himself into a sitting position, turning back the covers.

It feels as though I have been absent for so long I am invisible to him. There has been no time for us. For laughter and casual chat. For date nights. For sex.

During my time on the ward, I've seen other parents in our situation separate, the strain pushing them apart. I couldn't bear it if that happened to us. If you'd asked me before Lottie's illness to name a luxury item, I'd likely have said a designer handbag or a car but really the most important one is perhaps time. There's never enough of it.

'Wait.' I put a hand on his leg before he gets out of bed. 'Can we have a quick cuddle?'

He briefly hugs me before he lets me go.

'Sean. When Lottie's home in a couple of days, do you think –' I draw my knees up to my chest, cover myself with the duvet, feeling vulnerable as I ask in a small voice – 'do you think we'll be okay?'

'Mia, we are okay,' he says, already pulling on his socks.

'I don't know what you're thinking, feeling. It's like we're leading separate lives.' He had worn a new shirt yesterday that I didn't even recognise.

'We have been. But that's been unavoidable.'

'I can't believe it's nearly behind us.'

'The experience is but the feelings . . .'

He doesn't have to say any more. I know the terror of potentially losing Lottie has left an indelible mark on us all.

'But we've coped, haven't we?' I say. 'I'm proud of us.'

'I don't think I have.'

'In what way?'

I'm not expecting him to answer. He finds it difficult to express himself, but he grips the edge of the duvet with both hands as though to stop himself from getting up and walking away.

'I don't think I've come to terms with it at all,' he says quietly. 'You never expect to hear such devastating news; I'll never forget how I felt in that moment. It has changed me. I went from being Lottie's father, her protector to . . . She looked so small, didn't she, when she first got sick. It was as though she had shrunk. Was disappearing.' This is followed by a heavy silence, but I don't fill it. I'm holding my breath. He's finally opening up to me. 'There's nothing more I want than for things to be the way they used to be,' he says. 'But so much has changed.'

'But Lottie's coming home and—'

'I've been resenting you—'

'Me? Why?'

'Everything.' He sighs. 'I can't explain it all. I know some of it is unfair. You were the one to save her—'

'You wanted to.'

'But I *couldn't*, could I?'

I'm shocked. I try to put myself in his position. What if he'd been the perfect match? I'd have been pleased, relieved.

'What else do you resent me for?' My throat is closing with emotion. I'm asking a question that I'm not sure I want to know the answers to.

He turns to look at me. I watch thoughts I can't identify flicker across his face. It's as though he's battling with himself and I don't understand why.

He opens his mouth but, before he can speak again, from the bedside table, my phone rings. Alma's name lights up my screen.

We exchange a frightened glance before I snatch up my handset.

And then we're throwing on clothes, running out the door, racing towards the hospital.

As we run through winding corridors, we pass a mum holding the hand of her daughter who's dressed as a fairy. A memory comes to me of the time Lottie would put on plays for us.

We'd line up on the sofa and applaud as she spouted monologues constructed from imagination and nonsense with a liberal sprinkle of the dramatic. Waving her arms theatrically, the fairy wings hooked over her shoulders would shake, silver sequins catching the light.

She'd twirl around the room, tapping Michael Finnegan, a kitten then, gently on the head with her wand, *I grant you three wishes.*

I have only one wish now: for her to be okay.

I increase my pace, Sean matching me step for step.

'Alma.' I'm breathless when we reach her. 'I don't understand. She was fine yesterday.' I'm trying to control my voice, but it's already mostly tears.

'Infections can take hold hard and fast,' she says.

I feel I'm to blame. I had become complacent, thinking Lottie was okay. Sleeping in my own bed, worrying about the state of my marriage when I should have been here. I know that, moving forward, if she gets through this, once she's discharged, where we are, whatever we do, on some level, I'll be here. On this ward. Trembling and terrified. Expecting the worst.

'Can we see her?'

'I'll take you to her in a minute. She's being isolated again. You know the drill.'

'Will she be all right?' Sean asks the question that I cannot.

'It isn't ideal, but it isn't uncommon,' Alma says. 'Her immune system is taking another battering, but we spotted it quickly and we're treating her.'

'What if this had happened in another couple of days when she was supposed to be at home? What would we have done? You said infections take hold quickly?' I'm hyperventilating again.

'You'd have brought her back in straight away. I know

you're anxious to see her, but Dr Chadha would like to speak to you. Could you go and wait by her office?'

'Could you stay with Lottie?' I can't bear the thought of her alone.

'Of course.' Alma rubs the top of my arm before she hurries away.

Once more, Sean and I sit on those hard plastic chairs, waiting for news. Minutes later, he is on his feet. 'Christ, we forgot to wake Chris.' I don't need a mirror to know that anguish on his face matches mine. In rushing to one child, we'd forgotten the other one. 'I'll go and call him and Esther and grab us some coffee.'

I am left alone in an atmosphere that's immediately different in his absence. Heavier somehow, the silence has its own weight. I cannot bear it. The adrenaline inside me is urging me to move. Run. Do something.

I'm going out of my mind.

I take out my phone and begin to record, eyes stinging, my nails digging into my palm, forcing my tears to recede so the words can tumble out of me, unhindered. 'It's not fair. Lottie was doing so well. Was supposed to come home at the weekend. And now . . . now we risk losing her again. Every time I think we've hit rock bottom it seems there's always a new space to fall.'

I don't hear Sean come back until he thrusts a coffee under my nose and slumps onto the chair.

'I was just . . . This waiting is driving me insane.'

He doesn't answer. Doesn't look at me, doesn't approve. I slip my phone back into my bag. The distance between us is now so familiar it is unbearable.

Even at night the hospital is never still. Never quiet. Lottie is sleeping but I cannot allow myself to do the same. Sean has returned home. Because of the risk of infection, we decided that only I would stay. My mind strobes with images of her when she was a child. Images of me when I was a child. My dad on his final morning, 'I'm not feeling quite right.' Skipping home from swimming, hair damp, the smell of chlorine on my skin. Mum screaming and screaming and me, not quite sure what was going on, shaking him, 'Wake up, Daddy.'

I ring the buzzer by Lottie's bed and a nurse rushes in, not Alma. She's not on shift tonight.

'Please can you check her again?'

I'm being obsessive, I know. There are machines and alarms, but I'm petrified they'll malfunction.

'Of course. She is being monitored carefully, though.' I hear the impatience in her tone.

'Thank you,' I say as she leaves but I still can't relax.

She has given me no reason not to trust her, but I do not know this stranger and I long for Alma, who has spent more time with Lottie than anyone else here.

I think if she was here right now, I'd throw myself into her arms. Beg her to forgive me. Tell her all of it. Everything. Take responsibility for my part in that night. Trade the truth for my daughter's health as though Alma is a higher being and can make everything better.

But the truth would, perhaps, make everything worse.

Besides, she's been so lovely, I know she isn't holding a grudge, is she?

Chapter 12

Who's Watching You Documentary

Jake Lawler (host): Next up on the sofa is someone who can give us an insight into Sean Finch. A warm welcome to Aleksander Nowak.

Aleksander Nowak (former employee): (clears throat) Thank you.

Lawler: Now, you worked for Sean for a number of years, I believe?

Nowak: (shuffles on sofa) Yes. Sean employed me as a health and safety officer. I'm available for work actually. (glances into camera before staring into his lap)

Lawler: Hope you're not after my job. (laughs)

Nowak: No. I'm good at what I do.

Lawler: I'm sure you are. That was a joke.

(awkward silence) Tell me how Sean was as a boss.

Nowak: He was a good boss. A good man. He worked hard to build the business up, we all did.

Lawler: How many of you were there?

Nowak: Just three of us.

Lawler: And now I believe there is just Sean?

Nowak: Yes. Things changed after the pandemic, with people working from home and companies closing. One of the large firms undercuts every quote we give. We invested in new equipment and advertising, but nothing seemed to help. Although he tried his best, he let me go a few months ago.

Lawler: Lockdown was a tough time for everyone.

Nowak: There was furlough but, even when everything went back to (quote marks with fingers) 'normal', there just wasn't the work there. Sean paid us all out of his own money for a long time but eventually he couldn't do it anymore. Understandably, he wasn't as focused on the business once Lottie got sick. There was a time when she was supposed to be coming home that he was full of plans, but then she got an infection and it sounded pretty serious. Then she recovered from that and got another straight way. She was in hospital for months. I don't blame him for being distracted. (glances at camera) If anyone out there is looking for a—

Lawler: Were you friends outside of work?

Nowak: Sometimes we would socialise. Barbecues and things, but Sean was very close to his sister, Esther, and they all had children the same age so most of his free time was spent with his family.

Lawler: Interesting you say Sean was close to his sister, but you didn't mention Mia?

Nowak: Yes, they seemed happy before Lottie got sick.

Lawler: Yes, Lottie (hand covers heart) and how did Sean take it?

Nowak: Are you a father?

Lawler: Yes, I am. Every other weekend. (pulls a sad face)

Nowak: Then I'm sure you can understand how devastated Sean was.

Lawler: And how did he change during this period?

Nowak: He became quiet. Withdrawn. He didn't say much. He was a private person.

Lawler: It can't have been easy for him then, being all over social media?

Nowak: No. I remember we went to quote for a job, and they recognised Sean. Made a joke about how Sean was a health and safety guy and yet his kitchen was full of trip hazards. He laughed it off, but he said afterwards he kept asking Mia not to film him or their home but sometimes she did anyway. She didn't deliberately feature him, I don't think. Sometimes he wandered into the shot or was in the background. It can't have been easy when everyone was so interested in the family.

Lawler: Still are interested in them, I hope. (crosses fingers at the camera) Do you think that Sean and Mia—

Nowak: I'm not comfortable talking about their marriage.

Lawler: But you came on the show. I know, I know (holds hands up) you're not working so you have time to kill.

Nowak: I want to work. I am a good worker. I've kids to feed.

Lawler: Of course. One last question then. Can you tell me about the last time you spoke to Sean?

Nowak: Yes. He was in the café on Browning Square. I was surprised as it wasn't near his house but I was pleased to see him. It had been a few weeks. I went up to him, but he wasn't very friendly.

Lawler: Why not?

Nowak: He was with someone. Deep in conversation. I shouldn't have interrupted him really. I saw him again there the following week; that was the last time I saw him. I didn't speak to him that time because he was with her again.

Lawler: Her? Who was she?

Nowak: He did introduce us, but I can't remember her name. It was something like Ada? No, Ava. Yes, I think it was, no, that's not right. Alma. It was Alma.

@Lamadrama23 The nurse!!! Sean was shagging the nurse!!!

@Blackcat1970 Don't be crude. He was probably just talking about Lottie

@Jamie2983 All right 'Mrs I don't use social media'. This is the content I'm here for!

@Avocadomonkey I'm surprised this hasn't come out before in the papers #WWY researchers are brilliant

Chapter 13

Mia

Lottie is finally coming home today.

Yesterday, she'd been bubbling with excitement. Full of plans for Halloween. Socialising. I think, because she's spent so much time in bed, she doesn't realise quite how weak she is still.

'The first thing I want to do is go and watch a movie with Daisy.'

'Lottie, you'll have to be careful.' I was horrified at the thought of her sitting with all those strangers. 'You know your immune system is still very weak.'

'I'll be sitting down. Resting.'

'We have to be careful of infections. Look.'

On my phone I show her again one of the videos I'd posted the first day of her infection. How still she was. IV bag towering over her, tube snaking from her pale arm. I don't want to upset her but the fear of almost losing her again still lingers.

'I don't remember any of it,' she says quietly. 'I can't believe you filmed it all. I look dead. What if I had died? Would you have filmed that?'

'What? No. Don't even think that.'

'Would you have taken down the videos of me, if I'd died?' Then she looked past me, her face lighting up. 'Alma!'

'I wanted to see you before you go. I'm not on shift tomorrow. Here.' She looks around furtively before she hands Lottie a small, gift-wrapped box. I don't know whether she's meant to give patients gifts.

'It's supposed to protect you from negative energy.'

Lottie opens the box and gasps, but I don't see the expression on her face. I don't see anything in the room except the pendant nestled on burgundy velvet.

The evil eye pendant.

The same one that Alma was wearing all those years ago.

I tidy up the kitchen. Chris is scooping the last of his cornflakes into his mouth, milk dribbling down his chin. I hear Sean's footsteps march towards the front door.

I'm wiping down the worktop again. Spraying bleach over every surface.

'You know it's already cleaner than it's ever been,' Chris says. 'If it gets any shinier, I'm going to have to put my sunglasses on.'

'Sorry, it's just—' I run my cloth over the fridge.

'I know.' Chris dumps his bowl in the sink and gently takes the cleaner out of my hand. 'Why don't I give the house another going-over while you visit Grandma?' He's picked up on my anxiety. My desire that we eradicate all the bacteria we cannot see before Lottie comes home.

From the hallway, I realise I can hear Esther's voice.

'Look what Esther's brought.' Sean nods towards the giant cake box in his hands.

I lift open the lid and peek at the sponge, smothered with buttercream. The delicately piped *Welcome Home, Lottie* in swirling pink icing.

'That's gorgeous. You're still coming later?' We're not overwhelming Lottie with a big party, but Esther and Felix and Daisy are eager to see her.

'Of course. I just wanted to drop this off. I can't trust Felix not to eat it while I'm out this morning.'

'Off anywhere nice?' I ask.

'Lewis is taking me out for brunch.'

'Any occasion?' It isn't something they normally do.

'I'm hoping this is the start of spending more time together. He's always out. We've really drifted apart but I'm hopeful we can sort it out. I'm going to try and persuade him to work fewer hours. It isn't as though he can't afford the help. Anyway, I'd better go. He's waiting in the car.'

'Have a good time. See you this afternoon, sis.' Sean squeezes past me with the cake, towards the kitchen.

'I'll come out and say hello.' Lewis is engrossed in his phone. I tap on the car window, and he looks startled for a moment before he lowers it.

'Mia. You must be delighted Lottie is coming home today,' he says. 'I can't imagine how I'd have felt as a parent in your position. Everyone focuses on the mum, don't they, but dads matter too, don't you think?'

'Absolutely,' I say. 'Sean has had a really stressful time all around. Thankfully, though, Lottie has received the best care at the hospital. Her nurse Alma has been wonderful.' I watch his face; he met her when he brought Esther in to be tested for a match. Did he recognise her? The evil eye pendant she gifted Lottie yesterday is confirmation to me that it absolutely is her, but there's nothing in his expression to give him away.

'That's great. The NHS is such a valuable resource for those who can't afford private healthcare,' he says and my hands bunch tightly into fists.

He's so smug.

I say goodbye to them both and it isn't until his gleaming blue BMW has disappeared around the corner I realise my fingers are cramping.

On my way to Poppyfields to visit Mum, I notice how grim the town centre looks. Mum's favourite craft shop and the kitchen shop she liked have both closed down. She wouldn't recognise the High Street if she saw it now. When I reach her room it's devastating that she doesn't recognise me either. I'm distressed as I leave the care home, bumping into Sierra on my way out who's just leaving at the end of her shift.

'Sierra. Do you think she's getting worse?' I don't know why I ask the young assistant to confirm what I already know. What Mum's doctor has told me. I'm just wanting reassurance, for her to tell me that Mum still has plenty of good spells too, it's just that I'm not always around for those.

'Yeah, she is.' She twirls her strands of her hair around her finger. 'She keeps asking for Anthony.'

'That's my dad. Was. Was my dad.' The sadness is so deep I feel it cracking me open.

'Do you wanna collab?' she asks.

I can't figure out if she's offering me something I've never heard of to comfort me, but beneath her perfectly shaped eyebrows, her immaculately curled lashes, her eyes are hard.

'Sorry, a what?'

'Collab. You know, you feature me as a guest on your channel, and I'll have you on mine. Maybe we could both do something with Harlow? You know, I could be the one to bring you together. Her reputation took a hit after the joke she made about Lottie dying but she's still got a decent reach.'

I'm so stunned I can't speak. Dizzy with it. I'm amazed I am still upright. Her casually cruel request has yanked the metaphorical rug from under my feet.

Sierra takes my silence as a sign I'm thinking about it, and carries on babbling, 'I'm sure Harlow would be happy to do it. I've heard some of her sponsors dropped her, which is, like, totally unfair. That soundbite that circulated on all the socials with her saying 'Yes, your daughter is absolutely going to die', and then laughing, was taken so out of context. You only have to watch the whole section to see that she apologises and says that might have sounded like a cruel joke but, oh no, people judge on a five-second clip rather than spending a couple of minutes educating themselves on what actually went down. I finish in five minutes so we could record a teaser for it now. Then we can fix a time so I can come and make-over Lottie. She'll be quite pretty when her hair has grown back properly,' she says casually in a way that tells me she's never come close to losing anything that mattered to her.

I'm furious, possibly more furious than I have ever been, but it's as though I have a voice in my ear telling me to walk away because this despicable woman is still one of Mum's primary carers. So I force myself to keep calm as I hiss, 'Lottie's beautiful just as she is and, unlike *some people*, she's beautiful on the inside too.'

I stalk to the door, hearing her mutter behind me, 'You'll regret that.'

I had no idea then that I'd see her again just half an hour later.

Chapter 14

Who's Watching You Documentary

Jake Lawler (host): My next guest is Sierra LaRosa. (watches as Sierra walks onto set before she pauses, looks directly at the camera, and grins, waves)
Sierra, do come and take a seat.
(Sierra sweeps her blonde hair with green tips over her shoulders before strutting over to the sofa; hitches skirt up before sitting down, crossing legs)
Thanks for joining us.

Sierra LaRosa (carer): You're very welcome, Jake. (leans forward and touches his knee) I'm a big fan. (giggles)

Lawler: Now you work at Poppyfields—

LaRosa: *Worked.* I don't work there anymore. I'm concentrating on influencing. I'm on every platform as Sierra's Beauty Secrets.

Lawler: Right, sorry. Of course, but you did work at Poppyfields care home, and part of your job was caring for Beverley, Mia's mother?

LaRosa: What can I say, I'm a caring person. (twirls the ends of her hair around her index finger)

Lawler: Can you tell us a little about how you found Beverley?

LaRosa: A bit boring really. Most of them were. I mean (looks at camera) I still treated her well.

Lawler: And that *was* what you were being paid for. (flashes smile at camera) Did you meet the rest of the Finch family?

LaRosa: Yeah. Sean, Chris and Lottie all came to settle Beverley in.

Lawler: Did anything about them stand out at that time?

LaRosa: Nah. They were all really normal. Never thought they would get more followers than me. I was never a fan of Mia's, though.

Lawler: Why was that?

LaRosa: She was up her own arse. Only cared about herself.

Lawler: The impression we got of Mia at that

time was that she was a devoted mother, wife, daughter. Did she visit her mum much?

LaRosa: Well, yeah, all the time, but that don't mean she's nice.

Lawler: Was there anything in particular that felt off about her?

LaRosa: Yeah, I mean her channel blew up and mine was just starting and she could have invited me on to hers to collab and helped me, but no, I didn't fit her (commas with fingers) 'demographic'.

Lawler: So you didn't like Mia because she was more popular than you?

LaRosa: She isn't more popular than me. Everyone likes me. It's just, there are a lot of beauty channels out there; she had a USP.

Lawler: *Lucky* Mia having a sick child. (tight smile)

LaRosa: Yeah. (sad face) Even Harlow couldn't compete with that, could she?

Lawler: You told our researchers you had some information that you haven't shared publicly yet, but you didn't want to divulge what that was until you were on air? What is it you wanted to say, Sierra?

LaRosa: Oh, I have more than one piece of

information that nobody knows about, but this first one is something. (lips curl into a smile) Something that could be really important. (pauses) Someone came to visit Beverley. Just after Mia was arrested.

Lawler: (frowns) Was that unusual then? For Beverley to receive visitors?

LaRosa: Yeah. Nobody really came 'cept Mia. Not even the kids, really.

Lawler: It must have been nice for her then—

LaRosa: They made her cry. (leans forward) They *threatened* her.

Lawler: Threatened? (looks anxious) Are you sure you didn't misunderstand? Who was this person? Was it a man or woman?

LaRosa: Dunno who they were. I think, from the voice, it might have been a man, but it could have been a woman with a deeper voice, or someone disguising their voice.

Lawler: Disguising their voice? That's a bit disturbing. Somebody must know. Surely there's some sort of security? CCTV? You can't just wander in off the street? Threaten a patient?

LaRosa: We prefer to call them residents.

Lawler: Threaten a resident, then.

LaRosa: It isn't a prison. We can't stop people coming in.

Lawler: But the care home has dementia patients. What's to stop somebody wandering off?

LaRosa: Well, there's like a buzzer, the door is locked but anyone who buzzes is just let in. There's a visitor book everyone is supposed to sign but, (shrugs) we were really busy. Understaffed. We couldn't keep track of everyone. That day there was only me and Fat Phil on the ground floor where Beverley's room is.

Lawler: And did they sign in? This visitor?

LaRosa: Yeah. I mean we've gone back and checked because of all of this but it's ill . . . iledg . . . you can't read it properly.

Lawler: So nobody knows who they were?

LaRosa: Nah.

Lawler: Or what they wanted?

LaRosa: Nope. Beverley was really distressed. She was saying, 'I don't know you, get out of my room.'

Lawler: Is it possible that, because of her memory challenges, she did know them?

LaRosa: (looks at every camera, slowly) In my *expert* opinion, I don't believe she knew them. (folds her arms) She was scared. Crying.

Lawler: Crying? Because they wouldn't leave the room?

LaRosa: Because they was saying, 'I will find them. Even if you don't tell me where they are.'

Lawler: What do you think this mystery person was referring to?

LaRosa: Duh. The Finch family. Obvs. (eye roll) They said, (drops her voice) 'You wouldn't want anything to happen to your grandchildren, would you?'

Lawler: And then what happened?

LaRosa: She was crying harder.

Lawler: And you were just . . . listening? Did you go in and make sure everything was okay?

LaRosa: Nah, I was on a break. I was trying to livestream, but I had to stop because of all the noise. She began shouting louder, 'I don't know you.' Fat Phil went rushing into her room, well, as quickly as he could, you know, (puffs her cheeks out with air, holds arms out to her side and mimes a waddle) and (pause) the visitor (several beats) the *intruder* was gone. The window was open, and they'd vanished. Tell me now that isn't dodgy?

Lawler: Did you call the police?

LaRosa: Nah. It happens a lot with residents not remembering who someone was.

Lawler: But leaving from the window?

LaRosa: Yeah, well. That was a bit nuts, but they probably thought they'd get accused of something, the fuss she was making. It wasn't till one of the Finches went missing that I remembered them, the threat they made.

Lawler: And you told the police then straight away?

LaRosa: Yeah. Course. Well, after I'd sent a message to this show. I didn't want to vlog about it until I'd been on here because your reach is wider than mine and . . . well, I really want to do everything I can to help.

Lawler: But did you at least tell Mia?

LaRosa: No, it isn't as if she ever did me any favours, is it? One collab could have changed everything. Remember, find me at Sierra's Beauty Secrets!

@Blackcat1970 Who would scare an old lady like that?

@Avocadomonkey What if they did actually know Bev and she'd forgotten?!? #WWY

@Lamadrama23 Sierra's contouring is insane. I've subscribed to her channel!!!! I went to school with her, but she was called Samantha then!!!

@Jamie2983 She renamed herself after a cheap car – classy

Chapter 15

Mia

After picking up a few bits from the bakery for Lottie's homecoming, I cut through the park to reach my car.

I'm still reeling from Sierra's proposition when I see her. It takes me a second to place her outside the care home, but there's no mistaking her bright blonde hair, pink tips. To avoid her, I swerve and change direction, feet sinking in the soggy grass. Lost in my own thoughts.

'Mia?' I look up, expecting it to be Sierra who has called my name, but it isn't. It's Harlow.

I'm shocked to see her. We might live in the same town, but our paths have never really crossed. I'd seen her once from a distance before Lottie got sick but was such I fan I hadn't had the courage to approach her. Since I'd posted the video on her feed I'd been mainly in hospital with Lottie, I've rarely ventured out.

On screen she is always immaculate. Perfectly lined lips curved into a smile. Today, though, she's dishevelled. Her son, Marco, taller than both of us, is by her side. He's around seventeen, the same age as Chris, but despite the Batman t-shirt he's wearing, I'm finding the way he's glowering at me intimidating.

I hold my paper bags from the bakery, grease seeping through them, close to my chest like a shield. I might not be alone, but I feel as though I am.

'Are you happy?' Harlow asks but there's vitriol in the words rather than concern. 'You know I've lost sponsors, income, because of you?'

'I didn't . . . ' I trail off. It seems unkind, cruel almost, to say I haven't followed what had happened to her after the video I posted. That I hadn't thought much about her at all until Sierra just mentioned her. My time, my thoughts, have laid solely with Lottie. They still do.

'I have to go,' I say, although I don't move because the great British politeness has pinned my feet to the floor and she looks so upset. As I look into her eyes I recognise myself. A wife, a mother, desperately trying to hold it all together. But I know we are not the same when she says, 'My channel was *everything* to me. It was all I had.'

Uncomfortably, I glance at Marco. 'You have a family.'

'Had. *Had* a family. Javier doesn't want me anymore, Marco has had to leave private school and I'm living in the town centre now, *in a terrace.*'

She crosses her arms, waiting for me to respond, but what can I say? It sounds ridiculous, doesn't it? Overdramatic. That one video could cause her whole life to implode. Maybe it's a generational thing but, as much as I've liked using it as a distraction, it seems ridiculous to me that anyone's life can revolve around social media. That you can earn a good living from it.

'I'm sorry to hear that, but it's hardly my fault.' I begin to walk away but Marco sidesteps in front of me, blocking my path.

'It *is* your fault. Mum got so much hate, and she didn't

deserve it. People were twisting it that she was laughing and making jokes about Lottie dying. That's not what happened. People aren't even watching the original video for context. They're just reading the comments that she made a joke about Lottie dying, or watching the soundbite, and they've all piled on. It's not fair. Mum didn't know how sick she was.'

'I know that.' I try not to be intimidated by his expression, his tone. It's only natural that he wants to protect his mum. Chris would be the same with me, if he were here.

I'm glad he's not here though, glad nobody I know is here to witness the way my cheeks must be glowing, from the burn I feel in them, because I do feel responsible.

'The reaction sounds really extreme,' I admit. 'I am sorry about that, but I haven't encouraged it.'

'Maybe not but you could have *stopped* it. You could have controlled the response.'

'Mum's lost her sponsorship and her income *and* Dad,' Marco says.

I bite my lip because it's understandable he's devastated his parents are separating. He's seeing things in black and white. I'm sure Harlow and Javier had problems before this, but they've protected him from it. There's no way he'd have left her solely because of a misinterpreted video clip, is there?

'I'm sorry about your dad –' I turn to Harlow – 'and about Javier. And that you've had to move.'

'Yeah, well.' Harlow laughs but it's hollow. 'It seems he's a property developer who doesn't actually personally own anything. Everything is in his company name and—'

'Look.' Why is she telling me all of this? 'I do have to go.'

'That's it. Run away. You could have posted another video being a bit more sympathetic towards me.' Harlow's eyes glisten but I can't see any tears in them, only anger. 'I reached out to you about a collab.'

'I don't remember that.' I'm beginning to walk away.

'Convenient,' Marco mutters.

'I *did* have other things to worry about. I wasn't plotting your downfall, Harlow. I was in hospital with my sick daughter.'

'Ah yes, poor, poor Lottie. Worked out well for you, didn't it, follower wise? You've certainly milked that situation.'

It's akin to being drenched with an ice-cold bucket of water. The shock of it snatches my words away. I throw another glance at Marco, pitying him, rather than fearing him now. Imagine being raised by someone who seemingly has no compassion, no empathy.

'I bet you're so glad she fell sick.' Harlow smirks. 'It's turned you from a nobody into—'

'Oh, just fuck off, Harlow.'

I skirt quickly around her, the smell from the sausage rolls I am carrying turning my stomach. I hear her whisper to Marco before she is in front of me again.

'Why don't you fuck off!' she says. 'Everybody loved me, *everybody*, and then you made them pity you.'

In my peripheral vision I see a police officer in the distance, a lady before him gesturing with her hands as she talks. I turn to walk towards him. I don't think Harlow can have seen him because she pushes me, hard, and as I put out my hands to steady myself, the bags I am carrying splat onto the floor. The fresh cream from the cakes I'd bought for Lottie oozes out.

The palms of my hands sting as tiny pieces of gravel pierce my skin. My knee throbs as I scramble to my feet.

'I'm going to walk away and go and pick my daughter up from hospital.' I try to keep my voice steady but there's a wobble in it I just can't control.

'Lottie's finally coming home, is she?' Harlow tilts her

head to one side, mouth twisted into that cruel grin. 'You and Sean will live happily ever after. You'll lose viewers if that's the end of the drama. It would have been better for you professionally if she'd died so—'

There's a whooshing sound in my ears. I actually feel my heart rate accelerate as I lurch forward and shove her as hard as I can. She sprawls out on the floor in front of me and I stand over her, my hands already fists. I have never wanted to hit anyone before but every cell in my body twitches with the desire to smack her. I step back, though. It isn't who I am.

Then the policeman is at my side. I turn gratefully to him, my relief turning to dismay as he places us both under arrest.

Chapter 16

Mia

Six hours.

Six hours I have been at the station. My fingerprints have been taken, along with a mugshot where I stared at the camera and tried not to cry again. It was degrading to open my mouth while my cheeks were swabbed for DNA as though I was some sort of rapist or murderer. I've refused a solicitor, hoping to hurry things up. I'm desperate to leave, terrified I won't be allowed to. I was allowed to call Sean to tell him to pick Lottie up without me. Weeping at the unfairness of it all.

'What the fuck, Mia?' he had said.

'Harlow started it.'

'You're not twelve. You're a grown woman. A mother. This social media stuff is getting out of hand. This is Lottie's big day.'

Does he think I don't know that?

I've been endlessly dreaming of the moment we are all together again. Picturing Lottie's face lighting up as she sees the Welcome Home banner I had painted myself, knowing she'd appreciate the liberal sprinkling of pink and silver glitter. I've missed her delight in being reunited with Michael Finnegan, missed hearing his happy purrs. I was supposed to be there as she sank onto her favourite chair.

But thanks to Harlow, Lottie's homecoming is ruined.

I pace. Pace. Pace. Unable to settle on the hard bench in the room I'm in. Nothing on the walls to look at to distract me. Nothing to pass the time.

Nothing to occupy me but my own torturous thoughts.

Dropping to my haunches, I begin to cry again.

I thought I had reached rock bottom with Lottie's illness, but it's the same old story, isn't it? Every time I think there is nowhere left to go but up, I fall a little further.

Then there's the sound of the door unlocking. I'm both relieved and scared.

A different officer this time.

I raise my tear-stained face towards him, my entire body shaking as he says, 'We're letting you go with a caution.'

It is Esther who collects me. Guiding me towards the car as though I am ninety or mortally wounded. I feel as though I'm both. I can tell she's upset and I feel I have a million apologies to make, but first I ask, 'Is Lottie okay?'

'She's fine. Worried about you, obviously.'

'She doesn't know I've been arrested, does she?'

'I'm afraid so.'

'Esther!'

Her face crumples; she looks close to tears. 'Sorry but we had to tell her. She knew it would have to be something serious to stop you being there today.'

I nod. She's right. I'm being unfair.

'Are Lewis and Felix and Daisy still at the house with her?'

'The kids are.'

'And Lewis?' It's not that I want him there.

She doesn't reply, and when I glance at her I can see the tremble in her lip.

'Esther? Is something wrong with Lewis?' Although he looked fine when I saw him this morning, my mind automatically jumps to disease, hospitals, death.

For a moment she doesn't reply and I can see in her face that she's trying to compose herself

'He . . . Lewis . . . Well, he told me over brunch he wants to leave me.'

I stand still, shocked, as though I've had a bucket of cold water tipped over my head.

'Oh, Esther. I'm so sorry.' And I am. Even though I don't like him, he is her chosen person. 'That seems really sudden. I know you said you weren't seeing a lot of him, but I didn't know things were that bad between you?'

'Neither did I,' she says tearfully as she unlocks the car, but neither of us gets in. Instead we lean against the driver door. The autumn air chilling my cheeks, the tip of my nose.

'Why does he want to leave?'

'He wasn't specific but, reading between the lines, I think he has someone else.'

It's not as though I've ever liked him, but Esther loves him and she's distraught, so I suggest: 'Perhaps you can have some therapy? Sort it out?'

'I suggested that but he's adamant he doesn't want to. I really saw a different side to him today. It scared me. He was so emotionless, so, I don't know, hard. Cold.'

'Has he actually gone? Is there anything I can do?'

'Oh, he isn't physically leaving, apparently. He doesn't want me, but he wants to stay in the house.'

'What? Why? Does he want custody of the kids? Do Daisy and Felix know what's going on?'

'No. I haven't told them yet. We're going to tell them

together. Lewis doesn't want custody, he just doesn't want to move out.'

I can't get my head around it. 'He'll have to, though, won't he?'

'Apparently not. One of the mums at school is a solicitor and I called her as soon as I could for an informal chat with her. I'd like to think there is hope, but he sounded so final. I have to protect myself and the kids. I can't make him leave.'

'But . . . men are usually the ones to move out so the kids can stay in the family home?'

'Yes, but apparently they choose to because can you imagine how bloody awful the atmosphere would be if everyone that separated still lived together? I'm not sure if it's standard in every case, I'd imagine not with some women being at risk, but certainly in mine. Legally he doesn't have to leave. He isn't a threat to me.'

'What are you going to do? Can I help at all?' By help I mean I want to phone Lewis and ask what the fuck he is thinking, but I know that won't do any good. Anyway, I don't want it so to seem as though I'm threatening anyone, not when I received a formal caution half an hour ago. What would happen if I was arrested again? Perhaps I wouldn't be shown as much lenience now my altercation with Harlow is on record.

'I don't know what's going to happen, but for now I'm not going to think about it.' Esther climbs into the car. I do the same and we drive in silence. Both of us lost in our own thoughts. When she pulls up outside the house, I unbuckle my seatbelt and scramble out before she has properly parked.

I rush into the hallway. The smell of sweet and sour chicken lingers. The pink and silver balloons I had sellotaped to the lounge door bounce as I push my way into the room.

'Shh.' Chris holds an index finger in front of his lips,

gesturing towards Lottie, fast asleep on the chair. I drink in the sight of her. Does she look too pale? Trying not to disturb her, I lightly press the back of my hand against her forehead. Is she too warm?

'She's fine,' Sean says. 'Do you want a drink?'

'Please.' I follow him into the kitchen. Wrapping my arms around his waist before he can reach the fridge, resting my head against his back.

He stiffens and I think he's going to push me away, but then he holds me too. After everything we have been through, our love has taken on a new shape, but I don't yet recognise it. I don't think he does either. But one thing I do know is that love is not letting go even when it's hard. Especially when it's hard.

'Sorry,' I say.

He breaks away from me and leans against the worktop, crossing his arms. 'I can't believe you've got a criminal record.'

'I was cautioned, not charged.'

'Does that make it any better? You've missed such an important moment.'

'I know. I am sorry.' My voice wobbles as I slosh wine into a glass. 'I'm gutted I didn't get to pick Lottie up with you. Is everything okay?'

There's a beat before he says, 'Yeah.' He runs his fingers through his hair. I notice it needs cutting. Normally I'd book his appointment. So many things have passed me by. Will things just fall back into place? Can they? We've got through the worst, but it's altered the fabric of our lives, and we can't just smooth it back the way it was before. I take a sip, then a bigger one.

'Let's go back in,' I say.

While Lottie sleeps we catch up in whispers, Felix asking me what it was like being arrested.

I reach for the bag of prawn crackers. 'Don't you need to wash your inky fingers first?' Esther says.

'Inky?' I'm puzzled for a moment. 'Oh, from the fingerprints. Haha. They only do that in old films; it's computerised now.'

'Sorry, too soon for jokes?'

'Too soon.' I try to massage away the tension behind my forehead. I feel there is a permanent groove between my brows.

'We'd better go before we wake Lottie.' Esther senses it's all a bit much for me; I'm worried going home to Lewis will be too much for her but I don't want to say too much in front of Felix and Daisy.

'You can all stay, if you want to?' I offer.

'Thanks, but can you imagine all of us crammed here. It'd be bursting at the seams.' She mouths 'I'll be okay' while the kids are gathering their things.

At the door she turns. 'Serious question.' She lowers her voice. 'Was your mugshot worse than your passport photo? Because that really is fucking awful.'

For the first time that day, I laugh. Shoving her lightly on her arm.

'Help, assault,' she mouths.

I pull her into a hug. 'You're an idiot. But I love you.'

'Love you too.' She squeezes me tightly.

If I had known that would be the last time we would hug, the last time I would feel her hair against my cheek, the warmth of her skin, I don't think I'd have ever let her go. I come back to that moment over and over again in my mind. Those last few precious moments before my world started to spin at an alarming rate, at a different angle.

Chapter 17

Mia

'Mum!' Lottie rolls her eyes as I aim the red dot of the laser thermometer in the middle of her forehead. 'You've literally just taken my temperature.'

'I haven't,' I say but I know she's right. I can't help it. No one can properly understand my actions without knowing the depths of my fears, but I can't tell her that I'm so scared she'll develop another infection I'm waking up in a cold sweat in the middle of the night. Standing over her bed, watching the rise and fall of her chest the way I used to when she was a baby. Reassuring myself that she is here. She is alive. Because she'd gone downhill so quickly, I'm so afraid it might happen again, and I'd have missed the signs. That by the time we had rushed her back to the hospital it'd be too late.

I'm more exhausted now Lottie is home than I was when we were both sleeping at the hospital. At least there, I felt she was safe. Safer than she is here anyway.

What if I miss something? I aim the thermometer at her again. 'Just double-checking.'

'Chill out, Mum,' Chris says. 'Lottie's only been home a couple of days and you've already had to change the batteries in that thing.'

'Well, if you two didn't keep zapping it against the floor for Michael Finnegan to chase, they'd last longer.'

My mobile rings and the kids take the opportunity to bolt for the stairs.

'Keep an eye on your sister,' I shout after them before I answer the call.

'How's Lottie?' is the first thing Esther asks.

'She's good. Hanging out with Chris.'

'It's great they're so close. Same as me and Sean. Brothers can be so annoying but ultimately siblings always have each other's backs. It's the longest relationship you ever have, you know, the one with a brother or sister.'

'I wouldn't know.' I'm sad I don't have a sibling. Someone who could have looked around care homes with me. Reminisce about Mum the way she was, before this terrible disease started snatching her away from us.

'Well, it seems like most relationships in my life are going to last longer than my marriage,' she says.

'How are you?'

She thinks about this for a moment. I hear her breath coming down the line. I can picture her face, brow furrowed, trying to unpack the way she feels.

'Numb, I think. I feel . . . it's weird. On one level I'm absolutely devastated, telling myself I've been completely blindsided, but then I'm picking over the last few weeks, months, I don't know, maybe even years, thinking there was always some part of Lewis that he kept hidden from me.' She sighs. 'I just didn't expect *this*, though.'

'Is there anything I can do?'

'Probably. I haven't cried yet, you know. Not proper ugly sobbing. I just want to get through the practical first. We're going to talk again later about the living arrangements and when we're going to tell Felix and Daisy, and then I guess it'll hit me. When I see the kids' faces and they know I've let them down.'

'This isn't your fault.'

'Isn't it? I still don't really understand why . . . why I'm not enough.' Her voice is small and I wish she were in front of me so I could wrap her in my arms and tell her that she is enough. More than enough. Everything to so many people.

'Anyway, let's change the subject. I'm trying to hold myself together. Your turn to spill.'

'I'm okayish. Trying to stay calm but freaking out all the time that she's going to get ill again. It's not only the infections I'm worried about, but it is possible for AA to strike twice.'

'But statistically quite unlikely,' she reminds me.

'And things aren't great with Sean,' I admit. It's early days, us all being together again, but it doesn't feel quite right anymore.

She falls silent. I don't like putting her in the middle of us, but she understands him. Understands both of us.

'You know how he's been, a bit distant. I thought when Lottie came back he'd relax.'

'It's only been a couple of days. Maybe he has PTSD? I think that's probably possible when your child's life is threatened. Maybe you guys should have some therapy.'

'Maybe.'

'I wish Lewis would agree to mediation at least. I've asked him about our finances and what he intends to do financially in the divorce, and I have the statements for our joint bank accounts but there's not a lot in them. I know there are substantial savings somewhere, I just don't know where.'

'Surely a solicitor can access some sort of database?'

'The mum from school said there are a lot of ways of hiding money. It isn't as though he has a job with a normal salary. Consulting with businesses on how they can improve, sometimes investing in them; it's difficult to gauge how much he earns.'

'There must be tax returns? Accounts?'

'I'm sure there is but . . . I don't know. It'll figure itself out somehow. Mia—' she pauses '—have you seen it?'

'Seen what?'

'The video that was posted earlier?'

Without knowing why, my stomach begins to churn.

'Video of what?'

'It's from the park. You and Harlow arguing.'

'Oh no. Who posted it?'

'A new account. Someone who wants to remain anonymous, I think. You come out of it okay. Harlow can be heard clearly saying it would have been better for your numbers if Lottie had died. The reaction is, well, it's pretty bad. I don't think she'll bounce back from this.'

After the call ends, I watch the grainy video over and over again. There are links to both mine and Harlow's pages in the description. The comments are increasing with every minute. I click on my profile to make sure that the video isn't showing there.

I can't believe what I'm seeing.

My followers. My followers have leapt into five figures. I don't understand what's going on. I scan through all the new comments on my existing videos. Every single one of them references the video with Harlow.

Saw it on Instagram

On Facebook

TikTok

Reddit

Other sites I have never heard of. So many anonymous people pledging their loyalty to me as though this a war and they need to take sides. So many people asking if I'm going to retaliate. I think they want me to. That's why they're following me, I realise. Not because they necessarily care about Lottie but because they want a fight, the drama.

Everyone agrees, though, that Harlow saying it would have been better if Lottie had died is despicable.

Lottie.

Now that it seems to have been shared on every social media platform, she's going to see it, isn't she?

Reluctantly, I dash upstairs. Perch on the edge of Chris's bed. See the concern etched on my children's faces.

'Was that the hospital that called? Is something wrong?'

'No. It's . . . ' I don't want her to watch it, either of them to watch it, but better they see it here, safe in their own home, than out there, caught unawares.

Lottie's face crumples as they watch, while Chris's hardens.

'Harlow didn't mean it. She was upset.' I hold Lottie as she cries and vow once more that I'll do anything to protect my kids.

Anything.

The dishwasher whirrs as I switch it on. I'm shattered. Sean came home late so we've only just finished eating. It's been over a week since Lottie was discharged from hospital and the gap between us still hasn't closed. If anything, it feels even wider. Sean was furious about the video online of me and Harlow. Asked me if I'd delete all of my channels and, although I think I could perhaps stop posting now Lottie is home, I don't want to delete what's already up. There are some helpful posts for parents in similar situations and that's why I started it, after all.

Each night, he, I and the kids sit around the kitchen table. The top's scratched from the marks of a family over the years: Chris rolling cars over it; Lottie trying to scrape off blobs of pastel nail varnish; Sean sliding his laptop across it. We're each in the same chair we've always sat in, but it doesn't feel the same somehow. I had been so desperate to get back to normal, but I don't know what normal looks like anymore. Normal for me now is waking up in the middle of the night, panic fluttering around my heart, scared something has happened to Lottie. And then as darkness thickens, the light and shadows changing shapes as they shift around the room, my thoughts grow more ominous. Something terrible happening not only to Lottie but to Chris, Sean, any of us.

How did my mum bear it after Dad died so unexpectedly? Did she worry every time she couldn't see me? The space in my throat closes, trapping all the questions I want to ask my mum but, even if she were here now, it would be fruitless. She often doesn't remember me, remember him.

I want my mum.

The thought is sudden and sharp. I hunch over the worktop, a stabbing pain in my chest.

I'm not coping well, mentally, emotionally. The hospital recommended a support group, but I have been running on adrenaline, not wanting to stop and think about everything too much. I thought I had enough support with Esther. Remembering I had texted her before dinner, I check my mobile. My message remains unread.

'Wine?' The light of the fridge illuminates Sean's pale face as he lifts out another bottle of Pinot.

'No. What if we have to drive Lottie to the hospital? One of us needs stay under the limit.'

When did he start drinking so much? I cast my mind back, trying to recall the last time I saw him without a glass in his hand.

He sighs as though my answer is tiresome, or perhaps it is me who is tiresome.

'Go on. I'll have a small one, then.'

On the sofa, he splashes wine into one of the crystal goblets we received as a wedding gift. We only usually use them on special occasions, but I suppose there's no point saving things for a special occasion because we can't guarantee we'll ever have a cause to celebrate.

I *must* stop being so maudlin.

'Sean,' I begin at the same time he says, 'I can't do this.'

For a moment I'm confused. 'Do what?'

But I can see from the despair on his face. From the whites of his knuckles as he clasps the stem of his glass. From the way he is breathing.

'Us,' he says.

The minute I hear it, a low involuntary laugh escapes my lips because this is ridiculous, isn't it? This is Sean, me and Sean.

'But why?'

His silence is more unsettling than anything he might say, so I fill it. 'I've thought for a while you that you seem . . . ' I choose my words carefully. I'm not a doctor, I don't want to label him with depression, don't want to label him with anything at all, except husband. I want that so fiercely that I grasp at his hand. 'You seem down. And it's not surprising with everything we've been through this year. Men often bottle up their emotions. I've had Esther to talk to.'

'And your channel,' he mutters.

'Well, yes. But I've said I can stop now.'

'Your channel isn't the only problem.' He wriggles his fingers free of my grip. 'I've been waiting until Lottie is better, home, to see if we can fall back to the way we were, but I don't think we can.' His eyes well up. 'I don't think I can.'

'It's too early to give up. Of course it's not going to be the same as it was,' I babble, desperately. 'Of course. We're all different people, but that doesn't mean we can't be good again.'

'What if it isn't? I, I . . . ' He stumbles over his words. 'What if I don't want to be here, with you? Would you really want me to stay for the children?'

'Yes,' I say fiercely because he loves them. He loves me, doesn't he? Maybe he's seeing me in a different light. Constantly talking about medical stuff and smelling of hospitals isn't exactly sexy, is it? But after months of battling, Lottie is home.

'We'll have more time for us now as a family and—'

'I don't want that. I mean, I want the kids, obviously, but . . . ' he trails off before whispers. 'You. I don't want you.'

Chapter 18

Mia

The breath catches in my throat, and I swallow hard. He can't mean that he doesn't want me, us, can he? Unless . . .

'Is there someone else?' Fingers of dread squeeze my windpipe.

I cannot breathe.

'No,' he says emphatically.

Neither of us speaks until I ask, 'But then . . . why?' I'm afraid of his answer but at the same time desperate to hear it because I'm at a complete loss to know how to fight for my marriage when I don't fully understand what has torn it apart.

There's a slump in his shoulders. Shoulders that have now buckled under so much weight. His spine hunched in defeat. The same strong back that used to carry both Chris and Lottie as he'd race around the house on all fours. 'Giddy up, pony,' they'd say, Lottie's small hands clutching Sean's collar for balance, Chris behind her, his arms wrapped around her waist.

'Quit horsing around,' I'd laugh, and Sean would neigh,

rear up on his knees, hands already in place to catch the shrieking kids before they fell to the floor.

He'd always caught us – caught me – but he now no longer feels like my safety, my protector. But that's okay. It can be my turn to carry him.

'Should we make an appointment to see a therapist? Together or separately or—'

'I don't want to talk to anyone.'

What he means is that he doesn't want to fix this.

'But me? You'll talk to me? I deserve—'

'Deserve? It's always about what *you* want, isn't it, Mia?'

'No.' My anger rises to match his. 'I don't think it is *always* about me. I don't think it's often about me.' Like many women, I am many things, wife, mother, homemaker, employee. I'm not entirely sure I know who 'me' is anymore.

For a moment we sit in silence. I'm stunned. The walls of our marriage had been crumbling irreparably while I had been standing inside them, feeling protected. Loved.

'These past few months—'

'It isn't just these past few months,' Sean says, calmer again now.

'But I thought we were okay?'

Now.

We'd had tough times, of course. When Sean lost his mum it was particularly hard, him shutting me out. Putting on a brave face for Esther. Then there was that time when we had veered off track before Lottie came along. Chris was small and I was struggling to, well, to figure out who I was. Everyone's needs came before mine; they still do, truth be told. I just handle it better nowadays, except for times like these when Sean looks at me with such sorrowful eyes I'm immediately compelled to justify myself, holding out explanations and apologies just to keep us on the right course.

'I'm sorry I've neglected you.' I know this to be true, not just these past few months but perhaps, if I'm honest, as far back as I can remember.

'You haven't neglected me. It's right that the kids came first – come first – but . . . I always . . . I always thought I knew my place. Where I fit.'

'You fit right here with me. With us.'

'Something has changed.'

'*Everything* changed but now we can go back to the way it was before.'

'I . . . I can't. Inside me there's—' he covers his chest with his hand. 'Mia, this whole experience has taught me that life can be so short and so precious.' He's close to breaking, I can see it in his face, hear it in his voice. 'When I look at the rest of mine, I can't picture you in it anymore.' He looks at me with such infinite sadness my heart aches.

I've never really prioritised Sean, I can see this now, but I had always thought we were strong, our lives nothing extraordinary but there's comfort in the ordinary, isn't there? A familiarity in the routine. Then he tells me how he really feels about me, our life, and something breaks inside me because I know his decision is absolute. It is the end of us.

It is the early hours before I ask him. 'Have you any idea where you're going?'

He drops his head into his hands.

'Sean?' He won't look at me. 'I mean there's no rush to move out—'

'I'm not going anywhere.' His tone is one I don't recognise. A hint of shame?

'Oh. Okay.' I think of Esther when she was telling me that the solicitor had told her that Lewis didn't legally have to move out of their home. *Can you imagine how bloody awful the atmosphere would be if everyone that separated still lived together?* she had said but, in this case, I feel a frisson of hope. If we're all under one roof still then perhaps it isn't too late.

Sean utters something but I'm so lost in the happy-ever-after in my mind it doesn't register at first. But then, 'Sorry? What?' I must have misheard him.

'Esther and the kids are moving in here.'

'But they can't. There isn't enough room.'

'Esther doesn't want to live with Lewis anymore, and this is half her house. Our parents left it to both of us. It won't be forever, but Lewis isn't being transparent with money, and she has nowhere else to go yet.'

'Has she said this?' She can't have said this. She's my best friend.

'I went to see her after work.'

That's why he was late. Why she didn't reply to my text. She wanted him to tell me first. 'But where will we all sleep?'

Panic is already rising because he is right, this is their house. Yes, I probably have some claim on Sean's share legally because I am his wife but . . .

'Daisy and Lottie can share, and Felix can go in with Chris. Esther can have the bedroom, and I'll sleep on the sofa.'

And me? I want to ask. What about me? But I already know: he wants me to leave as much as I want to stay.

Drizzle blows against my face as I stand on Esther's doorstep the next morning. I've been turning things over all night, and I think there must be a solution to this if Esther and I sit down and talk about things properly. She may be Sean's sister, but she was my best friend long before I met him.

She opens the door, her face as pale as mine. Deep violet bags under her eyes. I feel a flash of sympathy. This must be awful for her too.

'Mia.' My name is barely a whisper. 'I can't believe this. I just can't.'

'Esther, can we talk?' She hasn't stepped aside to let me in.

'I don't know what to say to you right now. You can't expect me to take your side against my brother's.'

'Side? What? No. Sean and I are going to be amicable for the sake of the kids. Stay friends. We can all still be friends.'

'How?' Her voice is thick with tears. 'It won't be the same anymore.'

'But . . . we've been friends longer than I've been with Sean.'

'And Sean's been my brother even longer.'

'Look, I know you're close to him, but . . . I don't want to lose you too. I can't.'

She hangs her head. It's as if she's delaying her answer, forming it in her head before she says it aloud. 'I'm sure our paths will still cross. We can still be civil.'

'What? This isn't you. You don't speak like that. I don't want to be civil. Look, I know it might take some time, but I want everything to be the same.'

'But it isn't, is it?' She looks at me with such despair, but I also see the steeliness in her. The same steeliness Sean has. It's in their blood. I'm losing her. Losing everything.

'Do you really want to move into my house?'

'It's my house too.'

'Sorry. I know it's half yours, but it's my home, mine and the kids.'

'I'm not forcing anyone to leave,' she says.

'But you're making it impossible for me to stay.' I'm falling apart. Even though Sean is her brother, and they are close, I can't believe that Esther – Esther who held my hair back at uni when I threw up after a night out, who taught me how to express milk for Chris when my nipples were raw and I felt like giving up, who was my *bridesmaid* – is turning her back on me.

Tears stream down my cheeks and I see her eyes are glistening, her lip wobbling, and she begins to shut the door before she starts to cry too.

Seemingly, enemy lines have been drawn. Sean and Esther on one side, and I'm alone on the other.

So begins one of the worst weeks of my life, telling the kids, finding out about benefits, asking my boss if I can return to work straight away, agreeing maintenance payments with Sean.

Looking at the few properties that were available and affordable around Woodford, damp-ridden flats, mould clinging to the walls. Some people seem to think that if you're a single parent you can live the life of luxury with everything paid for, but that very much isn't the case. There are complicated claim forms, hoops to jump through, endless waiting and then trying to find somewhere within budget. Unscrupulous landlords that want to milk the system whatever the cost to their tenants.

And then a solution. On the outskirts of town, but Chris could still finish his A levels at sixth form.

That's when I moved into the glass house with the huge windows that would ultimately expose all of my secrets.

The fucking glass house.

Chapter 19

Who's Watching You Documentary

Jake Lawler (host): My next guest is Frank Johnson, from Woodford. Welcome, Frank.

Frank Johnson (local resident): Thank you. (sitting rigidly staring at camera)

Lawler: Just relax, Frank, focus on me, not the camera, this is just a chat.

Johnson: I ain't one to air me dirty laundry in public.

Lawler: I promise, I won't ask you anything personal, but you have more of an insight than most into the glass house.

Johnson: Yeah, well, me family lived there for generations. Not in that modern monstrosity but in the farmhouse that were there before.

Lawler: The farmhouse that was torn down so the glass house could be erected?

Johnson: Yeah, well, me parents passed and there were debts that . . . no, I ain't doing it. I ain't talking about me father's gambling.

Lawler: No one's asking you to. So your parents inherited that house from their parents who inherited it from their parents and so on?

Johnson: Yeah. We used to farm, though it's overgrown now with the trees and whatnot; you can't even see it from the road. It were beautiful once.

Lawler: And you and your brother couldn't keep it? (downturned mouth, hand over heart)

Johnson: Nah. Bills had to be paid out the estate.

Lawler: The property was sold. That must have been sad for you both?

Johnson: Not as sad as when the house were torn down. I was fuming. Bruce, though, he were a builder by trade. He did a lot of work constructing the glass house. Imagine how humiliating that must have been for him. That bloody hideous thing on our family plot. I'm amazed they ever got planning permission.

Lawler: But an honest day's work—

Johnson: But he weren't never properly paid, not in full. He were promised cash in hand, so there weren't anything he could do. I mean, he paid taxes and everything. As honest as the day is long. Anyhow, the house never got finished. The stress of it gave Bruce a heart attack.

Lawler: You must be very bitter regarding the house.

Johnson: It's an eyesore. It ain't even habitable, not really. Oh, I saw Miss Fancypants on the YouTube, but she were only sharing bits that looked good. Most of the walls weren't plastered, wires hanging out, plumbing exposed, no banister. It would never pass building regulations. It were a mess. Not where I'd want to raise *my* kiddies.

Lawler: I think Mia's choices were very limited if she wanted to stay in the area so Chris could finish his education and be in the vicinity of the hospital for Lottie.

Johnson: Well, I don't feel no sympathy; people in glass houses shouldn't throw stones.

Lawler: You think Mia was throwing stones?

Johnson: Yeah, well, I dunno. I'm just saying, she criticised that Harlow one, didn't she?

Lawler: If you class Mia correcting Harlow when Harlow had misunderstood the very grave illness her daughter was suffering from, then yes, I suppose that is '*throwing stones*'. (inverted quotes with fingers)

Johnson: (face reddens) I'm just saying what goes around comes around.

Lawler: You think the Finch family, those children, deserved to be terrorised?

Johnson: Well, no, there are people dead now and (glances up at the still image taken from the Finch Family's first video outside their old house) they ain't all here now, are they? I'm just saying there ain't no smoke without fire.

Lawler: Fire is literally the only thing that poor family hasn't been through.

@Lamadrama23 I've lived in Woodford for 10 years & I didn't know the house was even there!!!

@Blackcat1970 It's too modern

@Avocadomonkey Remember Mia filming the day she moved in? That huge vase of white lilies as a welcome gift? #WWY

@Jamie2983 The most my landlord ever gave me was a bill for a new carpet lol. Least I didn't get the threats she did tho

Chapter 20

Mia

'Oh no,' I can't help saying out loud as I read my emails. We've only been in the glass house for two days and everything is going from bad to worse. Really, everything is getting too much for me. The pain of moving out of our home was just as physical as it was emotional. I had chest pains as I tried to keep my feelings inside while I helped the kids choose what to pack, what to leave.

'Because we'll be coming back here to stay with Dad, won't we?' they had asked, uncertain, looking younger than they had in years.

'Absolutely,' I had swallowed hard, tried to keep my face from crumpling. 'Dad and I aren't going to make formal custody arrangements. You're free to see plenty of us both.'

'Promise?' Lottie had said.

'Promise.' I had forced a smile. Knowing that Esther and Lewis's messy separation was likely on her mind. He hadn't yet committed to a time to see Felix or Daisy.

But the universe has obviously deemed I haven't yet been through enough, because now, this.

Chris stops shoving cereal into his mouth, spoon hovering over the bowl, Coco Pops tumbling back into the puddle of chocolatey milk.

'What's up?' he asks.

'The online magazine don't want me back.'

'That's crazy. You're a great writer,' Lottie says.

'They said they've made cuts and are only using freelancers now. They've invited me to submit features.'

'That's promising?' Lottie says.

'That's speak for "we're only using AI, so we don't have to pay you",' Chris says.

'I think you're right.' I push my toast away from me. I've lost my appetite. 'Goodness, this world. Sometimes I feel it's moving too fast for me. So much has changed since I was your age.'

'You have to move with it, Mum, or get left behind,' Chris says.

'I'll have to look for something else, working from home.'

'You don't have to work from home.' Lottie sprinkles sugar over her cornflakes. 'I can go back to school.'

'You will go back to school, Lotts. Just not yet.'

'But when? I want to go.'

'She'd be okay, Mum,' Chris says.

The stupid thing is that she probably would but, every time I think of it – the throng of pupils fighting through the corridors, breathing their germs; unwashed hands touching the same places Lottie will touch – my mind spins me back to the hospital. Lottie small and frail under starched white sheets. The fear of losing her swells up and I can't actually breathe. I know, rationally I know, that the probabilities of her falling so ill again are low and I have to let her go sometime – I will – but there's nothing wrong with being cautious, is there?

'Let me think about a start date,' I promise her.

'I've an idea,' Chris says. 'What if we monetised your YouTube channel?'

'I'm not really doing it anymore though, am I?'

'Because Dad didn't like it. What's stopping you now?'

'But I started it to share Lottie's journey. To give hope to other parents who had a child with an illness. To raise awareness of AA. Now Lottie's recovering, there might not be anything to talk about.'

'People are interested in us still. Look.' Chris angles his phone towards me. 'Since that last video of you and Harlow in the park was shown on the local news, you've so many new subscribers. I've been reading up on the criteria and you have enough subscribers and watch time to qualify.'

'Surely I wouldn't bring in much of an income? I'm hardly that Tweety Pie you used to watch.'

'PewDiePie.' Chris shakes his head. 'I think, honestly, you wouldn't generate a massive income right now, but it'd be a start. The more views you get, the higher your chance of earning. We could also set you up on Instagram. Look at brand sponsorship.'

'Who'd sponsor me?'

'I dunno, Mum. I'm throwing ideas around. What products did you find useful when Lotts was in hospital for weeks on end? What made her more comfortable? What stopped her getting bored when she was getting better? There must be tons of stuff. YouTube can point towards your IG and vice versa.'

'I don't know if I'd have time. I'm going to home-school Lottie for a while.'

'Perfect. That's another demographic. We can—'

'*We?*' I grin.

'Well, yeah. Duh, you can't even work the remote properly.'

'There's a million different HDMI options on this TV.'

'What do you think? Nothing to lose? Add me to the accounts. You carry on making the videos and I'll do everything else.'

'I don't want to take time away from your studies.'

'No offence, but I can figure out the online stuff that would probably take you weeks in minutes.'

'Some taken. I guess it might be worth a go. Harlow said she earned a good income. You know . . . before.'

'Yeah. Looking at her previous numbers I'm not surprised.'

'But . . . perhaps she's a cautionary tale. I mean, look at what happened to her. How quickly people turn on someone. The mob mentality. Right now my community feels, well, like a community. I do love it. I do think it helps, and if I could earn some extra money that would be amazing. What do you think, Lottie?'

She shrugs.

The day passes quickly. Remembering what Chris said before he went to school about creating new content, I've already posted a video. Lottie has spent most of the day sorting out her bedroom. Unpacking her books onto a bookcase that the British Heart Foundation delivered, along with some other bits of furniture earlier.

I've had a good chat with Lottie's teacher and, although Lottie won't like what her teacher has said, I think it's for the best.

We're all quiet over dinner. Tired, I think. Thoughtful.

After I've washed everything by hand, because there's no dishwasher here, I'm walking through the hallway when I notice a brown envelope on the floor under the letterbox. I pick it up, opening it as I walk, praying it isn't a bill already.

I'M WATCHING YOU

The words blur before my eyes, my breath coming in short gasps. I turn the envelope over; there's no name on the front, but I have to assume it's for me.

I'M WATCHING YOU

I fling open the door but there's nobody there. My eyes scan the garden, the trees and bushes, shivering.

There's nobody out there that I can see, but I can still feel eyes on me.

'Mum?' Chris says, and I scrunch up the note, hoping he hasn't read it. 'I didn't want to tell you in front of Lottie but something bad happened on the way to school today that you need to know about.'

Chapter 21

Who's Watching You Documentary

Jake Lawler (host): I am delighted to be joined by Anastasiya Kravchenko, a teacher at Chris and Lottie's school. Goodness, (laughs) they say that when teachers look so young and beautiful then you're getting old.

Anastasiya Kravchenko (TA): I think that's policemen and I'm not sure about the beautiful—

Lawler: But you're—

Kravchenko: A teaching assistant. Not a teacher. And . . . and I don't work there anymore.

Lawler: Well, it's a very commendable profession however long you did it for. Perhaps you can tell me after the show how you came to do it. (grins) We could . . . (awkward pause; Lawler lightly touching his ear as though he's been told to move on) Anyway. You must have known Lottie and Chris quite well.

Kravchenko: I got to know Chris as I was based in his class with a student that needed additional assistance. Everyone knew Chris really as he was the sixth-form prefect. He was always helping people. Lottie, I never met, but I'd heard of her, of course. That's why I agreed to come on here today, because those poor children have been picked over and dehumanised in the press. Turned into nothing more than gossip fodder. I wanted to remind the public that the Finch family are real people, with real feelings.

Lawler: (hand covers heart) I couldn't agree more. People using those children as entertainment are despicable. Now, tell me something about Chris the public don't know yet.

Kravchenko: He's sensitive. We spoke about Lottie's diagnosis before class one day. He was trying really hard to control his emotions, but I could tell he was really afraid that Lottie might not make it. I said he should talk to his parents. That it was okay to want to look after himself too. He wasn't responsible for everyone's feelings.

Lawler: It seems unusual for a teenage boy to be so sensitive. The only thing my son worries about is reaching the next level on his Xbox games. (smirks)

Kravchenko: I get the impression that Mia placed a lot of pressure on him after Lottie was born to be the big brother and look after his little sister. She probably didn't even realise she was doing it. I think it's a role he takes very seriously. He's kind. He helped me settle in when I arrived.

Lawler: And I'm sure that was out of the goodness of his heart. Nothing to do with the way you look at all.

Kravchenko: He was kind to *everyone*. On Marco's first day—

Lawler: (leans forward) Marco Hernandez?

Kravchenko: Yes. I was walking into school when Harlow and Marco arrived, at the same time as Chris. Harlow asked if she could have a word with Chris.

Lawler: And you stopped too?

Kravchenko: I did. I knew what had happened with Harlow and Mia. I wanted to make sure she wasn't going to give Chris a hard time. You know, he got teased so much after that video went viral. At first, when Mia began gaining in popularity, nobody really took any notice. It wasn't the sort of thing teenagers watched or cared about but, after Mia was arrested, Chris came into class one day and pulled out his chair, but it had been handcuffed

to the table. Someone left him a muffin
with a nail file sticking out of it. There
were pictures stuck to his locker of Mia's
mugshot. Not the actual one. AI created.
Everyone talks so much about how social
media impacted Mia and Sean's marriage,
and Lottie. Chris gets forgotten about.

Lawler: And did Harlow? Give Chris a hard
time?

Kravchenko: She seemed incredibly sad.
She said, 'I've lost everything. You
know what that's like. I know you've had
to leave your home. Please, can you ask
your mum if she'll do a video with me?'
Chris said, 'No. I won't. I've seen the
video. I know what you said about my
sister.' Chris started to turn away and
Harlow grabbed his arm. 'I didn't mean
that. Of course I didn't mean it, I'm a
mum myself. I'm not a bad person, I just
did a bad thing.' She had gestured to
Marco. 'It's just that being cancelled,
it . . . it . . . ' She started to cry,
and Chris said. 'Look, so many people get
cancelled but only a small percentage
of them stay cancelled. I don't know if
there's any coming back for you, though.
Saying a child should have died is pretty
unforgivable.'

Lawler: What happened then?

Kravchenko: Harlow just nodded as though
she expected him to say no. She said,

'Please don't take it out on my boy.' Chris said, 'I can promise you I won't cause any trouble for Marco.' Chris walked through the gates. Marco caught up with him and yanked his bag and said, 'I might fucking cause trouble for you though, Finch.'

Lawler: Marco threatened Chris. (turns to camera) You heard this version exclusively here, folks. Don't forget to join in the conversation at #WWY. (hashtag appears on screen) What did Chris do? (turns to Kravchenko)

Kravchenko: Nothing. He ignored him because he'd promised Harlow. He has a very firm moral compass, Chris. He's very loyal.

Lawler: He wasn't so loyal when he was interviewed by the police and asked to provide an alibi though, was he?

@Blackcat1970 The video was probably edited that way

@Jamie2983 You can't edit someone saying something if they didn't say it!

@Lamadrama23 You can with AI!!! Deep fake!!!!

@Avocadomonkey Harlow never denied it was her. Still that arrest wasn't as interesting as the one still to come #WWY

Chapter 22

Mia

I'm staring at the TV. I've picked up a DVD player and some films from the charity shop because we don't have the internet yet or any streaming services. *Bridget Jones* has always been my comfort movie because it made me believe in true love, but without Sean I feel one step away from those giant beige pants and it's making me feel sad.

I switch it off.

Can't stop thinking about that note.

I'M WATCHING YOU

The threat behind it. I think it must be from Harlow. From what Chris told me, she knows we've left our house. Although the glass house is distinctive, it's been sat empty for years. Hidden from sight by trees and bushes. Not many people know it's here, but clearly she's aware of our address.

I'm not sure what to do about it. I really don't want to confront her. The caution from the police is still fresh in my mind. I don't want to report her either. She's been through such a lot. I do feel sorry for her. I don't think saying one bad thing makes someone a bad person, and in the days before smartphone cameras and social media no one would ever have known. Now one mistake can ruin your life because you never know who's watching you, do you?

I shiver. Pull the throw up to my chin.

That note.

I go upstairs to put a fleece on. I've got plug-in electric heaters in the main rooms that we use but it's still chilly here. I don't think they'll throw out enough heat deep in the depths of winter. We're barely warm enough now, in early November. I hear music coming from Chris's room. There's no noise coming from Lottie's and my first thought is that she is sick. I tap on the door before I quickly enter. She's curled on her side in bed. Arms wrapped around Mr Edward, her bear. The glow of her mobile on the pillow next to her. I wonder if she's been looking at photos of Sean. I keep doing that. I can't bring myself to change my screensaver.

'Are you feeling ill?' I'm pressing the back of my hand against her forehead as I ask. I hadn't been determined to stay around Woodford solely for the schools or for Sean. The proximity of the hospital, her specialist team, had been an important factor.

'No.'

'Are you sure?'

'Positive.'

'Scoot over.'

Her single bed sags as I climb onto it.

'Do you want to talk about it?'

'I wish we could go home,' she says in a small voice.

'Me too,' I admit. 'Maybe once I've seen a solicitor and Esther's divorce goes through—'

'I mean I wish it was how it used to be: you, me, Chris and Dad. Auntie Esther in her house with Uncle Lewis, Felix and Daisy. All getting together for picnics and barbecues and one of Grandma's roasts. It's never going to be like that again, is it, Mum?'

I breathe in deeply through my nose, trying to steady myself before I answer because knowing that I am the cause of my daughter's pain is unbearable.

'If Grandma tries to cook a roast now she'd likely burn the house down.' It's a stupid effort to lighten the mood and the minute I've said it I feel horrible and mean. What wouldn't I give for one of my mum's Yorkshire puddings, crispy potatoes. What wouldn't I give to have everything back the way it used to be? 'I'm sorry.' I pull Lottie tightly to me.

For a moment she sniffles into my chest, then she pulls back and says, 'No. I'm sorry. I get it. Sometimes adults don't love each other anymore.'

It stings – lemon juice on a paper cut – because, undoubtedly, I still love Sean. Despite everything, I like to think – hope – that he loves me too on some level. Perhaps that makes it harder. Perhaps it's easier to move on if there aren't any feelings left.

'We still care very deeply for each other.'

'Was it . . .' She's trembling. 'Was it my fault? The stress of my illness?'

'No! Absolutely not.'

'But you had to spend a lot of time apart when I was in hospital.'

'I promise you it wasn't that. If anything the two of you probably kept us together for longer than we would have been.'

'What was it, then?'

'I think,' I say carefully, 'that we'd just grown apart. We got together very young. It's sad but it happens.'

I stroke Lottie's hair.

'Want me to sing you a song?' I don't have a very good voice, but it always used to soothe her when she was little.

'You could tell me a story. On second thoughts, don't. If you put that on YouTube—'

'Hey. I don't put everything on YouTube.'

'I don't know what the kids at school are going to make of it all when I go back. Have you thought about a start date? Dr Chadha said to try a couple of mornings a week and see how I get on, didn't she?'

'Yes, but I don't think you're ready.'

'But I think I'm ready.'

'It's not like you can't learn stuff here. I can teach you.'

'But I'll be bored.'

'It won't be forever.'

'But when?'

I'm already feeling panicky hot at the thought of letting her out of my sight. I don't think she's strong enough yet. Or maybe I'm the one who isn't strong enough.

'It'll be Christmas next month and, honestly, all your class seems to do in that final week is watch films.'

'But I'm missing so much of my GCSE work.'

'Lottie, I had a chat with your teacher this afternoon. I was waiting for the right time to tell you because I know you'll be upset, but it seems that you're going to have to repeat the year.'

'Repeat? But all my friends will have finished. Daisy's already virtually best friends with Erika now.'

'Daisy will always be your cousin. She'll always have a place for you. You're so far behind. It isn't your fault, you're a clever girl.'

'But I've been doing coursework.'

'I know you've been doing what you can, but you've missed so much. Too much.'

She falls silent.

'I'm sorry, Lottie. It sucks. It really does, but things could be worse.'

'How?' There's a bitter edge that I haven't heard before.

'You might not be here.' It's blunt but true. Although everything seems a mess, we have so much to be grateful for.

'Maybe I don't want to be.'

'Don't say that. Don't *ever*—'

'Geez, Mum, I mean here in this glass house. Not literally on the planet.'

'I'm doing my best, Lottie.'

She stiffens in my arms. 'I know. I can never forget you saved my life.' She sounds so miserable.

For a few minutes we lie there in the half dark, and I can almost imagine we're in her old room. Posters of retro films on the walls. Hollywood mirror on the dressing table, lightbulbs illuminating her flawless skin as she slicked pink gloss over her lips. We must add some personal touches to this house.

'Anything else on your mind?' I ask.

I feel the rise and drop of her shoulders as she shrugs. 'Have you . . . ' she sighs. 'Have you seen the comments on the latest video?'

'No.'

'You told everyone my periods started again.'

'That's a good thing! They don't often return so quickly after chemo, sometimes not at all. If it gives some hope to women going through cancer treatments then I thought . . . Sorry, Lottie, do you want me to delete the whole post?'

There's a beat before she says, 'No. We wanted to help people, but Mum, basically there's this comment about me being a woman and . . . I don't want to repeat it but there are some real weirdos out there.'

'I'll go and get rid of that straight away.' I throw back the covers. 'I'll have to tell you the story of the princess in the tower another time.'

'It's okay, Mum. She rescues herself.'

I smile. I like the thought of that. 'Do you want to come downstairs and watch a film with me? You can choose.'

'Nah. They're all ancient. I'm going to grab a shower,' she says.

Sitting in the kitchen, laptop on the table in front of me, I hear Lottie clump downstairs to the shower. The one in the bathroom upstairs isn't yet wired in and she doesn't like baths. I've a glass of wine in my hand. Michael Finnegan is snoozing in his cat bed. For most of the day, he's been pacing, stopping every now and then to press his nose against the window, looking sadly at the outside, wondering why he isn't allowed in the garden. We've been keeping him in as a precaution while he gets used to his new environment, but I think we'll let him venture out in the next day or two.

I've hooked up my laptop to the hotspot on my phone and I'm livestreaming, sharing my plans to home-school Lottie, to perhaps do up this house, reading the comments carefully to see what people seem most engaged with. For the first time since that awful conversation with Sean, I feel a spark of excitement, hope. For the past few months I've loved creating content; the chance that I could generate any sort of income from it feels almost too good to be true.

I'm halfway through a sentence when, suddenly, a scream.

Lottie.

Not her I've-seen-a-spider shriek but one filled with pure terror.

I've scrambled to my feet, when she comes pelting into the room, fluffy white towel wrapped around her.

'Mum!' She throws herself in my arms. 'There's somebody outside.'

'What do you mean?' I glance at the windows. The

darkness outside coupled with the lights in the kitchen have turned them into a mirror.

'There was someone at the window. Cupping their hands against the glass. Looking in at me.'

'What's going on?' Chris runs in.

'Lottie thought she—'

'I didn't *think*. The window isn't frosted and there's no bloody blind. There was someone. It was too dark to tell if it was a man or a woman, but they had a black coat on and they were watching me.'

I'm watching you.

Who is watching us?

Is it Harlow or is it someone else?

Someone dangerous?

The kids are staring at me, waiting for me to do something.

I have to go outside and see who it is.

Chapter 23

Mia

Someone was watching my daughter through the bathroom window, and I need to find out who it is. If it is Harlow then surely there's nothing to fear, is there? Still, I feel a prickling of terror on my skin.

'Mum, who's out there? What do they want? Do something.' Lottie's still clinging to me. 'Call Dad.'

'He's working away this weekend. I'll go and check it out,' Chris says.

'You're not going out there.' I grab his arm. 'I'm going.'

'No, you're not. Call the police if you won't let me go,' Chris urges.

I deliberate. I haven't told the kids about the note or my theory about Harlow because Chris still has to go to school with Marco every day and I don't want to make things any more awkward than they already are. Besides, it seems like an overreaction, and you hear such stories nowadays about the emergency services taking hours to respond to serious crimes. A teenage girl, already unsettled by the new house, thinking she might have seen someone in the dark isn't exactly going to be a priority, is it?

But what if it isn't Harlow?

Every true crime documentary I've ever seen comes rushing in at me as I imagine the worst. That *Who's Watching You* series with the smarmy host who seems to revel in people doing terrible things. I'm catastrophising again. My heart galloping as I get myself in a state while trying to act calm in front of the kids. Pretending I'm in control, but I'm spiralling.

Oh god, what should I do?

I chew my lip while I mull it over, tasting blood.

Glancing at Michael Finnegan sleeping, wishing for the first time he were a dog who would bark at the first sign of a stranger.

My laptop catches my eye. I'm still recording, and the comments are going crazy.

WTF?

Who's out there?

Don't open the door!!!

'Sorry, guys, I'm sure everything's fine. I'm going to check. I'll post an update later.' I close the lid.

Then I fetch my boots.

The kids fall silent. I'm half expecting them to stop me, but they know – I know – that nobody will settle until someone has been in the garden and, as Lottie said earlier, a princess can save herself without the need for a prince.

I *can* do this.

But still, I'm trembling.

'Take a knife,' Chris says.

'I am *not* taking a knife. Lock the door behind me and have your phone ready to call the police, just in case. I'm sure everything is fine now. If someone was out there—'

'There was,' Lottie cuts in.

'Then they're probably long gone. Perhaps it's someone who walks their dog around here and thought the property was empty, a local. You probably scared them as much as they scared you.'

The children look reassured at this, but then they don't know about the note, do they?

I'm watching you.

My heart is in my mouth as I step outside. I can feel every beat fast and frantic in my throat. I turn and gesture for Chris to lock the door.

I've never had to use the torch on my mobile phone before and it's virtually useless. The pale light barely illuminating the ground in front of me.

The darkness here is absolute. I feel a fierce longing for Sean. Our old house, street lined with lampposts, houses packed tightly together, cocooned by the constant thrum of traffic.

A twig snaps and I jump before realising it was me who had trod on it.

I inch around the side of the house, sticking close to the wall. I've walked the length of the kitchen and am passing the hot tub that we'll probably never use. Around the next corner will be the bathroom. The place where Lottie saw . . .

'Harlow?' I whisper. 'I know it's you.'

But I don't really know that, do I?

I'm sweating. My feet feel like lead, unable to move. I steel myself before I push forward, make a sharp right. Adrenaline rushing through my veins, ready to run. There's a rustle in the bush to the side of me.

'Who's there?' I say. There's a tremor in my voice. 'Harlow? We've called the police.'

Low to the ground, I think I see a flash of something sandy brown. A hare? Do they come out in the dark? I've never lived this close to the countryside before. Under the bathroom window I crouch and shine my torch, looking for signs of footprints but there's a hard path rather than soft mud, so nothing is visible.

I finish scoping the perimeter and then I'm back in the warmth of the kitchen.

'There's nobody out there,' I say to the kids. But that doesn't mean there hasn't been.

We spend a couple of hours playing Uno, trying to relax. Usually there's much laughter and teasing when we slap cards down – *pick up four, you loser* – but tonight it feels forced. Eventually the kids go to bed and I'm locking up, checking the doors multiple times when I remember the livestream I was doing. I hope nobody has been too worried about us.

I open my phone and start recording, aware of how pale I look. How scared. I force a smile. 'Hi, guys. So. Just a quick check-in to let you know everything is okay. We haven't been murdered or anything! So, yes, some of you know that Lottie thought . . . Lottie said she saw someone watching her through the bathroom window earlier. I've been out there and had a good look and there's no sign of anyone. No crazed stalker waiting out there with an axe.' My laugh is hollow. It's too soon to make jokes really but I don't want to reveal just how worried I was – still am. 'I think it was likely a dog walker or neighbour who thought the property was empty and was checking we aren't squatters or anything. Anyway, I'm off to bed. Stay safe.'

I add a title 'Crazed stalker?' and some tags and post it before I collapse into bed.

I can't help checking my post one more time before I try to sleep. It's already gathered traction.

OMG how frightening.

Yours is my favourite channel. You're an inspiration.

Make sure you keep the doors locked, hun.

Have you thought about getting a dog?

We need to protect this family! Lottie has been through enough

This last comment is from Charlie's Angels, of course. But then:

@Joker666 You deserve everything you have coming to you

I've had the odd negative comment before but something about this one feels more chilling. I think it's the name, Joker666. I delete the comment, reassuring myself that at least they don't know where I live.

It's a long time before I fall into an uneasy sleep.

It's pitch black when I wake, heart thudding.

You know when you get a sense you're being watched? That's how I feel. Skin prickling. In that half state between sleep and awake, I'm sure there had been somebody standing over my bed.

I click on the lamp, squinting against the light as I scan the room.

There's nobody here but the door is wide open, and I know I would have pulled it to.

A sudden movement in the corner of the room.

Michael Finnegan on the chair, washing his paws.

Although he'd usually slip through the crack in the door, it's not unfeasible he could have been the one to knock it open.

Couldn't he?

I settle back down in bed.

Leave the lamp on.

Chapter 24

Mia

My eyes are gritty with tiredness. I flick on the kettle and add a teaspoon of coffee to a mug and then, yawning, add another.

'Holy shit, Mum –' Chris rushes into the kitchen, – 'have you checked the channel today?'

My stomach drops as I pull my phone out of my pocket. Usually sifting through the comments is the first thing I do when I wake, to make sure there's nothing negative Lottie can see.

'What's happened?' I open my app. 'Oh.'

'You've never had this many views before, never. And look how many new subscribers. This is great. I thought it had blown up after the fight in the park with Harlow, but this is something else'.

I take a moment to scroll through the comments. Chest tightening as I see one from Joker666.

Watch your back.

I delete it. Their comments are such a contrast to the sweetness of the ones from Charlie's Angels.

'It's because of last night,' Chris says when I don't speak.

'But I didn't finish my livestream and then only posted a two-minute video.'

'It's because of the title you gave the post, "Crazed Stalker"?'

'I don't get it.'

'Look at the comments. There's a lot of speculation that it was Harlow in the garden. People saying she's coming for revenge because that video of her in the park has ruined her reputation.'

'But how has everyone found the video? There are far more views than I have followers.'

'People don't get the choices they think they do. We've covered this in psychology at school. It's all about algorithms. Coders decide what you see. The posts that appear at the top of your feed aren't always the latest ones. Rather they're the ones the algorithms have chosen for you. Social media selects what you see, no matter what the people you follow are posting.'

'So algorithms prefer negative posts? I want my channel to be a positive place.'

'Algorithms have no preference between good and bad. They can't distinguish between positive and negative. What they do is show you things that will keep you looking at your screen. The more times users look at something, the more money the site makes.'

'But why not show people happy things? I want to inspire people, give them hope. Lift them up, not bring them down.'

'The algorithms' aim is to keep someone scrolling. Human nature drives people to spend more time looking at something negative for longer than they'd look at something calm. Even though the positive posts give more pleasure. It's called the negativity bias. When you labelled your video "Crazed Stalker?", it got picked up by the algorithm and, well, the engagement speaks for itself. It's like a car crash people slow down for. I bet nobody thinks they'd rather look at the wreckage than say, a group of rabbits frolicking—'

'Frolicking? You just said frolicking?' Lottie snorts with laughter as she joins us at the table. 'What are you talking about? Victorian times?'

My mobile rings. Sean.

'Hi. Everything okay?' He had said he was working away this weekend.

'You tell me? Esther says you posted a video that there was a madman in your garden?'

'Ah.' I glance at the kids before I push my chair back and retreat to the hallway.

'No,' I say in a low voice. 'Lottie thought she saw someone, but I went outside—'

'You went *outside*?'

'What did you expect me to do?'

'Call the police?'

'I wasn't convinced there was anyone out there. It's a new environment. Lots of trees and bushes we're not used to.'

'All those windows.'

'Yes. Honestly, if I thought we were in danger then I would have called someone.'

'Me, you could have called me.'

'Could I?' A frisson of anticipation runs through me as I wait for him to answer.

'Look,' he sighs. 'I want to make sure the kids are safe. That you're all safe. You've opened yourself up to the public and now some nutter—'

'There wasn't anyone there. I promise we're all fine and if we get spooked again I'll call you.'

'Okay. Can you tell the kids I'll call them this evening? I've got a meeting now.'

'Of course. Speak later.'

There's a warm glow as I end the call. He still cares. Esther is still watching my videos. Perhaps they both still care.

'Can I come with you, Mum?' Lottie asks as I zip up my boots.

I'm going to visit my mum in the care home and, while I'm out, I'll pick up a blind for the bathroom window.

I hesitate. I'm not keen on Lottie going out into the world, mixing. I'm scared she'll pick something up, but then I'll be with her.

'Rapunzel, Rapunzel,' Chris says from the table where he's studying.

'Lottie isn't a prisoner. Of course you can come and see Gran but, you know, she might not be having a good day.'

When we get there, Mum isn't in the garden of the care home or the resident's lounge. It's not always a good sign when she stays in her room.

We've just reached the second floor when a familiar figure steps out of the lift.

'Alma.' Lottie runs towards her and wraps her in a hug. 'Don't you work at the hospital anymore?'

'I do but I also do a bit of freelance nursing. Our pay isn't great.' She straightens up. 'How are you, Mia?'

'Good, thanks. We're here to visit my mum.'

'Beverley is such a gentle woman.'

'She is.'

'I'm glad you're still on the ward,' Lottie says. 'I've missed you. You're my favourite nurse.'

'Can I tell you a secret? Are you good at keeping secrets?'

Alma is looking at me as she asks this and a chill slithers down my spine.

'I am,' says Lottie.

'You were my favourite patient too.' Alma gives Lottie another quick hug and then says goodbye. 'I'm glad I still get to watch you on YouTube.'

She smiles at me before she walks away.

Mum not having a good day turned out to be an understatement.

She doesn't recognise me, doesn't recognise Lottie. Aside from not knowing who we are, she's agitated. Not herself at all.

Lottie immediately goes to give her a kiss.

'Don't,' I say sharply.

Lottie's face drops as she backs away. I didn't mean to frighten her, but Mum has been known to lash out when she's distressed. It rarely happens but I don't want to risk Lottie being hurt.

'Where's Anthony? I want Anthony.'

There is so much fear in her voice as she calls for my father, I'm transported back to all those years ago, trying to wake him up, not realising he'd never wake again.

'Mum.'

'Mum? I'm not your mum.'

'Sorry, *Beverley*.' It's an effort to keep myself composed so I don't upset her. I hate seeing her like this. This stoic woman who once dyed her hair green because I'd tried to dye mine blonde and it went wrong. I don't want Lottie to be seeing this.

Mum's trying to get up from her chair, but her knees are weak, and she can't manage without aid. It's horrible watching her, not wanting to help her stand because where would she go? She's not going to find the person she wants to see.

'Beverley?' I crouch in front of her, not too close, wanting to give her some space. 'Shall I read to you?'

Her eyes stop staring wildly around the room and focus on mine.

She doesn't answer but she's calmer as I reach for the book on the table. I'd brought it in for her a few weeks ago, *Anne of Green Gables*. It was her childhood favourite. I think the familiarity of it unlocks a sense of the safety of childhood.

'Mum?' Lottie asks in a small voice. 'What should I do?'

I glance over my shoulder; my daughter looks so distraught.

'Do you want to go and wait in the resident's lounge downstairs?'

'What if someone talks to me? What if they . . . you know.'

I don't know exactly what she means but it's clear she's uncomfortable.

'Do you want to wait in the library at the bottom of the road? I'll come and find you in half an hour or so?'

'Thanks, Mum.'

I don't watch her leave, I'm focusing on the story, on Mum, but I feel her absence all the same.

Almost an hour has passed before Mum falls asleep while I'm reading to her.

Sierra is in the reception when I'm heading for the door. Fiddling with her pink hair.

'You're welcome,' she shouts as I pass by her.

'Sorry, for what?'

'I was the one who posted the video of you and Harlow in the park.'

The look on her face oscillates between pride and doubt when she realises that I'm not smiling back at her.

'What?'

'I posted the video of you and Harlow,' she says, quieter now.

Hot sick anger claws at my stomach. 'What did you do that for?' There's a low, dangerous quality to my voice that she can obviously hear too because she takes a step backwards.

'To help you?' She looks uncertain now, afraid, and I think she should be because in this moment all I want to do is hurt her the way she has hurt my daughter. My whole family.

'I set up a throwaway account because I didn't want it to look like I'm taking sides, but it really helped you, didn't it?' She's more confident now, thinking of view counts, subscribers but not once thinking of people, feelings. The harm she has caused with one mindless post. 'I'm going to help build you, Mia. One good turn. Call me, we'll collab.'

'One good turn? I had to show that video to Lottie because it was out there. Watch her face as she listened to Harlow say it would have been better if she'd died.'

'You should have filmed her reaction. That would have been great content.' She's smiling again, thinking I understand her now, might even be grateful.

'Fuck off, Sierra,' I say.

I'm so close to lunging at her I have to force myself to turn and leave before I do something that could get me arrested again.

Normally when I arrive home the first thing I do is take my shoes off, but I'm dying for a wee. I've got a few paces down the hallway when I feel my trainers crunch over broken glass.

'Stop.' I glance over my shoulder, holding my palm up to Lottie. 'Don't come over here with bare feet.'

I look around but I can't see the source of the broken glass.

Someone has broken in and put it there.

'Chris?'

He doesn't answer.

'Chris?' I call, louder, already checking the downstairs rooms, racing upstairs, bursting into his bedroom. He's sprawled on the bed, headphones on.

'Mum! I could have been . . . well, getting changed or anything.'

'Sorry. There's glass on the floor downstairs.'

'Yeah. Soz, the photo of us with Dad got smashed. I thought I cleared it all up.'

Immediately my heart begins to slow. An accident that's all.

'Oh, don't worry. I'll do it. I'm not cross with you.'

'Why would you be? I didn't do it. I found it and assumed Michael Finnegan had knocked it off.'

It's a plausible explanation. Cats do leap and explore, but then I'd also blamed him for opening my bedroom door in the night.

If it's as simple as that then why do I feel increasingly scared here? If Harlow has sent the note, spied through the bathroom window, how far will she go? Has she got inside the house? How would she do that without keys? A locksmith is another expense I really don't need, but perhaps I should ring one, just in case.

I'm cooking dinner when I notice a florist's van pull up outside.

Immediately, I grab my phone. Begin recording. This is the upbeat content I want.

'A happier post today, someone has sent us flowers!' I smile into the camera as I head towards the door. I'm thinking the flowers must be from Sean. He had seemed so concerned when he called to make sure we were okay.

The florist is already back in her van as I open the door.

I glance down at the step, lowering my phone to film what's been left.

The delivery.

Not a bouquet for me at all but a wreath.

A wreath with a card attached to it.

RIP Lottie

Chapter 25

Who's Watching You Documentary

Jake Lawler (host): I'm pleased to welcome Dr Cade Jones to the show. Dr Jones is a clinical psychologist who's going to provide some insight into the psychology of social media. Welcome, Dr Jones.
(Dr Jones stands; the men shake hands before they both sit)

Dr Cade Jones (psychologist): Call me Cade, please. (glances at camera, straightens tie)

Lawler: Cade. (smiles) The publicity surrounding this case has the nation debating the perils of social media. The hidden dangers. We'll get into those in a moment but let's start with the positives, if we can. We know that before the phenomenal and, in Mia's own words, 'unexpected' success of her channel, that she'd spent a lot of times on various platforms, not necessarily interacting but . . . (stares intently into camera, lowers voice) lurking.

(pause)

Catfish, scammers, hackers. The internet is a dark place full of secrets. Full of people who aren't who they claim to be, who might have an ulterior motive for watching you.

Befriending you.

Lulling you into a false sense of security because, despite the privacy settings, social media really isn't safe, is it?

Jones: I can give you numerous examples of interactions gone horribly wrong but I'm not an IT guy so I really can't comment on password security and how locked down private profiles actually are. Mia was just a lurker though. That's a bit different to deliberately setting out to deceive someone.

Lawler: And what might she have gained from observing?

Jones: (clears throat) We know from multiple studies that social media can enhance the mental health of users. Sharing experiences can increase the sense of belonging. Even something as simple as joining an online book club can instil a sense of community, albeit a different definition of community than perhaps some of the older generation would recognise.

Lawler: The internet can bring people together, can't it?

Jones: Indeed. Many people have made life-long friends via, say, Facebook. For some people, particularly those who live alone, it can decrease loneliness. Sometimes online interactions are the only interaction with another human being that a person might have that day. (pushes black-rimmed glasses up the bridge of his nose)

Lawler: That all sounds great, but not everyone who uses social media can claim positive mental health benefits, can they?

Jones: No. Sadly not. There can be detrimental effects of social media on mental health.

Lawler: What sort of detrimental effects are we talking about?

Jones: The findings have been quite widespread. Anything from poor body image, and we particularly see this amongst young girls and women using Instagram. Comparing yourself to others is 'the thief of joy', as the saying goes. Users can sometimes begin to feel dissatisfied with their own lives, which can lead to lower self-esteem. Although fear of missing out isn't yet a recognised psychological condition, it's one we're seeing more and more of in clinic.

Lawler: I see. And Lottie. The entire Finch family were definitely missing out on life at that time. Shockingly, there are approximately 1.7 million under 16-year-olds in the UK classed as having a chronic illness. Approximately 35,000 kids admitted to hospital each year. What might the mindset be of a parent with a sick child?

Jones: (sips from a glass) There's no doubt that parenting a child with a chronic illness can cause immense strain to family life. Parents of children with chronic medical conditions are more likely to experience depression, anxiety and generalised emotional distress.

Lawler: So it's fair to say that parenting a sick child, over a prolonged period, can push you to breaking point.

Jones: I think that's far too generalised and the definition of breaking point ca—

Lawler: From the various crimes connected to the Finch family, I think that breaki—

Jones: I'm not here to provide a definitive explanation as to why the murder happened. Neither do I think it should be sensationalised for entertainment.

Lawler: (glares) And yet you agreed to come on the show? Sorry, (hollow laugh) emotions are running high because, it's just so . . . (hand covers heart) I'm finding the details so distressing. I'm a sensitive soul, but you're right. It would be highly remiss of me to imply that x happened because of y. It's far more complex

than that and we're here to unravel the
threads without judgement.
   (leans back on seat and rests arms
across the back of the cushion)
   Why would someone such as Harlow share
their entire life online?

Jones: I'm going to disagree with you
there—

Lawler: Again. (holds hands up and laughs)

Jones: You can perceive that someone like
Harlow, who made a living from influencing, shares their whole life online, but
in reality people only share what they
want you to see. Everyone has parts of
themselves, parts of their lives that
they want to keep hidden. I'm sure even
you have a skeleton in your closet, Jake.

Lawler: There's nothing in my closet
because my ex-wife cleaned me out. (tight
smile)

Jones: Hmm. (pauses, watching Jake for a
moment) Every time we notice likes and
nice comments on our posts, it initiates
the release of dopamine.

Lawler: What's dopamine?

Jones: It's a neurotransmitter. One of
the chemical messengers between neurons,
which are involved in both neurological
and physiological functioning.

Lawler: In layman's terms?

Jones: It's a feel-good chemical. It can be addictive.

Lawler: So the more popular an influencer becomes, the more dopamine they have and then the more they want?

Jones: Yes, it's self-perpetuating. But imagine in the case of Harlow how it must have felt to have adoring fans turn on you.

Lawler: Devastating. I hope I never experience it.

Jones: It was probably the whole series of events that led to Harlow's shocking actions. The first video she could have recovered from. The second video was harder for her to justify. But when people began blaming her for sending that wreath to Lottie and for scaring Lottie by spying on her through the bathroom window. It snowballed, didn't it? The hate was relentless. People who hadn't even seen the videos, weren't aware of who Harlow even was really, piled on. She was judged and found guilty by the internet. Well, what happened next was just so tragic. Perhaps avoidable, but we'll never know, will we?

@Blackcat1970 I don't get people who use social media. I never would

@Avocadomonkey You literally are right now #WWY

@Blackcat1970 Only to see everyone's theories

@Lamadrama23 Guys. Don't fight – we're getting to the good bit!!!

@Blackcat1970 It isn't good. It's heartbreaking. It isn't entertainment

@Jamie2983 And yet you're still here. Still watching.

Chapter 26

Mia

I'm gazing out at the garden. Lottie and Chris anxiously track Michael Finnegan, who is venturing out for the first time. Lottie had coated his paws liberally with butter the way we'd read about online. I don't know if it's a myth, but he doesn't seem to want to venture too far. Seems to know this is his home now.

The chicken is seasoned, the skin crisping in the oven. I'm whisking the batter for Yorkshire puddings. In truth, I usually use Aunt Bessie's but seeing Mum yesterday has left me gripped with nostalgia. It's as though replicating one of her legendary roasts can bring her back to me somehow.

Everything is falling apart.

A couple of days ago I was beginning to feel positive about the future. Swept away by Chris's vision for my channel.

Now, with the note, the lurker in the garden, the wreath and the ongoing backlash against Harlow after Sierra posted her video, I'm wondering whether I should just stop posting completely. I wanted to give back, make a difference. Perhaps I should look at other ways I can do that.

But it feels like something else I'm losing. That connection.

That sense of community. I know that I want to help others but also, maybe selfishly, I know I'd be lonely without it. I have to stop, though.

RIP Lottie.

Who sent that wreath? I find it hard to believe that it was Harlow. That another mother could have sent this. I had rung the florists to find out, but they said that customer information was confidential.

When I got off the phone, to my horror, I found the kids staring at the wreath. I should have hidden it straight away.

Lottie had been inconsolable, Chris holding her close while I rang the police. Got pointed to an online form to report it instead.

Are we in danger? That was one of the first questions.

How should I know? Isn't that their job to assess the risk?

I'd submitted my answers and hoped they didn't take too long in responding.

The wreath is now outside the back door. I don't want to throw it away in case it's evidence. I still have the note too.

It can't be someone with anything against Lottie, though. She's a child. It has to be someone with a grudge against me, but who? I seem to have upset everyone lately. Esther, but of course she wouldn't do this. Alma, but I don't think she knows what I did. Sierra, because I refused her stupid collab? Harlow, because once again all the drama has been stirred up? Joker666, whose comments are frequent and dark?

I'm suspicious of everyone.

Outside the patio doors, a sudden movement. My pulse races but it's just a crow landing on the lawn. I jump as he screeches, spreading his wings and soaring into the sky. Had something startled him? Someone?

I'm too hot.

There's an ominous sense of dread wrapped around me.

I'm on high alert. Knowing that something else is going to happen.

Something bad.

But not knowing when.

The timer beeps, telling me to drain the veg.

I lift the saucepan with two hands – it's heavy – and carry it over to the sink. As I begin to strain the carrots and peas, the steam rises. The window over the sink fogs up and words appear.

I WANT WHAT'S MINE

I drop the saucepan in the sink with a clatter.

I WANT WHAT'S MINE

I'm feeling lightheaded. Afraid. My skin tingling. Tentatively, as though they might bite me, I reach up and rub at the steam and the letters with my sleeve.

They disappear.

They'd been written on the inside of the window.

I don't think Michael Finnegan had knocked the photo frame from the table.

Someone has been in the house.

Sunday lunch was a strain. As soon as we'd finished eating, the kids went to play Mario Kart while I washed up. Now, I'm cleaning the window again, but I can still see those words.

I WANT WHAT'S MINE.

Did Harlow write them? Does it refer to her followers? Her sponsors?

Or is it someone else?

Alma? I can't exactly give her back what I took from her, can I? It's not as if she knows, though. Sierra?

Or is it some random person trying to scare me? Perhaps someone who thought they'd live in this house? Buy the land? I've heard the rumours that some old man blames the glass house for his brother's heart attack for some reason. I think his family used to live here.

I'm still trying to figure it out when Chris comes into the kitchen for a snack.

'I can't believe you're hungry again,' I say as he opens the fridge.

'I'm a growing boy.' He grins as he takes out the Branston pickle. 'Can I make a sandwich with the leftover chicken?'

'Of course. Leave a bit for Michael Finnegan, though. Something to reward him for coming home.'

'Mum,' Lottie shouts, her voice high and shaky.

Oh god, is there someone in the garden again, spying on us?

'Have you seen this?' Her obvious choking panic strangles her voice as she pelts into the kitchen with her laptop.

'Seen what?' My stomach plummets. Whatever she's about to show me clearly isn't anything good.

'It . . . it's so awful. I just can't.' She's wearing a pink unicorn t-shirt and she's shaking so hard the silver sequins that form the horn catch the light. I can't stop staring at them because I know instinctively I do not want to see whatever is on the screen.

'Whatever it is, it'll be okay, Lotts,' Chris says. But it isn't okay.

Ripples of Lottie's distress are spreading. I feel it too.

Someone is coming for us, and I don't know who or why.

Lottie puts her laptop on the table and opens the lid. Slowly, slowly. Before she sinks onto a chair.

'Words can't hurt us,' I say. 'Whatever they've said—'

'It isn't words. It isn't about me. About us.'

Lottie stares at Chris and me in turn, both bewildered and frightened.

'What is it, Lotts?' Chris asks.

'It's so awful. Watch.'

She presses play. I'm hit with such a strong sense of trepidation, I want to turn away from the screen.

I still hold the cloth in my hand from cleaning the window. I twist the end round and round my finger, tighter and tighter, my fingertip turning red.

A photo of Harlow appears and a male voice speaks over the top of it.

Social influencer Harlow Hernandez (35) has been found dead at her rented house. It is believed she has taken her own life.

I feel sick. My mouth is watery, and my stomach is lurching.

Harlow can't really be gone, can she?

Lottie drags the cursor on the video back to zero and plays the clip again. Once more, a smiling Harlow on the screen. Except she can't smile anymore, can she?

Dead?

It's such a complete shock that I feel both numb and really close to crying at the same time. I'm trying to be calm for Lottie's sake. For Chris's. They are both milk white. Trembling. I bite my lip so hard that it hurts, crushing the soft skin between my teeth in a bid to control myself, but it doesn't work.

Harlow has gone and, although I'm trying to be strong, I can feel the tears pouring down my cheeks. For her, for her son and for everyone who knew and loved her. So many people will be affected, so many more than she'd have realised.

I feel so sad, guilty, horrified. Myriad emotions.

Later, and I hate myself for this, the thought comes that perhaps now, that's the end of it. It's not relief that she's gone – of course not, it really is devastating – but the notes, the wreath, the threats.

I'd rather she was here to carry on tormenting me, but tragically she isn't and it's over now.

Isn't it?

Chapter 27

Mia

It's been three days since Harlow took her own life. I can't sleep. Am barely eating. I can't stop watching her channel. Playing her old videos over and over. Not the most recent ones, where dozens of red blood vessels streak the whites around her eyeballs as she'd begged the public to forgive her. The earlier ones. Where her poker-straight ponytail swished as she glided around the marble floor of her former home. When she'd share that it was tricky getting Marco to do his homework or eat vegetables. Could we all relate? And what do we all think of the glow on her skin? A new product she'd been sent that was 'totes amazing'. It seems like a lifetime ago.

I miss her.

I know that sounds hypocritical. I think it's that I miss those uncomplicated times. The times before Lottie fell ill and my marriage failed and I'd watch Harlow, wishing more than anything that my life could be like hers. All glossy and exciting.

Be careful what you wish for.

The truth is that in part I feel responsible. Perhaps even entirely responsible.

If I hadn't been so upset that she'd mocked Lottie's illness, not appreciating how serious it was.

If I had noticed her attempt to reach out to me afterwards.

If I hadn't ignored the video of her and me arguing in the park.

If I'd said publicly that I forgave her.

It's too late to forgive her now.

Whatever the situation, you always think there's more time, don't you? When I'd left the house with my mum, for swimming that day as a child, I never dreamed I'd never speak to my dad again. I've grown up valuing people, moments, thought I was aware of how quickly someone can be snatched away, but I hadn't expected it with Harlow. With someone so young and healthy. I want to gather everyone I know and hug them tightly because there isn't always more time, is there? More moments. More chances to say the things you wish you'd said.

And I think her death is going to be yet another thing that I never forgive myself for.

Nothing else has happened since. No comments from Joker666. No more deliveries to the house. Nobody lurking in the garden. No sense that anyone has been inside our home.

As the doorbell rings I hear Lottie rush to open it. I sit stiffly at the kitchen table. My hands clasped together. Waiting.

Sean traipses in the kitchen first, followed by Felix, Daisy, Chris and Lottie and then there she is. Esther. Eyes taking in everything. The exposed wiring. Bare plaster. Unfinished worktops.

'This is . . . it isn't exactly how it looks online, is it?' she says to me, so shocked by the truth of the glass house that she forgets she isn't really speaking to me.

'Smoke and mirrors,' I say.

'A lie.' Her eyes hold mine and the message in them is clear. We'll be civil for the sake of the kids, but we are not friends. Will never be friends again. She makes a show of dragging a chair around the table so she can sit next to Sean. I feel as though I'm on trial. Perhaps I should be.

'We wanted to talk to you altogether about Harlow,' I say to the kids. 'It's so shocking when someone we know takes their own life. It's natural to feel all kinds of emotions.'

It's a difficult subject to broach and, although it's upsetting, I feel it's really important to talk about it properly and sensitively. It isn't nothing. Harlow wasn't nothing and everyone is affected in different ways. No matter how alone someone might feel, they leave a loss, don't they?'

'How do you feel, Aunt Mia?' Felix asks. 'You didn't like her.'

The knot of grief in my stomach tightens. 'I didn't really know her properly, only what I saw online.' That's the way it is so often, isn't it? We don't get to know the whole person. Only what they choose to share. 'But I didn't . . . I didn't want this. But honestly?' We came together to be open, so I need to share. 'I feel guilty.

'Do you think it was because of our channel?' Lottie looks stricken. 'We would never have started if it weren't for me.'

'I think your illness set a lot of things in motion—' Esther begins.

'Esther!' Sean says sharply.

'Let me finish! I'm not saying it's Lottie's fault. Harlow made her choice, however difficult it is to understand.'

'Nobody thinks anything is your fault.' Sean takes both of Lottie's hands in his own. 'It's like your mum said. It's normal for us to all feel different things.'

'We had no way of knowing what she was thinking. No way. We couldn't have prevented it,' I say.

'I could. I was the last one of us to speak to her.' Chris trails off. The sadness of reliving that final conversation eclipses his ability to talk.

We wait.

I squeeze his hand. Letting him know it's okay to cry, but he hangs his head. His shoulders trembling. It's a moment before he can carry on. 'When she spoke to me outside the school I told her there was no coming back from the video in the park.'

'It isn't your fault.' Sean squeezes his arm.

'Harlow was very troubled,' I say.

'What do you mean, troubled?' Daisy asks.

'I think she might have been the one, you know, doing things to us. She's not here to defend herself so it isn't fair to sit here and speculate, but there haven't been any more incidents since,' I trail off.

Lottie nods. 'The last comment was from @Joker666 days ago. It said "Cute cat. Shame if anything happened to him." I literally haven't let Michael Finnegan out of my sight since.' She swivels her head around. Checking he is still curled up in his bed.

'But what we want you kids to realise is that you always have us to talk to. Always have options,' Esther says. 'There's very little that can't be fixed, no matter how hopeless things might feel.'

I catch her eye. She looks away.

I'm alone. Nursing a cup of milky coffee that's gone cold. A skin formed on the surface.

Sean and Esther have taken Felix and Daisy home and my two have gone up to bed. I stare out of the window. It's dark and all I can see is the kitchen lights reflected back at me.

I can't stop thinking about Harlow.

I take out my phone to record a goodbye message. My final post. I'm not going to delete the channel, I've decided. There are resources that I hope might help parents of sick children who might stumble across it in the future.

But it's time for me to step away.

That's what I intend to do anyway but then, as I head into the living room to film, I see it on the doormat. Another note.

**If you want to keep your daughter safe,
you know what you have to do.**

And I know that it isn't over at all.

Chapter 28

Mia

I've barely slept. I'm trying to act normal when inside everything feels as though it's shattered.

If you want to keep your daughter, you know what you have to do.

But I don't know. I don't know what I have to do. I haven't told the kids about the note I found yesterday. I haven't told anyone. I'm gripped by panic. Yo-yoing between wanting to call the police and trying to figure out a way to deal with it myself so the kids don't have anything else to worry about. They've been through so much this year. But the threat to Lottie is terrifying. I'd do anything to keep her safe, but how can if I don't know what this person wants?

It's Daisy's fifteenth birthday today. My fingers grip the steering wheel tightly as I drive the kids to our old house. My shoulders uncomfortably tense. Today, Esther and Sean are taking all the kids ice skating. Chris has only been once before, Lottie not at all; there isn't a rink locally. My no had been resolute when Sean had suggested it, choosing to wait until after he got home last night to call me.

'They want to go, Mia.' Impatience crept into his voice. 'I asked them before I left.'

'You shouldn't have asked them before me. If she isn't going to school, she can't go ice skating.'

'You're not the only parent.'

'I think you'll find—'

'I spoke to Alma. She said it's okay.'

I fell quiet for a moment. It felt as though he'd gone behind my back. 'I can't believe you already told the kids it's okay. Now I'll be the bad guy.'

Again.

He didn't reassure me, didn't tell me that I'm a good mum, because I am not his anymore and he's not responsible for soothing my doubts and fears away, is he?

'It'll be busy, won't it? All those people breathing—'

'People have to brea—'

'You know what I mean, Sean.'

'She's fine now, well on the road to recovery anyway. Her immune system is much stronger now. You have to let her live, Mia.'

Sean let that hang there. I wanted to tell him that it isn't his decision what I do and don't let Lottie do. It's not as though he's here, being a father, is it? But that isn't fair.

Sean loves Lottie. He didn't just turn that off when we separated. He wants the best for her, and it isn't like I don't have her best interests at heart too, but I see danger everywhere.

Germs advancing, silent and stealthy, the microscopic bacteria ready to attack.

'I was so scared she'd die, Sean.' I couldn't stop myself from blurting it out even though I've said it a hundred times before. A thousand.

'I know. We both were.'

For a fleeting moment, we were us again. The Finch

family, a team, battling an illness we didn't quite understand but were determined to defeat.

'But that's in the past. Things have changed.'

I picked up on his subtext that really everything had changed and not just Lottie's health, and it was all my fault, but I ignored it because I didn't know what to say. I feel I've apologised at least once to just about everyone and, sometimes, I'm not even sure what I'm sorry for anymore, but I still say it automatically because I have so much fucking guilt.

Guilt if I keep Lottie cooped up.

Guilt if I let her out and she gets an infection.

Guilt that Harlow isn't here anymore.

Guilt that after the latest note I know that this isn't over, but I haven't told anyone else that. Although everyone is incredibly upset about Harlow, their sadness was mixed with relief last night that she had been responsible and it was all over. Perhaps if I told Sean he'd understand that part of my anxiety is driven by my persecutor.

'Sometime, eventually, she's going to catch a cough or cold because people always do,' Sean said. 'Then her immune system will fight it off, because that's what they do. Let her go, Mia.'

In the way you let me go, is what I wanted to say, remembering the way he had spun me around during our first dance to 'No One' by Alicia Keys. Had I taken it for granted even then that I'd always feel his arms around me?

'It isn't just her health,' I replied. 'It's everything that's happened to us lately.'

'All the more reason for the kids to have a break, then. Some fun.'

A break from me, he meant. I knew he was right. But knowing it and embracing it are miles apart. Oceans. I felt sick at the thought of it, but we all have to try and forge a new sense of normality. 'You'll look after her, won't you?'

He didn't say, *I'm her father I'll always look after her.* Of course he didn't. I should take it as read that he'll do his best to protect her because that's what he does. He's a safe pair of hands and it's agonising that he isn't my safe pair of hands anymore.

'Can you drop her off?' he asked. 'I'll message you when we're back. Perhaps you could come in for a coffee or something when you pick them up?'

I didn't say that if Esther makes me a coffee she'd likely spit in it, because I wanted so badly to be able to curl up on our old brown velour sofa, my feet tucked under me, and chat about the kids, laugh, the way we used to.

'That would be nice.' I parroted the words I wanted to be true, but it wouldn't be nice. It'd be tense and awkward in the house that used to be my home. But somehow, despite that, I find that I still want to be there more than anything.

The front door is already open outside my old house. Lewis on the doorstep, speaking to Daisy.

'Please come skating with us, Dad.' She looks so dejected, rejected, my heart goes out to her.

'I can't, Daisy, I have to work.'

'That's what you call it now, is it?' Esther says from down the hallway.

Chris and Daisy look at me, worried.

'It's okay. You two go and have a great time.' I hug them both and they squeeze past Daisy, just as Lewis is promising her that he will come back later this afternoon.

'I'll bring your present and have a piece of cake,' he promises.

'Yeah, whatever,' she sighs, closing the door.

I'm already walking back to my car, noticing that I'm parked in front of Lewis. Am aware of his footsteps behind me.

I turn around as I'm unlocking to say an awkward goodbye but, before I can speak, he does.

Two words.

Just two words that turn my blood to ice.

And then it's obvious who has been tormenting me.

Lewis gives a slow, chilling smile.

It's as though, now he's not part of the family, he's let his mask slip. And showing who he really is makes it glaringly apparent that he knows my secret, just as I know his.

Terror has glued my feet to the pavement as he casually strolls to his car.

Move. I have to move before Sean, Esther and the kids come out.

I feel like I did on the fishing trip we went on once, legs wobbly, sickness in my throat.

I'm in no position to focus as I drive away from the house that used to be mine. A horn blares at me as I turn the corner. I'd forgotten to give way. I pull into a bus stop and drop my head onto the steering wheel.

I know who's been tormenting me and the knowing is a million times worse than the not knowing.

What am I going to do?

I'm shaking. Shaking. I cannot cope. I was barely coping before this, not really, and if the truth does come out then the fraying strands that are holding me together will unravel completely.

What am I going to do?

Ideas come and I dismiss them all because they are drastic and damaging and, despite everything, I think I am not a bad person. But one idea ricochets back at me time and time again. A pinball in a machine.

I can't.

I can't.

I can't.

There has to be another way. *Has* to be. But I cannot think of one.

Chapter 29

Mia

I can't believe that it was only a few hours ago that I dropped the kids off with Sean. That Lewis dropped his bombshell. It feels like a different day entirely. I feel like a different person.

What have I done?

It all seemed so . . . not simple in my head, far from easy, but . . . I don't know, it seemed like a solution.

What had I been thinking?

Oh god.

What have I done?

Blood has a taste.

A smell.

It catches at the back of my throat. I'm retching again. In the bath, on my hands and knees. Crimson-tinged water helter-skelters down the plug hole. Despite the steam rising, I'm shivering.

Oh, God. There's so much blood. I think that after this, whenever I close my eyes, I'll see it.

I can't breathe.

The acrylic is slippery as I rock back and forth. Whimpering.

What have I done?

Panic skitters around every cell in my body. I'm hot and cold.

I can't breathe.

Shaking, shaking. I don't know what to do but I can't stay here, in the bath. I need to hide the evidence from the children.

From everyone.

Thoughts of the kids bring another tidal wave of panic.

What have I done?

I try to calm myself. Remind myself that everything I do – everything I've done – is for them. To keep them safe.

Focus.

It takes a gargantuan effort to push myself back onto my heels. From the soap dish, I grab the brush I usually use to get the mud from my nails when I've been gardening. I scrub and scrub. Registering on some level that it hurts but welcoming the pain, feeling as though I deserve it.

Eventually, I raise my hands and examine the palms for blood, turn them over and check my nails.

Clean now.

But I don't think I'll ever really feel clean again.

But it will stop now, won't it? The frantic buzzing in my head. The panic that grips me each time I think about that message,

I want what's mine.

A noise?

My stomach lurches. Has someone come home? I can't let anyone see me like this.

Especially not the kids.

But they should still be with Sean, ice skating, shouldn't they?

Unless they've had an accident. Been hurt.

It's this fierce maternal instinct that drives me to my feet. My legs feel too weak to support me and it takes a moment before I can step out of the bath, one hand against the tiles, steadying myself. Almost crumbling as I catch sight of the droplets of water left behind, pink now instead of red. My mouth floods with bile.

Wrapping a towel around myself, I creep over to the door on tiptoes. Crack it open.

I'm motionless. Listening. But all I can hear is my own frantic heartbeat. My pulse whooshing in my ears.

'Hello?' I call out. 'Lottie? Chris?'

Silence wraps itself around me.

I hear something.

Behind me.

I start, spinning around. But it's just the glug-glug-glug as the last of the blood-tinged water is sucked down the plug hole.

I turn away from it. Turn away from my guilt.

I need a plan.

Focus.

Where is my mobile?

I hurry out of the bathroom. A knot of anxiety tightening in my stomach. I hadn't had anywhere else to go at the time I had moved into this modern glass house, and I'd thought how lucky I was. The patchwork of countryside surrounding it is stunning. But now I see it for what it is.

Too isolated.

Too conspicuous.

Because here's the thing. The transparent walls might allow me an unobstructed view of the outside, but it also allows unseen eyes to peer in. Frightened, my gaze is drawn to the darkness of the grounds as I hurry toward my bedroom. But with the lights illuminating the landing, all I can see is my own pale face staring back at me.

My guilty face.

All at once I feel such a sharp pang of longing for the life I had before, when I was unknown, invisible, but you can't change the past, can you? No matter how desperately you want to.

Can't rewind a month, a year, two years.

Not even just two hours. If I could do just that, then I wouldn't have . . .

Focus.

I drag my attention away from the windows because, even if there is someone lurking out there in the shadows, someone who has seen what I've done, I can't do anything about that now.

But there *are* things I can do.

Have to do.

I find my mobile on my pillow. My hand trembles as I pick it up.

There's a text on my phone from Lottie. She sent it about an hour ago: **We're heading back to Dad's now. Are you coming?**

I message the kids: **Sorry I'm going to be a little late. I'm not feeling well.**

That much, at least, is the truth.

I dress hurriedly. Black jeans. Black long-sleeved t-shirt. Hair tucked under my baseball cap.

In the kitchen, I grab the car keys, glancing at Michael Finnegan's empty mat, his bowl still full of the breakfast kibble Lottie had lovingly scraped into it.

Lottie.

Outside, the air is biting. My breath clouds in front of me. Despite the temperature, it's a clear evening. There's a velvety blanket stretched above, popping with stars.

Standing still, I take a moment to look up, overcome, because it's one of those things you take for granted, isn't it? The sky. The moon. That, whatever happens to us, the world will keep spinning, even though mine has been thrust violently off its axis.

The car park is deserted. There's the smell of hot oil and onions in the air from the burger place at the bottom of the road. A dull thud-thud-thud of bass coming from a club.

A crash.

My heart leaps into my mouth. In the distance, a stray cat darts out from behind the skip. Hurrying, I clench my car keys in my fist, ready to defend myself, wondering if I'll always feel this sense of being on high alert. Pre-empting danger around every corner.

When I reach the skip, I take a furtive look over my shoulder before tossing the bin bag amongst the other rubbish. Alongside the dress I had been wearing are our stripy beach towels and the Little Mermaid bathmat all splattered with blood. Charlotte had grown out of Disney years before but somehow the mat had stayed. Perhaps I have been clinging on to the last trace of her childhood before it fades away altogether. Perhaps we both have been because when Chris teases her about it and I offer to throw it away she won't let me.

And then I get back in my car, planning to head home and apply make-up with a shaking hand before I'll join my family at Esther's and pretend to be normal.

Pretend that everything is under control and, perhaps, now it really is.

Chapter 30

Who's Watching You Documentary

Jake Lawler (host): Now, our next guest is one I wish I was speaking to in different circumstances. (stares into camera, solemn) In a world exclusive interview, I'd like to welcome Harlow's husband, Javier Hernandez. Javier, (shakes hands with guest) I am incredibly sorry for your loss.

Javier Hernandez (Harlow's husband): Thank you.

Lawler: Please tell us why you wanted to give _Who's Watching You_ (slight smile) a world exclusive.

Hernandez: There's been so much written about Harlow online. People forget that she was a real person. A wife. A mother.

Lawler: And how is Marco?

Hernandez: Marco has made mistakes. We

all know that. But I'm not here to talk about his. I'm here to talk about my own.

Lawler: Go on.

Hernandez: People assume that Harlow did what she did because of all the online stuff and, yes, maybe that was the final straw, but she wasn't shallow. She was desperately unhappy before everything with Mia kicked off. Because of me.

Lawler: Are you talking about your separation?

Hernandez: Yes. There were so many comments that I'd left Harlow because of the feud with Mia but that was ridiculous. I left . . . I left because my business was collapsing, and I was too ashamed to tell her. When I met her she was Hayley Cook. She changed her name to Harlow when we got married because she thought is sounded glamorous, Harlow Hernandez. I'd promised her this amazing life full of amazing things and I . . . I let her down.

Lawler: Why didn't you tell her about your financial situation?

Hernandez: I'm a proud man and in a way it was easier to let her believe that I didn't love her anymore, rather than admit I was a failure. And then . . . and then . . . I wasn't there to protect her. I never thought she'd . . . I just didn't.

Lawler: I don't think anyone could have seen that coming. I'm so sorry. Please don't blame yourself.

Hernandez: But I do hold myself accountable. I'm not the only one either. I've had letters from so many people, including Mia Finch and, no, I'm not going to share what she said but I was glad she reached out. That's not why I'm here. I wanted to come on here and come clean because Harlow deserves the truth to be told. That the online stuff wasn't who she was. She seemed bitter in the video in the park, but I had made her that way. I want to say we shouldn't keep secrets. Lie. That love, love can be enough if we just trust it. I wish I'd have trusted it. (looks into camera, anguished expression) Trust in love.

Lawler: It's so brave of you to admit this.

Hernandez: After she . . . well, half the people were posting #BeKind while still speculating that Harlow had been the one stalking Mia. Of course, after Harlow had gone and Mia posted that video of the police cars with the flashing blue lights racing up her driveway, well. We all knew something terrible had happened and it wasn't Harlow's fault at all.

@Avocadomonkey That poor family #TrustInLove #WWY

@Jamie2983 It's his fault for dumping her

@Lamadrama23 It isn't anyone's fault! Be kind!!!

@Jamie2983 I'm ALWAYS kind!

@Blackcat1970 This is why social media is a bad idea

Chapter 31

Mia

The last thing I want to do is sit with Esther and play happy families, but already I am thinking about an alibi. The length of time I should stay.

Last night, when Esther had come to the glass house, I had offered her tea, biscuits, made her feel welcome, but she leaves me hanging in the doorway now, waiting to be invited in. To sit down. To be told where I can sit. It seems so callous, but she forgets how well I know her. The way her fingers keep lightly touching her mouth as though checking she's smiling. The way she's blinking more frequently than usual. This is tearing her apart too but that gives me hope. She misses me.

Esther's eyes don't slide up from the screen where she's showing Daisy a video she took earlier at the rink.

'Can you send it to me so I can share it with Erika, Mum? Should I send it to Dad? Where is he? He isn't replying to my texts, and he said he'd be here for the cake.'

'He's probably been held up. I'm sure he'll be in touch when he can.' Esther's voice is tight.

Felix and Sean are gesturing me over to the sofa, but all I can see is the room the way it used to be. Us with huge bowls of buttery popcorn balanced on laps as we watched a film. Lottie, unable to sit still, dancing around us in that fairy costume with wings that shimmered in the light.

The sofa is different now. Everything is different.

'Drink, Mum?' Chris asks.

'Oh, um, thanks.'

I follow him into the kitchen and what I see there is a punch to the guts.

'Oh no.' The walls and the door frames are freshly painted. Esther must have done it as though she could gloss over their history, as if they never existed here, and in a way that's true. The height chart by the back door has gone now. The pen marking how tall Chris and Lottie were at various ages hidden under a stark white.

The kids used to take it in turns to stand, spine against the wall, Chris breathing in, rod straight, trying to make himself as tall as possible.

Lottie shrieking, *Chris is on tiptoes. He's cheating, Mum. Dad. Look.*

Chris asking, *Have I grown? Have I grown?*

Somehow, despite Sean and I separating, despite the glass house, the loss of the height chart feels the worst of all, because it feels like the loss of Chris and Lottie's childhood.

It's ruined. Everything is ruined.

If I was barely holding it together before, I'm breaking apart right now.

'It's okay, Mum,' Chris says but the expression on his face says otherwise. He is grieved too.

I'm not thinking straight – who would be after the day I've had? – as I reach on top of the fridge for the pen I know Sean will still keep there.

With an unsteady hand I draw two black lines on the freshly painted wall: 'L' next to one and 'C' by the other.

My eyes meet Chris's, and I try to smile and pretend I'm fine, but I suspect I'm wearing my emotions on my face like a mask, so I turn away from him and fill a glass with water. We head back into the lounge.

'Didn't you want a coffee?' Sean asks.

'No, thanks.'

Esther disappears into the kitchen, and I hold my breath, waiting for the shout when she sees what I've done – she's going to be furious – but she can't have noticed because she's smiling when she comes back in. Birthday cake balanced on a silver board, pink and white striped flickering candles.

We sing 'Happy Birthday', Daisy's face flushed with happiness in the golden glow of the candlelight. She's the same age as Lottie but she seems so much younger.

Esther produces a sharp knife, and I stiffen as though Esther might plunge it into me. Instead, she cuts effortlessly through the sponge before balancing slices on napkins and handing them around.

Chris is given a huge slab of sponge sandwiched together with raspberry jam and swirls of buttercream. The piece Esther gives to Lottie, though, is nothing but a sliver. Before I can ask her to give Lottie more, Chris notices the way his sister's face drops and he swaps their plates over.

Daisy finishes her large slice, and Esther asks if she'd like another. 'No. I want to save some for Dad.'

At the thought of Lewis, a sour taste floods my mouth. 'We should be heading home.'

Sean stares into his lap. I'm longing for him to say we are already home, not because of the bricks and mortar that make up this house but because we are together again, though of course he doesn't. He probably shouldn't. I don't deserve it.

We all huddle on the doormat and hug our goodbyes. I notice Esther retreats pretty quickly once she has released Chris from her quick embrace. I don't think she's hugged Lottie. Then we are all outside in the cold. Both literally and metaphorically.

Our journey is slow and silent until we crunch up the driveway. Without sunlight glinting off the glass, it's possible to see directly inside. I shiver.

'Can you both go straight upstairs and get changed?' I ask.

'But I don't want to cha—'

'Do as you're told,' I say, sharper than necessary. It isn't their fault. None of this is their fault. But still there will be germs, bacteria, goodness knows what on their clothes, and I want to put them straight in the machine. 'You've been at that freezing rink and probably got damp and you'll both catch colds and—'

'All right, all right. Don't flip out.' Lottie climbs out of the car and slams the door. Chris jogs to catch her up.

They disappear inside. I open the garage door.

I'm just stepping back into the car to put it away when there's a terrified scream.

Lottie.

'Mum! Call the police!'

PART TWO

Chapter 32

Lottie

Ice skating was literally the best. I felt normal for the first time in such a long time. My hair is growing back, and I looked like any other girl. I didn't even mind so much that Erika came to the rink as well, although she was a bit annoying asking if I was okay every thirty seconds, but she's cool. I see why Daisy likes her. Felix was flirting with her, and I wondered whether Chris likes her too because he literally couldn't take his eyes off her. I felt all warm inside that he might find love but then sad because Mum will probably never let me out of her sight long enough to date.

Anyways, I felt relaxed.

Until I got home.

The scream tears through me even before my brain has properly processed what my eyes are seeing.

Not Michael Finnegan curled up snoozing on his mat the way he always does after dinner but . . .

Blood.

An empty mat where my cat should be, but isn't, and two bloody handprints on the glass of the doors as though someone had slammed their hands against them, trying to get in, after . . .

After what? Where has all the blood come from?

Who has all the blood come from?

I must be on that thing Dad says takes over sometimes when he has no recollection of driving home or whatever, auto thingy pilot, because I'm unlocking the door. Not caring what danger I'm putting myself in, only caring about Michael Finnegan.

On some level I know – I *know* – that the online messages, the comment about my cat, the wreath and all of that can't have led to this. It's . . . It's different, fucked.

Keyboard warriors, cyber stalkers, all the things I've heard people who do such things called, don't do things like this. They don't turn up at your house and kill your fucking cat, but I know deep in my gut that's what's happened.

I'm sobbing, shaking, like I feel my legs are going to just give way as I slide back the door, stumble into the garden.

It's dark but from the lights inside the house, I see it.

The hot tub cover discarded on the lawn.

I don't want to look but I'm pelting towards the hot tub, praying somehow it isn't too late.

Oh god.

Like, what the actual fuck?

Tears and snot are streaming down my face as I take in the blood, the lumps of flesh, intestines, floating in the crimson water. Is it . . . is it . . .

Now my knees do snap in half. I'm on my hands and knees, bile souring the back of my throat. The muscles in my stomach painfully contract as I vomit, grappling for air in between each painful retch, the smell of the blood, of the flesh, making me heave again.

From inside the house, I hear Chris calling my name, growing closer.

I don't want him to come outside, see this. I raise my head, 'no', spittle hanging from my mouth.

And then I see him. In the shadow of the moonlight. Watching me from the far side of the garden. The gap in the fence that borders the fields, big enough for a person to slip in and out of.

He takes a step and the bell on his collar jangles.

'Michael Finnegan!'

I stumble to my feet, weaving across the lawn towards him. His fur is warm and soft as I scoop him into my arms, the tears that won't stop falling soaking into his coat.

He purrs softly, not frightened, but he should be. I am.

I lurch back towards the house. Throw myself through the door just as Chris is about to come out into the garden.

'Lock it.'

'Lottie?'

'Chris, lock the fucking door.'

He turns the key and perhaps I should feel, if not safe, safer at least, but I don't think I'll ever feel safe again.

Chapter 33

Mia

Lottie's face has drained of colour. She's shaking as she clings on to Michael Finnegan; he mewls in protest and tries to wriggle out of her arms.

Chris is craning his neck, trying to track the blood with his eyes from the handprints on the window to the trail that leads across the decking.

'I should.' He reaches for the door handle, hesitant, throwing a glance over his shoulder at me, but I'm panicking as much as the kids, although I'm trying to hide it. He's trying to be the man of the house, feels he has to be, I suppose, but in this moment he looks younger than he's looked for years.

'Don't,' is all I can say.

'But Mum?'

'You can't go out there!' Lottie is hysterical. 'Someone has literally been murdered—'

'Murdered?' Chris covers his mouth with his hands.

'No one has been murdered.' My voice sounds odd. Too high. Too fast. I'm detaching from myself. Floating up towards the ceiling. The panic in my veins, the helium in a balloon. I'm lighter and lighter and—

'Mum!' Lottie's voice sounds dull and distant as though it's coming from somewhere else. 'There was so much blood and chunks of, I dunno, flesh?

I don't know what to say so I tell her what she wants to hear. 'It's just someone trying to scare us. Like the wreath.' I feel so wobbly, like I might faint, but I am the adult and I need to take charge.

'This is not the same as the fucking wreath, Mum. It's fucked. There is someone, or something, in pieces in our hot tub. Someone has been to our house. Someone, oh god.' Lottie begins to sway, and I guide her to the floor before she falls. Her pale face takes on a green tinge.

'I'm gonna chuck.'

Immediately, I am kneeling behind her, rocking her in my arms, stroking her hair away from her face. 'Sorry, sorry, sorry.'

'It wasn't your fault,' she mumbles, her words thick.

'Sorry you had to see it. That you went out there before me.'

'Someone put, someone is, oh god they could still be out there, watching us.'

'Shhh. Come on, let's move into the other room, away from this.' While she can still see the blood on the doors she isn't going to calm down.

Chris stands the other side of her and we both place hands under her elbows, heft her to her feet. When she's settled on the sofa, Chris says, 'I'll get you some water.'

I sit silently next to her, my fingers linked through hers. 'It's okay,' I say. Although it isn't but I hope that it will be.

It takes a few minutes for Chris to come back into the room, 'I've called the police.'

I. Cannot. Breathe.

'I feel sick again,' Lottie says.

She isn't the only one.

'I want Dad.' She's crying, trembling.

I want Sean too. There's that tightness in my chest again. The sense of everything spinning out of my control.

I. Cannot. Breathe.

'Ow, Mum.' Lottie snatches her hand away and I realise how tightly I must have been gripping it.

Heat rages through me. Sweat trickling between my breasts. My breath shallow and painful. The room closing in. The chest pains that had plagued me are sharp and relentless.

'You're having a panic attack, Mum.' Chris is crouching before me. My peripheral vision has disappeared and, through the tunnel I am looking through, my eyes find his.

'Inhale.' He tries to smile encouragingly, but he looks so scared, so out of his depth, the panic sinks its claws into me even deeper.

Why can't I breathe like a normal person?

Be a normal mother?

'Exhale.' He purses his lips together and exaggerates blowing out, the way I have with him and Lottie over the years. I copy him, hearing Lottie doing the same. Our breathing synchronises and we are in unison and, for the briefest smidge of a second, it's like we're united, us against the world, again.

'That's good, Mum,' he says. 'I'll call Dad and—'

'No.' I shake my head. 'I just need to . . . There's something I have to . . . ' but then there's the flash of blue lights outside the window.

'They were quick.' Lottie wipes her cheeks with her sleeve.

'Yeah, well, this is a murder.' Chris mutters.

'My breath must stink of vom. I'm just gonna go to the loo,' Lottie says.

'I'll let them in,' Chris says as he stands and heads out of the room.

Somehow, I force myself to my feet, my legs somehow carrying me across the room to the window.

I can't help slipping my phone out of my pocket and starting a livestream. The flashing lights of the police cars casting a blue hue on my already pallid skin.

'You won't believe what's happened today,' I say, shakily. Turning the camera to catch the vehicles outside, the uniformed officers making their way to the door, which is already open, Chris waiting to usher them in.

'Mum?' Lottie is back.

What am I doing? I snap off my phone. What have I become?

'Should we pack?' Lottie asks.

'Pack?'

'Yeah, if this is a crime scene we won't be able to stay here, will we?'

I'm caught in a web, partly of my own making, and I don't know how to break free.

But I know nowhere will be safe.

There is nowhere we can run to where they can't find us.

Chapter 34

Lottie

Chris paces around the room, unable to settle. I, on the other hand, can't move from where I sit cross-legged on his bed. My body feels weird. My mind too. I'm never going to get the image of the dead person out of the hot tub. Not just the image. The stench of it.

Her?

Him?

You wouldn't think that blood and flesh could smell so disgusting, but I can taste it in the back of my throat. I pull the sleeves of Dad's old black jumper I'm wearing over my hands, cover my face, and cry again.

'It's okay, Lottie.' Chris is rubbing my back. 'It was just some nutter. I bet it isn't even human remains. No more police have arrived yet. You'd think there'd be more cars, reporters or something if it was, you know, a person.'

It's quiet downstairs, too quiet.

'You think it's an animal?' I mumble. My tongue too thick for my mouth. I know this would be preferable to a person, but still. Finding it is the worst thing that's ever happened to me, and I've been through a lot. I don't believe it is an animal, though. There was a lot of it. Floating. Stinking.

'We know it's not Michael Finnegan so that's something.'

But that doesn't make it better.

Someone's or something's guts are spread around the garden, aren't they?

'Chris, where do you think we'll go? If this becomes a crime scene?'

'I dunno. Guess we could go to Dad's?' I don't think either of us knows how to refer to our former home. We don't call it Esther's, but it isn't ours anymore, is it?

'There isn't enough room for us.'

'I'd be okay kipping on Felix's floor. You could bunk in with Daisy.'

'There isn't enough room for us *all*,' I repeat, pointedly.

'Oh right, well. Mum will be okay, she could go to . . .' He frowns. Trying to conjure up a name, any name, but we both know there isn't anyone.

We have always been her entire world. Esther her only friend. It used to seem enough, but now it seems rather sad. 'She doesn't have any mates, does she?' Chris states the obvious.

'Neither do I,' I say.

'Of course you do. Once you go back to school.'

'I've been away forever. Everyone will forget me. Even Daisy seems friendlier with Erika than me.'

'They won't have forgotten you. They ask about you all the time.'

'Who?'

'Duh, everyone,' he says.

He lies. The girls I thought were my friends had drifted away after I was admitted into hospital because, I dunno really. Because they couldn't visit. I was too ill to video call. We had nothing in common anymore. They didn't want to hear about me puking after chemo or my hair falling out, and they probably thought I didn't want to hear about Scott Simpson snogging the face off of Ellie Perks, but I think I would have loved to have heard that. Something normal in a time where everything was upside down and back to front.

'Anyways, I can't leave Mum. I literally wouldn't be here without her.'

'Neither would I.'

'It isn't the same.'

'I know but, Lottie, you know Mum's . . . well, she's Mum. She's great, but you should be allowed to get back to normal now. Why don't you push back?'

'I do ask her, you know I do.'

'Yeah, but then you slink off to your room and cry. I've heard you'

'It isn't easy. If I tell her I don't want to live like this anymore, being stuck here, home-schooled, documenting my recovery then it would seem really ungrateful. If she hadn't donated—'

'They'd have found a match elsewhere. Dr Chadha said that kids have options and—'

'Yeah, but she stepped up for me when I needed it. She didn't have to just because she's our mum.'

'She doesn't own your life just because she saved it.'

'No but . . . ' It's hard to explain to Chris just how indebted I feel to Mum. The thought of hurting her feelings by telling her she doesn't know what's best for me anymore is just horrible. I don't want to damage the relationship we have by becoming a stroppy teenager. And I do feel lucky. Lucky that I have a closer relationship with my mum, because of what we've been through, versus most girls my age. Besides, I know this stage won't last forever even though it feels like it right now.

'Are you scared, Chris?' I pick at a stray thread hanging from my cuff. One hard tug and the jumper will probably unravel. I feels as though I might come undone too.

'Nah.'

'I am.' We're so exposed here in this house of glass. It doesn't feel like home. It's more like a property from a horror film that has an inbuilt AI that's a million times smarter than Alexa and might kill us one by one.

Oh god, what *was* in the hot tub? Why is it taking so long for Mum to come upstairs?

'It's just some sicko who thinks they can freak us out. It's pathetic really,' Chris says. 'There's a million other things they could have done that are worse.'

'Like?'

'Dunno.' He thinks. 'Skinned rabbits swinging from the tree.'

'Chris, that's, like, psycho shit right there.'

'Sorry, Lotts. Don't be scared. We're safe, I promise.'

'You can't know that. Nobody knows anything for sure.'

We both fall silent because we do know that. Perhaps better than anyone else our age. The future is quicksand, too precarious to try and step into.

'All that blood, Chris.' I can't stop fidgeting. Pushing my sleeves up, pulling them down, twisting that thread round and round my finger until the tip is bright red.

The blood.

Who would do something like that?

And why?

There's the click of Chris's door opening.

Mum looking like an actual corpse or something. Her face all grey and pinched.

She stands in the doorway, fiddling with a tissue in her hand.

I know, even before she speaks, whatever she says is going to be bad.

Really bad.

Chapter 35

Mia

'What did the police say? It's a person, isn't it? Is it someone we know?' Chris asks.

Lottie has shuffled back on the bed, against the headboard. She's drawn her knees up to her chest and wrapped her arms around them, trying to make herself smaller. Chris shuffles into her side the way he has a hundred times before. As they huddle together in front of me, I am transported back to being jolted awake in the dead of night. Bright flashes of lightning ripping the sky in two, thunder rumbling deep and low.

Stumbling out of bed while Sean slept on, my bare feet against the cold laminate floor as I'd rush into Lottie's room. She'd always hated storms.

One night, her bed was empty. Rather than waking me, she'd woken Chris, crawled in with him, knowing that while I'd snuggle down with her and try and soothe her back to sleep, he'd be the one to make her laugh.

What did the thunder say to the lightning? You're shocking.
What does a cloud wear under his raincoat? Thunderwear.

How does the rain tie its shoes? With a rainbow.

But he'd also be the one who would offer her an explanation she'd understand.

Counting between the bouts of thunder and lightning so they could calculate how far away the storm was.

My emotions had raged as frantically as the storm. On the one hand, it was reassuring that they had such a strong bond, knowing that Chris would always be there for Lottie if Sean or I couldn't be. But also, there was a teensy part of me that felt sad, as though I was no longer needed.

They need each other now, more than they know.

'Mum?' Lottie's gazing up at me, trusting.

'I've got something to tell you both.' I stand again. Too agitated to sit still. There have been a handful of conversations in my life that have stuck in my mind, word for word. The speech Sean gave when he asked me to marry him. The words he said when he told me he didn't want me anymore.

The phrase I used when I told him I was pregnant, first with Chris, then with Lottie.

Dr Chadha telling us just how sick Lottie actually was. *This.*

This will be one of those conversations. Something that will stay with me forever.

My mouth is dry, the words stuck in my throat. What I'm about to tell them might change the way they feel about me, but the truth always comes out, doesn't it?

Tell them.

When they were toddlers, and it was time to remove the Mr Bump plasters I had smoothed over grazed knees and elbows, I was never one to rip them off quickly; rather I'd peel the edges, little by little, trying to make it as painless as possible.

This will be painful, but dragging it out is only making it worse.

'You know the channel?'

'Your channel?' Lottie looks confused.

'*Our* channel. It . . . It's been, I mean, the viewers seem to like that we were being stalked and it's, I mean, obviously, it's not what I wanted but . . . '

'But what? Our stalker did this? What did the police say?'

'I'm trying to tell you. I . . . I love you both so much.'

In my mind, they shrink back to the kids they had once been, innocent, excited about everything.

We're the Finch family, welcome to our home.

Except we are not the same family, and this is not our home.

My chest aches for everything we've lost. More than anything, in this moment, I wish that Sean was by my side right now while I make my confession, his fingers threaded through mine, united. But then if he were here I wouldn't – *we* wouldn't – be in this position, would we?

'We know. We love you too,' Chris says. 'What about the hot tub, though? Have we got to move out? Is this a crime scene?'

'Is it . . . a person in the garden?' Lottie's trembling.

'No. No. It was offal, from the butchers. The remnants of cattle that had already been slaughtered for food. No one was hurt.'

'What sicko would dump that in our hot tub?'

I pause for the longest time. The stabbing pain comes again in my chest before I admit it.

'Me. It was me.'

Chapter 36

Mia

'It was me who dumped offal in the hot tub and I am so incredibly sorry that I scared you both.'

It was a despicable thing to do but, of all the secrets about myself I could share with them, this one is probably not the worst.

I give them a moment to process that I've just admitted to doing something so horrific.

'I'm so sorry.' I don't know what else to say, but I'm prepared to answer the many questions I know they'll have, even if I can't answer them all honestly.

I want what's mine, the message on the window had said, and even then I hadn't put two and two together. Suspecting everyone. Getting it wrong.

How can I tell them that two words from their Uncle Lewis had sent me spiralling into this? That I need money, a lot of money, and quickly, or someone will get hurt and, as the last note said, *If you want to keep your daughter safe, you know what you have to do*. I'm petrified it will be Lottie. If I was the one at risk then things might be different but my child – my children – that's another thing entirely.

Lewis had taken pleasure in ripping my world apart. He's such a bastard. I can't believe he didn't even turn up to see Daisy blow out her birthday candles.

'You put . . . what? What did you . . . why would you . . . why?' Chris stutters out questions.

They don't look angry or even shocked, just incredibly confused.

I sit on the bed again. Wanting to take their hands but afraid to. I need to tell them everything before I lose my nerve.

Not quite everything, though.

When Chris offered to monetise the channel, I thought I might make a small income, but it didn't seem important.

Until Lewis.

Then I remembered how my subscribers had rocketed since Lottie thought she saw someone in the garden.

'It was a stupid idea, the worst. I thought if I had another video go viral then we could make some serious money, quickly.'

'You needed something for the algorithms,' Chris states. Dully.

He's smart, my boy.

'It was fake? All of it?' He's putting everything together. 'The wreath, the smashed photo, the—'

'No. God no.' I shake my head furiously. 'I couldn't have put you both through that. I was behind the offal in the hot tub, but nothing else, I swear.' This much is true. 'You weren't even meant to see it. I asked you both to go upstairs and get changed when we came home so you *didn't* see it.

'And we're meant to believe anything you say now?' Chris can't even look at me.

Lottie, on the other hand, can't stop staring. 'Mum, I know you're not the stalker.'

'You don't know that, Lottie,' Chris says sharply.

'She'd tell us if she was. She's telling the truth now, isn't she?'

'Thank you, sweetheart.' I reach for her hand, but she snatches it away.

'That doesn't mean it's okay.' There is none of the usual sweetness in her voice. 'I can't believe you did that to me.' Her face crumples. 'I thought it was Michael Finnegan. I thought someone had killed my cat.'

'I'm sorry, sweetheart. Really, I am. I know it was terrifying.'

'You don't know.' She's shouting now. 'You don't know how it was seeing all that blood, flesh, *smelling* it. You don't know how it felt to not know if it was Michael Finnegan or a person and that I was, I am, so fucking awful I hoped it was a stranger rather than my cat. What sort of person does that make me?'

'You're a good person, Lottie.'

'I'm not. I'm really not.'

'It's natural to be relieved that Michael Finnegan is safe. I'm so sorry you thought it was him. I told you both to go straight upstairs, though, *I told you*.'

'Don't you dare fucking blame us.' It is the first time Chris has ever sworn at me, and I flinch as though he has struck me, knowing I deserve it.

'I'm not . . . I'm not blaming you. This was my fault, my choice, but I—'

I bite my lip, trying to stop the tears burning behind my eyes from leaking out. Knowing that I cannot begin to defend myself because I can't tell them everything. That if I cannot find some money, one or more of us will get hurt because people have been hurt before.

'Where did you even?' Lottie holds her hands out to me as though I can place an explanation in them.

'After I'd dropped you off at Esther's, I drove to the butchers in Hardingwick.'

'That's miles away.'

'I know. I didn't want to risk anyone seeing me locally.' I can tell myself that it was a spur of the moment act of desperation but on some level I had thought it through, hadn't I?

'What did you tell the police?'

'The truth.' I feel the heat in my cheeks. 'Well, I told them that I had put the stuff in the hot tub to film it for my channel, but I hadn't told you, not expecting you to see it. When you found it you were scared and rang them without me knowing.'

'And then? What? They just said okay?' Chris asks.

'Well, they weren't best pleased, but it isn't a crime. I told the truth.'

I don't tell them that I got a warning for wasting police time. That the officer had looked at me with utter disdain as I had admitted that I'd stuffed a bin bag with the blood-stained bathmat and towel in a skip in case it was discovered and reported. His voice was like steel as he said that my stupid 'prank' will be kept on police record. That it could hinder investigation into the report I had filed against the wreath, and the other things I had told them about.

'Your version of it,' Chris mutters.

'Do you think . . . ' I'm trying not to cry because I don't deserve their pity or their understanding, but still I hope for both of these things. 'Do you think that you can forgive me?'

They don't say no but they don't say anything and that's even worse.

'Do you want to come downstairs? I can make us something to eat, and we can talk some more?'

'We just want to be on our own, Mum,' Chris says. 'We need some space from you.'

'Do you think I can eat after seeing *that*?' Lottie gazes up at me, eyes bloodshot, cheeks tearstained, and I long to drop to my knees and tell her that I did it to try and keep her safe. But of course I don't. I can't, and as I trudge sadly out of Chris's room, I feel wretched because I can't tell them that it isn't over. I still haven't got the money. I don't know what to do.

But at least, tonight, we are all under the same roof. We don't know it yet, but it will be one of the last times.

Chapter 37

Mia

After a fitful night, it is the sun slicing through the window that peels my eyelids apart.

Immediately I am struck by a tidal wave of hopelessness.

I have failed my children.

All I ever wanted was to be a good mother. I think, perhaps up until now, I have been. I haven't always made the right choices, but I've done my best and ultimately that's all any of us can do, isn't it?

Until yesterday, I had always done my best.

Is everything ruined? Irrevocably damaged?

Will all the happy memories Chris and Lottie have carried with them be tarnished by this one godawful thing I did?

Will this, in years to come, be how they'll remember me?

Not as the mum who balanced them on a blue plastic stool, looped an apron around their neck and helped them measure flour carefully onto scales, laughed as they licked the remained of the mix from the bowl while lemon cupcakes rose in the oven.

The mum who supported every new hobby they wanted

to try. Shivered on the edge of football pitches under an umbrella, stitched badges onto sleeves.

Me, who gently rubbed calamine lotion onto chicken pox, doled out sticky pink Calpol throughout the night, sang nursery rhymes and made up stories.

Who has made a terrible mistake and who wishes, more than ever, they had a Dr Who TARDIS and could travel back, take it back, make everything better.

But I can't.

And even if the kids can one day forgive me, I know I'll never forgive myself because the children are my world, my everything, and if this has diluted, in their minds, the fierce love I have for them, then I will never stop questioning whether there had been another way.

Agonising over all the stupid decisions that led me to this.

One day, if they become parents themselves, they might understand the all-consuming love I feel for them. They might understand that parents don't magically have the answers. Are flawed, imperfect, the way we all are.

That try as we might, we don't always get it right, because not everybody does.

But we show up.

We show up every day and that, in itself, is something, isn't it?

I drag my grief-heavy legs out of bed, feeling as though I have lost the most precious part of myself, the part that always puts the kids first even though it may not feel like it to them.

In the bathroom, I splash cold water on my face and scrub at my skin as though I can wash away the person I am. I cannot meet my own eyes in the mirror.

The landing is silent. I check my watch as I hurry into Chris's room. I'm shocked it's gone nine. I can't believe I slept in so late. He'll have already left for his school trip to Norfolk.

His duvet is heaped on the floor. Rucksack missing. The teenage-boy smell lingering.

Next door, Lottie's room is empty too. Her bed neatly made.

She never usually makes her bed either, instead leaving the duvet crumpled, ready to slip back into. Seeing it smoothed out, the pillows fluffed looks so . . . so final. As though she never intends sleeping in it again.

'Lottie?' I race downstairs. My eyes darting towards the doormat, relieved there is no note today.

In the kitchen, Michael Finnegan is curled up on his mat. On the worktop, a note.

*I've gone to stay with Dad for a few days.
Need some space. Feed Michael Finnegan.
Don't call me.*

Oh god. How long's she been gone? Did she catch Sean before he left for work? Has she told him? I wanted to be the one to explain.

Don't call me, she has explicitly asked. Although part of me knows I have pushed things too far, that if I want her to come back to me, I do perhaps need to give her some space, I have to check in.

I call Lottie's phone, but it clicks to answer service. Sean's does the same. Instead, I text my daughter: **I'm so sorry. Call me!!**

And then I rattle off a message to Sean: **We need to talk. Is she really upset?**

The reply comes almost instantly: **Of course she's bloody upset. So am I. Furious. I can't believe you did that.**

My stomach flips. Before I can compose another text a

second message comes through: **And yes, we do need to talk but give it a couple of days so we can all calm down.**

A couple of days will feel like forever.

The chrome of the bar stool catches the light as I pull it out and sit on it. This house never felt like a home before. Now, without the kids, it feels even less so.

Michael Finnegan jumps onto the worktop, butts his head against me, purring. I scratch him behind the ears, remembering when we first brought him home, eight weeks old, a tiny ball of grey fluff. How Lottie's smile had been pure sunshine.

How I wish I could go back to those simpler times.

Begin again.

I have to get the money to keep us safe.

There's no other option is there, except . . .

Could I really do it?

Kill someone to protect my secret?

To protect my children?

Chapter 38

Who's Watching You **Documentary**

Jake Lawler (host): Now our next guest's occupation is what six-year-old me always dreamed of doing. Welcome to bus driver, Ron Starmer.

Ron Starmer (coach driver): Coaches not buses.

Lawler: Is there a difference?

Starmer: I'm hired for private trips. I don't pick up at stops.

Lawler: And, on this occasion, you were hired by Chris's school for a sixth form residential in Norfolk.

Starmer: (nods) That's right.

Lawler: And were you aware that you had celebrities on board?

Starmer: Not when I were booked, no. When I turned up, though, I recognised Chris

Finch and his sister Charlotte, along with Marco Hernandez. Poor lad. He hadn't long lost his mum.

Lawler: So their story was quite familiar to you?

Starmer: Dunno about familiar but my Rita, she watches them online. Soon as I recognised those lads I rang her.

Lawler: Why?

Starmer: She'd been going frantic the day before. That Mia had posted police cars with blue flashing lights racing up to her house and then nothing. No update. Rita was worried something terrible had happened but, with Chris on the trip, I knew they were okay.

Lawler: So you drove Chris and Marco to Norfolk. And were you booked to drive them home again?

Starmer: Yeah, I were booked to bring them all back again, only neither Marco nor Chris were on the coach on the way home.

@Avocadomonkey It must have been hard for Marco to be around Chris #WWY

@Blackcat1970 That doesn't excuse what Marco did

@Lamadrama23 Give him a break – he'd just lost his Mum!!!

@Jamie2983 Boo Hoo

Chapter 39

Lottie

'You sure you're okay with me going on this trip to Norfolk?' Chris asks.

He looks as crap as I feel. I barely slept last night. Every time I closed my eyes I could still see the blood. Smell it. Taste it. I've cleaned my teeth about a zillion times, but the metallic tang is still there, in the back of my throat.

'Yeah. I'm gonna hole up at Dad's until you get back. I don't want to be on my own with her right now. I don't know what to say.' Weirdly, I kind of understand why she did it. I mean, how someone can be driven to such drastic measures. Feel so desperate. Like Harlow did, I suppose, although it's too painful to think of another human feeling there's no other way out but that. What I don't understand is why Mum felt so desperate. Yeah, okay, we're hardly well off, but we're not exactly living on beans, are we? She didn't explain that, did she, during her half-arsed confession? Doing a bad thing doesn't make someone a bad person, though, does it?

Does it?

I really hope not.

'I don't even want to go on this residential anymore,' Chris says. 'I mean, if things are that bad financially, then I should leave school and get a job?'

His voice wobbles as he says this.

'No,' I say. 'You're so close to your exams. We'll figure it out.' Get me being the reassuring one.

The school looms in front of us. The coach already outside. It's too early for all the other pupils to be milling around, and I'm glad. I'd have felt awkward.

Part of things, but not. Standing out without a uniform. God, who'd have thought I'd miss wearing a tie. I really need to broach going back to school with Mum again. Properly. Chris is right, I'm living the life she wants me to live because I feel so indebted to her, but really it's not a life at all. I get what she says about the exams. I've missed too much to take them; despite the work the school sent me, I'm so far behind. I think I will have to repeat the year, which sucks, but I really think I want to be a nurse, and I'll need qualifications for that.

The truth is, I'm a little bit scared of falling ill again as well, but you can't live your life in fear, can you? One thing I've learned from my illness, from Harlow too, is that life can be much shorter than we think. I want to start living mine again. In a weird way, it feels like honouring Harlow if I do. I know she said some mean things about me, but we all make mistakes, don't we? Just not everybody's get found out and plastered all over the internet.

Making a decision about my future lifts the heaviness that's been dragging me down.

Despite the shit-show that was the hot tub, for the first time in what feels like forever I'm looking forward.

Looking up. Tilting my face to the sky, the freshness of the drizzle dampening my skin, and although I don't know anyone who has ever been to prison (and hope I never do), I imagine this is how it feels to be released.

Not exactly euphoric, with a sense of complete freedom, but relief to be out of confinement. Excitement tinged with apprehension about what comes next.

The engine of the coach is thrumming. The driver is leaning against the bonnet, gawping at us. Then he hunches over his mobile phone and is so engrossed he doesn't notice Mrs Harrison approach him with her clipboard. He probably wouldn't even notice if the engine exploded. And they say teens have an addiction to technology.

Chris slips his rucksack off his back and hefts it over one shoulder.

'Hey, Lotts.' Felix nudges me with his elbow. Daisy isn't with him; school doesn't start for a while yet.

'Ready?' he asks Chris. 'Christ, you look like shit. You okay?'

'Yeah,' Chris says, and I'm pleased he doesn't tell him why he looks so rough. I feel such a sense of loyalty to Mum despite everything.

'I didn't think he'd come,' Felix says in a low voice, looking at someone behind me. I turn around. It's Marco. I didn't expect him to be here either. He catches us watching him and I raise my hand in a wave, but his jaw tightens as he glowers at us.

'He'll think you're taking the piss.' Chris lowers my hand.

'I wasn't,' I say sadly. I can't imagine losing a parent. I can't imagine what he's going through. I wish we could all be friends. It isn't our fault our mums fell out. It would be nice to think something good can come from the ashes of something so awful, but it's probably too soon.

I do smile at him as I walk past, though.

He doesn't smile back.

Dad's van isn't outside; I've already missed him. Esther's Fiat is there, though. I'm not sure whether Daisy has left for school yet.

The doorbell has been removed. I remember when we were small Chris and I used to shout, *ding dong, ding dong, your nose is that long*, whenever it chimed, holding our fingers way out in front of our faces to Pinocchio proportions, collapsing into fits of giggles. I lift and drop the gleaming brass knocker.

Esther is drying her hands as she answers. 'Lottie?'

'Is Dad here?' I ask, even though I know he isn't.

'No. And if your mum has sent you to smooth things over then—'

'Smooth things over?'

'Drawing a height chart on my freshly painted wall because I'd painted over yours. Honestly, so childish. Then to text Sean this morning, asking if I'm still upset. Of course I'm bloody upset.'

'Aunt Esther. Can I please come in?'

I'm trying to contain my tears, standing on the step as though I am nothing more than a casual visitor.

She hesitates for a moment before saying, 'No.'

Those two small letters are a slap in the face.

'Why?' I think I'm intending to ask why I can't come in, but instead I finish the sentence with, 'Why don't you like me anymore?'

Her eyes break contact with mine. 'I don't know why you think I don't like you, but—'

'I mean, you're not smiling now or inviting me in. When we were all talking about Harlow you said . . . you said that my illness had triggered many things as though it was my fault. You didn't give me hardly any of Daisy's birthday cake. You didn't hug me goodbye.'

'Lottie—'

'Please don't tell me I'm imagining it. It just feels . . . different. You still seem to be okay with Chris. Have I . . . have I done something wrong?'

She looks upset as she rubs her now dry hands on the towel again. Glances over her shoulder, maybe to check no one else is listening or perhaps because she's got better things to get back to than me.

'It isn't that I don't like you.' I'm not sure how it's possible to sound both irritated and sad, but the tone of her voice conveys both. There's a sick feeling in my stomach as I realise it hasn't all been in my head. She *actually* doesn't like me.

My own aunt.

She must blame me for my parents separating, her brother's pain.

'You think it's my fault. That the strain of my illness was too much for Mum and Dad. That's what you meant when you said it triggered many things.'

'I didn't mean that.'

'Then what did you mean? It wasn't my fault I got sick.'

'I know it wasn't, Lottie.' Her voice is tight as though she too is trying not to cry.

'But you, I mean, you can't honestly blame me for them splitting up.'

It's barely an imperceptible raise of her eyebrows but I still spot it.

'You do, don't you?' Even though I'd suspected it, it still feels shocking and painful, like when I was little and Chris accidentally slammed my hand in the car door.

'No. Look . . . Come on in, Lottie.'

'No.' She didn't want me to before and I have this horrible feeling that if I step inside then I won't be the same person when I step back outside again. She knows something I don't. It's obvious.

'Lottie. I love you. I do, really. I'm sorry you feel I don't, but I can't talk properly right now. I have to get Daisy to school.' She begins to close the door, and I put my hand out.

'No. You don't get to dismiss me like that.' I've had enough of feeling I'm nothing. Fury rises through me. Really it isn't just fury at Esther, but at Mum, at aplastic anaemia, at everything that is out of my control. I'm out of control. 'You took our home.'

'I do own half this house. Lottie, I'm sorry you're upset. It wasn't your fault your parents split up, really. It was your mum's.'

'So something did happen?' They told Chris and me they'd just grown apart.

'I'm not the one you should be talking to about this.'

'Did she . . . was there someone else?' I think about the mystery landlord who is letting us live in the glass house.

'Lottie.' She's fighting tears. 'I can't have this conversation with you. It's not my place to say anything. I shouldn't have said it was your mum's fault.'

'If I ask her then she's not going to tell me the truth, is she?'

'Talk to Sean.'

'He hasn't been honest with me either.'

'I *told* him to tell you.'

'Will you tell me? Please, because . . . because I feel that everyone is lying to me and I . . . I . . . ' I begin to cry.

She wraps me in her arms, and I can hear the beat of her heart as she holds me tight.

'I'm so sorry,' she says into my hair. 'You do deserve to know, but I shouldn't be the one to tell you.'

'Please,' I begin to cry harder. And then she tells me and I kind of wish she hadn't.

'Lottie, Sean isn't . . . He loves you so much and that will never change, but he isn't your biological father.'

Chapter 40

Lottie

Sean isn't your biological father . . .

Why would Esther say that? Because he is. He absolutely is.

Isn't he?

He isn't your biological father.

She can't have meant that, can she? I wriggle out of her grasp and gaze up at her. Her face tells me she did mean it. She's crying too.

'Lottie, I . . . ' she begins, but she clearly doesn't know what to say. She wipes her cheeks with the heel of her hand. She looks as devastated as I feel. 'I'm so sorry. I told Sean to tell you.'

'Dad. Sean. He . . . he's not my real dad? Is that what you're saying?'

She's blinking an unnatural amount, clinging to the doorframe with one hand as though it's an anchor when, really, it's me who needs to steady myself. The pavement is rocking beneath my feet.

'It's true? He's really not my dad?'

Everything I thought I knew falls away from me. My childhood, my happiest parts, memories cracking and reforming into something not warm and fuzzy but cold and sharp.

It was a lie? Everything was a lie?

'You knew? Does everyone know?'

'Just Sean and your mum, I think. But Sean only recently found out. That's what I mean by your illness triggering many things. That's why he left.'

'Because of me? Because I'm not—'

'No, Lottie. No. Not because he didn't want to be your dad but because your mum has been lying to him for your entire life. He loves you exactly the same, I promise.'

Could that be true? He hasn't treated me any differently, has he? Still cuddling me. Still signing 'Dad' on texts as though I don't know who it is. He treats me just the same. Both of us. Me and Chris.

Does that mean . . . ?

'Is he . . . is he Chris's dad.'

'Yes.'

I don't know how I feel about this. Glad that Chris doesn't have to feel what I'm feeling right now but also as though I've lost something else.

Someone else.

Chris is no longer my whole brother. Half. Even as I think that, my love from him grows stronger; I won't let this affect our relationship, I won't. But how will he feel about me once he knows? It's altered the way Esther feels about me, hasn't it? She's hardly been able to bear to look at me, talk to me.

But she's been fine with Chris, who is still her nephew, her blood relative, hasn't she? I am no longer her niece.

'Lottie.' Tentatively she reaches out as though to hug me again, but I step back. 'I'm sorry. Really, I am. I'm sorry too if you thought I was being off with you. It certainly wasn't purposeful. It's your mum I'm angry with. Come on in. I'll make you a hot chocolate and we can talk properly.'

I shake my head. Tears falling. I don't belong here. I don't know where I belong.

'Who is my real father?'

'You should be talking to—'

'I'm talking to you.' My words harden along with my resolve. Aunt Esther has blown my world apart and I'm not leaving until she hands me at least some fragments to try and rebuild something.

'Sean wouldn't want—'

'This is about what *I* want. For once. Me.'

'But it isn't—'

'I won't tell him.' Secrets. Everyone's been keeping so many secrets. I'm good at keeping them too. 'If you ever cared about me, even the smallest amount—'

'Oh Lottie, I loved you very much. I still do. You're my niece.'

'I need to know who I am.'

She swallows hard. Sniffs. 'Okay.' She nods to herself. 'Okay, but Lottie. I need you to know how sorry I am you've found out this way. We're all still a family, I swear. I know it's not the same, nowhere near the same, but I'm hurting too. The bond I shared with your mum when we went through two pregnancies together. I thought we were the best of friends, but she lied to me.'

'She lied to everyone.' I can't even begin to unpick how I feel about her right now. I thought the hot tub was the first time she'd ever deceived me. 'Who is my biological father, Esther?'

She bites her lip, and it honestly seems like such a cliched thing to do I'm expecting her to wring her hands next.

'Who?' My anger spikes.

She glances around as though she expects to see him before her worried eyes land on me, but I don't care how she's feeling. How conflicted she is.

'Esther.'

There is a long painful pause before the silence buckles under the weight of his name, 'Your biological father is called Gabriel Solas.'

Gabriel Solas.

I have his name now. It's something that reveals nothing but feels like everything.

I stare at Esther. She's so close I could reach out and touch her, but she's a lifetime away from me now. I feel a sad, desperate flare of love for her. For the life I thought I had that is slipping through my fingers. I want to ask her if she remembers that time she came to babysit me. She knew I'd be upset because Mum and Dad were taking Chris to a football match without me. I try not to read too much into being left behind now. I'd always believed it was because I didn't like sport, couldn't sit still, but now I wonder whether it's because they were a three, bound by blood, and I was . . .

Anyways, Esther came to babysit. I was going through my fairy phase, and I still remember how my insides had fizzed with excitement when she'd walked into my bedroom. Shimmering blue fairy wings on her back bouncing as she walked. Swirling her wand around as she promised me a magical day, and it had been. Now all my memories are tainted because of *him.*

Gabriel Solas.

'And? Who is he? This man who was so irresistible Mum just couldn't help herself.'

I'm trying to sound as though I don't care, but I've never cared about anything more. Mum and Dad are, were, so happy. I just can't see Mum as the having-an-affair type.

But then, before yesterday, I couldn't see her as the 'dumping offal in our hot tub and pretending it was a stalker' type either.

Who is she? Do you ever really know someone?

'I think, and again it really isn't me you should be discussing this with, but from what Sean has told me, it was a one-time thing. Nothing serious.'

I don't know if that makes it better or worse. That she didn't have any feelings for Gabriel, that I wasn't conceived out of love.

'So I'm the result of a one-night stand. She, what? Met him in a club or something?'

'No. No. She worked for him.'

'He was her *boss*?' It really is the day for cliches. 'Where?'

'The business doesn't exist anymore.'

'So where can I find him? This *Gabriel*?' I'm not entirely sure I want to meet him, not now, not ever, but information is power. That's what Mum used to say when she was endlessly researching aplastic anaemia.

'I don't know where he lives. Really.'

My shoulders sag. I guess I can google him, but I need more to go on.

'What was his company called?'

'He was a restaurateur.'

That throws me. I didn't know Mum ever worked for a restaurant, but then I guess I don't know much of her before-me life. She's just Mum.

'Where?'

'It was in Little Haven. It was called "Nine, The Square", after its address.'

'Sounds wanky,' I mutter.

'It does sound pretentious. It closed down years ago anyway.'

But it's enough information to find him if I want to.

I think I want to.

I think I have to so I can see he's just a name. He doesn't hold any power over me.

As I walk away from Esther, each step triggers such an overwhelming onslaught of loss that my chest aches. I turn to look at the woman I once called Aunt, and I wonder if I'll ever be able to call her that again.

Or if it would be just another lie.

Chapter 41

Mia

There's nothing as corrosive, nothing as hurtful, as lies.

Nothing as damaging as keeping the truth from someone.

The kids will never forgive me for the things I've done. Just as Sean hasn't forgiven me. It was a shock when he tearfully revealed he knew that Lottie wasn't his that night he told me we were over.

'Sean, please. Talk to me.' I sat next to him and, as the cushion dipped, I tried to tell myself that Sean had shifted away from me to make himself more comfortable, but from the way he stared into his lap it was obviously so much more than that.

My hand hovered, unsure whether to take his, watching the way he curved his fingers into his palm, placing my own hands on my knees that were already trembling.

How had we become so broken?

We had both been so centred on Lottie there hadn't been time for us, and when there was, there was this. This uncomfortable silence.

'Sean, I know that—' I began at the exact same time he said, 'I'm leaving.'

'You're . . . what? Why?'

At first he didn't reply and, although I was desperate for an explanation, I resisted the urge to shake him, make him tell me, because if he didn't elaborate, it couldn't be true, could it? He wouldn't leave me. Us.

He raised his head for the first time. Bags hung under bloodshot eyes. Dread was a freight train slamming into me.

He means it.

He means it.

He means it.

'I know.' His voice had cracked as he'd uttered that scant sentence that meant the end of us, the end of everything. He cleared his throat and said louder, the two words draped with bitterness, 'I know.' Yet, as he stared at me, under the cold anger was a flicker of hope while he waited for me to respond. While he waited for me to tell him that it wasn't true.

While he waited for me to shatter his heart.

'I . . . I don't.' I licked my dry lips.

I don't know what you mean.

I don't want to tell you.

It was the strangest sensation, being confronted by the truth. I'd imagined it, of course I'd imagined it, running different scenarios through my mind. Forming conversations in my head while I showered. Giving both the questions and the answers. Hanging on to the steadfast belief that we could work it out because we were Mia and Sean. Sean and Mia. Sometimes I didn't know where I ended and he began. A light touch of the hand, a look, both of us knowing what the other was feeling. Needing. We had been through so much already that nothing seemed insurmountable.

But still I hadn't told him.

I think because, perhaps, deep down, I was afraid of this. This enormous gulf between us even though we are sitting almost thigh to thigh on the sofa.

'How?' It's all I can say. Not really wanting to incriminate myself with excuses and explanations in case there was still some minute chance we were at crossed purposes.

'I got to the hospital before you after my meeting with Lewis. I asked Alma how close a match I was, and she said . . . she said I wasn't at all, but that it was rarer to find a nonbiological match. She thought I knew I wasn't related to Lottie. She was upset when it was apparent I wasn't aware. I just . . . I had just wanted to find out if I could take your place. Spare you going through it.'

It's such a Sean thing to have done. If he had to, he'd run into burning buildings for us, take a bullet for us.

But everyone has a limit, don't they? A line that when shoved across they can't come back from.

'Alma shouldn't have—'

'You *should* have.'

I nodded. He was right. Tears were running down my face and I swiped them away, angry with myself. Lottie is not Sean's daughter.

Why hadn't I told him before?

Instead of being honest from the beginning, I was always, always turning it over and over until I was dizzy with it.

Sick of it.

As years passed, it didn't seem so important. The fact that Sean wasn't Lottie's biological father shrank in my mind until it became insignificant in the story of us. For what is a dad? A mistake? DNA? Or is it sitting by a child's bedside, soothing them from nightmares. Driving them to endless hospital appointments. Making her laugh with robot dancing and terrible jokes during the worst of times.

Camping in the garden, toasting marshmallows over a crackling fire, pointing out constellations.

Showing up. Being there.

Sean *is* Lottie's dad. He was the first one to hold her. Loving her instantly.

My mouth dried. It was hard to get the question out. 'Are you going to tell her?'

His expression slid from hurt and confused to disgust.

The trust vanished from the eyes that had gazed lovingly into mine when I'd pushed a gold band onto his finger and promised him forever.

'I mean, I'm sorry. I'm so, so sorry. But as far as Lottie's concerned, you're her dad.'

Oh god, had he been waiting until she's well before he breaks her apart again?

'I thought we were getting back to normal. Well, our normal.' I tried to slow down the words that were surging from my mouth before I had even thought properly what I wanted to say. I was one step away from dropping to my knees and begging for forgiveness. Perhaps that's what I should have been doing because that's what I wanted more than anything. Not forgiveness, not yet, that would be asking for too much, I know. But for understanding.

'Who was he, then?' He tried to sound casual, but I could see the clench in his jaw, the curl of his fists.

'Gabriel. It was one time. A mistake. It was when Chris was young, and we were going through such a rough patch.'

Anger flashed in his eyes.

'Chris is yours, you know,' I said hurriedly, in case there was any doubt.

'I know,' he said scathingly. 'I did a test.'

'You . . . ' I bit my tongue. Considered what I wanted to say against what I should say. What had he subjected Chris to?

'It's okay. He didn't know.' Sean read me. Could still read me. 'I brought one of those home kits and sent off a sample of his hair and a sample of mine.'

I couldn't imagine how that must have felt. Both the humiliation and the fear.

'You didn't ask—'

'I couldn't trust you to tell the truth.'

'I mean, you didn't ask me about any of it. How have you kept this from me for months?'

'You've kept it from me for years,' he threw back.

'I wasn't sure at first. I thought about telling you. God, I wanted to. But I didn't want to hurt you.'

'Very selfless,' he muttered.

'Okay. Yes. It wasn't only to protect you. It was to protect us, our family. I was never certain. When Lottie was born and you held her in your arms, I felt such a rush of relief. She looked so much like you.'

Even the midwife thought so. 'You have your daddy's eyes,' she had said, and I held that statement close to me as affirmation, regarding it as science almost, this medically trained figure of authority who delivered my baby in her starched uniform was sure Lottie was Sean's.

But as time went on, her mouth changed shape, her nose, and I began to have doubts. I folded them up and shut them in a drawer in my mind. But now that drawer has been yanked open, my secrets and lies exposed.

'We can work this out, can't we? Talk. Look, I know—'

'Don't make this any harder than it already is.' Sean angrily swiped away tears that were spilling down his cheeks. 'Spare me that, at least.'

I had chewed the inside of my lip until I tasted blood. I fought against giving him the space he needed or trying to convince him that somehow we could move forward, if we both wanted it enough. But that's the thing with marriage, any relationship really. To make it work, both parties have to be invested, and I could see that Sean had already mentally checked out. But what we had was worth fighting for.

'Surely—'

'At the time,' he said quietly. 'At the time I could probably have forgiven you. But this . . . this is fifteen years of lies, Mia. It's too much. I don't know who you are anymore.'

'Does Esther know?' What must she think of me?

'I told her today. She feels as betrayed by you as I do,' he says. 'I didn't want to tell her when I first found out because I didn't know if we could perhaps sort this out, but I've been talking everything through with Alma to get it straight in my head, and there's no going back for us.'

'Alma? You're seeing *Alma*?'

'Not seeing, no. But she's the only one who knew. The only one I could talk to. I thought if we were to get through this then Esther needn't know. That things could be the way they were, but I can't move on. I just can't.'

Outside, a flash of red as a car raced past the window. The driver eager to get to wherever they were going. What was next for us?

It turns out the glass house was next for me.

In truth, and it was only after I'd moved out of the house I realised, I'd been horribly lonely for the longest time. Even though I'd been surrounded by medical staff at the hospital, had children and a husband I adored, I'd felt so alone because that's what carrying a secret does. It isolates you. Separates you from everyone, even yourself.

I don't know why I'm thinking about all this right now. I think it's because I'm rarely alone. I have more time to think.

But Gabriel is not someone I want to dwell on.

Not someone I ever want Lottie to find out about.

Who her father really is.

How dangerous he is.

Chapter 42

Lottie

I'm looking for my dad.

There's a sense of danger cloaked around me. I don't mean a physical danger or anything, just that I'm chasing information that will change my life, and I don't know if I want that. If I'm ready.

After I left Esther's, I'd turned my phone off. I couldn't cope with anything. Not knowing what I'd do if Chris texted, or Mum or the man I thought of as my father. I wanted to shut myself away from everyone. I'd walked into town and, really, it was kind of a whim to jump on the bus when I saw it coming, 'Little Haven' displayed on its front.

Fate?

I'd got the bus to Little Haven because I felt I had nothing else to do, nowhere else to go. I could have googled him, Gabriel, and saved myself the trip but I was killing time. It's not like I thought I'd achieve anything by coming here. It's not like it's still a restaurant but, well, like I said, I didn't know where else to go right now. I had thought about texting Alma. We've always kept in touch. She was my favourite nurse and made my stay in hospital a lot less scary, but if I messaged her and asked to go to hers, I'd have to tell her why.

I'm not ready to tell anyone why I can't go home.

I'd stared aimlessly out of the window all the way, wondering what passersby saw when they caught sight of me. Someone as lost as I felt?

At Little Haven, I'd wandered around. I could have switched on my phone and used Maps, but I didn't want to. I'd left it up to fate again. If I found the square, it was meant to be.

Anyways, I'd stumbled across it and, basically, now I'm here I don't quite know what to do.

The square is small, shabby. Stupidly, it isn't even actually a square. There's an 'L' shape row of what looks like derelict properties, bordering what I guess was once a communal garden, now just chipped black railings fencing in a tangle of weeds.

What would have been the rest of the square is rubble surrounded by construction hoarding. There are various signs stating, 'Private Property', 'Trespassers will be Prosecuted', and 'Beware Guard Dogs', but there's nothing here to protect. What might have been a thriving market town has been left to rot.

Nine, The Square, just like everything else, is now empty.

Graffiti sprayed across the steel shutters. Some of it is pretty good. A woman in a cloak, hands on hips, hair billowing behind her as though she's facing strong wind. She isn't real but there's a determination about her that I draw from.

Above the shutters is a sign, weatherworn and faded, Wilson & Sons. Obviously a family firm.

Just not my name. Not my family.

Family.

Does this Gabriel even know I exist? I wish I'd asked Esther that. If he does, and he's chosen not to be in my life, well, that's pretty shitty. Not that I want him in my life.

Dad is . . . and when I think of Dad I think of Sean; of course, this bloke, this Gabriel, is nothing more than shared DNA. Nothing to me, not really.

But still, there's a part of me that feels so . . . needy. So wanting to belong, to be loved but, much as it pains me to admit it, Esther was right. Mum is the one I should be talking to. Finding out what happened between her and this guy. Did she love him? Could she have loved him even if it was just one night?

But then, how can I trust anything she says? The hot tub thing, I mean, I'd thought that was as bad as it could get, you know? What lie could be bigger than that? But this? This is bigger.

I can't trust Mum.

The thought buckles my knees, and I sit heavily on a mossy bench. Registering the damp seeping through my jeans but glad of it, glad to feel something other than this horrible, horrible numbness.

It's hard to stop mentally travelling back. Analysing everything with fresh eyes. With mistrusting eyes.

When Mum had said she didn't have a single doubt about donating bone marrow to me, did she mean it?

When she swore she'd rather be at the hospital with me more than anywhere else in the world, was that the truth?

When she said she loved me?

An old woman stares at me as she walks past. At first I think she recognises me, but she's ancient, like fifty or something, so probably hasn't even heard of YouTube let alone watched it.

Sometimes it feels as though the world knows who I am but, of course, even though Mum's channel blew up, it's really only a small proportion of people, spread all over the globe. It's not like everyone knows who we are.

Other than the whole thing with Harlow, there isn't a lot to know us for. We're an ordinary family.

Were.

Were an ordinary family.

Now we don't feel like a unit, and I don't know where I fit.

Rain trickles down my neck. I must look a state. Sitting crying on a bench, soaked through. No wonder she was looking at me weird.

The thought occurs that if Mum saw a girl sitting alone in a storm, distressed, she'd approach her. Ask her if she needs anything, because she's kind like that, but then I wonder if she really is as compassionate as she seems.

If her kindness has all been an act too?

If everything is pretend?

I'm crying harder. Covering my face with my hands when I feel a hand rest lightly on my shoulder.

Thinking the woman has come back, I look up.

But it isn't her.

It's a man.

Something inside me recognises him. It's as though I've seen him before, but I know it isn't that. It's because he has the same nose as me. The same shaped mouth.

It's as though something in my body recognises that his blood runs through my veins.

This man, I know with certainty, is my father.

Chapter 43

Mia

Although I'm exhausted in a way I haven't been before, I can't stop pacing. My chest is tight all the time. The pain has morphed from sudden and sharp to a constant dull ache.

I really don't feel right.

It's okay that Lottie turned to Sean, and I know he will be looking after her, but I can't help worrying.

I really shouldn't.

No matter what biology says, Sean is still her dad and she's safe with him.

He is good and kind, not like her biological father.

Again, there's a flash of relief that she doesn't know Gabriel exists.

That he doesn't know she exists.

She wouldn't be safe with him at all.

Chapter 44

Lottie

He might have owned a restaurant, but he doesn't look like a respectable business owner. Dishevelled, unshaven. Blond hair touching his collar. Rather than the sense of safety and security I get when I'm with Dad, and I mean the-man-who-raised-me Dad, all I feel right now, as I gaze up at this stranger, is uncomfortable.

Awkward.

His green eyes study me. 'I was going to pass by when I saw you sitting there in the rain, but then . . . Something made me stop.'

His eyes scan my face, and I wonder whether he's noticing the familiarity too.

For what seems like minutes, we stare at each other until I look away. He turns his head too and one quick glance reveals the same profile as mine.

'That used to be my restaurant.' He follows my eye-line across the road. 'It isn't my premises anymore, but I retained the maisonette next door, not that it has much value now. A developer offered to buy it, but I held out for more money.

Big mistake. The project has been abandoned. Still, we all make mistakes, don't we?'

The words seem loaded, meant for me. I sneak a glance, wondering if he's looking at me with tears in his eyes, but he's still staring across the road.

'I've been away. It was a shock to come back and see it like this. Sad, really.'

It's an odd thing to blurt out to someone you don't know, and the only explanation is that he instinctively knows who I am too. I wish I hadn't come. It was stupid. It's not as if I want him in my life, is it?

Is it?

Truth is, I just don't know. The whole thing has been such a bombshell, I haven't had time to process it. To ask the right questions – any questions. To find out what happened between him and my mum. I mean, they worked together so they must have been friends. More than friends obviously because, well, there's me. But beyond that, I just don't know.

'Are you okay?' he asks, but as I watch his mouth move all I see in my head is the way Dad's lips have always curled into a smile whenever I walk into the room. Not because I'm doing anything particularly funny or clever but because I'm just there. Because I exist.

Suddenly my cheeks are burning with shame that I even came here. Even though I never thought he'd be here, the restaurant long gone, the bitter taste of disloyalty burns so fiercely on my tongue that I cannot speak. Instead I nod – I'm okay – and gather my things and my thoughts and, slinging my bag over my shoulder, I turn to walk away.

'Charlotte?' he says and my stomach literally drops onto the pavement. I mean, I can feel my guts actually moving. 'It is Charlotte, isn't it?'

'Yeah,' I say as I spin around, because I can't exactly ignore him, can I?

This man is my father.

It's all I can think of as I stare at him, wiping my cheeks, embarrassed that the first impression he'll have of me is a snotty, snivelling mess.

But then I begin to wonder how he knows who I am. Questioning why, if he knew I existed, he hasn't ever wanted to see me.

'So your mum told you about me. What did she say?' He scratches at the stubble on his chin, fingertips stained nicotine yellow.

'Nothing. She doesn't even know that I know. I only found out about you today and decided to check you out.' I straighten my spine a little as though I'm in control. Not sure why I feel the need to impress him. Wanting him to know that I've made the effort even if he never has. 'So.'

His eyes travel across my face and I wonder whether he's seeing himself in my features. I search his eyes for some kind of clue as to how he's feeling. Some kind of affection, but there's nothing I can identify.

He's a stranger to me.

Suddenly, he smiles and, despite my misgivings about being here, I can't help smiling back. I'd been so scared of being rejected.

'We can't just stand in the rain. Come in, come in.'

He begins to walk across the room, but I don't follow.

He's a stranger and stranger danger is something that's been drummed into me from such a young age.

He turns back to me. 'Charlotte?'

I'm freezing and soaking, and it'd be nice to get dry and warm. He isn't really a stranger, is he? He made me, after all. And although I could turn around now, call Mum and demand an explanation, how can I trust what she'd tell me? She's proven herself to be a liar, hasn't she?

Here, I can ask Gabriel everything I want to know. I can compare his version with Mum's version later.

I'm not committing to anything if I follow him inside, am I?

It's not like that means I want a father–daughter relationship with him, does it?

I take another look at the graffiti woman and imagine myself in that cloak.

Powerful.

It'll be okay. I'll be okay. Anyways, I can leave anytime I want to.

Can't I?

Chapter 45

Lottie

The door to Gabriel's place has peeling blue paint and a rusting letterbox. Something is stopping me walking through the entrance. A gut feeling that this won't end well. I'm bound to be unsettled but is this feeling something else? Something more?

'Charlotte, come on in.'

It's like one of those, what do you call it, pivotal moments in a horror film. You're screaming at the girl to leave but instead she goes deeper into the building.

'Charlotte?'

'Sorry. This is a bit weird. You're a stranger.'

'God. Sorry. Is this really inappropriate? Do you want to go somewhere public? The café shut down, you can see we don't have much in the village anymore, but there is a bench in the park that's under cover. We could go there, or we could call Mia and ask her to chaperone?'

'No. Don't call Mum.'

'Does she know where you are?'

'No.'

'Does anyone?'

'Mum thinks I'm with Dad tonight. I told her I need some space.'

'You should let your dad know where you are then if he's expecting you.'

''S all right. I haven't told him I'm coming over yet.' My voice is wobbling all over the place, so is my lip probably. I feel like a stupid kid trying not to cry. 'It's a bit fucke— a bit of a mess.'

'Oh dear. Shall we go to the park? A chat might help?'

I glance over my shoulder. The rain is torrential. I feel silly dragging us both back out in it again, because of what? A weird feeling? This *is* a weird situation. It isn't exactly going to feel normal, is it?

And because I don't trust my gut anymore, because it had never told me that my childhood was fake, I step inside and close the door behind me.

My first mistake.

It's gloomy, there's a musty smell. Stale cigarette smoke. Gabriel heads towards a narrow staircase and begins to climb.

To where? The bedrooms? I step backwards towards the door, the handle poking me in the back. I'm fumbling behind me for it, trying to act casually as I ask, 'Where are you going?'

'To the lounge. Sorry, I should give you a tour. The kitchen and the bathroom are down here.'

My cheeks blaze, hoping that he doesn't know that for a second I thought he might be, what, a paedo? I berate myself for being an idiot as he leads me through to the back of the, not a flat, what did he call it, a maison something or other.

The kitchen has weird orangey-coloured wooden cabinets. The work surfaces are clear – Mum would love that – but the coffee machine and food processor we have out that she calls clutter make it feel like home. This is stark. From the window behind the sink, rain pushes in and pools around the taps.

'Need to get round to fixing that,' Gabriel says.

'You said you've been away? Anywhere nice?'

'It was kind of a work thing,' he says. 'Bathroom if you need it.'

This is grim. Black mould creeping across the ceiling. The smell of damp is overpowering.

Then we head upstairs. Thankfully it's warmer. As I walk into the lounge there's a hiss. A blast from the plug-in air freshener fills the room with the scent of mint. It's like stepping into a giant stick of chewing gum. I can't help coughing.

The view stretches across the square, not that there's much to see.

'Sit down,' Gabriel says. 'Sorry, I should have offered you a drink. Tea? Coffee?'

I shake my head. 'Hot chocolate?'

'No.' He looks deflated. 'I have orange juice?'

'Great. Thanks.'

I'm not thirsty really but as his footsteps thud back downstairs I take the time to gather myself. To dart into all corners, not sure what I'm looking for, but wanting to get a sense of who this man is. The furniture is dark, old fashioned. On the sideboard there's a photo of a much younger Gabriel with an older woman who looks so much like me it takes my breath away. I think she must be my grandmother. There's a constriction in my throat as I trace the shape of her face with my fingertip. It's mad I have a whole other family.

'That's my mum.'

I start. I hadn't heard Gabriel come back into the room.

'This was her place actually. She lived here until very recently.'

'My grandma. My other grandma –' it feels weird saying that – 'she's in a care home.'

'Sorry to hear that. My mum lived here until she passed away.'

'Oh.' I don't know what to say. Ridiculously, tears prick at the back of my eyes. I never knew her, but I could have done.

I could have done if Mum had been honest with me.

He sets my drink on a side table, and I take the seat nearest to it. Suddenly, I remember that no one knows where I am. I take my mobile out of my bag so I can switch it back on and text Chris.

'Mum always wanted grandchildren. She'd have loved you. She was so natural. I don't know much about kids, I'm afraid. Other than the fact you're all glued to those things.'

I look up, guilty. I haven't even booted up my phone yet, but I don't want to seem rude, disinterested in him, so I put it down on the table and then we sit, stare at each other awkwardly before we both begin to speak at once.

'Do you have—'

'Are you—'

We both force a laugh.

'You first,' he says.

'Umm. You don't have any other kids then?'

'No. Never married.'

'Why not?' In my head I'm imagining that he's been in love with Mum all these years.

'My job made it difficult to form long-term relationships.'

'Is that because you're away a lot?'

'Yes. Can I ask a question now?'

'Yeah.'

'How did you find out about me?'

'My aunt told me. Esther. She said you and Mum worked together?'

'Your mum used to work at my restaurant.'

'And you . . . I mean you two.' I can feel the heat in my cheeks.

'We did.'

'But she was *married*.' Loyalty for my dad flares.

'She wasn't then. Look, we . . . I can't speak for her, Charlotte. I know you must be confused, but relationships can be complicated. It wasn't that we set out to deliberately deceive anyone; it was a one-off.' He scratches at his bristles again. The sleeve of his shirt slips and I notice an intricate twist of tattoos on his arm. 'I think you should speak to your mum about this.'

'Yeah, well, she doesn't always tell the truth,' I mutter, angrily pulling at a stray thread on my jumper. Not caring if it unravels, because that's what I feel is happening to me. I'm unravelling. I'm sitting in a strange flat, in a strange town with this dude who is my actual dad.

My chest tightens. Breath shallow. I hunch over, trying to control my breathing. Hearing Mum's voice in my head, *one, two, three. Slowly in, slowly out.* Feeling it calm me and hating that, after everything I've learned today, it still does.

'You okay?' Gabriel is watching me, making no move to comfort me, probably feeling as out of his depth as I do. How long has he even known I existed?

'Yeah.' I pick up my glass and sip at the orange juice; it isn't the one I like that we have at home, the one with the bits in it, but I finish it anyway.

It's probably just because it's a different brand that it tastes funny.

Chapter 46

Lottie

'Did you know? About me?' I ask.

'Your mum never told me,' he says.

I'm her dirty secret.

The thought pops into my head and I feel the toxicity of it leaching into my bloodstream. Poison flowing through my blood.

I am something to be ashamed of.

I can't cope anymore. I need fresh air. Space.

'I've gotta go.' I reach for the strap of my bag.

'Please don't go, Charlotte. I know this is hard, but I'd really like to get to know a little about your life. You might decide you don't want me in it after today.'

I hesitate. He's right. I don't know if I'll want to see him again. I already have a dad, don't I? The best dad. But then . . . this doesn't make sense. Gabriel knew who I was. Outside. He *must* have known about me.

'One thing to know about me is that I don't like liars.' My tone is steel. 'You knew who I was when you spoke to me.'

He glances down at the threadbare carpet before raising his face to mine. 'You're right. But I only found out about you last week. A mutual acquaintance told me. I know it's a shock to both of us. I've been wondering what to do but then I saw you, and you look so much like me I felt this immediate bond. I knew it was you. Please. Let me get to know you a little.'

'What do you want to know?' I perch on the edge of my chair, but I don't let go of the strap of my bag.

He takes his time choosing his questions. I guess he's scared that at any second I might run away. I'm already sitting in an awkward position, twisted at the waist, my feet are pointing towards the door.

'What's your favourite subject at school? Oh, shouldn't you be at school or is it the holidays?'

'I've been sick so I'm off.'

I'm waiting for the questions about my illness, but they don't come.

'There's a lot of that cough and cold virus about. I guess it's no hardship staying home. Where do you live? What's your mum up to?'

'She's an influencer.'

'A what?'

'On social media. She makes videos and stuff about our lives.'

'Right. I see,' he says, although from his face it's apparent he doesn't. According to him, he's had a week to research me, us, but it appears he hasn't bothered. 'I meant, what does she do for a living?'

'That is what she does. Companies sponsor her, you know, paid adverts and stuff.' Even though she's not at this stage yet, she is on her way, and I want him to think she's a success.

'And that's a job?' He shakes a cigarette out of a packet and clamps it between his lips.

'Some people make millions, you know, live in mansions and everything. Swimming pools, the lot.'

He sparks a lighter and takes a deep draw on his cigarette. The tip burns red and smoke curls towards me as he exhales. I cough and cough, lift up my glass but it's empty.

'Sorry.' He stubs his cigarette out. 'That's the last thing you need if you've been poorly.' He picks up his phone. 'Show me what your mum does.'

Embarrassed, I take the handset. Not really wanting to show him. Not wanting him to read the comments about me, my changing body, but then perhaps if he knows what I've been through he'll, I dunno, care?

I find us on YouTube and pass him back his phone.

He watches a video, whistles.

'That's a nice house you live in.'

'Yeah, well, I liked our old house but after Mum and Dad split up we had to move.'

'I didn't realise your parents were separated. So your mum lives in that big glass house alone?'

'Hardly alone; she has me and Chris.'

'Of course. I just meant it's a big property to afford by yourself. She must really be doing well. I'll get you another juice.'

I want to tell him not to bother because I'm not staying. It sounds as though he's trying to get to know Mum rather than me. I wonder if he's still into her.

When he returns, I take the glass from him, and I drink it all quickly. I want to leave as soon as I can.

'I really should get going.'

'Oh.' He sounds disappointed. 'Before you go, can I

show you some photos of my parents? Your grandparents? Also there's my aunt, who would be your great-aunt, of course.'

'Umm, yeah, okay.' The temptation to see blood relatives is greater than my desire to leave.

He lifts out an old-fashioned album. There's yellowing tissue paper in between the pages that crinkle as he turns them.

'This is me as a baby.'

'You look like you're wearing a dress.'

'It's a christening gown. It's been passed down through the generations.'

I expect him to ask me if I was christened but it doesn't seem to occur to him. Perhaps he isn't religious.

He points out his parents and tells me stories about them and then about his grandparents. Making Christmas pudding with his nan, stirring coins into the mixture.

'What did you do that for?'

'It's lucky if you get one in your portion.'

'Not so lucky if you choke.'

He laughs. 'Not sure if I ever had any luck, but now you're here I think my luck has changed.'

I don't reply, uncomfortable. Just because we share DNA, he's sharing his history, doesn't mean we have a relationship.

He flips over the page again.

'Oh, a cat!' I point to a black cat sitting on the windowsill in the next photo. 'I have a cat. He's called Michael Finnegan.'

'That one was called Smokey. We had him for about eighteen years.'

'Wow.' It's cool to know he lived that long. I can't imagine life without Michael Finnegan.

'When he was a kitten he disappeared. It was one of the

first times he'd been out on his own. We made up posters for lampposts and knocked on all the neighbours' doors. Asked everyone to check their sheds. We couldn't find him. Days passed and we thought we'd never see him again.'

'What happened?'

'We were walking home one night, I'd been to Boy Scouts, and there was a terrible storm. Bit like today really, rain pelting down. Anyway, over the wind and the thunder I heard this faint mewing. Mum thought I'd imagined it but then I called his name, and we heard him, mewling. He'd climbed a tree and got stuck. I ran home to tell Dad, and he came back with his ladder and rescued him.'

'Was he okay?'

'Soaked through and hungry. He felt very sorry for himself. Anyway, after that he never strayed far from home again. That was a good thing. Never crossing the road.'

'Did you have any other pets?'

'I had a rabbit once.' He's telling me about him but it's like he's talking slowly or something. I can hear his words, but they are all stretched and bent out of shape, and I don't understand them.

I try to focus on the photo he's pointing out to me, but my head is fuzzy, and I can't see properly.

What's happening to me?

I think it's probably stress. Panic. This isn't exactly a normal situation, is it?

I try to conjure Mum's voice.

Breathe in deeply.

One.

Two.

Three.

But my skin is hot and cold and it's like I have the flu or something but, oh god, it feels a bit like when I was sick. Has my aplastic anaemia come back?

'Mum.' It's an effort to move my mouth. I try to lift my head to tell Gabriel that there's something wrong with me. To tell him to get my mum.

I should have listened to her. I shouldn't have come outside where infections lurk ready to take hold of me.

But . . .

My mind is trying to put it together. I've only been out the house for . . .

Breathe.

One.

Two.

Three.

I felt all right until I came here, until I drank this . . .

Momentarily I focus on Gabriel's face. He's watching me in that detached way again as though I'm an animal in a cage. Why did I follow him here? I don't even know him.

Panic spikes but exhaustion is winning. My eyes begin to close.

I force them open. I have to stay awake.

Breathe.

One.

Two.

Three.

I think I feel Mum's hands in mine but I'm slipping away. I can't fight it. My head lolls back, dribble spilling from the corner of my mouth.

Get.

Out.

Of.

Here.

I need to stand. My legs won't work.

Calm. Breathe.

One.

My eyes are closed.
Two.
Head swimming.
Three.
Nothing.

Chapter 47

Mia

Lottie is safe.

Perhaps safer with Sean than she is with me right now. I have kept reminding myself of that through this endless day, hours dragging long and slow. Sean may be furious with me. Lottie, too, but they're together. Although that last note had terrified me – *you know what you have to do* – Lottie is secure at Sean's house. It's not as though she's wandering the streets with friends or anything.

Nobody can get to her.

I still have time to sort this out – but how?

The sharp pains in my chest are so frequent I almost don't register them anymore.

Chris has texted me from Norfolk, sent a picture of the accommodation to let me know he's arrived safely. He hasn't typed a message to go with it. Usually he'd have written something like 'at the Jurassic coast but haven't seen a dinosaur yet' but I guess he doesn't know what to say to me right now. There's been nothing from Lottie, but I didn't really expect there to be after her note.

I'm fighting the urge to go to Sean's and try and talk to her. It isn't just the shame I feel at what I put Lottie through with the hot tub that's stopping me. The revulsion that will likely be on Sean's and Esther's faces when they next see me. It'll be a look I recognise; I see it every time I look in the mirror.

It's more the fact that Lottie has asked for some space and the least I can do is give it to her. If she ever wants to live with me again, and I hope to God she wants to live with me again, I'm going to have to learn to loosen the reins a little.

To stop fearing something awful will happen to her if she's out of my sight. I just need to somehow appease the sender of the threats and then we can begin our new normal. Lottie can return to school. Live her life again. Learn to live with germs and infections and everything else that we all have to deal with because, ultimately, she isn't sick anymore.

I can let go.

Breathe.

We can learn to be us again.

Tonight will be a good trial run for us both. Her being out in the world without anything terrible happening while I make a plan.

She is safe.

Chapter 48

Lottie

Danger.

My mind flashes the word, but I cannot get my body to react. My thoughts are muzzy, everything woozy. It feels a little like that time that Daisy and I drank cider in the shed. Sweet and sharp on my tongue. Giggling. Giggling. Giggling. Having fun.

This isn't fun.

This isn't the same.

Panic shakes me and I try again to move but something is cutting into my wrists, my ankles.

I can't move. Can't move. Can't move. God, it's so hard to breathe.

Help. I want to scream but something is covering my mouth.

Blackness beckons me again and, as I slip into oblivion, I try to form the word, but I know it's in my head. That no one can hear it but me. Still, it is my last conscious thought.

Help.

Chapter 49

Who's Watching You Documentary

Jake Lawler (host): (paces, turns, paces, stops central to camera – anguished expression) The Finch family had already been through so much and had no idea that there was another death just around the corner. Everyone had rooted online for Charlotte since she first fell ill but, ultimately, her ending was tragic and not what any of us would have wanted for her. I get tearful now just thinking about it. (hand over heart)

Mia bravely, selflessly, donated bone marrow. Imagine going through all of that to protect your daughter because you were scared the illness might take her and then . . . (shakes head sadly) There's more than one way to lose a child, isn't there?

@Avocadomonkey As a mummy I can't imagine. How does Mia cope?

@Blackcat1970 Fame always has a price

@Lamadrama23 Mia paid the highest price of all!!!

@Jamie2983 She brought it on herself

Chapter 50

Lottie

It's dark.

My eyelids feels as though they're stuck together. It's an effort to peel them open. Rain drums against the window. A faint amber glow filters in through the window.

A lamppost?

But we don't have any lampposts around the glass house.

There's a pulsing pain in my head, like one of the pickaxes from Minecraft bashing me again and again the way Chris used to swing at the rocks to build his world.

But Minecraft isn't real and neither can this be.

Where am I?

Panic kicks in quickly because, although I feel so groggy, I know something is wrong.

I am not in bed.

I can't seem to think straight. Can't remember where I am, but I know I'm not at home.

I'm dazed. My whole body aching. A foul smell filling my nostrils.

I'm on the floor. Face pressed against a carpet that was

probably once a soft pile but is now crusty with, urgh, I don't even want to think what it might be.

My hand is numb, pins and needles where I've been lying awkwardly. I try to move my arm, but I can't.

My hands are bound together.

My ankles too.

I open my mouth to scream but my terror is muffled by whatever is tied tightly around my head, covering my mouth.

For a moment I slump into this situation that is so far out of my control. Mind ticking over.

Think.

Fragments of memory filter in and I try to slot them together like one of the jigsaws Chris and I used to do, but I don't have an image to work from, and half of the pieces are missing, the gaps too vast to guess what should be there.

Blood.

I smell it, sickeningly sweet.

See flashes of crimson. Taste the metallic tang on my tongue.

The hot tub.

I remember finding all that flesh floating around the water.

I swallow, tasting blood now, realise I must have bitten the inside of my cheek or something. I try to swallow but it's difficult lying down.

I can't breathe.

I'm going to die.

I cannot breathe.

My chest is so tight I wouldn't be surprised if it literally exploded.

I'm going to die.

Nobody knows where I am.

Why didn't I tell someone – anyone – where I am?

There's isn't enough air. Is it possible to suffocate if your mouth is covered? Snot is blocking my nose. Oh god. I try to force my tongue out of my mouth, to dislodge the fabric stretched across my lips. Tasting blood.

The last thing I ever taste will be my own blood.

I am sick. Dizzy. Afraid.

I try to calm myself. There's air in the room but that's no consolation when I'm inhaling the stale smoke on the material around my mouth – a tie?

Breathe.

One.

Two.

Three.

But I can't breathe. I just can't. Huge wracking sobs are trapped inside me. They're going to tear me in two, leave me in pieces in this unfamiliar place.

Where am I?

With a gargantuan effort, I turn myself over. Eyes scanning for something familiar, but vague and amorphous shadows loom in all corners of the room. They could be pieces of furniture but could equally be people, monsters, somebody watching me.

I whimper.

The rain pelts louder against the window. I have a vague recollection of getting wet. Rain gusting into my face, wind snatching at my hair.

An image comes to mind.

A warrior in a cloak, her hands on hips, green-eyed stare challenging me.

Think.

I am so confused. It feels as though I have sea sickness the way I had when we had taken the ferry to the Isle of Wight. Mum urging me to keep sipping at ice-cold water as I felt the unsteady ground shift beneath my feet.

Think.

Just like I had during that crossing, I feel a sloshing in my stomach. Then, I had leaned over the railings as a flock of seagulls overhead screeched out their hunger. There's a noise in my head right now. Not birds this time but, *He's not your father.*

Esther's voice clear and cutting.

Somewhere in the depths of my mind I remember going to Dad's.

Blood.

The hot tub. Mum had filled the hot tub with offal, and I didn't feel safe with her.

I am not safe now.

He's not your father.

Gabriel. A man called Gabriel.

My mind is clearing a little, but my eyes are closing. I'm fighting against something chemical, I know that. Every teenage girl is aware of the dangers of leaving their drink unattended. Having something slipped into it.

Orange. I taste orange.

I'd drunk juice. Given to me by that man, that man that looks like me.

He's not your father.

I remember a man.

A name.

A restaurant.

A maison something or other in a derelict square.

Gabriel.

What does he want from me? Why has he done this to me?

I have to fight sleep. Have to get out of here. Have to.

He has a plan. I need to make one of my own.

'Not sure if I ever had any luck, but now you're here I think my luck has changed.'

Christmas. Sixpence in the pudding.

Make a wish.

Chris.

I want my brother more than anything right now.

I begin to jerk. Flapping around on the floor like one of those red plastic fortune-teller fish we'd find in our crackers.

I'm going to get out of here.

True.

True.

True.

Chris. Chris will come and find me, won't he? Mum? Dad? They'll all know I'm missing by now.

They'll be searching. Searching.

Being rescued is my last conscious thought as whatever I've been drugged with drags me under once more.

Chapter 51

Lottie

I've never felt so scared. I want to go home. I don't even care if that's Dad's or the glass house. I want to be anywhere that isn't here. I'm freezing cold, a draught pushing in from under the door, but at least it's daylight now. The shadows that had last night seemed so terrifying – lurking figures out to get me – are now revealed as a pile of boxes and bags, an emerald green dress slung on the top. A tailor's dummy. There's a dark mahogany dressing table with an oval mirror, a stool with a pink seat. Is that where my grandmother would get ready? I've never met her, but I judge her harshly now because she raised a monster. Did she know? Were they close? Was it her passing that pushed Gabriel over the edge? Because he's clearly unhinged.

Oh god.

My eyes flicker towards the dress, back to the dressing table. What if he wants to dress me up like his mum? What if he's a complete nut job like Norman whatsit in that *Psycho* film Chris made me watch that gave me nightmares for weeks?

I scan the rest of the room for a rocking chair, not exactly relaxing when there isn't one, but it does quell the mad panic a bit.

On the wall there's a framed photo. It's hard to make out from here but I squint. It's the restaurant. Perhaps opening night. The 'Nine, The Square' sign clearly visible behind the people standing in front of it. Two men and two women. I narrow my gaze. Is that Mum? I think it might be. One of the men is definitely Gabriel; I've never seen the other one before. The second woman is taller than Mum. There's something about the heart shape of her face, though, that reminds me a little of Alma, my nurse, and I feel a lurch of longing for the safety of the hospital ward.

Think.

When I was young I'd put little plays on for Mum and Dad, roping Chris in. Sometimes I'd make him shuffle across the carpet on all fours, pretending to be Scooby-Doo. I'd throw him a chunk of Rich Tea biscuit and call it a Scooby Snack, and we'd solve an impossible mystery. Escape from peril. Take deep bows from the waist as our parents applauded.

I can do this. I can pretend I am a character. That this is make-believe. Find a way out. It was me who was responsible for us breaking the record at that Escape Room we went to before I got sick. As far as I know, The Fantastic Finches are still top of the leaderboard.

My bladder is full. Uncomfortable. It makes it hard to focus. I squirm; adjusting my position does nothing to ease the need to wee. It doesn't really help the ache in my muscles either.

Oh god.

I'm going to wet myself.

Please no.

At this point in time that thought feels worse than anything else. The humiliation.

Get a grip, Lottie.

But I can't. I need the toilet so badly I begin to cry. All thoughts of formulating a plan evaporate.

I can't get out of here.

I can't.

I. Just. Can't.

Then all thoughts of everything disappear as footsteps loom closer and closer.

Oh god.

Oh god.

The handle of the door begins to move.

He's coming.

But what does he want with me?

Chapter 52

Lottie

The door creaks open. Yeah, like actually creaks like this is a fucking horror film, and that's what this feels like. The villain come to kill off the hero so they can't tell on them, but I've never felt less heroic. I haven't even done anything with my life yet. 'You've been the hero of your own story,' Mum had said once when I was in hospital, sad I was missing out on so much.

But I'm only fifteen and so much is left unwritten. Is this my final chapter?

I don't want to die like this.

Not here.

Not now.

I don't want to die at all, not when I've been through so much to live.

I'm panicky sick. Rocking my body back and forth on the floor, that fortune-teller fish again, knowing that I can't break free but something in me driving each movement I make.

The survival instinct, I guess; we did it once in Biology. That intrinsic desire to live. Yeah, I have that right now.

For a moment, when Gabriel steps towards me, I stop moving. Curl into myself, trying to become as small as possible. Invisible.

Breathe.

One.

Two.

Three.

I can't, I can't. I screw my eyes shut.

I feel his fingers on my skull, tugging, a pulling of my hair, and then the gag is off. My lips are dry, and I lick them before realising this is my chance. I open my mouth wide, and he covers it with his palm. It too smells of stale smoke.

'It is very unlikely anyone will hear you if you scream. You've seen how derelict it is here. Half the square has been demolished. There are no neighbours.'

My heart sinks, knowing he's right, but then I remember the old woman yesterday, walking her dog. There must be residents somewhere, mustn't there?

He removes his hand, and I take a chance. 'Help!'

The crack to my cheek is sudden and sharp. Instantly, my voice shrivels to nothing.

'Lottie. I'm trusting you to behave and if you don't I'll gag you again.'

He hit me.

I stare at him, my eyes wide.

It's not like I thought he'd be a contender for father of the year or anything, I mean, look at what he's done so far, but still.

He hit me.

What the . . . I mean, like, no one has ever struck me before. My skin smarts but I'm too shocked to cry.

'That's better.' He takes my silence for submission. 'Now. I'm not used to looking after kids,' he says without a trace of irony. 'But I'm guessing you're probably hungry?'

'I . . . ' I can't look at him. 'I need the toilet.'

He appraises me. I don't want to beg but I'm so scared he'll say no, bring me a bucket or something, or worse, just leave me here to lie in a puddle of my own urine.

'Please.'

He crouches down and unties my ankles before yanking me up with my elbow as though I'm a marionette, unable to move by myself, and that's what it feels like. My feet are tingly. I sway, the after-effects of whatever he gave me moving the floor beneath me.

He drags me downstairs to the bathroom, his fingers digging into the top of my arm. When we reach the door, he pulls it open and for one horrible moment I think he's going to come into the room with me.

Watch me.

I begin to sob, and he turns me around. Unties my wrist.

'Charlotte –' he doesn't say anything else until I raise my tearstained face to look at him – 'I don't want to hurt you. Really.'

My still-smarting cheek tells another story.

'You're my . . . look, this is a confusing situation for both of us.'

'What do you want with me?'

'Go and use the bathroom, clean yourself up a bit and then we can talk.'

He steps into the room with me, and I begin to cry humiliated tears. I can't use the toilet in front of him, but my bladder feels like it's about to burst. Before I can decide what to do, he strides over to the medicine cabinet and opens it. He peruses the contents before taking out a pair of nail scissors and some bottles of medication. 'Mum's sleeping tablets,' he tells me. They must be what he gave me last night.

Then, finally, he leaves the room and I'm alone. The

mirrored door of the now empty cabinet hanging crooked from its hinges.

I glance around the room for anything I can use as a weapon.

He's smart.

I have to be smarter.

Chapter 53

Lottie

I'm back in the bedroom. There was no window in the bathroom. No way of escaping. There wasn't even a bottle of shower gel I could perhaps have squirted in his eyes to buy me time to run down the stairs.

With my hands tied in front of me, I nibble at the toast he's brought me, the thickly spread strawberry jam giving me a sugar rush. My stomach is contracting; I'm hungry but it's hard to force it down. Not when he's watching me.

We sit, facing each other, like an interrogation scene from a movie. Any minute now I expect a spotlight to shine in my face or him to start waterboarding me or something.

My vision keeps narrowing. I think my mind is trying to shut down my senses, block out what's happening to me because my hearing is all weird too. Like I'm wearing my thick yellow hat over my ears like I do when I play snowballs with Chris.

Chris.
Mum.
Dad.

Will I ever see my family again?

I'm determined to get out of here. As I eat, I take furtive glances around the room, hoping that something will spark some sort of plan. I don't really fancy my chances, but I have to try something.

I have to.

'You must have a lot of questions,' he says, taking away my plate when I've swallowed the last of my breakfast.

I don't say yes because, although I do have a lot of questions, I don't want to ask them because I'm terrified of what the answers might be.

Are you going to let me go?

Are you going to hurt me?

Are you going to kill me?

He's waiting for me to say something and so I force out a thin, 'Why?'

He carefully sets the plate on the floor, offers me more water, but I shake my head.

'I always wanted children.'

It's so ridiculous I want to laugh, but there's a wistful expression on his face and I think somehow he means it. I can't tell him he'd have made a great dad because, obvs, but I do offer a tentative, 'You have me, a daughter.'

You have me tied up because you're a fucking psycho.

'I never got the chance to have a wife and family.'

'Why?' I don't understand.

'I've been away a long time.'

'Yeah, but surely that . . . Oh. You've been in prison?' That's why he said he had nothing to offer me.

He pushes up the sleeves of his jumper. My eyes travel over his pale skin. The crude tattoos under thick black hair. Shapes that look like they've been carved into his arms.

The strawberry jam rises up in my throat. What has this man – this criminal – my father, done?

Something that Mum found out about, and what? Reported him? Testified against him? Is he trying to get back at her for something? I really don't want to know.

'It isn't too late for you. You're not that old. Men can have—'

'No. This isn't some sort of petty revenge. I haven't really given your mum a single thought over the years, but then, you turn up and I saw the big fancy house you live in, and I knew. It isn't the sort of place you live in if you're poor. You said influencers can become millionaires and—'

'Money? You think Mum has money? We're not rich. Mum rented the house for cheap because it isn't finished properly. Nobody else wanted to live there and the owner didn't want it left empty so vandals didn't break in or anything. It's not that great on the inside, really.'

'I think it's pretty flash on the inside. Yeah, with your kitchen with the marble work surfaces, that huge American fridge-freezer. That posh bath on legs where you can lie and look out at the fields. I watched more videos last night. She's a good actress, your mum, I'll give her that.' He puts on a high-pitched voice, 'I'm so scared I have a stalker and we're getting all these threats from the Joker666, and I don't know who it is.'

'She isn't making that up. There is a—'

'Oh, I *know* there's a stalker and I know *exactly* who it is.'

Of course he does. His gaze is unflinching. My blood runs cold. It is me who looks away first. What exactly is this man capable of?

The doorbell rings.

We both react at the same time, me opening my lips to release a scream and him roughly wrapping his tie around my mouth so the sound is muffled.

He makes no move to go downstairs. Probably hoping

whoever is down there, the postman, delivery driver, will go away.

But then there is a thumping on the door, so loud and so angry we both flinch. A voice calling, 'Gabriel. Open up. You know what'll happen if you don't.'

Gabriel suddenly looks smaller. Scared. He raises his finger to his lips – shhh.

'He won't help you, he's an evil bastard,' he whispers. 'He thinks I owe him money from before I was sent down.'

I see something flicker in Gabriel's eyes, fear, and my stomach contracts sharply. If he's afraid then I know that I should be terrified. But the voice outside is familiar to me.

The thumping comes again. 'I'm warning you, Gabriel.'

Gabriel flinches before he hurries out of the room. I hear his thumping footsteps on the stairs.

He's gone to open the front door.

But he hasn't locked me in again.

This is my chance to escape.

Chapter 54

Mia

These glass walls feel like a prison. Again, I find myself wanting to escape from the life I've created.

The first time I felt like that was sixteen years ago.

Sean had been working, always working, and I know he was putting in extra hours so I didn't have to. Before we had Chris, we'd talked about the parents who had raised us. The type of parents we wanted to be. We had both lost our fathers, but both grown up with our mothers waiting for us after school to walk us home. Cheering us on at sports day, applauding louder than everyone else during the nativity play as though we had been cast as Mary and Joseph and not a star and a donkey.

Sean and I had got together because we fancied each other but it was our shared family values, our moral compass, that had kept us together.

Or so I had thought, then.

Chris wasn't a difficult baby, he really wasn't. Other than a few weeks of colic when he was tiny, motherhood hadn't yet brought the challenges I had read about. The fussy eating, the temper tantrums. So why, then, did I feel so dissatisfied? Why did I feel a pang of jealousy every time I waved Sean off to work, Chris balanced on my hip, opening and closing his pudgy fist – *bye, Daddy.*

Sean was exhausting himself paying the rent on the tiny Victorian cottage we had settled in. I had fallen in love with the original features. We'd purposefully chosen Little Haven because of its location: not exactly halfway between his mum and mine, but it wasn't closer enough to either to offend the other. We were geographically nearer to Esther than anybody else. She'd married Lewis and become a stay-at-home mum too. Our boys were around the same age, but she glowed with contentment while I felt increasingly on edge. Waiting for – willing – something to happen, but I wasn't sure what. Now, looking back, I wonder if I had the baby blues, but I hadn't wanted to voice it then because I had felt like a failure and was scared of being judged.

And then came the day I met Gabriel.

The day everything changed.

It had been a light, bright morning but I remember it now in shades of grey. The vibrant blue of the sky diminished to a thick charcoal in my mind, perhaps because that's the way I sometimes think it should have been. Moody clouds and the threat of rain. Because then I wouldn't have strapped Chris into his pushchair. Stuffed the last few slices of bread into my bag. Headed off towards the murky patch of water I optimistically called a pond, where noisy ducks slid off the slimy surface. But no, despite everything that happened, I can't really regret meeting Gabriel, can I? Despite the heartache and pain and fear and the stress of the court case, there was that one thing that made it all worthwhile.

Lottie.

I had cut across the square. The wheel of the pushchair catching against the kerb, stuck. I leaned against the handle, shoving hard. The pushchair suddenly skew-whiff, wheel rolling down the gutter.

'Shit,' I muttered under my breath. Peering over the top of the hood, both reassured Chris was sleeping and wasn't scared, and pissed off that he wasn't awake and we might as well have stayed at home anyway.

I didn't know what to do. I didn't want to let go of the handle in case it tipped over. Frantically, I looked around for someone to help.

'Hey!' I shouted over to a man standing outside one of the properties on the square, the sun illuminating his blond hair. I had been watching the renovations for weeks, guessing what it might be, until the tables and chairs were added and it became apparent it was going to be a restaurant. Not one we'd be taking the kids to with the starched white tablecloths and candles as centre pieces.

He glanced over his shoulder.

'Have you got a sec?' I called again.

He began to saunter across the square.

'I need help.'

He broke into a jog.

When our eyes met, god, it's so corny to say there were sparks but I felt a jolt that travelled through me, a heat building between my legs. A desire I hadn't felt since before I fell pregnant, all in the space of about five seconds.

It was crazy. We still hadn't spoken.

Quickly he assessed the situation, green eyes travelling towards the gutter and back to Chris. He picked up the buggy with a still-sleeping Chris inside. 'You get the wheel,' and he strode off towards the restaurant with my child while I carried out his instructions before chasing after them.

The smell of the fresh white paint that coated the walls still lingered in the restaurant. It was the kind of clean space I'd tried to create in our lounge, but I'd spent so long trying to scrub off sticky toddler fingerprints and crayon, I'd resigned myself to redecorating in a more child-friendly shade. Something dark and forgiving.

'Wow. This is amazing.' I slowly spun around, appraising the different sizes of brass shades suspended from a rope pendant. The contemporary art, swirls of oranges and yellows and greens, bordered with a thin black frame. Then I lifted my sleeping child and cradled him against my chest while the man tipped the pushchair onto its side.

'Glad you like it. I'll just grab some tools.'

While he was gone, I opened one of the menus. The options were limited. Expensive. Difficult to pronounce. I'd detected the trace of an accent. What cuisine was this? French?

'You like to eat?'

I sucked my stomach in automatically, conscious I'd never really lost the baby weight.

'Yes, but my meals are all eaten one-handed now.'

He looked puzzled.

'Because of this one.' I nodded at Chris. 'Most of the time my food is cold, or it ends up all down my top.'

His eyes flickered to my chest and instead of feeling embarrassed I subtly shifted my position so my shoulders were back, spine a little straighter.

'There you go.' He righted the buggy again and stood up.

'Thank you so much. Oh, I don't even know your name?'

'Gabriel.'

'You're French?' I'd been trying to place his accent.

'*Oui*.' He smiled and it was like being bathed in golden sunshine. 'Well, my father was. My mum's from Dublin. That's why I sound like this. Do you want a coffee?'

It was my sliding-doors moment. My life could have taken an entirely different path had I said no. But then, in that alternate universe, Lottie might never have existed.

I didn't want to leave that pristine grown-up space with polished oak floors and tables with sharp corners. It was a world created by adults for adults and I longed to remain in it. Thankfully Chris was still napping.

We sipped coffee. Chatted.

'My mum used to run this shop, she was a dressmaker.'

'Was?' My brow creases.

'She's okay.' He laughed. 'She lives in the maisonette next door actually.'

'Is she involved in the restaurant?'

'No. I do have a silent partner, but family and business don't really mix. What's your story?'

'I don't really have one,' I said sadly, staring down into my espresso cup.

He leaned across the table and placed two fingers under my chin, tilting my face until our eyes met. The gesture was so cheesy, I mean, like something you'd see in a romcom, but it was also intimate and strangely erotic. I wanted to take his hand and place it against my cheek. I wanted to . . .

'I'm in a relationship.' I leaned back in my chair, widening the gap between us. 'Very happily,' I said firmly. It wasn't a lie. I loved Sean, I really did – still do – it wasn't him that I was unhappy with, it was myself.

'Okaayy. And what do you do, in this happily-in-a-relationship life of yours?' He grinned as he picked up his second coffee. I drained mine before my feelings poured out of me. The way I had never been entirely sure where I fit, what I wanted to do, even before Chris came along.

'I'm rubbish at maths, good at English. That's what my degree is in. I always dreamed of writing a book but, you know, how do you even do that? How do you get published? When I met Sean I was working as an estate agent. I love property, always dreamed of building my own lavish house.'

'With a writing room, of course.'

'Yeah.' I wanted it all. 'I thought it's important for Chris to have me at home, but I don't know what will happen when I want another job. I have a giant gap in my CV.'

'And do you want one? A job?'

'Are you offering?'

Was I flirting? I caught my fingers twirling strands of hair and I dropped my hands into my lap.

Stop it.

'We're due to open in a couple of weeks and we're looking for a manager.'

'A manager? I don't think I'm qualified.'

'Oh, I don't know. You organise schedules, mediate disputes.' He cups his mouth with his hands and whispers 'tantrums' with a nod towards Chris. 'I'm sure you can budget, there would be some basic bookkeeping.'

'Did you hear that part when I said I'm rubbish at maths?'

'I think you'd be perfect.'

That sentence ran through my mind until it transformed into 'I think you're perfect' and then I realised what a dangerous game I was playing.

Sure, a little daytime flirting with a stranger was one thing, but I loved Sean, and despite it sometimes feeling like a hamster wheel, I loved my life, and so I spewed out a list of reasons why Gabriel shouldn't hire me.

I was talking too fast, aware of the flush of my cheeks, the caffeine twitching my knee.

'You're forgetting the one reason to hire you.'

'What's that?'

'I want to.'

I want you.

A Frank Sinatra album streamed in the background. 'Fly Me to the Moon' coming at me from all the discreet Bose speakers slotted into alcoves, attached to pillars. I could fly to the moon. I could do anything I wanted to.

'Okay.' I nodded. 'I'll have to talk to Sean.'

'You need his permission?' Gabriel said lightly.

'No. But it'll mean a change for us all. Childcare. I'm sure Esther, his sister, would help out. Sean and I are equals.' My gaze was unwavering; I needed him to understand that. 'We make the decisions together. I think you should meet him.'

It was a test more than an invitation. A this-is-purely-a-job. A you-are-solely-my-boss.

'I'd like that,' he said. 'And you should meet the rest of the team. Bradley, he's my protégé. And my girlfriend too, Alma.'

Chapter 55

Lottie

I have to get away from Gabriel.

Furious voices come at me from downstairs. Gabriel's and . . . Oh. My. God.

The man shouting at him. The familiar voice.

It's Lewis.

Uncle Lewis.

How does he know Gabriel? I don't dwell on this; the most important thing is getting out of here.

I'm about to find some way of making a noise with my chair to signal for help when something stops me.

What did Gabriel say?

He won't help you; he's an evil bastard.

What if Uncle Lewis already knows I'm here? What if it's his fault that I am? Did he tell Aunt Esther to give me this address? But why would he do that? But then why would he know someone like Gabriel? Nothing is making sense.

Think.

I'm scared of Uncle Lewis right now. That's one fact that I'm sure of.

It's hard to think of him as just Felix and Daisy's dad when he's threatening to kill Gabriel if he doesn't repay him. It's bonkers that I'm scared of him, but the sense that I should be is so strong it prevents me from trying to signal to him. It's not as though I'm a blood relative of his, is it? I'm not any sort of relative now I know I'm not related to Aunt Esther.

I have to get out of here.

Think.

My hands are still tied together in front of me.

I lean forward, my fingers tugging at the knots on the rope that is wrapped tightly around my feet. If I could just get them free.

My nail snags; I wince but I don't slow down for a second. I don't know how long I've got. I resist the urge to look around the room. Try to focus on what I need to do first.

One step at a time.

That's what Alma used to say.

She said every journey begins with one single step.

I don't know if I can walk out of here. I'll throw myself out of the window if I have to. Being broken and bleeding on the pavement is preferable to this.

Quickly.

My throat swells with emotion. Really, I just want to bawl, I can't untie it.

I can't.

But that princess who saved herself didn't waste time with self-pity, did she?

I can do this. I can. But even as I keep repeating that in my head like a mantra, I'm doubting myself.

Shit. Silence.

But then the arguing starts again. This time from the lounge.

If they're both out of the hallway then I can reach the front door without them seeing me.

Quickly. Quickly.

I wiggle the knot. I think I'm pulling it tighter together. Making it more difficult.

I can do this.

Years ago, Daisy and I joined the Brownies. Knot tying was one of our badges.

I can remember some of the loops, but it doesn't help me untie them.

Or does it?

I practised at home, taught Chris. We played escapologists, timing each other.

Breathe.

I close my eyes. Letting my muscle memory kick in. Not consciously thinking and not mindlessly yanking either.

There's a loosening, a give. The rope falls away from my ankles.

I'm free.

Chapter 56

Mia

There was a freedom that came with working. A different environment. My own income. My hours were erratic. Esther helped out with Chris when Sean wasn't around. She said it gave her something to do other than spend Lewis's money. I never really knew what he did for a living – 'an entrepreneur' he would say – but they had a lovely home. I looked forward to buying things for ours. I'd been hoping for lots of tips but although we had space for twenty covers, over half of those were empty on Friday and Saturdays, what should be our busiest evenings. There were much less than that in the week.

It seemed overkill to hire more staff until business built up so, although I was officially the manager, and Alma was front of house – she had chosen her role – we both waitressed as well. I tried really hard to make friends with her as she was the boss's girlfriend, complimenting her hair, her make-up, the evil eye pendant she always wore that gave me the creeps.

Bradley brought the Labrador-puppy energy. Only in his

early twenties, he shadowed Gabriel with an enthusiasm that made me smile.

Gabriel and Bradley weren't blood relatives but Gabriel would clap him on the shoulder, 'All this will be yours one day if you play your cards right,' as though he was running an entire empire and not – from what I could see – a so-far-failing restaurant.

Upstairs was a private room. Gabriel was often in there, smoking, playing cards. Friends would visit him, coming in through the back door. I never knew who. Despite the fact that Alma was his girlfriend, there was a spark between us.

Often I'd turn around to find him appraising me with his eyes and I'd smile, ask him what he was looking at.

'I like watching you,' he'd say, and I'd turn away to hide my own smile.

But it was more than that.

I felt, because I'd been there from the start, that we were in it together. I often took ideas to him, ways to build up the business.

'We need to advertise. Perhaps contact local radio and the paper and—'

'Mia, I don't want to be one of those tacky places.'

'Tacky?'

'You know. All special offers and themed nights.'

'I didn't mention—'

'Word of mouth. That's what builds a great reputation. No amount of advertising can buy that.'

'But if there aren't enough customers talking about it?'

'Last night was busy.'

'How busy?' It had been my night off.

'You'll see when you do the books. Takings are healthy.'

And they were. The food was expensive, and most people seemed to pay cash.

'It always seems to be busy when I'm not here. I hope I'm not putting people off.' I was only half-joking.

'Mia, you couldn't put anyone off. You're the heart of this place. We're all moths to a flame around you.'

My face flushed with guilt as I realised Alma had overheard him say that.

'There's nothing going on between us,' I told her, even though she hadn't asked.

'Be careful, Mia.' Her tone made it sound like a warning rather than a threat and I began to notice how unhappy she seemed. Gone was the bright smile she had beamed into the camera as we all stood outside 'Nine, The Square' on opening night, posing for photos.

As Gabriel and Alma seemed to grow further apart, I'm ashamed to say Gabriel and I grew closer.

Lingering looks, fingers brushing a hand, an arm, shivers shimmying down my spine each time we 'accidentally' touched. Looking back now, I'm not even sure if I found him that attractive. I think what drew me to him wasn't the person he was, but the person I became when I was at the restaurant. My crisp white shirt free from splatters of strawberry yogurt, hips swaying as I sashayed in heels. Heels! It all sounds so superficial, I know, but it's as though, when I became a mum I gained something so precious, and I was grateful for that however I'm coming across, really. But I also felt I lost part of myself. At playgroups, the nursery, I was Chris's mum. With Sean at his networking events, I was 'Sean's partner'. I was fading away. Here, I was just Mia.

Me.

And then came that night. Oh god, that night.

It had begun like any other. Nine, The Square was still closed when I got there to prep, locked. I let myself in but, before I pushed the door to the kitchen open, I hesitated. I could hear raised voices. Bradley and Gabriel.

'I can't believe you've been so stupid.' Gabriel sounded furious but, not only that, there was something else in his tone. '*He'll* find out, you know.' Fear. It was fear I could detect. I wasn't sure why, but goosebumps sprang up on my arms.

'He won't, boss. It's foolproof—'

'You're a fool and I'm *not* your boss. Not anymore. Christ, he's going to think that—'

'You can't sack me off. Please. I'm sorry.'

'It's too late for sorry.'

'It isn't. What if I go and see him? Explain?'

The sound of the front door made me take hurried steps back into the dining area.

'Hi,' Alma said. 'Is Gabriel here yet?'

'I don't know.' I wasn't sure why I lied but I knew I'd overheard something I shouldn't have. 'I've only just got here.' I made a pantomime of taking my bag off my shoulder, shrugging off my coat, proving a point.

The atmosphere was weird all night. I didn't see Bradley again and Gabriel squirrelled himself away upstairs.

After a couple of hours, I went upstairs to tell him I'd locked up. There weren't any customers and I was going home. This time, it was he and Alma arguing.

'I can't believe you sent Bradley into the lion's den. He's just a baby.'

'His choice. Anyway, if he's got any sense he'll have left town and hope he's never found out.'

'I can't believe you're still . . . ' Alma was stifling sobs. 'You said that this was real. I don't want this anymore. I don't want you. It's over.'

'Alma, don't—' Gabriel began but suddenly the door was yanked open. I pressed myself against the wall as Alma strode downstairs.

'Alma, are you okay?' I asked.

She shook her head but didn't stop. I was about to follow her when there was a light touch on my arm.

'Sorry about that.' Gabriel next to me.

'What's going on? Alma's quit? I should go and check on her.'

'Leave her. We've decided to separate, and emotions are high right now. It's been a strain starting up a business. She worries too much.'

'Does she, though?' I voiced my own concerns. 'I . . . I don't understand this. We're virtually empty most of the time and you don't seem to care, and yet the books show we're making a profit.'

'Have a drink with me.' Gabriel headed back into the lounge area and poured from a bottle of Malbec.

'I have to get home.'

'Come and have a drink with me first, please?'

'Sean will be waiting.' I said his name aloud almost to remind myself that he existed, as much as a reminder to Gabriel that I had a partner even if he didn't anymore.

'I wanted to talk to you about your ideas for growing the business. I think we should start to implement them. Please, I need your help even more with Alma gone. Bradley too.'

'Where is Bradley?' Nothing I'd overheard really made any sense but I was worried about him.

'It turns out he wasn't cut out to be a restauranteur.'

'But what about—' I didn't finish, taking a deep breath, finding myself nervous but not sure why. 'I overheard you talking to Bradley earlier. You said someone would be furious. Who? Why?' My gaze was challenging. Bradley was the youngest here and I felt a sense of responsibility towards him. I think he made me wonder what Chris would be like when he grew up. Who he'd be. I hoped there'd always be someone looking out for him.

Gabriel sighed. 'I didn't want anyone to find out and think badly of him, but you know I have a business partner?'

I nodded although I'd never met them.

'Bradley has been stealing. Some customers pay in cash, and he's been pocketing it.'

'Are you sure?' I was disappointed in him, disappointed in myself for not noticing. 'And Alma? Why has she left?'

'The spark has been gone for a long time. I'm all alone now. I need you, Mia.'

I studied his expression, trying to find sincerity in it. 'Really?'

'Really. One drink?' He tilted the bottle, and I nodded.

The proverbial sheep.

'I can't believe how much I adore this place.' Gabriel twisted the stem of his wine glass around in his fingers. Crimson liquid sloshing. We'd somehow almost finished the bottle. He was listening to my plans, though. Seemed excited by them.

'I adore it too but then I knew, the second I walked in here that day, that I would.'

'Did you? I never thought I'd enjoy this.'

'So why did you open it then?'

'It was . . . it was something that I felt, I don't know, worth a try while I figured out what it is I really wanted to do, but I've fallen in love with the place, with the menus and the customers, and actually I think this is it for me. This is my future. Christ. Me a restauranteur, who'd have thought? Maybe it's being in such close proximity to my mum that makes me want to be a better person. I want to make her proud.'

We chinked.

'And how about you, Mia? What does your future look like? Are you going to stay with me?'

The candle flickered, the wine warming. I tucked my legs

under me on the sofa. With the rain drumming against the window, I felt as though there was nowhere else I'd rather be. I felt . . . and I hate admitting this now, but I felt as though I loved him.

'Do you want me?' I'd intended to finish that sentence with 'to stay'. But my words fell away from me as he ran his forefingers over the back on my hand. My head swam with wine and thoughts I should not have been having.

I was drunk but that was no excuse.

He leaned forward. An invitation.

I tilted my chin, waited.

His lips brushed against mine for seconds before we were tugging at each other's clothes.

Afterwards, he pulled at the blanket that covered the back of the sofa and draped it over us, and I snuggled into him, contented.

'Shall I fetch another bottle?'

'I'll do it.' I wrapped the blanket around me. 'There's a bottle in the cellar I've been wanting to try.'

I padded downstairs in bare feet. The door of the cellar was open, light spilling up the stairs.

A noise.

Everyone had gone for the night.

Alma?

I froze. Aware I was naked under the blanket. My instincts telling me to run away but curiosity pushing me forward.

Tiptoeing.

Crouching at the bottom of the stairs, peering into the cellar seeing, not Alma, but a man with his back to me. I watched what he was doing in shock, fear.

My breath hitched in my throat.

This wasn't right.

I couldn't let him see me.

Slowly, slowly, I retreated backwards up the stairs, towards the music Gabriel was playing. Mind full of questions as I rushed through the tables in the restaurant. Catching one with my hip. The glass candle holder sliding to the ground, smashing.

Freezing.

Footsteps.

The figure emerging from the direction of the cellar.

Lewis.

Chapter 57

Mia

I clutched the blanket tightly to cover my naked body, desperately wanting to turn away from my brother-in-law, to go upstairs and get dressed, but I was held rigid by shame and fear. The rest of the restaurant fading away in my peripheral vision. Lewis's face flickering in and out of focus.

I was going to lose everything.

'Lewis? What are you doing here?' My voice a whisper.

'I could ask you the same thing.'

'You know I work here? Esther must have told you?'

'She did but I didn't realise that you'd taken on out-of-hours duties.' His eyes travelled salaciously over me. I gripped the blanket a little bit tighter, my stomach churning.

'Well, I was upstairs, and I spilt something over myself so I'm letting my clothes dry,' my voice brittle with lies. I didn't want him to know about me and Gabriel. I didn't want him to know that I'd been anywhere near the cellar either. 'I just came downstairs to go in the kitchen and fetch—'

'Save it,' he says. 'Esther told me that there's nothing much going on in that department between you and Sean, so I don't blame you.' I felt the flush creeping round my neck. 'Let's just say you never saw me here, and I never saw,' his eyes flicked over me again, 'so much of you, and leave it at that.'

I nodded. The wine rising hot and sour in my throat.

What had I done?

Regret hit hard and fast. I couldn't love Gabriel, even though it had felt that way a few moments ago. I ran upstairs, not answering his questions as I began to scramble back into my clothes, and when I heard the engines, the slam of doors, it didn't really register. Not until the ambient glow was flooded with blue flashing lights. Police barrelling in through the front door, the back door. Me standing, frozen for the second time that evening.

Gabriel stood behind me as the police surged into the room, both of his hands on my upper arms, fingers digging painfully into my flesh. He shoved me towards them so he could get away. The feel of the rough carpet against my knees for the second time that night. This time I was moaning in pain, not pleasure, as I fell hard on my wrist, twisting it.

Scrambling across the floor, my back against the sofa, knees to my chest, arms covering my head as a lamp flew in my direction, smashing against the coffee table. Gabriel darting, left to right, punching a policeman to the ground, realising the exit was blocked. Swooping down to the floor before straightening up. Noticing the glint of the corkscrew in his hand. The manic look in his eyes as he lunged towards me. The sickening realisation that he wanted to use me as a hostage.

He wanted to use me again.

Me screaming as Gabriel was simultaneously jerked backwards. The snap of the metal handcuffs around his wrist.

'Gabriel Solas,' a police officer said, breathless, his lip bleeding, 'I'm arresting you on suspicion of money laundering. You do not have to say anything. But it may harm your defence if you do not mention when questioned something which you later rely on in court. Anything you do say may be given in evidence.'

Alma's earlier words to him came back to me: 'I thought it was real.' I'd thought she meant their relationship but perhaps she had meant the business all along. Maybe both.

I was mute with shock as he was led downstairs. Cradling my wrist. Fearful of handcuffs being used on me. Of me being arrested too.

Numb as I was helped onto the sofa. Asked to confirm my name and role.

'We need you to come to the station tomorrow and make a formal statement.'

Tears fell harder as I realised they were letting me go as if they already knew that I wasn't involved. That's when I realised someone had tipped them off.

Alma?

I was told to vacate the premises; already the search had begun. My teeth chattered while I walked shakily home. Sean took one look at my pale face when I stumbled through the door and wrapped me in his arms.

'What's happened?'

'Gabriel,' was the only thing I could say before I dissolved into tears again. Feeling Sean's grip tighten around me, the tension in it. I gathered my composure because I knew he could smell the fug of alcohol clouding me, could tell his mind was hopping from scenario to scenario and, although he'd never had reason to doubt me before, I didn't want him to land on the truth. 'The restaurant was raided, and he's been arrested,' I said.

I filled Sean in with as much as I knew and he ushered me

into a hot bath as though I was sick, bringing me a cup of sugar-laden tea. Perching on the toilet seat while I sank into coconut bubbles, washing away the scent of another man. I didn't really know what money laundering was.

'It's where someone is making cash from something illegal,' Sean explained. 'Like drug dealing or selling weapons, something like that. It's suspicious if someone spends vast amounts of money they haven't been seen to make in a legitimate way so they might buy a restaurant or another business, particularly somewhere that deals in cash, like a car wash or something. They mix the takings from their criminal activities with the takings from a legal business. It can then be deposited in a bank and spent.'

I couldn't believe this had been going on without me knowing it. It was me who used to deposit the cash takings in the bank. I felt sick that the police might think I had been involved.

As it turned out, though, only Gabriel was charged and found guilty of money laundering, resisting arrest and assaulting a police officer. I was traumatised by it all. Especially hearing about his violent past. By the time I discovered I was pregnant, it was easy to pretend he didn't exist. I buried the truth, but secrets have a way of clawing to the surface, don't they?

I know now he is free.

Lewis told me in those two words that had chilled me to the bone: 'Gabriel's out.'

Those two words that brought immediate clarity. I knew the meaning of the notes, the message on the window.

I knew I was in trouble, and I knew why.

Chapter 58

Mia

The night of Gabriel's arrest, Sean had pulled the duvet up to his chin as he rolled onto his side. I curled myself into him, hoping that the heavy rise and fall of his chest would lull me into a deep sleep too. I had cleaned my teeth, but I could still taste the wine sour on my throat, could still taste Gabriel.

When I closed my eyes, I saw the flickering candlelight, his face looming towards me, felt the roughness of his lips on mine. In my mind, though, I pictured a different outcome. Me pushing him away, saying no.

Why hadn't I said no?

I pressed my fingertips against my eyelids as I tried to contain my sobs so my body didn't shake.

Spinning. Everything was spinning. Alcohol and remorse and a cold fear rocking the bed, the floor.

I thought I was going to throw up.

Tomorrow, I had to give a statement. Sean had already said he'd come to the station with me because he's a good man.

Why hadn't I said no?

Although the room was pitch-black, I was seeing clearly for the first time in what felt like forever. There had been a physical distance between Sean and me because he had been working so hard building a future for us, trying to fulfil our dream of someday owning our own house, my dream of someday building one. The emotional distance, though, was down to me. I'd taken his exhaustion as a lack of interest in me. Self-conscious about the way my body had changed since pregnancy. I'd blamed my exhaustion on him not helping out with Chris. The more I'd nagged him, the further he had pulled away, when what I really should have been saying is, *I love you, I need help*. Because the momentary excitement I had felt with Gabriel earlier, that fleeting euphoria, highlighted to me how low I had actually felt since Chris had been born. I adored my baby with every fibre of my being, but I hadn't felt like *me* since. I'd been carrying around this low-level anxiety, the perpetual feeling of impending doom. I should have told someone, rather than thinking it was a failure of sorts, that I'd be a failure if I didn't smile brightly at the doctor, the midwife, the health visitor: 'everything is fine, I've never felt better.' My feelings confused and conflicted. I had a healthy child, surely I shouldn't be feeling so down.

I wanted Sean and I to be the best parents we could be. I also wanted us to be us again.

I wanted the pressure, the crushing weight of expectation that I had placed upon my own shoulders, to lift. And wanting something to be okay is the first stage to making things okay, isn't it?

I couldn't magic-wand-abracadabra into our happy ever after but . . .

What if?

The same thought kept battering me and I tried to ignore it, resist it, change it into something else, but that proved entirely fruitless.

What if?

And so I slipped out of bed. Slipped out of the house. Really, looking back, I can't believe I did it. I think I was in shock. It was as though I also slipped out of my own skin. Became someone I didn't recognise. I think, honestly, looking back, I haven't recognised myself since that night.

The restaurant was in darkness when I skulked down the street, dressed in black, sticking to the shadows. I wasn't certain what I was going to do because I didn't know what I'd find. In truth I had envisaged blue and white crime scene tape to be stretched across the entrance, or possibly a policeman guarding the entrance, maybe even the search still taking place, but there was nothing. In a way it would have been a relief if I hadn't been able to slide my key into the lock after furtively checking over my shoulder and let myself in, because then I wouldn't have had to make a decision.

What if?

It was eerie standing in the empty restaurant. I'd expect the police search to result in disarray, tables and chairs upended, contents of drawers emptied like I'd seen once on TV but, although there were things that had been moved and not returned to their rightful place, you wouldn't know what had happened here only hours before.

With only the dim light of the streetlamp casting through the windows, I made my way towards the door upstairs. I could hardly bear to go in the room where I had betrayed Sean, but I had to. I didn't look at the sofa, didn't look at anything except the picture hanging on the wall.

My heart was hammering in my chest as I lifted it down. Behind it, the safe unlocked, empty. The takings from the restaurant, or what Gabriel was pretending were cash takings, were gone. Of course.

A noise.

I held my breath. Forehead beading with sweat. I didn't know if I was breaking any laws, but my behaviour was questionable, to say the least.

Again, I heard a scraping. I realised it was from the maisonette next door, Gabriel's mum.

My heart twisted. Did she know about her son? I thought of the way he'd spoken earlier about her. That conversation made sense to me now. He'd bought the restaurant as a front but ended up loving it. He'd wanted to be better for her, a better son. I wanted to believe that.

I headed down to the basement. Where I had seen Lewis earlier with his arm stretched high up into the chimney flue.

I opened the iron door and shoved my hand inside. I couldn't feel anything. Any gaps. Any hiding places. I knew what I had seen, though.

Frustrated, I pushed at all the bricks. Nothing moved. I pushed against them again, this time at an angle.

There was a give.

I pulled the loose brick out and thrust my hand in again, feeling for the bundles of paper. I pulled them out one by one. Stacks of notes held together with grubby elastic bands.

I couldn't believe the police hadn't found it.

It was my next sliding-doors moment.

What if?

Quick as a flash, I could see a life unfolding where we could buy a house, Sean wouldn't have to work so hard, and I'd spend the rest of my life trying to make up for the things I could not tell him.

Or I could go home.

Stay safe.

I was trembling so hard as I sank to my haunches.

What if?

I could take the money: the police didn't know it was there; Gabriel would never give up his secrets and tell them. If there was enough evidence to arrest him then surely he'd be detained, prosecuted. He'd hardly expect it to still be there when he was released, would he? He might even assume a dodgy officer took it.

What if?

What if Lewis came back for it? I did't think he'd been arrested as well, or Esther would have called either Sean or me.

What if?

What if this came back to haunt me and I regretted it for the rest of my life?

My mum's voice echoed around my mind: 'You only regret the chances you didn't take.'

I felt detached from myself as I dropped the money inside my bag, slipped out of the back door.

Went home and pretended to be normal.

I've been pretending ever since.

Finding six figures of cash that no one was going to report missing is a dream, isn't it? But here's the thing: it isn't the 'fix-all, life-changing, dreams-come-true experience' you might think. There's not a lot you can do with it, not quickly anyway. If you take it to a bank then there'll be questions, a lot of questions. If you suddenly drive around in a sports car you've paid cash for, well, you might get away with it, but you'd be likely be drawing attention to yourself.

I had all this money and in the following days I found I just couldn't tell Sean. How could I explain it? He'd be horrified.

Esther and Lewis came round. I tried to avoid being alone with him, but it was inevitable.

'Did you know?' he asked me.

'No. I was just the waitress.' He studied me but I held his gaze.

'Did you take anything?'

'No. I haven't even been paid for this last week. I don't know how we're going to manage.'

He nodded. He knew that financially we were struggling.

'Maybe Bradley will know where it is?'

'Bradley was gone before the money was taken.'

Gone?

There was something in the way Lewis said this that sent a chill crawling down my spine. The last thing I'd overheard Bradley say to Gabriel was that he was going to go and visit '*him*' and make it right. Now I knew that '*him*' was Lewis.

Gone?

His mouth twisted into a grin. 'Don't worry, Mia. Bradley won't talk.' He leaned in and whispered in my ear, 'He can't. You be careful what you say. We wouldn't want Sean to *disappear* too, would we?'

And so I believed, rightly or wrongly, that Lewis had, if not killed Bradley himself because he had stolen from him, paid someone else to do it, and I was terrified that he might carry out his threat and hurt Sean.

We continued to struggle because I couldn't arouse Lewis's suspicion by spending the money I wasn't meant to have. After Esther and Sean's mum passed away, we moved into the small house they'd been raised in. All the time I kept buying the kids things from charity shops. I went to the supermarket late in search of yellow-stickered items. I sensed Lewis watching me. I kept quiet.

Every time I wanted to tell Esther who the man she

had married actually was, I chickened out. Scared of the repercussions. Scared for Sean, the kids, all of us. It might sound weird but, over time, I separated that Lewis the criminal from Lewis the family man, the brother-in-law I rarely saw but heard lots about from Esther. Then, in my mind, I could also separate the Mia I had been from the one I wanted to become. The one who had never slept with Gabriel. In my head we became two different versions of Lewis and Mia and it made everything a little easier to bear.

Building a house had always been my dream. There was a plot of land that wasn't expensive; it was in an area that had flooded in the past. Buyers were wary so I bought it in cash. Then came the painstaking build. In my head I thought I'd create my ideal home, nothing too flashy, but I'd always wanted a house made of glass and then, one day, I'd share it with Sean. Enough years would have passed with us going without so Lewis wouldn't suspect anything other than the truth I'd create. I'd pretend I'd won one of the property raffles you see online but think nobody ever really wins. I don't really know how I thought I'd explain it, hoped Sean would be so excited he wouldn't ask too many questions.

It took such a long time to construct. Everything was paid for in cash (and builders love cash, I've found) but I couldn't do too much at once for fear of creating gossip. There was problem after problem. Eventually I ran out of money and the glass house remained my broken dream. So many times I thought about selling it but then it would all have been such a waste.

It wasn't until Sean and I separated and Esther decided to move back into my – her – house that I really considered living in it. It was easy to convince everyone I was renting it cheap because it wasn't finished.

My dream home, my nightmare scenario without Sean.

A constant reminder that one day Gabriel would be released.

That he might suspect it was me who took his money.

That he'd want it back.

Chapter 59

Lottie

I'm straining really hard to hear what Gabriel and Lewis are saying. Their voices are muffled but the walls are thin, and I can make out most of it.

'I've been really patient while you've been inside,' Lewis says. 'I haven't wanted to be associated with you, but I told you last week, now you're out, I want my money.'

'And I told you I don't have it. It doesn't seem like you need it anyway. I've heard you've invested in loads of restaurants now.'

'That's beside the point. Anyway, I'm going through a divorce. I'm going to need every penny.'

'I kept quiet about you. There wasn't a paper trail to you, but I could have given the police your name and had them investigate all your dodgy—'

'I'm a reputable businessman.'

'Only because you let others do your dirty work.'

There's a low laugh. 'I should be on *Dragons' Den*.'

'Look, I told you last week that someone must have

taken the cash. It wasn't here when I got back. Do you think I'd have hung around if it had been here?'

'And I gave you time to find out who.'

'I've been thinking about Mia.'

'I'm sure you've thought about her a lot in the last few days since I told you she'd had your kid.'

'I don't mean thinking about the kid. I mean that Mia could have taken the money.'

'Nah. Her and her deadbeat husband have lived in poverty for years. He used his own money to pay his employees, sad bastard. If she'd have taken the cash I'd have seen her spend it over the years.'

'But she lives in this huge glass house now.'

'She rents it cheap. Felix says it's a complete shit-hole. Never finished. It wasn't Alma either before you start. She's a nurse now and living in a tiny flat. I've spoken to her.'

'Look, I still think Mia—'

'I don't really care what you think. I care what you do. I'll be back in a few days and if you haven't got my money you won't be walking out of here. Remember Bradley?' Uncle Lewis's voice is calm now and somehow it's scarier than when he was shouting.

Hurry.

My fingers tug the gag away from my mouth, pushing it down so it's draped around my neck like a scarf, but if feels more like a noose.

I lick my lips. They're dry and sore where I've bitten them over and over during the past twenty-four hours in an effort to stop myself bawling, so afraid that I wouldn't be able to breathe under the gag if I gave way to my emotions.

My hands are still tied, and I tug at the knot with my teeth, aware that I'm wasting time, but I'm also thinking, not sure what to do.

There's a thud.

Not a person being hit but a wall perhaps or the door?

It sounds more frightening down there than it is in here. With a light tread, I'm at the window. I pull back the yellowing net curtain that is stiff to the touch, peering out of the grubby glass. The square is deserted, the weather still vile. Where is the old lady who was walking the dog yesterday? I glance downwards and see a car and for a moment my heart lifts and my palms get ready to bang on the window, but then I realise it belongs to Uncle Lewis.

I lift up the handle on the window. Maybe I can shimmy down a drainpipe or clamber up onto the roof or something. I can't even think about the consequences if I slip. I'm so desperate I don't care.

The window won't open. At first I think it's stuck because it's perhaps been shut for a long time so I put my weight against it, but it holds fast.

Shit.

I bounce up and down on my toes, frustrated tears welling.

I want Mum.

Chris.

Dad.

But the only one here is me. Trapped by angry voices and my own insecurities, but then I think, *Fuck it*, remembering when I put on my plays. *Pretend to be someone else. Pretend this is all an act.*

I'm a character. Nothing more. This is not me. Not my life.

I am that princess who saved herself.

Slowly, slowly, I tiptoe towards the door, holding my breath with every single step. I'm on the landing. There are two other doors up here. I know one is the lounge. I head towards the other room. Another bedroom I think. I know that doesn't have a way out. I head towards the other room. There might be a window that opens or a phone or something.

The room smells of stale smoke. The curtains closed. The wallpaper is faded roses, bedspread pink and frilly. On the dressing table are bottles of perfume, talcum powder. There's a sepia wedding photo in a tarnished silver frame. The couple look so happy as they gaze into each other's eyes. My grandparents, great-grandparents perhaps. This must have been my grandmother's room and it's so weird that I'm here and she's not and everything is fucked.

Behind the curtain, this window is also locked. I scan the room for a phone but there isn't one. I thought old people always had one of those handsets that plugs into the wall in case they fell over or something like Gran had before she moved into the home.

I wish I had my bag, my mobile.

I head for the door and shuffle towards the banister, crouching low so the men can't look up and see me.

I can see the back of Gabriel, and the legs and feet of Lewis.

They're heading back towards the front door and . . .

Oh god.

I'm scuttling back to the room, sitting on the chair, hurriedly pulling the scarf around my mouth, rope around my ankles, wrists. Heart pounding. Pounding. Pounding out of my chest.

Gabriel looks as scared as I feel as he comes back into the room.

I don't look at him. I'm sweating. Will he notice that the ropes aren't tied properly?

'Tell me again about your mum, the glass house. Your brother.'

'Chris?' Why does he want to know about Chris?

'I need to know everything, Lottie. I need to make a plan.'

Chapter 60

Mia

At first, when someone began tormenting me, I'd been convinced it was Harlow. Then, when it became tragically apparent that it wasn't, my suspicions had turned to Alma. I'd taken something from her – Gabriel. I quickly dismissed this, though, because she was then – seems to be now – really sweet-natured. Besides, the last note had threatened Lottie directly and I know Alma thinks the world of her.

When Lewis whispered those two words – *Gabriel's out* – with a chilling smile on his face, it had all fallen into place.

I want what's mine.

Garbriel wants the cash I took.

I don't know how far he'll go to get it. He's hurt people before, that came out in the trial. I think he must have hurt people since, inside, and had his sentence extended.

I'm cutting up a pineapple. It's Lottie's favourite fruit and I'm hoping she'll be home today. The ringing phone startles me and my knife slips. I wince and suck at the blood as I check my mobile.

Chris's teacher, Mrs Harrison.

'Mia, this is a bit awkward, but have you heard from Chris?'

'No. He's on the trip in Norfolk. Hang on, aren't you on the trip in Norfolk?'

'I am but . . . I don't quite know how to say this, but Chris has disappeared.'

Chapter 61

Who's Watching You Documentary

Jake Lawler (host): Next, we welcome Mei Chen who works at the outward bounds centre in Norfolk where Chris Finch and Marco Hernandez went for their residential trip. Hello, don't look so nervous, I don't bite (curves fingers into claws) unless you want me to. (laughs)

Mei Chen (activity co-ordinator): (clears throat) Thank you.

Lawler: Now, can you tell us in your own words what happened on that trip?

Chen: Yes. (shifts on seat, looks at camera, looks away again) The first day was tense. You could sense something was going to happen between Chris and Marco.

Lawler: Did Chris antagonise him?

Chen: No, not at all. Chris let him go

first in the dinner queue. Let him play pool before him, even though Chris had been waiting for longer.

Lawler: So how did this tension escalate?

Chen: Marco was playing pool against Felix, Chris's cousin. Felix won and made a joke about Marco being a loser, and Marco lunged at him. Chris stepped between them to try and calm things down. Marco had his fists up and Chris kept saying, 'I won't fight you.'

Lawler: But he did.

Chen: He didn't. Marco punched him around three times. Chris was on the floor and Marco kicked him. That's when the teachers came to break it up. Chris's nose was bleeding, his mouth too, but he just . . . he just took it, as though he felt he deserved it.

Lawler: And then what happened?

Chen: Marco's father was called to pick him up immediately. Chris, though, he took off. Everyone was going frantic looking for him. His family were called. It was only later, of course, we learned that he'd made his own way home.

Lawler: They must have ruined the trip for everyone. You put a lot of effort into planning these things, don't you?

Chen: Nobody was angry. It was just so incredibly sad. You can't help thinking that if their mothers hadn't put themselves and those poor boys on social media, their lives would have been very different. Maybe Mia would still have both of her children with her.

@Lamadrama23 Marco was out of order having a pop at Chris!!!

@Avocadomonkey Javier apologised for his son when he was on the show tho

@Blackcat1970 It makes you think, doesn't it? That's why I don't agree with sharing so much of yourself online

@Avocadomonkey Hard disagree. My kiddies will love it when they're older. Seeing all their childhood documented forever

@Blackcat1970 Will they, though? I think social media can be dangerous

@Jamie2983 And yet you're STILL here

Chapter 62

Mia

Chris is missing. I'm frantic as I call Sean.

He answers the phone with a curt, 'Hello.'

'Chris's school have just called me and—'

'He's fine,' Sean says. 'I just was going to ring you.'

'But he isn't at the residential?'

'He texted me. There was some sort of fight with Marco Hernandez.'

I draw breath sharply.

'He says he's not hurt. But he got on a bus and he's on his way home.'

'Right.' Knowing Chris is okay, that he isn't missing, is a huge relief, but I can't help feeling wounded that he'd called Sean and not me. 'Well, that's good.' I hesitate. Wondering if he's going to fill the silence, but he doesn't. He hasn't hung up, though. That's a good sign but the iciness between us chills me. I need to try and explain why I put offal in the hot tub the best I can.

'I know you're angry with me.'

'I'm furious.'

'For what it's worth, I am sorry.'

I'll be apologising throughout this conversation, I know. Throughout every conversation I have these next few days, weeks, as long as it takes my family to, maybe not forgive me, not straight away – I don't expect, deserve, absolution – but to understand. Understanding, accepting even if you don't like something, is the first step on the path to peace, isn't it?

'What were you thinking?' He doesn't sound so angry anymore, just incredibly weary.

'I wasn't. I think . . . ' I pinch the bridge of my nose. I won't cry. I want to explain myself the best I can but it's difficult to choose the right words. I can hardly say that once I stole a lot of money and the person I stole it from wants it back. That I'm so desperate. So scared that someone will get hurt – that the children might get hurt – I staged a stupid stunt that terrified them.

'It was an impulse decision.' I bite my lip, the wrong phrase has escaped. Even though I didn't really give myself time to think it through, I had to drive to the butcher's to get the offal. There was plenty of time for me to have changed my mind. I just chose not to. 'I mean, I didn't want to hurt anyone.' My voice breaks.

'I know you didn't, Mia.' Sean's tone is softer now. 'But you have to accept it isn't our house anymore and Esther has spent a lot of time and money making it her own and—'

'What? What's the house, Esther, got to do with this?'

I can't figure out what this has to do with what I did at the glass house with the hot tub.

'Well, everything. I know it's upsetting, if I'm honest it upset me, but who wants a height chart with someone else's kids—'

'Height chart? I don't know what you're talking about?' I'm so confused.

'You drew lines on the wall, by the back door? Wrote Chris and Lottie's names on the fresh paint?'

A beat.

'On Daisy's birthday.'

'Yes.' It comes back to me know but it seems so irrelevant in the face of everything. I don't know why he's bringing it up when our daughter turned up on his doorstep yesterday, distraught because of the terrible thing I did. Sean sounds as though he doesn't know, but he has to know. We were messaging about it, weren't we?

I'm doubting myself as I lower my phone and scroll again through my messages. The first one I sent him:

We need to talk. Is she really upset?

Of course she's bloody upset. So am I. Furious. I can't believe you did that.

And yes, we do need to talk but give it a couple of days so we can all calm down.

As I reread them, I can see where the confusion lies. I hadn't used Lottie's name when I'd asked if she was still upset. He thought I was messaging about Esther. I feel a little zing. Lottie can't have told him what I did. That means she still feels some semblance of loyalty towards me. She still cares.

Perhaps she even understands.

If she hasn't told him by now she likely never will. Chris won't tell him either if I ask him not to when he gets home from his trip. I'm uncomfortable with the thought of putting him in that position but it's hardly the worst thing I've done, is it? I can figure something out with Gabriel. A way to repay him without doing anything else so stupid. I can maybe shift some of this weight that's always pressing down on my chest.

'I'm sorry about the height chart. It was childish. A knee-jerk reaction. I just saw the blank space on the wall, and I remembered.' My voice cracks.

'Me too. I know it's hard. It's tough for me living here, expecting to come home after work every day to find you here, the kids.'

'How is Lottie today?' I focus on why I'm calling.

'How would I know? She's with you.'

Dread curdles.

'No. She stayed with you last night.'

'Why would she? It isn't my day.'

'Because of—' I stop; it would take too long to explain. 'Did you see her at all yesterday? Speak to her?'

'No. Mia, you're scaring me. What's going on? Where is Lottie?'

Chapter 63

Mia

Sean tells me that he'll call the police on his way round. That I'm to stay put. Try to call Lottie. Chris.

Lottie's phone is going straight to voicemail.

Has he taken her? Has Gabriel taken her?

I can't quite believe he has. There hasn't been any ransom demand, has there? The thought of this doesn't calm me. Where else could she be? I run through her friends. Most of them disappeared when she first went into hospital.

I call Chris, praying he doesn't reject my call. I don't usually ring him; he prefers to communicate via WhatsApp. I'd only call if there were something wrong.

Pick up.

Pick up.

Pick up.

'Mum?' He sounds cautious.

'Do you know where your sister is?'

'She went to Dad's. She left you a note.'

'She isn't with Dad. He hasn't seen her. She's been gone all night.' My voice is verging on hysteria, and I know I should be trying to be calm so I don't scare him, but I can't control the panic that is forcing me to pace, pace, pace as I grip the handset so hard my fingers hurt.

'Can you think of anywhere she might be? Anyone she might be with?'

'She only really has us, and Daisy. There's Daisy's friend Erika. All her old friends abandoned her.'

'I'm going to start ringing round. Call me if you hear anything.' I hang up. Then punch out an 'I love you' message to Chris because I need to say it and he needs to hear it right now.

Then I begin to call the contacts I have in my phone. Mothers of children who have not been around to hang out with Lottie for such a long time. It's fruitless. No one has seen her.

Does Gabriel have her?

What if he does? I don't have the money to give him to get her back.

What am I going to do?

The only way out of this mess is to pay Gabriel.

Or kill him.

The thought pops into my head, unbidden, and I dismiss it straight away.

I'm not a killer.

But I am desperate.

No.

No.

No.

But . . .

No.

My head is muzzy. It's like there's a swarm of bees buzzing around my brain, frantic and directionless. There's a constant noise I cannot quiet.

I cannot think clearly.

Where is Lottie?

Where is my daughter?

Sean arrives, so deathly pale I push a glass of water in his hand and make him sit down. Minutes later, the police. The officer is the same one who came here a couple of days ago. Then, the blue lights had flashed on his car; there had been a sense of urgency in his movements after Chris's frantic call that someone had been murdered.

Today, although the response time has been impressive, he regards me with suspicion.

'I was in this area, but I certainly wasn't expecting to see you again this week, Mrs Finch.'

'My daughter is missing,' I say at the same time Sean asks, 'Again?'

'Is this another "prank" to boost followers?'

'No. It isn't. I prom—'

'Can one of you tell me what's going on?' Sean has a hard edge to his voice. 'My daughter is missing and—'

'Yes. She must have been very distressed after your wife's little stunt.' There's the hint of a smirk on his lips.

Regret and shame are a crushing weight on my chest.

'Mia?' Sean says sharply.

I take a shaky breath, tell him what I did, and I swear to God I will never forget the revulsion on his face. He physically recoils from me as though I am a monster, and I think perhaps I am.

'No wonder she's upset. She's run away, hasn't she? I'm going to look for her myself.'

'But—'

'I'll try the places she loved as a kid. That picnic spot on the top of Hope Hill.'

He runs from the house and jumps into his car before I can tell him that I don't think she's run away.

'If she doesn't turn up—' the policeman begins.

'No.' I grab his arm as he turns, releasing it quickly as his face darkens. It doesn't matter if my secrets are exposed.

If I have to admit I am a thief and a liar, I need him to track down Gabriel and see if he has her.

'I think she's been taken.' I remind him of the notes. Explain about the wreath. The threats on the comments. The fact that someone had been in the house, written a message on the window, but I can tell he doesn't believe a word I'm saying.

I am the boy who cried wolf.

Just then there's a crackle on his walkie-talkie. He speaks into it, in a low voice.

'I've got to go, Mrs Finch.' He's walking away again.

'You can't just leave. Haven't you listened to anything I've been saying? I can give you a name. An address.'

'And you have proof?'

'No. But—'

'There's been a stabbing.'

My knees buckle.

'It isn't a girl.' He realises what I must be thinking. 'But I have to go. Come down to make a statement at the station if Lottie doesn't turn up soon. I think her dad is right, though. She was upset about your little stunt, and she ran away.'

He's already climbing in his car. Driving away.

Sean isn't right.

Sean isn't her father.

I snatch my car keys.

I think Gabriel has her and if the police won't go and get her, then I will, but where do I even start? Little Haven would be a dead end. I've driven through it several times over the years and it's a ghost village now. No amenities. Most of the properties on the square gone.

Where would he have gone?

I'm about to call Alma to see if she can think of anywhere he might be when my phone rings.

News.

Chapter 64

Lottie

I've tried to answer all of Gabriel's questions without giving too much away. The thought of him anywhere near Chris makes my stomach roll. I don't ask him anything about Uncle Lewis or Bradley. I don't care about anything other than staying alive and getting out of here right now.

'Fuck's sake,' he mutters as he scrolls through his phone. 'You're all over social media.'

'Yeah, well.' I don't know what to say about that. 'I told you Mum started a channel.'

'I don't mean that. This.' He thrusts his handset in my face and I flinch, scared he's going to hit me again.

'What is this?'

I scan the posts he's showing me. Gabriel is right. I am all over social media. #LookForLottie is trending.

My heart lifts. Chris must have done this.

They know I'm missing. Someone will find me.

'The whole country will be looking for me,' I say.

'Of course they won't,' he says, but he sounds unsure. He's been away. He doesn't know about the power of social media, the good and the bad. The TikTok detectives who will already be tracing my last steps.

'They will.' #LookForLottie will stir everything up again, Mum and Harlow, all of it, but right now I'm glad of it because I think it just might save my life.

'If you let me go now I won't tell anyone where I've been. I promise I'll—'

'Got it.' He lifts his head and smiles, and the smile is the creepiest one I've ever seen. Worse than that Pennywise in *It*. That clown had freaked me out so badly when Chris and I watched it but not as badly as this. What does he mean, "Got it"?'

'I'm going to ask your mum for the money she owes me and as soon as she's paid then you'll be free to go,' he says.

'But she doesn't have any money.'

'Lottie, that huge glass house—'

'I told you. It isn't finished. We live there cheaply because the landlord—'

'There is no landlord.' He shoves his phone at me again, but I don't really understand what I'm looking at. 'Your mum. Your mum owns the house.'

My head is reeling. How can Mum own the house? It's impossible. And yet he has proof and, yeah, basically it makes more sense than some dodgy agent renting out somewhere that's such a hazard.

Again, I feel so let down. Is there anything she hasn't lied to me about? I can't trust her at all. I certainly can't trust that she'll figure this out and come and save me.

But then, in the distance, I hear a car.

Chapter 65

Mia

When Chris called and said that as a result of his #LookForLottie campaign someone had given him an address where she was, I had been doubtful. I've seen from the comments on our posts, from @Joker666 and every other weirdo, that the internet can bring out the worst in people. This could be a joke. A trap. But then it seems like the internet can also spawn amazing things because the address he gives me is so familiar to me I know in an instant that this lead is genuine.

The drive to Little Haven is fast and frantic. I abandon my car outside a house with boarded-up windows just before I get to the square. I can't believe Gabriel came back here when he was released. Everywhere is derelict.

I walk to the edge of the square. I can see the restaurant, but I don't approach it yet as I try and formulate a plan because, now I am here, I don't quite know what to do. I can hardly knock on the door and demand he gives her back, can I?

I don't know what I expected to find. Lottie sitting on

the bench opposite the restaurant, waiting for me. Hoped. It's what I'd hoped to find.

Would he hurt her?

I'd like to think not. She's just a child. His child.

But then, he doesn't know that she's his daughter, does he? I never told him I was pregnant. To him, she's mine and Sean's. A stranger. A bargaining chip.

Does that make her more in danger?

And I don't know him anymore. I don't know the ways in which years in prison might harden a person. I suppose I never knew him, not really.

I'm lost in thought. Vaguely aware of the sound of a car engine. A door slamming. Footsteps pounding behind me. Suddenly, hot breath on the back of my neck.

A hand gripping my arm.

I spin around.

'Chris?' I blink rapidly, unable to trust what I'm seeing. My son. My boy. Black eye and split lip. My stomach pitches. What have my children been through because of me?

'I got off the bus and got a cab. What's the plan?'

'I don't know,' I admit. 'Do you know who got in touch with you after seeing your #LookForLottie posts and told you to come here?' The thought it might be Gabriel laying a trap is much on my mind.

'It was Erika. You know, Daisy's friend.'

'But how did she know that—'

'Shut up. I'm telling you. She'd been upstairs yesterday, in Daisy's room while Daisy was in the shower. She heard the bell ring and because Daisy's door was open she overheard Esther and Lottie talking.'

'Lottie went to Esther's? But—'

'Mum! *Stop* interrupting. Esther told Lottie that Dad – Sean – isn't her dad.'

His words dry my mouth. I cannot speak. Cannot move.

I'm held in his contemptuous gaze, a spider caught in a web of my own making.

He knows.

Lottie knows.

'Esther gave Lottie this address. Erika didn't tell Daisy, didn't tell anyone. It wasn't until she saw my #LookForLottie campaign that she realised Lottie was missing. I've come to get my sister back.'

The ground is shifting beneath my feet. Esther told Lottie.

I feel my fury rise at her because it's easier than being angry with myself. How could she shatter Lottie's world like that?

She's clearly ashamed that she did because she obviously hasn't told Sean about that conversation, has she? Or he'd have mentioned it to me.

I swallow hard, hot and uncomfortable under Chris's glare.

There's so much I want to – need to say – to him, to both of them, but now is not the time.

'Where's this restaurant?' Chris asks.

'It was there.' I point towards the empty building. My eyes are drawn towards the maisonette next door. It seems unlikely that Gabriel's mum would still live here. Not when everything is in the process of being torn down, but I have to check.

'I think now we're certain she's here, we should ring the police.' I don't care about the consequences to me.

'Why? She's just come to meet her dad. She'll probably be glad of a lift home now.'

'Chris.' This gets worse and worse. What a tangled web I've weaved and how hard it is to try and unpick it. 'I don't think she's still in there voluntarily.'

'I don't get it.'

'Her father . . . Gabriel. He isn't a nice person. He's been in prison and . . . ' Oh god. 'I took, I stole something from him. I think he might be keeping Lottie until I pay him back.'

'What the fuck, Mum? Just pay him back.'

'I can't. I don't have the money.'

Chris gnaws on his lip. Thinking. 'That's why you staged the hot tub thing?'

'Yes.'

'If we call the police will they even believe you? They can't get in there if he doesn't let them in without a warrant. Would they even get a warrant? How long would that take?'

'I don't know, Chris.' I don't have all the answers. I don't have any of them.

'On TV it takes about an episode, an hour?'

'I don't think anything works like it's portrayed on TV.'

'Then we have to get her out,' he says.

'I'm going to knock on the door. See if he's there. See what he says. Reason with him.' I say even though I know there is no reasoning with a man like Gabriel. 'Wait here.'

'No. I'm coming with you.'

'You're not. You either stay here or I'll call Sean and we'll wait together for him to come and take you home and—'

'Okay. Okay. I don't want leave Lottie in there any longer than we have to.'

Chris leans against the wall and crosses his arms resentfully.

My legs are shaking as I head towards the front door. It seems as though I've got it wrong. Gabriel didn't take Lottie. She came here of her own volition. He'll know that Lottie's his daughter if she's turned up and told him.

I'm confident he won't hurt her.

I'm not confident he won't hurt me, but I can take it. I can take anything as long as my kids are safe.

Once shiny and blue, the door is now all flaking paint
and rusting letterbox. I lift and drop the tarnished knocker.
Shout through the letterbox.
'Lottie? Lottie?'
Silence.
Until . . .
Slowly, slowly the door swings open.
Gabriel.

Chapter 66

Mia

'Mia.' Gabriel doesn't look surprised to see me.

He has her.

Oh god, he really has her.

'I'm looking for my daughter.'

'*Your* daughter?'

He does know.

His smile is ice. As he takes a step forward, I hold my ground. I might be intimidated by him, but I won't let him see that I am. I can smell the coffee on his breath. See every open pore on his nose. Feel the threat radiating from him. The ugliness.

How could I ever have thought him attractive?

'Yes. *My* daughter,' I say firmly. I'm trying to pretend I am not intimidated but my knees are weak. I am so, so scared right now.

'And why do you think she's here?'

My mouth dries.

He knows.

'The police know where I am.'

'Do they? Did they come to that big glass house of yours for a chat?'

I inhale sharply. It was him who came to the house, left the notes. I suspected as much but . . .

'Had fun scaring me in my own home, did you?' I try to sound nonchalant.

'I don't know what you're talking about. Remember that night. The night I left the restaurant?' He picks up strands of my hair and twirls it around his fingers. I smell the nicotine on them as I slap them away, stomach roiling as I remember them running over my eager naked body.

'Left? Was marched out in handcuffs, you mean.' I try to sound braver than I feel. 'Where's Lottie? Is she here?'

'Maybe.' He gives that a moment while I swallow back down the vomit that is rising in my throat. I try to push past him, but he pushes me back.

'Not so fast. I might have something of yours, but do you have something of mine? Some money. Only it wasn't mine and if I don't pay the person back I owe it to them.' He runs his index finger across his throat.

Panic is twisting my internal organs; he has my daughter, I know it.

He thinks I have his money, and he has her.

And he's desperate.

Suddenly he grabs hold of my coat by the neck and drags me inside. I'm kicking fingers, trying to prise his hands off me.

My chest hurts, my heart thumping against my rib cage.

'Lottie!' I'm screaming. 'Lottie?'

And then, from upstairs, a noise.

Chapter 67

Lottie

I hear Mum yelling my name. I'm stamping my feet on floor. Trying to scream through the gag.

Help.

Help.

Help.

And then the door opens.

Chris is there and I sag with relief.

I am saved.

But, although there are three of us and only one of him, I know that Gabriel won't let us walk out of here without a fight.

Chapter 68

Who's Watching You Documentary

Jake Lawler (host): Next on the sofa is Detective Inspector Russell Sinclair, who I'm sure will be giving *Who's Watching You* yet another exclusive. (grins into the camera) Welcome. (turns to detective and holds out his hands) I'll come quietly. (smile drops as detective doesn't smile back. Hands return to lap) So, Russell—

Detective Inspector Russell Sinclair (lead detective in Finch case): Detective Sinclair.

Lawler: (tight smile, muscle in jaw pulsing) Detective. I'm delighted you have chosen *Who's Watching You* for your one and only TV interview.

Sinclair: You have the biggest reach.

Lawler: Yes, (smiles at camera, hand covers heart) I can't take *all* the credit for that, though. Our research team is brilliant. I'm sure you can give us a rare insight into—

Sinclair: I'm not here to discuss the case.

Lawler: (frowns) Then why—

Sinclair: The *only* reason I've joined you today is because you fuel the fires of armchair detectives, and I want to reiterate how dangerous it can be when social media jumps on a theory and doesn't let it go. TikTok especially can be damaging. However well-intentioned people are, they can hinder the case, prejudice opinions.

Lawler: Here on this show—

Sinclair: It's exactly the same. Your researchers are glorified armchair detectives. Tossing theories around and speculating.

Lawler: I'm sorry but who found Lottie in the end? It wasn't the police, was it? It was Chris's #LookForLottie campaign, the so-called armchair detectives who found a vulnerable girl who—

Sinclair: Let's not beat around the bush. There was no big mystery, was there? Nothing to sensationalise? Lottie was at her friend Erika's house all along.

Lawler: Yes, and we'll be hearing from Erika later on in the show for another exclusive. Now, Detective Sinclair, if we could just talk about the arrest—

Sinclair: No.

Lawler: The murder—

Sinclair: I've said all I'm going to say.

@Avocadomonkey Shame he won't talk about the murder. Did anyone see the leaked photos of the crime scene? #WWY

@Lamadrama23 All that blood!!!

@Blackcat1970 He's right. Social media can interfere with investigations

@Jamie2983 I wish you'd just piss off

@Avocadomonkey #Bekind

Chapter 69

Mia

Lottie is home. We're all home. The three of us sit stiffly on the sofa. Almost touching but further apart than we've ever been.

Sean is on his way.

'Is everyone going to know now?' Lottie says in a small, sad voice. 'That Sean isn't my dad and Gabriel kidnapped me and we . . . we . . . ' Her voice is flat. Emotionless. She's in shock.

We're all in shock but on some level I know what we have to do.

'We need to stick to the same story.'

When the kids were younger they had a game called 'Buzz Off'. You'd slide a metal loop around a wire and if you lost focus for even a second the results were disastrous. If I don't focus now, the consequences will be devastating. But I can hear the buzz of that wire in my head, louder and louder. I cannot think.

'We tell the police you were at Erika's, Lottie,' Chris says when I don't speak. 'That you ran away because of what Mum did with the hot tub. When I came back from Norfolk I joined Mum in looking for you when Erika texted to let us know you were at her house after she'd seen my #LookForLottie post.'

'But Erika would have been at school.'

'She felt so awkward at being around Daisy after overhearing Esther tell Lottie . . . well, you know, that she went home. Her mum was at work so she won't know whether Lottie was there or not. It'll be fine.'

'But Gabriel—'

'Lottie, you don't have any connection to him,' I say. 'Nobody knows about Sean except immediate family, and we can keep it that way. Nobody has to know anything that has just gone on. You're home now and we can all spend the evening together playing Uno and everything will be fine,' I say, but I neither sound nor feel convincing.

One wrong move and it's game over.

'I'm going to have a bath.' Lottie slowly stands with a weariness I see at the care home when I visit Mum in the elderly residents whose joints creak in protest when they move.

'I'll come and run it for you,' I offer.

'No, Mum.' She trudges out of the room without looking back.

I'm deliberating going after her anyway when I glance at Chris. His poor, battered face. With a jolt I'm reminded I have two children and right now it feels as though I'm failing them both.

'Does it hurt?' I reach out a hand and softly touch his cheek.

'You should have seen the other guy,' he says with a weak smile as he pulls away from me.

'What happened?'

'Marco Hernandez.'

I'm scanning his face, noting his injuries, before I move to his hands. I take them in mine, check his knuckles. There's no sign of bruising or swelling.

'I didn't hit him,' Chris says quietly.

'You didn't try and defend yourself?' I know Chris isn't the violent type, but human instinct is to protect yourself, isn't it? At the very least to cover your face with your hands.

'No. I . . . ' he sighs. 'I get it. He's grieving, angry and I . . . It didn't seem right to fight back.'

'I know he's lost his mum, and even at my age I can't imagine how that feels, but that doesn't give him the right to attack you.'

'Maybe not but I felt, I dunno. Not that I deserved it, but I understood it. And there is a part of me that wonders if Harlow would still be alive if it wasn't for –' he shrugs – 'you know.'

I nod, too overcome with emotion to speak because I do know. The same thought runs through my mind all the time. 'I think if you choose to live your life online, the dopamine hits from all the likes and positive comments leave you craving more, but the lows . . . the trolls, I mean . . . I don't think anything can prepare you for that. Harlow was a human being and every negative post about her must have been so hurtful. We don't know exactly why she did what she did, but I know I'll feel guilty about my part in it, every single day.'

'Me too.' Chris leans his head on my shoulder.

'You haven't done anything wrong, Chris.'

'Neither have you, but that doesn't make it easier, does it? I can't help thinking how I'd feel if I lost you, Mum. Marco is my age.'

'You'll never lose me.' I hug him tightly. 'I promise I'll always be here for you.'

I didn't know then, of course, that I'd made a promise that would be impossible to keep.

After a night of fractured sleep, I'm at the supermarket, randomly throwing things in a basket. Things I stopped buying after Lottie's AA diagnosis when I because obsessed with nutrition. It's not as though Jaffa Cakes and Flaming Hot Doritos will make a difference to the way she feels about me, but I have to try.

If I'd been paying attention I might have noticed the glow of blue lights as I approached our house.

As it is, I am so distracted, on autopilot really, when I spot two police cars. There's a policeman leaning against the bonnet of one, talking into a radio.

Our eyes meet and my mouth instantly dries. There is no reassuring smile. No this-is-just-a-routine-visit.

The lack of friendliness in their faces shows me that it's more than that.

There's the click of my door opening.

My numb fingers fumbling for the catch on my seat belt.

And the words.

Oh god, those words.

'Mia Finch, I'm arresting you on suspicion of the murder of Gabriel Solas.'

Dark spots flicker in front of my eyes. Vision tunnelling. Sounds muffled.

Words running into each other except the one that's all-consuming.

Murder.

I shake my head. I can't make sense of it. I can't make sense of anything.

'Mum?' Chris hesitates at the bottom of the driveway. Our eyes meet and the unspoken passes between us as I give an almost imperceptible shake of my head.

Then I'm being led away.

How did I get here?

But I know how I got here.

I know how my story began.

Once upon a time, I had fallen in love.

But as I'm manoeuvred into the police car, a hand covering the top of my head as I duck inside, I don't know how my story will end.

PART THREE

Chapter 70

Mia

Murder.

Those six letters swell in my head, until there's no room for anything else. They take up all the space in this tiny cell I find myself in, sucking out all the air.

I cannot breathe.

Murder.

Sweat sticks my shirt to my body.

For my entire life, aside from taking that money, I've been law-abiding. The perfect citizen. I even returned to Tesco once, clutching my bag of shopping and my receipt, after I realised the self-service checkout hadn't scanned all of my items. I've always been too scared of the consequences of breaking the rules to deviate from the straight and narrow path I've stuck to, and now I've been arrested.

Arrested *again.*

Only this isn't arguing in the park, breaching the Public Order Act.

Murder.

The word has always sent chills down my spine.

Murder.

It sounds so terrifying, doesn't it? So final, which of course it is, but it's more than that, more than death. It represents brutality. A lack of choice. Someone playing God, deciding when someone should die.

And why.

Somehow I feel both numb and scared at the same time as I rock. And rock. And rock. But then my adrenaline begins to ebb away, and my legs feel so shaky I sink down on the bench that masquerades as a bed. There's no luxury here. No duvet or pillow. I lay down, exhausted with it all, my eyes struggling to stay open. I'm not sure if it's bedtime or not. My watch was taken away when I was booked in, but this isn't the usual type of tiredness. It's shock that's shutting my body down.

I wonder what the kids are doing. What they've had for dinner.

Wonder what they think of me right now.

Murder.

I begin to weep. For my children and then for myself, shamefully; for the life I might not get to return to. I cry for Sean, for the way we were. I cry for everyone except Gabriel.

I should feel sorry he's dead.

I *should*. But I don't.

I'm only sorry I am here because of it.

I am only sorry for the poor postman who thought there was something wrong because the front door was ajar and had gone in to investigate, discovering his body.

There's a throbbing behind my temples. The occupant of the cell next door won't stop shouting. Slamming their hands against the door, making demands.

But nevertheless, I curl myself up into a ball and somehow, despite the noise, the light, the uncomfortable heat, despite everything, I cry myself to sleep.

I wake with a start from a nightmare. I had been standing over Gabriel's lifeless body, telling him he deserved it. Perhaps my subconscious was trying to justify that he had it coming to him but, whatever he has done, nobody has the right to take a life, do they?

Somebody has to pay.

And then the sound of my name. My stomach clenches painfully before everything feels so loose that I fear my bowels are going to open.

I am asked the same questions over and over.

'Mia, why were you at Gabriel Solas's house?'

I am given the date and the address.

'I wasn't. I was with Chris all day, and then with Chris and Lottie all evening.'

'Chris was on a school trip in Norfolk for part of the day. We've spoken to him. Is there anything you want to tell us?'

'No.' This is the story we'd agreed on using if we were questioned when we called the police to tell them we'd found Lottie, but then, they hadn't asked for details. I expand on my answer. 'I mean, I reported Lottie missing because I thought that she was. When Chris came home from Norfolk we spent the rest of the day together, looking for her before Erika, a friend of hers, texted Chris and said she was with her. She'd seen on social media that we thought Lottie was missing. We brought her home, played a few games of cards and then all went to bed. None of us went out again.'

The trick to lying is to stick as close to the truth as possible. This is almost the truth.

I'm poised to get up, to walk out of the room, when they say, 'The thing is, Mia, Chris says you weren't with him at all. He didn't spend the day with you. In fact, he says he distinctly remembers hearing you leave the house once he was in bed. He even got up to check and you weren't at home.'

The walls are sliding in, the ceiling dropping.

There isn't enough air in the room.

This tiny, oppressive room that I know there's no chance of me leaving now.

Chapter 71

Who's Watching You Documentary

Jake Lawler (host): It's a delight to welcome to the show a guest that many of you will know online under her profile name 'Charlie's Angels'. Here she is, as herself today, Erika Vaughn. Erika, I'm so pleased our researchers managed to track you down.

Erika Vaughn (Charlie's Angels): (knee jiggles up and down) Yeah, my identity was plastered all over socials.

Lawler: We're still happy to have you.

Vaughn: Well, I came on because you said you'd been tipped off that the media are going to portray me as some sort of weird stalker because, you know, I've been watching Mia's posts since the beginning and my life would be ruined if I didn't put my side across but I'm—

Lawler: I'm sure nobody said 'ruined'.

Vaughn: I can show you the email. (fumbles for phone)

Lawler: That won't be necessary. Why don't you tell me why you were so interested in the Finch family? I'm aware you're friends with Lottie's cousin, Daisy. But I'd have thought a girl your age would be more interested in a channel like Sierra's Beauty Secrets?

Vaughn: Nah, well. (sniffs) I dunno why Mia's video popped up on my feed, but I had . . . I had . . . (begins to cry)

Lawler: Here. (hands a tissue)

Vaughn: (wipes eyes) I had a sister, she was the same age as Lottie, and she had, not AA but . . . she died, and I . . . Lottie reminded me of her so much. I didn't really know her at school before, but I became so invested in her journey. It was like, if she didn't make it then I'd have lost my sister all over again. That was why I watched everything. Not because I'm a weirdo. (wipes eyes again) Do you think people will leave me alone now?

Lawler: I'm sure everyone's rooting for you. Can I ask, where did the name Charlie's Angels come from?

Vaughn: Oh, um, there was some ancient programme my mum was watching on one of the crappy channels called *Charlie's Angels* and I thought, Charlotte, you know. I didn't want anyone to know it was me.

Lawler: And our researchers tell me that at the time Lottie went missing and the #LookForLottie campaign started, she was actually with you?

Vaughn: (gazes into lap) Yeah.

Lawler: Well, our brilliant research team have uncovered a secret, Erika.

Vaughn: Oh god, what? (pales, begins to cry) I didn't—

Lawler: Please. (touches her knee briefly) I didn't mean to upset you. I'm sure everyone will be thrilled that as well as making friends with Lottie, rather than only watching her online, you're dating Christopher Finch now. You *are* dating him?

Vaughn: Oh, (cries harder) yeah.

Lawler: Sorry. Thanks to our researchers, we let the secret out of the bag. Sometimes they're just *too* good. (bright smile) That's what keeps *Who's Watching You* the most accurate true crime series out there!

@Blackcat197 It's not right. Erika was manipulated to go on the show

@Avocadomonkey She's dating Chris Finch! Great exclusive #WWY

@Jamie2983 The papers are right then – she IS obsessed

@Lamadrama23 I'm obsessed with them all!!!

Chapter 72

Mia

'I repeat, why were you at Gabriel's house?'

'I've never been there.' It's a stupid reply. I notice the slight wince of the duty solicitor. I've been told to keep saying 'no comment' but I think that would make me look like I'm hiding something.

'We know you were there.'

Do I keep denying it? Is there any point now Chris isn't on my side? Now that he's said I left the house later that night after we had brought Lottie home.

But they can't prove I was there, can they? There definitely weren't any neighbours. Any witnesses. Even if Chris isn't providing me with an alibi, it doesn't mean I'd been at the square.

'I wasn't there.'

'We know you were. The forensic team have confirmed it.'

Too late I remember Gabriel dragging me inside the front door. My fingerprints as I'd clung to the frame. I wonder if it's like on TV – all white paper suits, masks and gloves.

I feel myself sinking, feet in quicksand, unable to get out of the hole I have made.

'Look, I might have . . . I mean, my fingerprints might have.'

'Your fingerprints were. We ran the ones we found at the house through the database, and you were found to be a match. You've been arrested before after your altercation with Harlow Hernandez.'

'But I wasn't charged.'

'We still have your details. I'm sure you were informed when and how you could request for them to be removed after you weren't charged. *On that occasion.*'

Sweat trickles between my breasts.

I've already said I've never been to Gabriel's house before, but my fingerprints have proven me to be a liar. How can I expect them to believe anything I say now?

'Okay, well, to be honest—' I wince as that trots out of my mouth. Has a truthful sentence ever started with 'to be honest'? I place my hand on my knee to stop it jiggling up and down, aware that everything I am saying, doing, my entire body language, is making me appear guilty. 'It's complicated.'

'It was a yes or no question, Mia. Not even a yes or no question. We already know that you *were* there.'

I feel the eyes of my allocated solicitor on me, glance at her and see the frown on her face.

'You don't have to answer that, Mia,' she says but if I don't answer, if all I offer them is no comment, then they'll keep me here, won't they? I've already been told that they can hold me for up to ninety-six hours and I want to go home as soon as I can. If I can just convince them that I'm not the only suspect, then they'll have to release me, won't they? Being there doesn't mean I killed him, does it? They need more than that.

They need cold, hard evidence I did it, and they won't find that.

'I want to tell them.'

'My client's fingerprints being found at the scene doesn't mean she killed anyone,' she says but that's as much for my benefit as for theirs. My fluttering heart slows a little. I'm not alone, she is on my side, and yes, fingerprints don't mean I'm guilty, do they? There's probably hundreds of different fingerprints in there.

'Mia, your fingerprints were also found on the poker, which we believe to be the murder weapon.'

Bizarrely, I feel a strange urge to giggle. Mrs Peacock in the library with the candlestick.

This cannot be real.

'There was also blood at the scene, on the body, that didn't belong to the victim. I see you've cut your finger, Mia?'

'I was slicing a pineapple for Lottie and the knife slipped.'

'We found drops of blood on the victim and the DNA matches the DNA we have on file for you.'

I grip the table because the floor is falling away from me. I'm too deep in that quicksand, sinking. Sinking. Then, strangely, floating, looking down on myself.

They have my fingerprints on the murder weapon.

My DNA.

They know it's my DNA on Gabriel.

The victim's body.

Gabriel is dead and they have my DNA on file.

DNA is irrefutable.

As though I'm taking my final breaths, my life flashes before me. The kids aging backwards in my memory. From teenagers to toddlers. Silver fairy wings and superhero capes.

My throat aches.

I try to hold on to those memories but they're slipping away from me. My life is slipping away from me as I whisper, 'Okay.' I nod. 'Okay.'

My solicitor asks for a break, a private chat, but I shake my head. I don't want one. I have to say it before I lose my nerve.

Tell them.

Playing Cluedo around the kitchen table on a Sunday afternoon. Me, Sean and the kids. We were all so happy once.

Tell them.

'Mia, would you like a drink of water?'

Spinning. Everything is spinning. What I'd like is my life back.

Tell them.

'I used to work for Gabriel Solas, at the restaurant. Years ago, before he went to prison for money laundering. There was cash hidden in the basement. I discovered it and I . . . I took it.'

I hang my head. My tears spill onto the tabletop and automatically I clean it with my sleeve.

Wiping crumbs from the Cluedo board, kids begging for one more custard cream.

Oh god, the kids.

Tell them.

'When Gabriel was released, he came after me. Threatened me. You know about the notes, the wreath. It was all him. He wanted his money back and I . . . I didn't have it, so . . . I went to see him at the old restaurant. I tried to beg for more time, but he said he'd hurt me, the children. I couldn't . . . I'd do anything to protect my children.' This is the truth. 'So I picked up the poker and I . . . '

My voice sounds as though it's coming from someone else's mouth.

Speaking someone else's confession.

'I killed him.'

Chapter 73

Lottie

One Week Later

I haven't felt safe since, well, you know, everything.

When I was small, I'd curl up on the sofa with Mum, snuggle into her side, our hands dipping into sticky sweet popcorn, eyes trained on the TV.

'I didn't like it,' Simon Cowell would say to the person stood trembling before him. 'I loved it.'

'They were rubbish,' Dad would mutter from behind his book; he always pretended to hate reality TV, but he'd be as caught up in it as Mum and me.

'It isn't solely about the voice,' Mum would explain again. 'It's having the X factor. The undefinable thing that makes people want to watch you.'

'Lottie can sing better, though.' Chris would snap another Lego piece into place on his latest creation.

I'd scramble to my feet, the bowl on Mum's lap wobbling precariously, and launch into a song, dancing as I sang, not caring if I knew all the words or not.

'And she has the X factor,' Chris would applaud.

I wonder now if he was right. If I do have – if the entire Finch family has – the X factor. That special quality that draws people to us. Not only because of the way our channel blew up, but now, I am still being watched, followed, as I head towards the prison.

'Take a photo, it'll last longer,' Chris shouted once as a bearded man had stared at us as we walked to Tesco, but then the guy had raised a camera as though he'd been issued an invitation.

I'm a robot moving along an assembly line as I go through the security checks. I glance over my shoulder to reassure myself that Dad is still there, waiting for me. Usually he'd have to come in with me because I am under eighteen but there is nothing usual about today's visit.

No one smiles at me, but I try to be brave as I queue to provide my ID, to have my fingerprints taken, not by rolling my fingers in ink the way Chris and I used to do when we'd play detectives, but by pressing down on a touchscreen. The slow walk through the scanner that feels like a gaping jaw as I step into it, ready to swallow me up and spit me out. I need to get used to this. Mum hasn't been sentenced yet but there won't be a trial now she's admitted it. We're just waiting to find out how long she will serve.

'Don't worry, it's just like going through airport security,' the family liaison officer we'd been issued had explained and I'd nodded, not sharing that I've never been to an airport. Never been on a plane. The world, which sometimes feels so big thanks to the internet, so accessible, can also feel too small. My world does anyway.

Then I'm queuing again.

Traipsing into a private room.

And then there she is.

Mum.

Chapter 74

Lottie

The sight of Mum triggers such an overwhelming onslaught of guilt, I cannot physically move towards her. Everything about her is new and strange – the grey prison clothes that drain the colour from her face, the haunted look in her eyes – and yet, somehow, she's achingly familiar. Tucking her hair behind her ears with the same fingers that soothed me as a child, spooned out pink sticky medicine, tickled me until I laughed so hard I thought I'd never stop.

In those last precious hours before she was arrested, I had barely spoken to her. Traumatised from my ordeal at Gabriel's flat. I had so many questions to ask her about him, but I was hurt and angry and I thought there'd be plenty of time. But now, he is dead, and Mum has confessed to killing him and . . . and . . .

Oh, Mum.

She's as conflicted as I am, I see it on her face. She wants me to both run towards her and run away, but my chest is tight, my vision blurs and I find I can do neither.

I feel the hot gaze of the guard studying me and I don't

know whether she is viewing me with scorn or sympathy, but I really don't care.

I can't stay here. I just can't.

I turn to flee. But then, just as guilt is trying to push me away, a desperate need for my mother engulfs me, propelling me forward. I didn't think we'd be able to hug but we can.

'I'll give you two some space, but I'll be right outside the door,' says the guard.

Although I'm grateful we're alone, I know we've only been granted this privacy privilege because I need to tell Mum that her mum – my gran – has passed away in the care home. I can't quite get any words out yet, though.

'Are you okay?' Mum asks the question I should be asking her. I shake my head rather than answer because if I try to speak I'll cry and if I start to cry I won't be able to stop.

For a second, as I sit down on the uncomfortable plastic chair, I imagine this room, this building, flooding with my tears. The walls buckling under the sheer weight and volume of my sorrow. Mum and I swimming away in the chaos. It's the kind of crazy play I'd have invented when I was a kid but I'm not a child anymore, am I? Whatever innocence I once had has long gone. The traces that remain will be left behind once I leave here, along with this woman who used to be my entire world, but now?

I don't know who we are to each other right now.

I tug the sleeves of my jumper down over my hands and furiously swipe at my damp cheeks. The smell of this place is already clinging to the wool. It's a smell I've never encountered before. Fear? Despair? Rage? Something dark and dangerous bubbling away under the surface. The combined energy of the prisoners electric. Who knows how far someone who has nothing to lose might go? Later – soon – when I stand outside, my face raised to the sky, and drag in a lungful of fresh air, I know that I'll still smell it.

It is the realisation that Mum's hair won't carry the scent of the rosemary shampoo we've both used as far back as I can remember that tips me over the edge. Causes me to shake so hard my teeth are rattling in my head with the memory that, after yet another hospital visit, she'd run me a bath, cuddle me afterwards.

'There. You smell like home again,' she'd say and I always wanted to tell her that the smell of home didn't come in a bottle, home was . . . it was her. The softness of her as she held me, the scent of her skin when I'd buried my face into her neck.

Perhaps it does come in a bottle, though. Perhaps if I keep using that same shampoo then I'll never again feel as truly alone as I do right now.

'Lottie?' she now says gently. 'Look at me.'

But I can't. I'm staring at the table but not really seeing it. My foot won't stop tapping as anxiety races through my cells, snatching my senses away from me.

'Lottie.' Her voice comes from far away. 'Look at me.' She's firmer now. Somehow, even though my head feels too heavy for my neck, I raise it. She smiles encouragingly. 'Good girl. Now we're going to breathe together. One.'

We fall back into our old routine. Breathing in deeply through our noses. Out through our mouths. The way we have a thousand times before when the nurse had approached me with a needle or I had to say goodbye to everything familiar for weeks on end to isolate. The ritual calms me.

I was wrong when I said I didn't know who we were to each other right now.

We're us.

I guess it's who we'll be in the future that scares me.

'I'm sorry,' I say.

'You've nothing to apologise for.' There is conviction in her words, but I know that's not true.

'How's Chris?'

'He's okay. He wants to visit but I wanted to come and see you on my own this first time.'

'And Dad? He's looking after you?'

'He hasn't poisoned me yet.' I give a weak smile. Dad is many things, but a good cook isn't one of them.

'I'm sure his meals are better than I get in here.'

'I'm sorry.'

'Lottie, that was supposed to be a joke. It's fine. Everything is fine.'

'What do they give you to eat?'

'I had cereal for breakfast. Lunch is usually a sandwich but there's fruit too. Dinner last night was a curry. It's okay.'

'You've lost weight.'

'Well, that isn't a bad thing. I didn't realise how often I dipped into the biscuit tin until it wasn't there.'

I can't do this. I can't sit here and pretend this is normal. Fine.

Our small talk peels away the edges, exposing the thing neither of us really wants to talk about, but we have to. Because it festers between us, fetid and toxic and impossible to ignore.

'Why did you say you killed him? Why don't you deny it? Fight it? Try and get out of here? I know you didn't do it. I know you're not capable of murdering anyone. Mum, please.' My words fall out in a garbled rush as I gaze at her imploringly. Whoever she is, whatever she has done, she's still my mum. The person who has always been able to fix everything. She fixed me, didn't she?

'Lottie. I know this is hard for you but—'

'Hard?' I'm verging on hysteria. She makes a downward 'shush' motion with her hands. 'Hard?' I'm whispering again now. 'Mum, this isn't fair.'

'Life often isn't. You know that better than anyone.'

'But . . . ' I glance around, even though we're alone. Discreetly I run my hands under the surface of the table. I don't know what I'm expecting to find, some sort of bug? All I know of prison is what I've seen on TV. It doesn't seem like anyone is listening, recording us, but can I be sure? Surely the guards would want to? But then there's a lot of prisoners here. A lot of secrets. 'Are we being monitored?'

'Well, if you produce a cake with a file in and try and break me out, then—'

'Mum. This isn't funny.'

'I'm not laughing. We're safe to talk.' She studies me carefully. 'But we really don't have to.'

'But . . . It isn't . . . Can't you . . . ' I pause to pull the fragmented pieces of what I need to say together, to pull the fragmented pieces of myself together. 'You said you killed him.' I may not have to say it, I may not even want to but, really, how can I not? 'But we both know you didn't do it. Why did you tell them that you did?'

'Oh, Lottie.' She looks at me with such compassion. Such love. 'I told them that I killed Gabriel –' she straightens her spine, takes a deep breath – 'because I didn't want them to find out that it was you.'

Chapter 75

Mia

My darling girl crumples before me. Did she think I didn't know it was her who killed Gabriel? Did she think I could just tell the truth – my truth – and I'd be released? That the police would just say, 'Oh, okay, sorry,' and we'd be free to get on with our lives? That they wouldn't want to prosecute whoever was culpable?

That they wouldn't lock my daughter up?

I didn't give birth to her, I didn't donate bone marrow, I didn't save her life so she could spend half of it in a cell.

'Mum, I . . . ' I wait for her denials to come but they don't because if it wasn't me, there is only one other person it can have been.

'Have you always known?' She can't meet my eye.

'At first I was confused. How could my DNA be at the scene when I wasn't? My blood on Gabriel's body?' I had been over the day Chris and I had gone to Nine, The Square in my mind.

I had been grappling with Gabriel when Chris leaped onto his back. Lottie behind him, standing still and silent.

Hands clasped over her mouth. Gabriel let me go and flung Chris to the floor. Kicked my darling boy in the stomach. I grabbed the poker and waved it at him, 'Stop!'

He turned around but his eyes weren't on me. They were on something behind me. I twisted my head around.

Lottie was brandishing a knife.

'Don't hurt my brother,' she said in a voice that didn't sound like hers. I advanced on him with the poker while she advanced on him with the knife.

Gabriel held up both hands.

With one hand I had fumbled for my mobile. Pressed the call button.

'Don't ring the police,' he had shouted.

'I'm not.' I wasn't going to call them until I'd found a way to protect Lottie from all the media attention this would bring. And yes, okay, to protect myself. 'I'm calling Lewis.'

'No. Don't.'

Gabriel had looked genuinely terrified, so I'd ended the call.

'You can go. Sorry. Lewis told me you can't have taken the money but—' he ran his hand through his thinning hair and the despair on his face was one I recognised on mine. The desperation to repay a debt and the lengths you'd go to do it. There's a world of difference between my hot tub stunt and kidnapping a child, but I kind of understood it.

We walked out of that house, knowing that he wouldn't come after us.

On the way home, Lewis had called me back.

'Mia. Everything okay?' I was surprised he'd returned my call. Wondered what he would have done if Gabriel wasn't back. 'I'm just about to board a flight for Dublin.' In the background I could hear the airport Tannoy.

'Yes.'

'Good. We wouldn't want someone's release stirring anything up, would we? We remember Bradley?'

He won't talk. He can't. We wouldn't want Sean to disappear too.

'I remember. Everything's fine.' I hung up. If it weren't for Lewis being out of the country, I might have initially thought he had been the one to kill Gabriel. Gabriel had been alive when we left The Square. How had my blood, my DNA, been on his body when I hadn't touched him? But then I recalled what we learned at the hospital. 'Lottie, do you remember how Alma told us that recipients' DNA can change to match their donors? It was the only thing that made sense. That and the fact that Chris told the police I had gone out that night when I hadn't.'

Lottie tells me what had happened.

'I told Chris to tell the truth. I *told* him. After you'd been arrested, I ran upstairs. Pulled out the bag of clothes I'd been wearing the night before that I'd stuffed under the bed. Clothes that were covered in Gabriel's blood.'

'"What are you doing?" Chris had asked.

'"I'm taking them to the station, to get Mum out. I'm going to tell them the truth. That I killed Gabriel."

'"But they'll keep you instead." Chris had looked so broken.

'"Mum didn't do anything wrong."

'"I'll take them." Chris had held out his hand. "You stay here, and I'll go and tell them that he kidnapped you, that it was in self-defence. You didn't mean to kill him. It'll all be okay, Lotts."

'While he was gone I threw up three times. I wrote out instructions on looking after Michael Finnegan. Wrote letters to you and Dad. I thought Chris would come back with the police, but he came back on his own. Said that he'd got rid of the clothes. That I wasn't to say anything, that you wouldn't want me to. The evidence was gone, and Chris wouldn't tell me where.'

'He's right, I wouldn't have wanted you to tell the police the truth.'

'Then I heard you'd confessed. Oh, *Mum*.' There is heartbreak in those three letters. 'You must hate me. Chris must hate me.'

'I'd never hate you. You must have gone back to the house for a good reason. Chris would know that. He had a choice between you and me, and he chose you. It's okay. I chose you too. I confessed because all the evidence was there. I'd touched the poker. My DNA on his body. Now they have my confession too along with my motive that I'd stolen from him. You're in the clear.'

'I'm sorry. I'm so sorry. I was so scared, but I want to tell the truth now. It was an accident. Self-defence.'

'I know it must have been. I can't imagine how frightened you were. But it doesn't change the fact that you fled the scene. Lied to the police. I lied to the police. We could both be prosecuted for so many things.'

'But what if we're not? What if I just tell them and—'

'Charlotte.' I use her full name because I want her to feel a sense of detachment right now. To take the emotion out of the equation as much as she can. 'There is a chance, if we tell the police what happened, that you could walk free. But there is also a possibility that you might be charged with manslaughter. That you could serve years in prison. I can't – I won't risk that. Besides, I told the police that I killed Gabriel because I stole his money. I admitted I'd taken cash from the restaurant. And he'd come after me when he'd been released with the threats and the wreath and everything to scare me into paying it back. I've proven I bought the glass house with it. They think it was all about money. No one has any idea he's your biological father, and it's better for you that it stays that way.'

'But—'

'This is my choice, Lottie,' I say firmly. 'If I wanted to I could tell them the truth. But I don't want to tell them the truth. If it's a choice between you and me being branded a killer?' My voice catches in my constricted throat but there's a sincerity to my words. 'I choose you. Every. Single. Time.'

'You might not, if you knew everything,' she says.

Chapter 76

Lottie

Mum knows it was me. Of course she does.

Who else could it have been with her DNA at the scene?

Our DNA.

Donating bone marrow has saved me but it has ruined her.

'I went back to the square for my phone,' I say quietly.

I see the flicker of disappointment on her face. She thinks she's given up her life for my mobile.

'I'd left it there and there were things on it . . . well. I didn't want anyone else to ever see them. I thought Gabriel would have run away. Been scared of Uncle Lewis coming or of being charged with kidnap and sent back to prison.'

'Oh, Lottie.'

'I went back when you and Chris were asleep. The house was dark. I got in the same way Chris had, through the broken kitchen window.' I take a break, the fear of that night coming at me. 'I crept upstairs and found my phone, put it in my pocket but then . . . he was . . . he was there.'

'You must have been terrified.'

'I was. He lunged at me and . . . and I panicked. I grabbed that sharp heavy thing, you know, that was by the fire. It cut my arm as I swung it at him. I didn't want to kill him, just hurt him a bit so I could get away, but he kind of . . . he just crumpled to the floor. He wasn't moving. It was horrible. I threw down the thingy and tried to shake him so he woke up, but he didn't move and so I ran away.'

'It's okay, Lottie. I don't blame you. Why you went back doesn't change anything. You must have been scared for your life. Particularly as he'd already sent a wreath with your name on it.'

A heavy weight rolls in the pit of my stomach. I feel so sick. So scared. But I have to do this. I have to say it. Mum has made a choice, but it isn't an informed choice because she doesn't know everything.

Not yet.

I keep my breaths slow and measured, trying to summon the courage to say the unthinkable. Knowing that once I've said it, it can't be unsaid. Knowing that Mum might change her mind. That I could be the one sitting in her place while she is walking out the door.

Say it.

Out of all the horrific, heinous things I have done, this perhaps is the hardest of all.

Say it.

Perhaps the most unforgivable. Not accidentally taking a life while terrified for my own.

But something cold and calculated.

Say it.

It is a day for unburdening. A day for truth.

A last chance for me to lay all my cards on the table and see if Mum will still want to play when she sees what my hand is comprised of.

Because the murder, well yes, it is something I did.
But it isn't the only thing.
The only crime.
I did a bad thing.

Chapter 77

Lottie

'I have something to tell you. It wasn't *him*.' I can't call him Gabriel as though he is a friend, and I won't call him dad. We don't need to rake over him again. Mum made a mistake, and she regrets it. I know that. The thing is, I've made mistakes too. She just doesn't know about all of them yet.

I'm standing on the precipice of lies; the truth is waiting for me below, sharp and shameful. I step off the edge and hope my mother's love is ready to catch me as I fall.

'Gabriel didn't send the wreath, Mum. It was me.'

'You?' She shakes her head, disbelieving. '*You* sent a wreath to *yourself*? How? Why?'

'I took the money from Grandma's purse at the care home and ordered it with cash while you read to her.'

'I don't understand?'

'It was me. It was all me. There was never an intruder in the garden. I made that up.' Mum opens her mouth to speak but I hold out my hand to silence her. I need to get this all out before I bottle it.

'I wrote the note "I'm watching you". I came into your room at night while you were asleep and stood over you. I smashed the photo. I wrote on the kitchen window. All of it. It was me.'

I'm out of breath as though I've run a race.

'I don't understand,' she says again.

'I hated it. *Hated it*. Being all over social media. Not having any choice in it.'

'You did have a choice. I asked you.'

'You asked when you'd already started it, when I was really sick. I could see what it meant to you, how comforting it was to you and . . . and how could I say no? You saved my life.'

'But not so you could hand over yours, if that's what you felt you were doing?'

I nod.

'That's what you meant when you wrote on the window? 'I want what's mine'. Your life back?'

'Yeah.' I'm tugging my sleeves down over my hands, making them disappear. Wishing I could disappear.

My lungs constrict as though someone has tied a rope around me, and that is what I feel like. Constricted. Trapped.

'The note, "I'm watching you", it was meant . . . meant to scare you, I suppose. Make you think how I felt with all those people watching me. I was so angry when I wrote that. The other note. The "if you want to keep your daughter" . . . you were losing me, Mum. Losing me because you kept sharing me and you didn't even see it.'

Her skin is ashen. 'I had no idea.'

'You'd filmed the day that I'd started my periods again, Mum. That's, like, totally embarrassing.' I focus on my lap, not on her crumpled face. 'It wasn't enough that there's a ton of footage out there of me with no hair? I'm a teenager. I can't. I just can't even.'

I'm crying and, when I look up, Mum is too.

'I wanted to tell you I'd had enough, I did. I was determined to, but then Chris said you were both going to monetise the channel and I felt so guilty that you'd lost your job because I was sick and . . . '

'You did . . . all of it?' She's visibly shocked but she's shaking her head, not believing it, and all at once I want to weep. She knows I am capable of murder and yet she doesn't think I'm capable of this. She's still seeing the good in me when I can no longer see any in myself.

Her mouth opens and closes. Opens again, the one word, the only word that makes any sense leaves her lips and comes to rest on the table between us.

'Why?'

'I felt as though social media had become my whole life, the thing that defined me. That would always define me. Ten years, twenty, when I go to a job interview, fall in love, meet my in-laws, one quick google and there I am, at my weakest, with every little detail laid bare. The meds that gave me constipation. How happy you were when I eventually "went". Mum, I hated every second of it.'

Even as I speak my thoughts out loud, I know they don't hold the same element of truth they once did. I hadn't hated it all. There were times I'd been glad, happy even. When somebody would comment they'd donated bone marrow because of me, feeling I'd made a difference.

Of all the ways this visit had gone in my head, it had never ended up with me hurting Mum this way.

I came here to tell Mum about Gran. I don't really think it was for this. Not to reveal that I had been the one to scare her and Chris. I had blurted it out because it is torturous, seeing the way she still looks at me as though I am the most wondrous planet in the universe, when I don't deserve it.

I don't deserve her love or her loyalty.

Perhaps now she'll tell the truth and I'll be the one stuck in this drab place, with drab clothes, my future stretching long and laborious. It's what I deserve, I know, but the thought of being trapped here terrifies me. My breath is shallow. Heat prickling under my arms. There's a pain in my chest.

'You're having a panic attack.' Mum's voice reaches me, and I shake my head. A tiny piece of me wishing I were having a heart attack because then I'd get to leave.

'I can't . . .' I'm hyperventilating. 'I can't . . .'

I know that everyone here likely feels the same, but all those days, weeks, months, stuck on a ward have left me with some kind of claustrophobia. I had felt – stupidly – that the hospital was some kind of prison and, once I left there, confined to the house with Mum filming my every move had been another kind of prison.

I know now that I was wrong. I had taken so much for granted. I just hadn't realised it.

The ceiling is pressing down, walls are drawing in.

'Lottie, breathe,' Mum commands and it grounds me. She glances at the clock, and I try and gather myself because I don't know how long we've got left and I can't leave this half said.

'You saw the comments, Mum.'

'But I deleted the negative ones straight away and those sorts of comments were few and far between. Most of them were really positive. You inspired so many people.'

'Yeah, well, maybe, but it's the bad stuff that sticks in your head, isn't it? That stuck in mine. And then I was, you know. Changing.'

Growing a nice pair of tits there, Charlie.

I could give you something to make you feel better, if you know what I mean.

If you want money to raise awareness of your disease,
I'd pay for your virginity.

'And everyone was looking at me. Judging me. You didn't
want me to go back to school, and I felt like I was an animal
in a zoo. Being constantly stared at. Unable to escape.'

Mum looks completely bewildered. 'I thought we were
making a difference. I thought you wanted to make a
difference.'

'I did. When it was solely about aplastic anaemia, you
know, giving support to other parents, hope to other kids,
it was, I dunno, I knew it took your mind off of stuff. And I
guess it made me feel, I dunno . . . like there was still a point
to me. A purpose, you know, but it became so much more
than that, Mum.'

'People were interested in us. Invested in us. Following
your journey, wanting you to be well.'

'But then I was well, and it became about Dad and you
guys splitting up. Imagine how it was for me and Chris.
Not really understanding why he left us, but old enough
to know that you needed our support. Moving out of our
home into that . . . that fucking goldfish bowl. And then all
the terrible things with Harlow.'

'Lottie, I—'

'All the dark stuff. How crazy everything got after she
took her own life. How awful that she did. Sometimes I
wondered whether people were waiting for you to do the
same. All that stalker business. Mum, why are people so
much more interested when things go bad?'

'Chris explained it to me once, it's because—'

'I hated it. Hated knowing that complete strangers knew
so much about us, or thought they did anyway. It's like,
remember that old film we watched once? The dude that
didn't know his entire life was fabricated for entertainment?'

'*The Truman Show*?'

'Yeah. I watched that again, and I thought, at least he didn't know. For the longest time he didn't know everyone was watching him, but it was the first thing I thought about when I woke up. When I looked in the mirror in the morning, thinking I looked pale and ugly but knowing if I put make-up on some sicko would think it's for them.'

You're all grown-up, Lottie. Fancy a fuck?

'You told everyone when my periods had restarted.'

I'll have to wear a condom.

'Because it's a sign of health. I . . . Oh god.' Mum drops her head into her hands. When she raises her face again, there is such anguish in her eyes that my heart turns over.

'Why didn't you tell me to stop? I would have stopped if I'd have known.'

'I couldn't. You gave me life. Twice.' We're both sobbing. Struggling to speak. 'If it wasn't for you, I wouldn't have been born, and then you donated. Without you, I wouldn't be here.'

'If I hadn't donated then someone else wou—'

'You don't know that I'd have found a match, or found one in time, or that my body wouldn't have rejected it. Mum, you saved me. I owe you everything.'

'But surely—' she looks so confused. 'Surely if you can see that, appreciate that, then you must be aware how much I love you? How I'd do anything for you? All you had to do was say stop. I thought, I thought that you and Chris—' she swallows hard. 'Does he hate it too?'

'Not in the same way I do. You don't feature him too often.'

'But he still hates it?'

I shrug. 'I dunno, but he gets a hard time about it at school.'

If I'd thought she looked defeated when I walked in, she looks utterly broken now.

She whispers, 'I really didn't think you minded?'

'I just wanted to be normal.'

'You were normal.'

'I didn't feel it. I was just something people could look at and laugh at.'

'Lottie, nobody was laughing at you.'

'They were, Mum. All that stuff about my weight and appearance.'

'But you were advocating for body positivity. I thought—'

'You thought.' Anger swells. 'But you didn't ask.'

'I'm sorry I didn't ask. I'm asking now, though, if you've told me everything?'

'Not quite.'

Chapter 78

Mia

I don't know how much more I can take. I can't process the fact that there was never a crazed stalker. It had all been Lottie. If she hadn't sent the notes and I hadn't suspected Gabriel, I'd never have put the offal in the hot tub. She'd never have run away to Sean's. Esther would never have blurted the truth about her biological dad out.

He might still be alive.

If.

If.

If.

But then, the truth is freeing her. My darling girl.

'What else do you need to tell me?' I ask.

She shrugs, before she stares at the table. 'Joker666 that was trolling us, well, that was me too.'

'You? You were sending yourself threats?'

'Yeah. That's why . . . that's why I went back for my phone. My Joker666 profile was still logged in and I didn't want it to get into the wrong hands. Gabriel knew what I was doing. He said that he knew exactly who was stalking us. The only way he could have known it was me was if he had checked my phone.'

Before I can respond, the door creaks open.

'Time's up,' says the guard.

All too quickly, Lottie hugs me, and I never want to let her go. But then she's heading out of the door, shoulders rounded, body convulsing with sobs she's trying so hard to supress the way she used to when she was small and she'd hurt herself, trying to keep up with Chris.

I can ride a bike without stabilisers.

I can reach the top of the climbing frame.

I can jump from the swing while it's still moving.

'It doesn't matter. I still love you. I'll always love you,' I call after her.

Then the guard touches my shoulder as I'm watching my daughter leave.

'Sorry for the loss of your mother,' she says, and I realise why we were granted the privilege of a private room.

Just how much I've really lost.

Chapter 79

Lottie

There are certain memories from childhood that stay with you when you grow. Sometimes, seemingly trivial things are, inexplicably, the things easily recalled. For me, I can't remember my first day of school, the first time I lost a tooth. What I can bring to the forefront of my mind, in glorious technicolour, is the first time Mum filmed Chris and me for YouTube. We'd become obsessed with the channel after Chris had watched a clip called 'Charlie bit my finger' at a friend's house. We had begged Mum to film us. Esther, Gran, Felix and Daisy had been visiting, and I wanted everyone in it.

She had attached her phone to a tripod, and we'd gasped as it had wobbled and almost fallen when she'd turned around. Dad diving to catch it. 'Just call me Joe Hart.'

'Joe Hart,' Chris had said instantly, and we'd fallen about in stitches.

'If you earned the money of an England player, we wouldn't live here,' Mum had said, smiling, and I'd stopped laughing.

'I love our house.' I had straightened my spine proudly, as though we lived in Buckingham Palace and not in a small terrace, on a street littered with empty crisp packets and crumpled cans. I had loved our home, though. I still wish we'd stayed there, or perhaps I just wish we'd stayed in that time when everything was less complicated.

When we were a family.

Anyway, the tripod had been broken. Dad – *Dad* – had said, 'I'll film you all.'

'No.' I can't remember if it was Chris or me who had said that; probably both of us. 'We all have to be in it.'

'Excuse me.' Mum had intercepted an elderly lady who was walking her Jack Russell. 'Would you mind filming us, please? It will only take a minute.'

The lady's face had lit up. I don't know whether she was lonely or whether she just wanted something exciting to tell her family. I hope it was the latter because we never spoke to her again after that. Never invited her in and befriended her. We were so wrapped up in ourselves. Even then, the thought of our online audience was somehow more enticing than anyone physically present.

After Dad had showed her what to do, we had put on our biggest, brightest smiles.

'Hello. We're the Finch family. Welcome to our home.' We had waved. Followed this with, 'We can't wait for you to get to know us.'

Now everyone thinks they do know us, but they don't. Not even close.

We hadn't been able to think of anything else to say, so Mum had eagerly taken the phone back and we'd crowded around the screen, right there in the street, playing back the clip. The lady's dog had been tugging at his lead while she'd recorded us, and the resulting footage was shaky, but we didn't care.

'We're going to put it online,' Chris had told her. 'Millions of people will watch it.'

'I don't know about millions.' Mum had looked worried then.

'Going to be famous, are you?' the lady had asked.

Of course, none of us knew then that we'd be infamous.

I wonder if the lady is still alive. If she's seen us on the news. If she's told everyone she filmed the first ever clip of us – the Finch family – before everything fell apart.

If she voices her opinion regardless of whether anyone asks for it or not: 'They seemed so *normal*.' Whether she's tried to sell her story to the paper. Everyone else seems to.

Chapter 80

Who's Watching You Documentary

Jake Lawler (host): So we've come to the end of our Finch Family edition. (covers heart with hand)

It isn't the end for Charlotte that anybody wanted, although losing her mum meant she was reunited with her father, and Sean seems like a really good dad.

We just have time for one last guest. Mrs Norris! Now, you filmed the original footage of the Finch family all those years ago, didn't you?

Mrs Norris (passerby): Yes! (straightens hat) I couldn't believe it when my grandson showed me the clip. 'You used to live around there, did you know them?' he asked me. 'I filmed that!' I said. Lottie and Chris were only small then, and of course Beverley, Mia's mum, was still alive.

Lawler: Did you have any idea then, what Mia was capable of?

The cameras stop rolling. The crew begins to leave.

The video is still on a loop and Jake should perhaps feel something, a pang of sympathy for the kids as he reaches to turn it off, but he doesn't.

We can't wait for you to get to know us.

And he does know them, doesn't he? Their secrets anyway. As for their hopes and dreams, well, he doesn't want to think too deeply about those. It would make them too human. And that's the thing about true crime, isn't it? We know, on some level, it happened. But we all sleep better if we think the people aren't real. Not like us. So we tell ourselves it's just a story.

The Finch family.

He had known as soon as Mia's fight with Harlow happened and they had both been arrested that they were worth investigating. That's why he had gone to Beverley's care home – Mia had mentioned she was in Poppyfields during one of her videos. He'd tried to persuade Beverley to give him Mia's home address. Told her that he wanted to keep the family safe, her grandchildren, but she'd become hysterical, and he'd had to leave through the window.

His hunch had been right, though.

The Finch family were pure gold.

Someone asked him recently in an interview if his work gave him nightmares. Immersing himself so fully in the grim details, the worst of human nature.

'I feel I'm doing a public service,' he had said. 'Everyone deserves to know the truth, don't they?'

Except his second wife or his mistress, he thinks, a smirk on his face.

Unbidden, Harlow crosses his mind, but he pushes the thought of her away. If you do something stupid and get cancelled then you deserve everything coming, don't you?

He clicks off the video. The children fade away as the screen goes black.

'Mr Lawler?'

Jake looks up at the two blonde interns awkwardly shuffling in front of him. He doesn't know why they all seem to go about in pairs now.

'Mr Hanson wants to see you.'

The big boss. Jake wonders if he's getting a pay rise. Smiles all the way to the head of network's office.

'Ken.' Jake sinks into one of the leather armchairs. 'No whisky?' He looks around for the usual bottle and two glasses.

'Not today,' Ken says.

'Happy with the ratings? They're up on last season. Everyone was obsessed with the cult at Oak Leaf Farm but now Mia, Sean, Chris and Lottie are all everyone is talking about on socials. I can't wait until next month when *Who's Watching You* is covering the notorious Madley Murders at Newington House. That twist was insane, wasn't it?'

'It was. I think the public are going to lap it up. The thing is, Jake, you won't be presenting it.'

'Won't be?' Jake laughs. 'What do you mean? This show would be nothing without me. My fans love me.'

'There's been a complaint about you. Inappropriate behaviour.'

'Oh, that teaching assistant from Chris's school led me on.'

'There's been more than one complaint. Not just from the guests either.'

'Banter, that's all it is. These snowflakes wouldn't know a joke if it hit them. You're a man of the world, you know what it's like. You can't say anything without offending someone.'

'It hasn't just been words though, Jake, has it?'

'What? I don't know what you mean. Oh, well, there was that one time. That intern didn't say no, though. She's only kicking off now so she can sell her story. I haven't done anything wrong.'

The door to the office opens. Jake swallows hard as he sees the police officer framed in the doorway. In his pocket, his mobile vibrates with notification after notification. He has a google alert set up for his name. What's everyone saying?

They'll all be on his side.

It's just banter, isn't it?

As for the other stuff, it's her word against his.

His fans will stand by him, won't they?

@Avocadomonkey OMG!!! Have you heard about Letchy Lawler? So glad he's gone #WWY

@Lamadrama23 Me too!!! He's a creep!!! That was something his brilliant researchers didn't see coming!!!

@Jamie2983 Oh, I think they probably did!

@Blackcat1970 It isn't funny. The world is horrible. I'm going to deactivate my account

@Jamie2983 Byyyeeeeee!!!!!

Chapter 81

Mia

Six Months Later

Despite the bars and the clanking of keys and the jeers and the endless, endless hours sat with nothing to do but think, I'm still me.

Perhaps more me than I've been in a long time.

It's not as though I'm relaxed here, far from it. My guard is something I never drop. I was worried that, being thought to have killed someone, I'd have something to prove here. I've watched the TV dramas, after all, I know there's a hierarchy, but I keep myself to myself and it's been fine so far.

Well, not fine, obviously. But I'm coping with incarceration better than I thought I would. I suppose it's the knowledge that it's me in here or Lottie, and faced with that choice again I'd choose me.

Every.

Single.

Time.

That's what being a mother is, isn't it? Sacrifice. Putting everyone's needs before your own.

Let them all think I killed Gabriel. No one knows the truth except me and Lottie and Chris, and I'll do what I have to do to keep it that way.

Anyway, here, in this tiny cell, there's no responsibility. No pressure.

Of course I'd rather be on the outside. Cooking, cleaning, locating lost PE kits and seemingly always driving someone somewhere, but I've had time to think. Really think about the person I used to be, before. Not before Gabriel. Not before Sean and the kids, even. But before Lottie's illness.

I see now that the desire to keep my children safe, and the sudden loss of my own father, have been the driving force behind everything I've done. Not in the healthy every-mum-does-the-same way but merging into something darker. Dangerous. The years I spent trying to shield Lottie from the truth about her father, tying myself in knots. It wasn't only because I wanted her to believe that Sean was her father, but because Gabriel was a terrible man who did terrible things.

Trying to protect her from the things I thought could hurt her, germs, bacteria, the entire world. Not letting her go back to school after the doctor said she could. I thought the world might cause her to become sick again. Even though, statistically speaking, Lottie was really unlucky to develop AA, and it was so unlikely she'd ever get it again, once you've had that fear of loss it never really leaves you. Once you've sat silent and scared in a hospital room, trying to absorb the fact that your daughter is chronically ill, well, it changes you. That sense of loss still lingering beneath the surface even once she was discharged.

In the end, it wasn't disease or the infections that almost took her from me, but my lie. If I'd have been honest about her parentage to start with then Gabriel might be a vague and amorphous figure hovering on the periphery of our lives.

He might still be alive.

I might not be here.

I shift my weight on my narrow bed. The thin mattress does little to soften the metal of the frame as it digs into my hips.

But then things might never have changed. I might not have loosened my grip on Lottie, and she might have ended up hating me.

It broke my heart when she told me how she really felt about the channel, about everything, how indebted she felt to me. There's a fine line between feeling indebted and feeling resentful, isn't there? She was zigzagging across it, confused, hurting. Now she's . . . I don't want to say free. Because my greatest fear is that she'll never be free of the guilt of killing Gabriel, but she's out there, living life in the way that other sixteen-year-old girls do.

So yes, in a weird sort of way, this is good for me. Good for us all.

I'm not going to lie, it raises my anxiety knowing she's out there and I'm unable to reach her if she needs me, but she has Sean, Chris, Esther, a whole team of people who love her, and I have to trust, not only them, but her.

You can't always keep everyone safe. Sometimes you have to have a little faith it will all work out.

I have faith that this will all work out.

Even though it's as though our lives were already drenched in petrol and the truth was the match that burned everything to the ground.

But out of the ashes there's hope for the future.

A guy called Jake Lawler kept applying for visiting orders. Sean told me Jake was making a documentary about us, the rise and fall of the Finch family. I'd felt sick, ashamed, guilty, but then I'd felt something else.

Empowered.

It was my story – our story – and although Jake claimed that *Who's Watching You* is the most accurate true crime series out there, no one knows us as well as I do.

After talking it through with Lottie and Chris, I reached out to a publisher, and I've been offered a book deal!

Everything has cycles of popularity, and books, it seems, are a big thing again.

'We need to strike while the iron is hot,' my editor had told me. 'Once the documentary airs, everyone will be super interested again.'

So I agreed to tell my story. If Harlow's family agree to it, I'd like her to be part of my book too. Not just her public persona but how she was as a person, *who* she was as a person. A wife. A mother. A daughter. A friend. To remind readers that we're all human. Flawed. Fallible.

I'd vowed to tell my editor everything, warts and all, but of course there are things that will remain close to me.

Hidden.

Sometimes I worry that the truth will always come out. That the uncovering of one thing will spiral into the whole sorry mess being unearthed.

But that won't happen, will it?

Will it?

Epilogue

Alma

Prison has an indefinable smell. Not like the ward where Alma spends most of her time, where you can pick out disinfectant, vomit, urine. This, this is something else. The same smell as the prison Gabriel had been in. She had visited him just once. After he was arrested, he had used his one phone call to contact her. Not because he loved her, but because he wanted her to go and retrieve the cash hidden in the restaurant basement. He'd told her this quickly, using innuendo. Vague statements she pieced together. She wasn't sure if that meant their conversation was being listened to or recorded. She had been terrified as she'd returned to Nine, The Square under the cover of night. She thought she saw someone coming out of the front door and she had run away and hid, thinking it would be the police. Although she hadn't had anything to do with Gabriel's illegal activities, she had been aware of them. She thinks now that knowing, being complicit with a crime but keeping quiet, is perhaps akin to committing one. Anyway what she was about to do would definitely be a crime even if she wasn't sure what. Hindering an investigation? Hiding evidence?

But still, after crouching behind some bushes for the longest time, she ventured forward again.

For love?

For money?

She doesn't like to think too much about why.

Anyway, the hiding place had been empty, and she assumed that the figure she had seen had been Lewis. Waves of heat and cold shuddered through her every time she thought about it. What would he have done if he'd caught her there? The same as he had done to Bradley?

Falteringly, she had told Gabriel face to face. Wanting him to see she wasn't lying. Wanting him to believe her. And yes, she supposes she still wanted him to want her. To tell her that the money didn't matter as long as they had each other. That once he got out, they'd start a new life together. She hadn't been with him long, but she had loved him. Loved the promise of a different future to the one she'd envisaged. One where she'd be able to shop freely without using a calculator, choosing what to put back on the shelf when she reached her budget. And children. She'd always wanted children.

Gabriel had raged against Lewis. Raged against the injustice of being locked up. Raged against Mia, who hadn't come to see him despite the fact they had slept together. Alma had sat there, tears welling, her mouth gaping open with horror at that revelation, but he hadn't noticed. He hadn't seen her.

When she left, she knew she wouldn't see him again. Wouldn't go back.

She had nightmares for weeks about the noise, the glare of the other prisoners.

Who'd have thought she'd be visiting a prison once more?

'Mia,' Alma begins to stand as Mia approaches the table but then sits again. Not sure what the protocol is here. Not wanting to get into trouble.

'Thanks for coming to see me.'

'I was surprised you wanted to see me. How are you?'

'Well, I was trying to keep my head down, stay anonymous, but a lot of the prisoners watched or were at least aware of that documentary that's just aired – *Who's Watching You.*'

'Ah. Even in prison you can't escape Jake Lawler. I didn't know anyone could watch TV here.'

'We have access to quite a few forms of media, although some of it is moderated, and costly.'

'I guess you know I was a guest on the show then?'

'I do. For the most accurate crime series, he got a lot wrong. Despite his insincere *hand on heart, I'm so sad, this is what happened but we're here to share the facts* claim, as it turned out, he didn't know that much at all.'

'He's been cancelled now.'

'Good. Anyway, I wanted to see you because . . .'

'Everything.'

A beat. Mia holds Alma's eyes with her own and Alma feels the connection there. The shared experience they have never talked about.

'Yes. You took a chance going on the show. I'm glad the *brilliant researchers* didn't uncover your connection to Gabriel. Weren't you worried?'

'A bit, but we weren't together for long, and he was dead. I did deliberate for a long time when the WWY team called me, but a lot of years have passed. I'm older, considerably larger, my hair is a different colour. I wear glasses now. I saw the way you studied me sometimes. You weren't sure it was me, were you?'

'No. If it wasn't for you still using "Alma", it probably wouldn't have crossed my mind.'

'I couldn't turn down the chance to raise awareness of AA. Donating bone marrow. Well, you know. You've been on a ward. Lived it. They promised me they'd focus on that angle, but they didn't.'

'It was a good thing to do. You're a good person. You really care about your patients, don't you?'

'Yes, especially Lottie. I knew when Sean's DNA test came back and showed he wasn't her biological father that she was Gabriel's. Even if he hadn't told me he had slept with you. They look so similar.' That's why Alma had given her an evil eye pendant to protect her.

'I have to ask you, Alma. You and Sean. I know you're together—'

'Only very recently. We'd been meeting for coffee as friends. He just needed someone outside of the family to talk to, I think, to try and process everything, but then . . .'

'Is it because of me and Gabriel? Some sort of revenge?'

'No. I really care about Sean. About Lottie and Chris too.'

'How are they?'

'Happier living back at your old house. It was handy the house next door coming up to rent for Esther, Felix and Daisy. Esther is hoping to buy it once her divorce from Lewis is finalised. It's nice for the cousins to be neighbours. To help each other through, you know . . .'

'Having criminals as parents.'

HMRC had launched an investigation into Lewis's business after someone tipped them off, and he was arrested for tax evasion and fraud. Who knows what else might be uncovered about him?

Murder?

Sean, Chris and Lottie have become a family to Alma, and it has made her think about Bradley's family. The closure they've never got. She's still unsure whether to tip the police off, though, because of the impact on Felix and

Daisy. Sometimes it's difficult to know what the right thing to do is.

'Alma, did you know about the missing money? That I took it?'

'I knew it was missing but Gabriel and I both thought Lewis had taken it. When Lewis brought Esther to the hospital to be tested as a match for Lottie, I'd recognised him and made an excuse to leave the room so I could gather myself. He followed me out into the corridor.

'"I wasn't sure it was you until I saw your face when it dawned on you who I was," he said. "If you speak to Gabriel, tell him that I know he's getting out later this year and I'll want my money back. Remind him about Bradley. I'm not messing around." I told him that I hadn't had any contact with Gabriel for over fifteen years. That I was surprised he was still inside. "Time added for bad behaviour," was all he said before he went back to join Esther.

'Later, it did cross my mind that you might have taken it, but once I found out about Lottie being Gabriel's daughter I thought, even if you had, you deserved it.' Alma licks her dry lips. She wishes she'd bought a drink from the vending machine. 'Mia.' She leans forward and clasps her hands together on the table. 'You're not going to reveal Gabriel is Lottie's father in this book you're writing, are you?'

'Of course not. I wanted to talk to you about the book. The kids have told me it's okay but then they said that about my channel and, well . . . ' Mia trails off.

'Lottie is fine with it. She thinks it might put a stop to the constant requests for interviews. You know, the book says everything there is to say and that's the end of it. Please don't worry too much about her. I am looking after her, both of them, and they're pleased that Harlow's going to be included in such a positive way.'

Alma loves Lottie. Loves Chris too with a ferocity she

hasn't experienced before. Her, Sean and the kids. Her new little family mean everything to her. She'd do anything to protect them. She wants to tell Mia that she understands why she took the blame for Gabriel's murder when she didn't do it but, of course, she doesn't because she isn't supposed to know. No one is.

Alma drags in a deep lungful of fresh air as she steps out of the prison gates. She raises her face to the sky and for a moment stands still, feeling the cool breeze on her skin, thinking how lucky she is.

There but for the grace of God . . .

Then she texts Lottie as she's making her way back to her car. **Your mum was in good spirits.** She'd been honest with Mia about her love for Lottie, for Chris. She will take care of them. They've quickly settled into life as a family because Lottie already felt safe with her. Trusted her. Chris too.

Alma remembers the terror that had wrapped itself around her throat when she saw Chris's #LookForLottie when she'd switched her phone on after her shift. Immediately, she had texted Sean, **I've just heard about Lottie. Any news?** Standing, frustrated when the message wasn't instantly read.

Although it was such a long shot, she couldn't help wondering. She knew from Lewis that Gabriel was due for release. She knew he was Lottie's father. It crossed her mind that perhaps Sean had told Lottie that fact as she'd tried to persuade him to do. That perhaps Lottie had run away to meet Gabriel.

She went to the restaurant, hadn't realised by then that Lottie had been found.

The square was deserted. Dark with the absence of streetlights. The creamy moon illuminated number nine. It was here she had fallen in love for the first time. Had her heart broken. She hadn't realised how derelict it was. There was no chance anyone was living here now, but still the past tugged her forward.

As she drew near to the maisonette where Gabriel's mum used to live, she noticed the soft glow of a lamp through the crack in the curtains upstairs.

Her heart stuttered. Someone was here. Every instinct told her to run away. No good would come from her seeing Gabriel again, but if there was even a smidgeon of a chance that Lottie was inside then she had to find out.

She knocked on the door.

Waited.

Pushed it open.

Called out for Gabriel. Lottie.

Creaked her way slowly up the stairs, all the while her heart pounding.

It was the smell that hit her first. A smell that she was so familiar with because of her job.

Blood.

A moan from the floor.

She lowered her eyes, inhaling sharply as she saw Gabriel sprawled on the floor, a gaping wound on his head.

Alma dropped to her haunches. Not touching him. Aware this might be a crime scene. Glad her hair was tied up tightly, that she was still wearing her scrubs that covered her body.

Confusion crumpled his face as he looked at her, 'Alma . . . Alma, is that you?'

He blinked several times before he studied her again, 'Alma?'

'Did Lewis do this?' She ignored his question as she snapped on a pair of the latex gloves she always carried in the mini first-aid kit in her bag. She hadn't thought he'd recognise her, but there had always been something between them, hadn't there?

'Lottie,' he mumbled.

'Is Lottie here? Is she okay?' Alma glanced around.

'Lottie did this.'

Shock snatched the questions she wanted to ask from Alma's mouth.

Lottie did this? Her sweet Lottie, who she'd nursed through such terrible times.

'But . . . why?'

'She won't get away with it,' Gabriel said. 'Help me, Alma.'

Alma peered at the wound on his head; still she wouldn't touch him. Perhaps even then she knew.

'I can't. You need a hospital. Proper treatment.'

Her fingers closed around the mobile in her pocket. What if she rang for an ambulance? They'd have to inform the police.

Even if Gabriel didn't say it was Lottie then, if he recovered, it wasn't like he'd forget.

If he recovered.

She could make sure he didn't. Keep Lottie safe. The whole family. She loved Sean. Respected Mia as a mother. The Finch family had been through so much. She couldn't risk Lottie being convicted, because the only thing Alma was certain of was that Lottie must have had a good reason for this.

She is a good person. Gabriel was not a good man, and he had no one who cared about him.

She looked around. Saw the poker on the floor that had obviously inflicted this terrible wound.

So many thoughts raced through her head and then, nothing.

A blankness as her she wrapped her gloved fingers around it.

A detachment as she brought it down once more on Gabriel's head.

Dizziness as she left the man she had once loved dead on the floor.

It wasn't until she pulled off her gloves outside and touched her cheek that she realised she was crying.

She had done a bad thing.

But she didn't tell anyone. She really does hate that Lottie is carrying the guilt that she killed Gabriel, and if Lottie had been arrested Alma would have confessed, of that she had no doubt. But it was Mia who confessed after her DNA had been found at the scene. She remembered how she had told Mia and Lottie how DNA could be altered after a transplant.

'That's so cool,' Lottie had said.

It had saved her.

Guilt spasms through Alma now as she starts her car to drive away from the prison. She should be the one in there, she knows, but Mia had taken so much from her.

Gabriel.

The money that should have been hers.

Her phone buzzes. A message from an unknown number.

Saw you on the documentary, nurse. I recognised you from Little Haven. You were at Gabriel's house the night he was killed. I'll be in touch to tell you what I want and, in the meantime, don't do anything stupid. I'll be watching you.

Alma rests her forehead on the steering wheel, sickness swirling in her belly. Who sent that? Where did they send it from?

She raises her head and casts an uneasy glance around the car park.

That's the thing with life in the digital age. Even if you don't know it. Even if you can't see them. There is *always* someone watching you.

Reader Letter

(CONTAINS SPOILERS)

Hello,

Firstly thank you so much for spending time getting to know the Finch family. I really hope you enjoyed *I Did a Bad Thing*. If you did and could spare a few moments to pop a star rating or review on Amazon, it really does make a difference to the visibility and success of a book.

This book wasn't the result of one big idea. The first thing that inspired me was overhearing an argument between a mother and a daughter in a coffee shop. The daughter didn't want her mum taking her photo and putting it on Instagram but her mum said she didn't have a choice. I found this both sad and distressing. The teenager was clearly upset. It really made me think about the way we live our lives, the photos we use to document it and how things never really disappear once they've been posted. I thought about the girl while I was driving home and, by the time I reached my front door, Lottie was fully formed in my mind.

I wasn't sure why Lottie wouldn't tell Mia directly not to feature her on social media until a conversation with my son Finley a few months later. He told me that he'd read about a crime where the DNA found at the scene belonged to somebody already in prison. Nobody could understand how this had happened until it came to light that the DNA of recipients of bone marrow can change over time. Along with finding this fascinating, it also gave Lottie a reason to feel indebted to Mia after Mia had saved her life and to further explore that bond between mother and daughter when Mia is arrested for a crime she believes Lottie committed.

While researching aplastic anaemia, it has been a real privilege sharing the stories of both patients and their families. No two journeys are the same. I hope, in some small way, to raise awareness of the importance of donating bone marrow. If you are interesting in learning more about this condition, please do check out the Aplastic Anaemia Trust.

For details of special offers and to be kept up to date on my latest releases (my next thriller is all about a mother and is SO twisty), do sign up to my newsletter. You get two free short stories for subscribing.

Until the next time,
Louise x

Acknowledgements

It feels odd to be bringing out a book where my mum will never see the cover, hear the title, or read it and so I wanted to start by giving her a very special mention. She is greatly missed.

As ever, thanks to my publishers, HQ: marketing, PR, production, design and everyone involved in bringing a book to life, especially my fabulous editor, Manpreet Grewal. Manpreet understood what I was trying to do with this story and her suggestions made it so much better. Thanks also to my agency, The Blair Partnership. In particular, Hattie Grunewald and Rory Scarfe.

Ellie Dawes at The Aplastic Anaemia Trust has been instrumental in my research. Any mistakes are purely my own and any artistic licence taken solely my decision. Thank you so much for being so generous with your time, Ellie.

Big thanks to all you readers! I appreciate all the support I've been shown over the years. Seeing my books featured on Instagram and social media feeds still gives me such a thrill. A special mention to my weekly Sunday Bookshare community on my Facebook Author page (even though your recommendations have made by TBR wildly out of control!).

Love to my friends and family. Particularly Sarah, Hilary, Clare, Cheryl & Natalie. Pauline & Mike. Jo, Leigh & the gang. My sister, Karen.

Tim, one day we'll relax!

Callum, Kai and Finley, my absolute world.

And Ian. Of course. Always.

Book Club Questions

(CONTAINS SPOILERS)

1. Who did you suspect throughout this book and why?
2. Mia starts her channel as a way of feeling connected to people and also to support other parents in similar situations. Have you ever turned to an online community for support? Would you? If not, why not?
3. Has this book made you think about the way you use social media?
4. There are more and more influencers. What do you think the positives and negatives are of living a life online? Have you had a particularly positive or negative experience online?
5. Do you listen to true crime podcasts or watch documentaries? Have you ever questioned the validity of them?
6. Lottie didn't want to be featured on social media but she felt so indebted to Mia for saving her life that she felt she couldn't say no. Did you grow up with social media? What was your experience then and how do you feel about it now? If not, do you wish it had been around?

7. Sean might have forgiven Mia if she had been honest about Gabriel even if Lottie turned out to be Gabriel's daughter. He couldn't forgive her concealing it from him for fifteen years. Do you think trust can ever be rebuilt once it has been broken?
8. It is implied that Bradley has been murdered by Lewis. Mia was terrified to report this after Lewis threatened Sean. Can you understand why she didn't report this or do you think she should have?
9. Jake Lawler ends up getting fired from hosting *Who's Watching You*. What are your views on cancel culture?
10. Were you satisfied with the ending?

Don't miss another addictive and pulse-pounding psychological thriller from Louise Jensen!

The Abbotts' new lodger Luke hasn't told them much about himself, but they can't expect to know everything about a stranger who's just moved in.

But Luke keeps asking about their family photos and looking through their things. Why does he want to know everything about them? And why does daughter Jen think someone is watching her?

Then, suddenly, Mum Mel texts the family to say she needs a break. But Mel has never gone away alone before. And now it's been days, and no one has heard from her.

The Abbotts' house is full of secrets.

They say people never tell the whole truth.

They're right.

Make sure you've read this nail-biting suspense thriller full of twists and turns!

The perfect opportunity . . .

A manor house available rent-free to house-sitters is an offer too good to miss for Cass and James, who have been saving for a deposit on their own home for so long.

Although it had been abandoned for almost thirty years, after a home invasion left almost all the inhabitants dead, it is an amazing chance for them to build their future.

But is it worth the price?

Shortly after moving in things take a sinister turn. Objects disappear and turn up in odd places, the clock always stops at the same time, the house is strangely oppressive and sometimes it feels like Cass and James are not alone.

Newington House may have bad energy, and a dark reputation. But surely there's no reason for history to repeat itself, is there?

Another unmissable and gripping psychological suspense thriller from Louise Jensen!

She promised not to tell. They made sure she couldn't . . .

At her surprise 40th birthday party, Kate Granger feels like the luckiest woman in the world but just hours later her fifteen-year-old daughter, Caily, is found unconscious underneath a bridge when she should have been at school.

Now, Caily lies comatose in her hospital bed, and the police don't believe it was an accident. As the investigation progresses, it soon becomes clear that not everyone in the family was where they claimed to be at the time of her fall.

Caily should be safe in hospital but not everyone wants her to wake up. Someone is desperate to protect the truth, and it isn't just Caily's life that is in danger.

Because some secrets are worth killing for . . .